The Iron Angel

AND OTHER TALES OF THE GYPSY SLEUTH

EDWARD D. HOCH
(Photograph by Michael Culligan)

EDWARD D. HOCH

The Iron Angel

AND OTHER TALES OF THE GYPSY SLEUTH

Crippen & Landru Publishers
Norfolk, Virginia
2003

Cover painting by Carol Heyer

Cover design by Deborah Miller

Crippen & Landru logo by Eric D. Greene

ISBN (limited edition): 1-885941-90-0
ISBN (trade edition): 1-885941-91-9

FIRST EDITION

10 9 8 7 6 5 4 3 2 1

Crippen & Landru Publishers, Inc.
P. O. Box 9315
Norfolk, VA 23505
USA

www.crippenlandru.com
CrippenL@Infi.Net

FOR PAULA SMITH

CONTENTS

INTRODUCTION

Graham Greene once wrote, "*Brighton Rock* began as a detective story and continued, I am sometimes tempted to think, as an error of judgment." My Michael Vlado series began as detective stories, and though I would never call them an error of judgment, they certainly didn't develop as planned.

The series had its beginning in 1984 when Bill Pronzini invited me to contribute a story to *The Ethnic Detectives*, an anthology he was editing with Martin Greenberg. I pondered a number of possibilities, including an Eskimo detective, before deciding on a Gypsy detective. To my knowledge there had been only one prior Gypsy sleuth, Martin Cruz Smith's Roman Grey, who appeared in just two novels in the early 1970s. (I had forgotten Fergus Hume's *Hagar of the Pawn-Shop*, an 1898 collection about a Gypsy pawnbroker in London, but as Michele Slung has pointed out she was more a problem-solver than a true detective.)

Next I did some research on Gypsies and found that those living in Romania were not as nomadic as their brethren for some reason and tended to settle in one spot. This seemed to be best for a series character so I decided to set the first story in Romania, never suspecting how much traveling my Gypsy would do over the course of twenty-seven stories. For a name I wanted something not too foreign, and when I determined that my Romanian Gypsy would have been born during the final year of King Michael's reign ("Mihai" in Romanian), I named him Michael Vlado. The surname, of course, was suggested by the country's legendary Vlad the Impaler.

With the first story, "The Luck of a Gypsy," sold to the anthology, I asked Eleanor Sullivan, the astute editor of *Ellery Queen's Mystery Magazine*, if she would be interested in a series about a Gypsy detective. She was, and I immediately set to work on a second story. My records show that I received a copy of *The Ethnic Detectives* on April 18, 1985. "The Luck of a Gypsy" was the only story in the series not to appear in *EQMM*, and this collection marks its first reprinting. Four days later, on April 22, I received the July 1985 issue of *EQMM* containing the second story, "Odds on a Gypsy," and a series was born.

Everything was quiet during those early years. But soon the geography of Europe began to change. The Berlin wall fell and the Soviet Union collapsed. A number of other Socialist governments collapsed or were overthrown, including that of Romania. President Nicolae Ceausescu and his wife were tried on charges of genocide and executed on Christmas Day, 1989. I was more than a little surprised to learn that the exiled King Michael, my character's namesake, was still alive and anxious to return to his country at age 68. Much of this became part of my series, together with the increasing persecution of Gypsies throughout Europe. Often, when Gypsy villages were burned or walls erected to keep them confined, Michael Viado was on the scene. It hadn't been planned like this, but events had overtaken him.

Still, for all its unexpected turns, I believe the European history of the late Twentieth Century has helped to make this a better and more meaningful series. The fifteen stories collected here, published between 1985 and 2000, take Michael Vlado from his own Romanian village to Moscow and Italy, to the Greek islands and England. Along the way you'll meet Michael's wife Rosanna, his good friend Captain Segar of the government militia, and some very clever murderers.

A full checklist of Michael Vlado titles may be found at the end of this volume. Again, my thanks to Sandi and Doug Greene for publishing this handsome edition, and to Janet Hutchings, my editor at *EQMM*, for keeping Michael Vlado alive and well.

Edward D. Hoch
Rochester, New York
July 2002

THE LUCK OF A GYPSY

In Romania, in the foothills of the Transylvanian Alps, men like Captain Segar no longer worried about vampires. Their concerns were the more mundane evils of life in the late twentieth century — gold smuggling, drugs, illegal border crossings and the like. And because Captain Segar could speak the Romany tongue so well, his special concern had become the Gypsies. In his region there were those who roamed in caravans and those who lived quietly in the little foothill villages like Gravita, with its dirt roads and grazing horses.

He had driven to Gravita that brisk May morning to confer with one man who knew more than he did about the way of the Gypsy and the workings of the Gypsy mind. In another time, another place, Michael Vlado might have been mayor of his village, or even an official of the central government. He was a wise man, a friendly man, and a natural leader among his people. The Gypsies of the area had gradually become farmers, toiling in the wheat fields in the shadow of the distant mountains. Romania was not an industrialized nation like the other members of the Communist bloc, and it still depended heavily upon its annual crops of wheat and corn.

Even in such a setting, Michael Vlado was near the top, and as Segar left his dust-covered car in search of the dark eyed Gypsy, the people of the village quickly informed him that Michael was presiding over a dispute involving a bride-price. Segar slipped into the back of the council hall to listen.

A number of Gypsy tribes, including the Rom of Eastern Europe and the Balkans, still maintained the institution of bride-price, whereby a payment was made by the family of the groom to the family of the bride, to indemnify them for the loss of a daughter. Captain Segar had always thought it an odd custom, the opposite of the dowry a bride's family supplied in some cultures. But while the dowry was generally a thing of the past, the bride-price was a matter of pride and honor among these Gypsy families. Here, in the informal court or *kris*, both sides had brought their dispute to be decided by Michael Vlado.

As Segar settled onto one of the hard wooden benches, a Gypsy named Ion Fetesti was arguing his case. "I appeal to this *kris* to find in my favor! I have paid a suitable sum as a bride-price to the family of Maria Malita, and my son should be allowed to marry her."

Behind the great oak judgment table, Michael Vlado turned his dark eyes to the other man who stood before him. "We have heard Ion Fetesti's side of the dispute. Now what do you have to say, Arges Malita?"

The bride's father was a slim, muscular Gypsy whom Segar knew slightly from previous visits. His clothes were not as expensive or colorful as Fetesti's, and he made that point at once. "My family is poor, as all of you know. Maria is our greatest asset, able to work long in the fields and still help her mother with the kitchen chores. To take her away from us for a few pieces of gold is an insult to the Rom tradition!"

"I have no—" Fetesti started to interrupt.

"You have everything!" Malita insisted. "You have a television, and tractors to pull your plows, and the only camping vehicle in the village! Your son will marry my daughter and both of them will work your fields. For this loss you offer a bride-price of a few gold pieces!"

Both men were stirred by emotion, and Michael Vlado must have felt it too. Instead of rendering an instant verdict, he announced, "I will take the matter under advisement. Return here tomorrow noon for my decision. The *kris* is adjourned until then."

There was grumbling from some of the spectators on both sides, but they filed out peacefully. Captain Segar caught up with Michael as he exited by a side door. "Hold on there, Gypsy! I've driven a long way to speak with you."

Michael Vlado's weathered face relaxed into a smile. Though just past forty he had the commanding presence of an older man, and Segar often had to remind himself that they were contemporaries. "The government's police have arrived! Am I under arrest, good Captain? Is my village surrounded?"

"Hardly that. But all this talk of money and wealth in a Communist state seems wrong."

Vlado smiled indulgently, as he often did at Segar's statements. "You forget that Gypsies do not live in a Communist state. We are subject to our own laws and our own social structures."

They were strolling away from the village buildings, across a field where the first wildflowers of spring were just beginning to appear. "Let's not have the old arguments again," Segar told him. "You're citizens of Romania and you must obey Romanian laws."

"As we do, when they do not conflict with our own! Have I not directed the Gypsy energy into farming and away from our more traditional pursuits? A decade ago my people were blacksmiths and horse traders, peddlers and fortune-tellers."

"Many of them still are."

"Of course! But by the next generation it will be different. We will enter the mainstream of life while still clinging to the old customs. It can be done, Captain."

"Perhaps," Segar admitted. "But the renegades among you are still a problem. A problem for me, at least. That is why I'm here."

"What is it? An old Gypsy woman taking money for curing someone's arthritis?"

"A bit more serious than that. A Gypsy caravan crossed the border at Orsova, heading this way. You know the border there, at the Danube. The traffic from Yugoslavia is heavy with local people on weekends, and security is lax. They checked one truck of the caravan and found several gold ingots hidden beneath it, taped to the frame and coated with grease. Unfortunately by that time the rest of the caravan had been allowed to pass through the checkpoint."

"Gypsies with gold! They are good people to know. Perhaps there is one among them who will offer a better bride-price for Maria Malita."

"This is nothing to joke about, Michael. The gold might be smuggled in to foment unrest. The Americans – "

Michael Vlado laughed. "Gypsies do not work for the Americans, any more than they work for the Russians."

"Still, there is fear of counterrevolutionary activities. I am to remain in this area for the next few days, in the event the caravan comes this way."

"And why should they?"

"To stay with fellow Gypsies."

"We are well integrated with the culture here, Captain, despite our clinging to the old ways. And we are sedentary. Only ten percent of Balkan and Eastern European Gypsies are nomadic, unlike our brothers in Western Europe. These people who cross the border will keep moving like the nomads they are. They will not seek out our village."

"We'll see," Segar told him. "Have you reached a decision yet in the matter of the bride-price?"

"I must sleep on it. Young Steven Fetesti is a fine lad, and it would make a good marriage. Still, the rights of the Malita family must be considered."

It was Steven Fetesti who brought them the news, an hour later, that a caravan vehicle carrying two strange Gypsies had arrived in the village.

There was a king of the Gypsies in Gravita, and it was to him that Michael Vlado carried word of the strangers' arrival. He was called King Carranza, and Segar had met him on previous visits. Once he'd been an active blacksmith, the strongest man in the tribe, but a runaway horse had crippled him ten years earlier. He was still the king, for what little the title meant, but it was Michael who exercised the power. Segar knew someday he would be a king like Carranza.

"Strangers?" the king said, lifting his mane of iron-gray hair. "Is that what brings the police?"

"It is," Segar replied, answering before Michael did. "We believe they smuggled gold ingots across the border. Now that they have reached the village I will have to stop and search them. I hope your people will cooperate."

King Carranza turned in his wheelchair. "Gypsies must stick together."

"These are strangers," Segar insisted. "You owe them nothing."

"We shall see."

Segar's hand dropped to the leather holster he wore on his belt. He had never drawn his weapon in the village of Gravita, but he was reminding them he still carried it. "I will search their vehicle," he said again.

The Gypsy king waved his hand. "So be it. Michael will assist you."

They left him in his room behind the blacksmith's shop and walked down the street together. In the distance they could see the shiny white vehicle where it had stopped. "It is nothing but a camper – identical to hundreds of others." Michael said it with a trace of scorn. "When I was a boy Gypsy caravans were pulled by horses, and each one was decorated in the manner of that family. They were colorful things of beauty, and no two were alike."

"Times change," Segar remarked. He was anxious to search the vehicle.

The two Gypsies who'd come in it – a young man and woman – stood by the side of the road talking to a beautiful young woman he recognized as Maria Malita, object of the bride-price dispute. Segar reflected again that Steven Fetesti was a very lucky man. A woman like Maria was worth any price.

Maria turned as they approached. "These strangers are on their way to Bucharest. They need directions."

"A bit out of your way, aren't you?" Segar suggested.

The two, who spoke a form of Romany mixed with some Greek words, introduced themselves as Norn Tene and his sister Rachael. They claimed to have gotten lost on the back roads after crossing the border at Calafat. Captain Segar did not believe that any more than he believed they were brother and sister.

"You did not cross at Orsova?" he asked.

"Orsova?" Norn Tene repeated. "No, no. Calafat."

Segar studied the dust-covered Greek license plate on the back of the vehicle. "You came from Athens?"

"That's right."

"I must search your vehicle for illegal cargo."

"Search?" The young woman pretended not to understand.

Segar dropped his hand to his holster, and Michael Vlado spoke up. "He has the permission of King Carranza. I am to see that you cooperate." There was just a hint of a threat in his voice.

Norn Tene shrugged. "We have nothing to hide."

Segar crawled beneath the vehicle and inspected it with his flashlight. There was plenty of grease but no sign of any gold. Next he entered the camper with Tene and looked in any place large enough to hide gold ingots. Again there was nothing. "Are you satisfied?" the Gypsy asked.

Captain Segar studied him carefully. "I am never satisfied when I am outwitted by a Gypsy."

"In Greece there was no police harassment. Gypsies could move about with complete freedom."

"Then go back to Greece!" He stormed out of the camper.

"Did you find anything?" Michael asked.

"Nothing."

"Can they be on their way?"

"I suppose so." He would have to telephone back to headquarters and admit his failure.

"Perhaps only a few vehicles in the caravan were carrying gold," Michael suggested. "Or perhaps these two are telling the truth."

Segar had another thought. "You two – let me see your passports."

Norn Tene handed over two grimy Greek documents of a sort easily forged. They were not stamped with the town of entry, but Segar knew the border guards were sometimes lax on weekends, especially with a large caravan traveling together. It proved nothing.

"May we go now?" the woman Rachael asked.

"Go!" Segar almost shouted.

He watched the vehicle pull away and then called out to young Steven Fetesti. "Where did you first see them corning into town? Were they traveling on the road from Calafat or from Orsova?"

"It was my father who first saw them, on the Orsova road. He sent me to tell you."

"The Orsova road," Segar repeated. He turned to Michael. "That gold is somewhere in the vehicle. I'm certain of it."

"But where? You searched it yourself, Captain." His tone of voice seemed to express little regret that Segar had been outwitted.

"I'm going after them," Segar decided. "Come along."

They went in the government car, going down the road in the direction the camper had taken. "I'm going with you only to protect you from harm," Michael assured him. "You must not do anything rash."

"I don't need protection. This is my lucky day."

"Of course," Michael agreed. "The luck of a Gypsy. The Rom have an old saying: *If in the morning a Gypsy you meet, the rest of your day will be lucky and sweet.*"

"And I've met plenty of Gypsies this day," Captain Segar agreed. He was keeping his eye on the road ahead, searching for a sight of the white camper. "Starting with you. How were you given a name like Michael, anyway?"

"After the last Romanian king. I was born in August of 1944, in the very month that he took power. Of course the Russians forced him to abdicate three years later, but he was a national hero for a brief time. He switched Romania to the Allied side, against Hitler."

"And Vlado is from Prince Vlad, the model for Count Dracula?"

Michael Vlado chuckled. "No, no – the legends of Transylvania are even more bizarre than those of the Gypsy. Vlado is a common family name among Gypsies, known even in America, where much of the Rom tribe has settled."

"Where are you from originally? India, as the legends say?"

"Northern India, most certainly. But we were as much outcasts there as we have been ever since."

"But now you wander no longer."

"Nine or ten centuries of wandering is enough for any tribe. Perhaps there is another saying: *The world shall know no peace, till the Gypsy's wanderings cease.*"

"There it is!" Segar said suddenly, catching sight of the white camper parked just off the road. He pulled in behind it and they got out.

The driver's door was standing open, and as they neared it Segar saw an arm dangling almost to the ground. He drew his pistol without a word. Norn Tene had toppled sideways from the driver's seat, and blood was running from two bullet wounds in his head, dripping onto the ground beside the car. In the passenger seat, the girl Rachael was crumpled and bleeding from wounds in her head and breast.

"They're both dead," Captain Segar said with something like awe in his voice.

This time Michael Vlado helped him search, but there was no sign of the gold. In fact there seemed to be no personal possessions at all in the camper except for some food and bedding. "Whoever killed them took it," Segar decided. "Do you agree?"

"There was no time for the killer to search the vehicle," Michael pointed out. "We were less than five minutes be hind them. Besides, you'd already looked for the gold."

"I might have missed it," Segar said, though he didn't really believe that. He had not risen to the rank of Captain by missing something as large and obvious as gold ingots.

"The ingots might be of small size," the Gypsy pointed out.

"Those seized at the border were large enough. They were hidden beneath the camping vehicle, coated with grease."

"Perhaps there was some other motive for the killings." But Segar could tell that the words lacked conviction. They both knew the two had been killed for their gold, by one of the village Gypsies.

"There is no other motive," Segar said. "I want the killer, Michael, and I want the gold."

"I cannot give you what I do not have."

"I want the killer or I will have the militia up here, tearing apart every house in Gravita."

"You cannot do that."

Segar's temper boiled over. The killings seemed like a personal affront to him, and seeing the bodies not yet drained of their blood made him want to strike back. "I can do anything that I wish, Michael Vlado! You are nothing but a band of Gypsies, remember. You are beyond the protection of the law. I can have everyone in this town arrested if I wish."

"We have lived here all our lives. We are citizens."

"Then act like a citizen! Give me the killer of these two people."

"I cannot give you what I do not have," he repeated.

"I will call the authorities now to deal with these bodies. You have until morning to deliver the murderer to me. Otherwise you force me to take drastic action."

Michael Vlado merely shook his head and said nothing. Segar used the police radio in his car to summon assistance. Then he returned to the Gypsy, his temper calmed a bit, and attempted to show a degree of moderation. "You could start by listing for me those Gypsies known to possess guns."

"All of us possess guns, Captain. It is a farming and hunting community."

"And do all of you possess gold ingots?"

Michael Vlado sighed. "You must talk to King Carranza. If he approves, I will give you what help I can."

It was thirty minutes before the district police reached the scene, and Segar saw at once that they had little knowledge or skill in dealing with the double killing. Some of his own men arrived soon after, and he ordered the government police under the Ministry of Justice to take jurisdiction in the matter. It was late afternoon before he was able to leave the scene and drive back to the village with Michael Vlado. At King Carranza's blacksmith shop they found they were not the only visitors. Steven Fetesti and Maria Malita had come with a special petition.

Steven, his young face troubled and intense, was pacing the floor of Carranza's living room while the crippled king sat hunched over in his wheelchair. He was obviously mak ing a final plea that his marriage to Maria be allowed to proceed as scheduled. "It is our life, King Carranza, and a dispute over the bride-price should not be allowed to disrupt the ceremony!"

The king raised his hand for silence as Segar and Michael Vlado entered. "What new troubles do you bring me, Michael? I have already heard of the tragic killings on the north road."

"That is why I come. Captain Segar wants my cooperation. But tend to these young people first."

It was Maria who spoke next, and she addressed herself to Michael. "We know our fate is in your hands because you will rule on the bride-price controversy tomorrow noon. But we cannot accept a verdict that denies us the right to marry unless a few more *leu* or a few more gold necklaces are paid."

"You must abide by the ruling of the *kris*," the king told them. "That has always been the way of the Gypsies."

"Then it's time that way was changed," Steven told him. "If necessary we will leave Gravita. We will run away to Bucharest and be married there!"

Michael placed a hand on the young man's broad shoulders. "Wait until tomorrow, and see what happens. I urge you not to do anything rash that will bring shame on both your families."

Maria Malita seemed reassured by his words, and she took Steven aside. Finally they promised not to do anything until the following day. When they had left, King Carranza said, "Your judgment in the matter must not be swayed by sentiment, Michael. If the bride-price is unfair, you must rule that way."

"Right now we have a more important matter before us.

"The killings? They were nomads, were they not?"

"They were Gypsies, from Greece. It seems obvious they headed in our direction because they sought safety with us. Instead they received bullets."

"From whom?"

"That we do not know."

"An outsider – "

"Not likely. One of our people saw the captain searching for smuggled gold.

He – or she – waylaid them along the road and shot them both. The killer no doubt planned to search for the gold himself, but heard our approaching car and escaped into the woods. We were only minutes behind."

"Why do you say *she?*"

"We cannot rule out a woman," Michael said. "A woman would be more successful in getting them to stop in the first place, and she might have hidden a rifle under her full skirt."

But Captain Segar shook his head. "The murder weapon was more likely a pistol. The camper door was opened on the driver's side before the shots were fired, because there were no bullet holes in the glass. I think the killer was standing nearby, and at that range rifle bullets would have passed through the bodies. These bullets didn't. Also, a rifle or automatic pistol ejects its cartridge cases. There were none on the ground, and the killer wouldn't have had time to pick them up. I would guess a revolver was used."

Carranza's eyes twinkled. "You are a good detective."

"A detective, yes – but my knowledge of the Rom is limited. I speak your language, I know something of your customs, but for this investigation I need Michael here."

"You ask that he betray a fellow Gypsy?"

"The victims were Gypsies, and guests of this village."

"They were only passing through," Michael corrected. "But we had a responsibility for their safety."

The king nodded. "Perfectly true, and the Rom is a strictly moral society. We do have responsibility to uncover the killer if he is one of our people. Can we still insist that our unmarried girls be chaperoned when we let a double murder go unpunished?"

"I will help you," Michael told the captain, "if it is King Carranza's will."

"It is," the man in the wheelchair said.

"Tomorrow morning?" Segar asked.

"Tomorrow noon."

Captain Segar remained at the village overnight, sleeping at the Vlado home. Michael's wife Rosanna, whom Segar had not met before, proved to be a pleasant but withdrawn woman who took little interest in her husband's affairs. She carved little wooden animals which were sold in one of the village shops, and late in the evening warmed toward Segar enough to get out a deck of tarot cards and tell his fortune.

"She's good with those," Michael said, watching his wife with unconcealed admiration as she predicted a long and happy life, and many children, for

Captain Segar.

"I have four children now," he told her. "Do you see more?"

"A fifth, at least. A girl."

Captain Segar smiled.

He slept downstairs on a worn sofa, and sometime past midnight awakened enough to see a shadow move across the front door of the little house. He started to reach for his gun but then he recognized Michael, slipping out of the house. Perhaps he was on his way to meet a woman or find a murderer. Either way, Segar knew he did not want company.

He woke at dawn, and saw that Michael was already sitting fully dressed at the kitchen table. Perhaps he had not slept at all. Segar rolled off the sofa, rubbing the sleep from his eyes. He went into the bathroom without speaking, and when he came out he said, "You promised me a murderer before noon."

"By noon, I think I said. First I must dispose of the matter of the bride-price."

"Never mind the bride-price. Do you know who killed those two people?"

"Yes."

"And where the gold was hidden?"

"Yes, that too."

"Where did you go during the night?"

"All in good time, Captain."

After breakfast they walked through the village and Michael Vlado spoke to everyone they passed. He wore a colorful new vest his wife had made, and seemed especially proud of it. "You are happy today," Segar observed.

"The weather is warming. Soon the crops will be planted. When my people have things to occupy them, there are not so many temptations about."

"You will lead them someday," Segar observed. "You will be their king."

"Carranza is their king. To go against his wishes would bring a curse upon the entire tribe."

"You still believe the old superstitions?"

But Michael did not answer.

When they reached the council hall, well before the time set for Michael to deliver his verdict, the rival fathers were already on the scene. Arges Malita was pacing back and forth, eying Ion Fetesti with open dislike. "Ah, Michael Vlado," he said as they approached, "do you have a verdict for me today?"

"I have. You will hear it at noon."

"Your daughter is not fit for my son!" Fetesti shouted suddenly, and Arges Malita hurled himself toward the other man. Segar moved quickly to keep them apart. Family members led them in separate directions, trying to calm them.

"I thought Gypsy marriages were arranged by the families," Segar said as they entered the building.

"Usually they are. But with Steven and Maria it is true love. The fathers were never friendly, and this business of the bride-price has driven them even further apart. I think Malita would have objected no matter what price the Fetesti family offered for Maria."

"Was there trouble when you and Rosanna married?"

Michael chuckled. "Nothing like this. But Gypsies are hot-blooded by nature. It is to be expected."

The spectators gradually filed in, taking their seats on opposite sides of the room. The families were divided, except that Steven and Maria sat together in the last row on his side. Just before noon Segar was surprised to see King Carranza wheeled in, his chair pushed by Michael's wife.

Segar stood at the back of the small room while Michael sat behind the judgment table. "This *kris* is now in session," he announced. "Although my judgment is informal, and has no legal sanction in the eyes of the state, it is binding in our community. Ion Fetesti and Arges Malita, please rise." When they had done so, he continued. "We find that the bride-price offered by the Fetesti family is a fair and reasonable one, and must be accepted by the family of Maria Malita."

There was cheering from the family of Steven Fetesti and silence from the Malita clan. Captain Segar glanced at King Carranza and thought he detected a slight smile. In the last row, Steven kissed Maria gently on the lips.

"There is one other matter," Michael announced as some of the family members began to file out. "Though it is not the official business of this *kris* to investigate crimes, we cannot let yesterday's terrible event pass without notice. Two travelers, Roms like ourselves, were brutally robbed and murdered while passing through the village. For this the killer must be brought to account. I have investigated the matter, and it is now my unpleasant duty to name the guilty party."

There was dead silence in the room as he spoke. Segar tensed, waiting for the next words.

"Ion Fetesti, you are the murderer!"

Fetesti, basking in the triumph of his victory on the bride-price, looked dumbfounded for just an instant. Then his hand streaked beneath his coat and came out holding a revolver. Segar's own shot was just a second too late, and he saw Michael topple as the killer's bullet struck him.

It was Rosanna who insisted that Michael be carried to their house, and it was she who worked on his shoulder, digging and probing until the bullet had been removed. Segar took it to match with the slugs from the other two victims, though the result would be of only academic interest. His own shot had blown off the back of Ion Fetesti's head.

When Michael could sit up and talk, there were questions from Rosanna and King Carranza, as well as from Segar. "It was a foolish thing, I suppose, announcing his name like that," Michael admitted. "But I had no way of knowing he'd be armed. I suppose he brought the weapon to protect himself from Maria's father."

"How did you know he killed those two?" Captain Segar asked. "You must have had some knowledge I lacked."

"No, no – you saw and heard all that I did. My midnight journey last night was only to confirm what I already knew. Our first sight of the victims' camper, parked in the village yesterday, showed that it was shiny – not dusty like your own car, Captain, after traveling these dirt roads. And yet the Greek license plate on the back was dusty. What does that suggest?"

"My God! They switched plates!"

"Or to be more exact, they switched campers. You did not find the gold ingots when you searched for them because you were searching the wrong vehicle. That camper came from this village, and they simply attached their plates to it. If you were listening during yesterday's *kris* testimony, you know that Ion Fetesti owned the only camping vehicle in the village. And I remarked myself how much alike they all looked. Is there confirmation of this theory? Yes, because young Steven told us his father first saw the visitors and sent Steven to tell us. While he was telling us, his father warned them the police were in the village and struck a deal with them. He emptied his own camper of his personal possessions, quickly switched license plates, and allowed them to drive it into the village. They did it in such a hurry, no one noticed the dusty license plates. Fetesti would have avoided getting his fingerprints on them as much as possible if he was planning a crime."

"He planned to kill them from the beginning?"

"Perhaps not. But while they were in the village with us he found the gold ingots fastened beneath the camper. He needed money – for his son's bride-price if nothing else – so he decided to keep that camper with its gold. He met Norn Tene and Rachael at the agreed-upon rendezvous outside the village, but instead of returning their camper he killed them."

"Where did you go during the night?" Segar asked.

"To Fetesti's house to look at his camper. I guessed he would leave the ingots safely where they were for the time being, and I found them just where you said, covered with grease."

"Why didn't those Gypsies simply remove the gold bars and leave them with Fetesti, rather than change campers?"

"They didn't trust him enough to show him what they were carrying. And when I examined them they were well hidden and difficult to remove from the camper's chassis."

Rosanna finished bandaging her husband, the rings on her fingers catching the light as she worked. "What about the wedding?" she asked, "now that Steven's father is dead?"

"Ion Fetesti must be buried first," Michael decided. "Then the wedding will go on as planned. A fair bride price has been decided upon."

Gypsies, Captain Segar thought, remembering the young couple. There are good ones and bad ones. "I'll be going soon," he said. "Take care of yourself, Michael. That bullet might have killed you."

Michael Vlado smiled. "I have the luck of a Gypsy."

"It didn't help Fetesti today."

ODDS ON A GYPSY

In the spring of that year, Captain Segar often made the long drive through the foothills of the Transylvanian Alps to the village of Gravita. He had grown friendly with the Gypsy leader Michael Vlado who was attempting to educate his people and instruct them in the ways of farming.

In the few short months they'd known one another, Segar had learned a great deal about Gypsy life in general and Michael in particular. Though Gypsy caravans still roamed the back roads of Romania, Michael Vlado and his people were not nomads. Like most Eastern European Gypsies, they had settled in one place and were attempting to integrate their culture with that of the general population.

Still, the old Gypsy ways died hard, and one of Segar's special treats on a spring afternoon was watching Michael and the others as they trained the horses. The races run in the old pasture near Michael's house were as exciting as those he'd seen in Bucharest, and even in Moscow. It was after an especially exciting race won by Michael's horse Rom Way, that Segar first mentioned his brother.

"That horse should be racing for high stakes, Michael. He's every bit as good as some of those old plow horses that run at the Moscow Hippodrome."

Michael merely smiled, as he often did at Captain Segar's pronouncements. "What do you know of racing in Moscow, Captain?"

Segar, who'd spent half his forty years as a member of the government police, did not like to be thought of as a provincial man. "I have visited my brother there," he answered stiffly. "Konrad is in the Agriculture Ministry in Moscow, and they run the Hippodrome. I've spent many days there on my vacations."

"I apologize. You may speak with authority."

"I say this much with authority, Michael. Rom Way could beat most of the horses in Moscow. Who is that young man who rides him ?"

Michael called to Tanti Slatina, the young Gypsy farmhand who served as his jockey. Tanti was short and lightweight, perfect for riding in races, and he had an irrepressible enthusiasm that made him willing to try anything. "Did I ride well?" he asked Michael, leading the big chestnut horse over to Vlado and Segar.

"Very well, Tanti. You know Captain Segar, don't you?"

"Of course." They shook hands and Segar studied the young man, barely out of his teens.

"You like to ride, don't you?"

"Of course ! I would rather do it than anything !"

"He rode Rom Way at the district fair last summer when the horse was only two," Michael said. "This year he'll do much better."

But Captain Segar shook his head. "Rom Way and this young man are both wasted at district fairs. My brother from Moscow is visiting me next week, Michael. Let me bring him up here to see them run."

"For what reason?"

"Perhaps he can advise you about the horse. This could be a money maker for us all."

The Gypsy smiled. "What sort of talk is that, coming from a socialist captain of police?"

Segar waved away the words with his hand. He always resisted any talk of politics. Like many Romanian officials his attitude toward Moscow was ambivalent. The country had not endorsed the 1980 Soviet invasion of Afghanistan and had taken part in the 1984 Los Angeles Olympics boycotted by Russia, but the two nations remained friendly. "Will you talk to my brother or not?"

"Very well," Michael agreed. "Bring him along. We'll give him some good Gypsy food."

Michael Vlado was not the King of Gypsies in Gravita but the old man who held that title had long ago passed on all real authority to Michael. It was he who presided over the informal village court to settle disputes according to Gypsy law and he who took on the role of father and protector to his people in times of trouble. On the day Captain Segar arrived at Michael's small farmhouse with his brother Konrad, the Gypsy was mediating a land dispute between two families. Michael's wife Rosanna, a quiet woman skilled in the carving of wooden animals, spoke pleasantly with them until her husband's return, showing off some of her latest work.

"This horse is lovely," Konrad said, passing the carving to his brother. "Don't you think so, Nicol?"

"It is indeed," replied Segar who rarely used his given name. Having Konrad back for a visit reminded him of more than his name. It reminded him of the family dispute twenty years earlier when Romania had disagreed with some Russian economic policies and Konrad, five years older than Nicol, had left home to work for the Soviets in Moscow. His rise in the Agriculture Ministry had been slow but steady, though he was the first to admit he'd never pictured himself as one of those operating the Moscow racetrack.

With Michael's belated arrival, the tempo of the conversation picked up. He took them out to the stable to see Rom Way at once and within an hour Tanti Slatina had saddled the chestnut for a romp around the oval track "A bit makeshift," Michael admitted to his visitor from Moscow, "but we make do with it."

Konrad Segar did nothing to conceal his interest. He was a big man, who clearly had led a better life than his brother. He asked about betting and about how Rom Way performed against other horses. When Michael staged an actual race, using the horse of a neighbor as competition, Konrad seemed genuinely impressed by the time of the big chestnut. "He is a Gypsy horse."

"That he is," Michael agreed.

"He should race at the Hippodrome," Segar's brother decided. "You bring him there."

The Gypsy laughed. "Moscow is nine hundred miles away."

"Since when was a Gypsy afraid to travel? You could drive that in one day."

"Not pulling a horse trailer."

"Two days then. I will furnish all the necessary papers to get you across the border."

"Rom Way has never run at an official track. He has never run in Russia at all."

"Our racing statistics are very poor," Konrad Segar admitted. "The program lists the past five finishes and times, but not when or where the horse raced. Often even these meager statistics are omitted."

Young Tanti Slatina had caught the man's enthusiasm. "Can we go?" he asked Michael. "Can I race in Moscow?"

The Gypsy leader turned to Captain Segar, "What do you think?"

"If you race in Moscow, I will come to see it myself."

Michael promised to think about it over dinner. Later Segar saw him consulting briefly with his wife and then he told Segar he was going out to speak with the parents of his young jockey. When he came back he was smiling. "All right," he decided. "We are going to Moscow."

Racing at the Hippodrome was only three times a week – on Sunday afternoon and Wednesday and Friday evenings – and involved a complex mixture of trotting and conventional races run on an outer and inner track. Captain Segar felt he knew the operations of the track by heart from the time he'd spent there and from having heard his brother talk so much about it. He'd taken leave during the period in June when Michael and Tanti and Rom Way would be making the trip, planning to drive along with them, saying there was plenty of room in the car they were taking.

Rosanna Vlado came out to see them off, having packed lunches for them to eat en route. She did not seem overjoyed at her husband's absence from home but apparently had made no effort to stop him. He had made his decision, and in a Gypsy household there was nothing more to be said. A horse trailer was hooked up to the back of the car and Rom Way was coaxed inside. The big chestnut seemed tense with anticipation, as if aware that big things were expected of him.

"Are there gypsies in Russia?" Tanti asked as they reached the main highway and turned north toward the border.

"A great many of them," Michael Vlado assured him, "Though not as many as there were years ago. The Rom have always been well treated in Russia even under the Czars."

"What must I do to be a jockey in Russia?"

"The rules for racing at the Hippodrome are quite loose," Segar assured him. "Generally horses come from the state training facilities in the country or are trained in Moscow. Jockeys and horse trainers each receive a fixed salary of four thousand rubles a year plus about thirty percent of the horse's winnings. Winnings are not large – a few hundred dollars at best – nor are the bets. The average jockey might race from May to August and then work in a factory the rest of the year."

"But Rom Way is not from a horse training farm," Tanti said, perhaps fearful he would not be allowed to race at the Hippodrome after all, "and I am not even a Russian citizen."

"My brother has taken care of all that," Segar assured them.

Behind the wheel of the car, Michael Vlado smiled. "Perhaps he expects to make a big killing on Rom Way."

"It could hardly be that. The maximum bet at any one window is ten rubles. A winning horse might return less than one ruble. Of course, bettors hurry from window to window to get down as many wagers as possible, but with as many as seventeen races on the card there is very little time between them. Often the horses are already loosening up on one track before the previous race has finished on the other track. There is no time to collect one's winnings before the next race goes off, so bettors often operate in teams with one betting while the other collects."

They crossed the border into Russia and continued north, bearing to the east. At first, the countryside appeared much the same as it had in Romania, but as they traveled farther north they entered a more industrialized region and came upon a modern divided highway.

After a night's sleep along the road in the car, Michael tended to the horse and they ate a meager breakfast. Then they were on the road again taking the divided highway that would lead them directly into Moscow. As they approached urban areas, Tanti was surprised to see women with brooms along the highway, sweeping the grass free of litter and leaves.

Once in the city itself they drove directly to Konrad's apartment in a high-rise building of recent construction. As a government official his quarters were better than most and more spacious than the apartment Segar had seen on his last visit. As they entered, a man was leaving – a small man who pushed past them without apology and hurried to the elevator.

"Don't mind him," Konrad said lightly, greeting them with handshakes all around. "His name is Vladimir Kosok. He's one of the trainers from the Hippodrome. With them there is always trouble of one kind or another. Come – sit down. What do you think of Moscow so far?"

"The streets are so wide," Tanti Slatina answered. "And so many buildings! I'm not used to the crowds."

"You had better get used to them if you are to ride at the Hippodrome. There you will see crowds, believe me."

He took them to dinner that evening at a nearby restaurant, and then showed them the one-room apartment he had arranged for them in the same building as his own. Michael and young Tanti were to share it, while Segar stayed with his brother. Konrad had arranged for everything, including someone to stable Rom Way until he could be properly entered at the Hippodrome in the morning. Segar was pleased and he could see that his Gypsy friends were enjoying their first sights of Moscow.

The Hippodrome was a massive monument to a Russia long past – a century and a half old and still showing a sort of squalid grandeur. It was located in Begovaya Street, northwest of the central city and not far from the Moscow zoo. At its entrance, a dozen high Corinthinan columns supported statues of rearing horses, but inside the grandstand's marble steps were badly worn and its walls and floors soiled. The infield within the double track was overgrown with early summer weeds. Still, Segar thought, one could marvel at the columns supporting the lavishly decorated grandstand roof that dated back to Czarist times and imagine for an afternoon that one had entered another age.

By Sunday noon, the place was already filled with some 5000 spectators in preparation for the 1:00 pm start of the first race. They seemed to be working people of all ages – old veterans wearing medals and brash young men in tight western-styled jeans. Although no drinks were sold, some of younger ones drank vodka from flasks. It was a good-natured crowd.

Rom Way had been given stable space in the huge area that housed more than five hundred horses. He would work out on Monday and Tuesday in preparation for his first race on Wednesday evening. To Segar it all seemed too casual but he assumed Konrad knew what he was doing.

"Is this a summer track only?" Michael asked as they waited for the first race down near the rail. "In Romania we hear of the harsh Moscow winters."

"No, we have learned to make money in the best capitalist tradition. It goes, after all, to subsidize the Moscow theater and the Bolshoi ballet. In February we hold troika races here, with horses pulling sleighs. And the harness racing continues year round."

A fountain in the infield began to gush water and the public address system came alive with martial music. Then a clanging bell signaled the start of the first race.

Though Segar was hardly a betting man, the small amount of the wagers frustrated him. Michael and Tanti managed to bet a couple of winners, but it was pure luck. The racing programs were incomprehensible and the computerized tote board – made in Finland, according to Konrad – indicated which horse had drawn the most bets but did not report the actual odds.

Konrad appeared with black caviar sandwiches for everyone – a delicacy sold for less than a ruble each at the track. "We took in twenty million rubles in bets last year," he said proudly, " and we may top that this year."

The long card of races dragged on until 7:30 that evening but long before that they had abandoned the grandstand and were inspecting the stable area with Konrad. Along the way, their party acquired another member – a slender blonde woman name Alexis, who seemed to be on intimate terms with Konrad. Segar had known of his brother's divorce for some time, but he was surprised that this attractive young woman should find Konrad desirable.

"Have you seen the sights of Moscow yet?" she asked as they strolled in the stable area, carefully avoiding the constant parade of horses to and from the track. "Lenin's tomb, the Kremlin, the Bolshoi?"

"We arrived only late yesterday," Michael told her.

She was obviously taken with his handsome dark features. "Konrad tells me you are a Gypsy, Michael. Do you travel in a caravan?"

"No, I live on a little farm in Romania with my wife and children."

"His wife tells fortunes," Captain Segar told them. "She has predicted a fifth child for Helga and me, but it has not come yet."

Konrad chuckled and made a ribald comment about his brother. Everyone laughed except young Tanti, who had not understood it. He was more anxious to get back to the horse he would be riding the following morning.

The Hippodrome stables were under the care of a burly old man named Fritz Leiden, a former German soldier who'd remained in Russia after being freed from a prison camp after the war. He was good at his job and seemed to welcome newcomers he could impress. "You think you can race at the Hippodrome, boy?" he asked Tanti.

"I hope so sir !"

"A Gypsy jockey! A rarity, surely, but not the first we've had. We'll see how you do on the track tomorrow and Tuesday morning."

"He's passed his twentieth birthday," Michael said. "He's no longer a boy."

"We'll see how he rides," Leiden said. He walked with a bit of a limp and Segar wondered if it was from an old war wound or a balky horse. "This is the oldest and most important of Russia's fifty two racetracks. Not just anyone can ride at the Hippodrome. Arabian horses from Turkey were running here when Karl Marx was still a teenager." For all his pride he might have been a native-born Russian. "I will be at the rail in the morning, watching you, boy."

True to his word, Fritz Leiden was out at 7:00 am when Michael saddled up Rom Way and gave Tanti a hand up. There was no opportunity for sleeping in Konrad's apartment once the alarm had awakened them, so Captain Segar was there too, feeling foolishly informal in casual clothes his brother had provided. "You look like a police captain, Nicol," he'd told him, "even out of uniform. At least wear this shirt and pants so you look more like the rest of us on a day off at the racetrack. You and your Gypsy friends are too colorful."

Michael led Rom Way onto the track where a dozen other horses were already working out. He spoke a few words to Tanti and the jockey took the big chestnut around the first time at a canter, letting him grow accustomed to his surroundings. On the next lap, at a sign from Michael, the horse was speeded to a full gallop.

"Very good!" Konrad said, checking the time with his stopwatch. "He could be a winner against the second-rate horses here."

Michael was looking beyond Konrad, at something in the grandstand. "It seems as if we're not the only ones timing Rom Way. Isn't that the man we saw at your apartment ?"

Konrad turned to follow his gaze. "Yes. Vladimir Kosok. I think I'll see what he's up to."

After another gallop around the track, Tanti pulled up the horse and Michael decided it was enough for the first day. "Walk him around a bit and we'll give him another run tomorrow."

When Konrad returned to the group, Nicol knew his brother well enough to see that he was disturbed. "That Kosok is too interfering for his own good!" Konrad said. "He has some horses running on Wednesday and he's afraid this Gypsy chestnut will run right over them. He wants us to skip that day and wait until Friday. I told him we would not."

"Did that satisfy him ?" Segar asked.

"Oh, he made some threats about reporting me. He seems to think I'm making money on this horse somehow."

"Why do you put up with him?" said his brother. "He's only a trainer."

"We were friendly once. And we had some dealings. It was he who introduced me to Alexis and she is still a friend of his."

"Do you owe him anything?"

Konrad thought for a moment and answered, "No, nothing. But in this country one must be careful of his enemies. A word spoken in the wrong place can be dangerous."

The conversation bothered Segar. As a police officer, he couldn't help wondering if his brother was involved in something shady. Suddenly the whole journey to Moscow with the gypsies and their horse seemed a mistake.

Michael continued to work out Rom Way on Tuesday and the big horse circled the track a half second faster than before. They spent the morning at the track and then off sightseeing in the afternoon. Konrad was at work and was only able to join them in the evening. Surprisingly it was Alexis who appeared on Wednesday morning, nodding briefly to Segar but obviously directing her attention toward Michael Vlado.

"How is your horse running?" she asked. "Should I bet him tonight?"

"There he is, just coming into the home stretch. Judge for yourself."

"He runs well. He runs like the Gypsy outlaw he is."

"We are not all outlaws," Michael replied with a slight smile. Segar could not be sure, but the woman might have been flirting. "Tell me," she continued, "is it true that Gypsy men must pay a bride-price for their women, the opposite of a dowry?"

He nodded. "The custom exists in China and some other places, too. It is not exclusive with gypsies."

"And do you travel in caravans and deliver Gypsy curses?"

"I am merely a farmer and horse breeder."

"Come now! Gypsies know many things."

They were standing by the rail and Tanti was just dismounting when there was a shout from the stable area. Fritz Leiden was calling for help. Segar broke into a run with the others following, his police training taking over by instinct. He reached the German and took him by the shoulders. "What's happened?"

"In there," Leiden said, pointing to the nearest stable.

Segar went in and bent over a man lying on his face in the straw. A wound to the head was open but there was very little blood. "He's dead," he told Michael.

"It's that Kosok fellow," Tanti said.

Segar lifted the man's head slightly and they saw that it was indeed Kosok. "Did you see anyone near here?" he asked Leiden.

"Only a stable boy with his wheelbarrow doing his daily cleaning chores! I didn't see Kosok or anyone else."

"You'd better call the police."

Later, as the police were completing their formalities, Alexis said, "I knew him quite well. Do you think I should admit it?"

"Not unless they ask you," Segar advised her. "Never lie to them, but don't volunteer anything either."

"That's right – you're a police captain yourself, back in Romania."

"Konrad told us he met you through Kosok. What was the man, besides a horse trainer?"

She shrugged. "He gambled some. I don't know where he got his money."

The police had finished with Fritz Leiden and Michael asked him: "Whose stable is this?"

"It belongs to Dmitri Ivanov. He trains several horses. All the stables along this side are his."

Ivanov himself soon appeared on the scene. He wore jodhpurs and riding boots, giving the appearance of an English country squire until he began conversing in Russian. That particular stable had been unoccupied, he said, since three of his horses had been shipped out to other tracks after Sunday's races. "Of course I knew Kosok," he replied to the police investigator's question. "He was at the track almost every day. Sometimes he trained horses, other times he just hung around. He was always eager to make an easy ruble or two."

The investigator, whose name was Nevsky, made notes in a black book. "Who were his enemies, his friends?"

A few names were mentioned and Konrad Segar was one of them. It was

Fritz Leiden who said he'd often seen the dead man talking with the official from the Agriculture Ministry. When Investigator Nevsky perked up at this, Segar wondered if the mention of a government official had made him nervous. Then one of the other detectives came over to Nevsky and told him they'd found something of interest and they moved off to anther area of the stables, with Segar and the others following along.

"Do you think this will delay tonight's races?" Tanti asked anxiously.

"I doubt it," Michael replied. "They make a great deal of money from it. You'll get your chance to ride."

Nevsky and the other detective were examining one of the large wheelbarrows the stable boys used to remove horse manure during their cleaning chores. There seemed to be nothing in it but a pair of stable boy's overalls and a shirt. The pants cuffs had been turned up but there was only a bit of straw in them. Then the detectives found something else in the folds of clothing – a large hypodermic needle of the sort used to inject horses. "Have its contents analyzed," Nevsky ordered.

The trainers and jockeys who had gathered around at the news of the killing gradually dispersed and Michael and Tanti went off to Rom Way's stable nearby. Tanti led the horse into the fresh straw and as he gave him a bucket of water Michael toed at the straw deep in thought.

Segar was still following Investigator Nevsky about when Konrad arrived. Word of the murder had reached the Ministry office. "What happened here?" he demanded of the detective.

"A man named Vladimir Kosok was killed by a blow on the head. It seems to have happened an hour or two before the body was found. You knew the man, Comrade Segar?"

"I knew him, yes."

"When did you last see him?"

"I came here to ask questions, not answer them. My office is in charge of operations here, as you know."

"I understand that." Nevsky reached into a plastic evidence bag he was carrying. "You see, Comrade, this box of matches was found clutched in the dead man's hand."

Segar and his brother both stared at it. On the side of the box was the symbol of the Agriculture Ministry. Segar had seen some like it at Konrad's apartment. "He might have gotten that anywhere," Konrad said. "No doubt they've been left here on occasion by myself and others from the office."

"But he was clutching it as if he had just grabbed it from his killer. And we found a hypodermic needle, too. Its contents are being analyzed."

Konrad was grim-faced. "To answer your earlier question, I saw the dead man here yesterday morning while I was watching the horses work out."

"Very well." Investigator Nevsky made another note in his book. Segar saw that he must take some action. "Perhaps you would allow me to aid in the investigation. I am a captain of police back in Romania."

"We can handle it quite well," the Russian assured him, closing his notebook and walking away.

"They suspect me," Konrad said. "I could see it in his eyes."

"Surely your position – "

"I am not important enough to sway a murder investigation."

"But you had no motive for killing Kosok."

"Some might think my love for Alexis was motive enough. He resented our affair. On Sunday when you saw him leaving my apartment he had been there to warn me away from her."

"I didn't know," Segar said quietly.

"I must go find her."

"She was with us earlier, watching the workout. She may be with Michael at the stable."

They found her there, patting Rom Way while Michael brushed him down. When he heard of the latest developments the Gypsy was troubled. "We did not mean to bring you problems," he told Konrad.

"You have not brought them."

"I hope not. Some feel the coming of gypsies brings an ill wind."

"I urged you to come," Konrad reminded him. "I'll be cheering you on tonight."

Segar managed to get Michael aside. "The official police want none of my help. But you have aided me before in investigations. Do you see anything we might have missed?"

"Many things," the Gypsy said. "But let us await the results of the investigation and of tonight's races."

Rom Way ran in the fourteenth race, near the end of the evening's card. He took an early lead and then dropped back as Michael and Segar cheered him on from the rail. Konrad and Alexis were there too, adding their encouragement. One of Ivanov's horses had surged to the lead and Alexis shouted, "I hope he loses! Come on, Rom Way !"

Tanti used his whip just once but it was enough to spur RomWay on. He came even with Ivanov's horse and then in the home stretch edged him out by half a length. Rom Way had won his first big race.

The exhilaration they all felt in watching could hardly match Tanti Slatina's in riding the winner. He jumped down from his mount to accept Michael's enthusiastic hug and a kiss from Alexis. When they'd all calmed down, Segar saw Michael draw the young woman aside. "Why were you so anxious that Ivanov's horse lose?" he asked.

"Ivanov and Kosok were partners on that horse," she replied.

"Partners? The horses are owned by the state. The men were only trainers."

"Partners in wagering. They had a system for betting large sums of money – more than is allowed by law. They bribed a cashier to punch out extra tickets for them so they wouldn't have to run between windows buying them." She took a deep breath. "I wouldn't be telling you this if Vladimir were still alive. I really did love him once."

The small purse for winning the race was awarded and they started off to celebrate. There was talk of entering another race on Friday evening but Fritz Leiden informed Michael that the Friday card was already full. "Perhaps on Sunday," he suggested.

That was when Investigator Nevsky appeared, grim-faced as ever. "I understand your Gypsy horse was the winner," he said with a trace of distaste.

"You should have bet on him," Michael Vlado replied with ease. "The payoff was very good. If they posted odds, he would have gone at about ten to one."

"It is highly irregular for a privately owned horse to race at the Hippodrome or anywhere in Russia. You must be aware of that. One wonders if Kosok was threatening to report this to the proper authorities."

"We received no money," Michael assured him. "Only the regular trainer and jockey fees and our percentage of the purse. Russian horses travel to Berlin and Dusseldorf. Certainly German horses race here on occasion. You know as well as I do you have no basis for threats."

Nevsky's lips twisted into a slight grin. It was the first time he'd attempted anything approaching a smile. "I can have you arrested on suspicion this very minute. No one will care what happens to a Gypsy."

"Perhaps we'd make more sense if we worked together," Michael suggested.

"What sort of Gypsy name is Michael anyway?"

"A Romanian sort. I was named after King Michael, our country's last monarch before it became a communist state."

"And a poor communist state it is," Nevsky grumbled. "Neither a Gypsy nor a Romanian receives my sympathy."

"If you intend to arrest me, tell me one thing first. What were the contents of that hypodermic needle?"

"Is that any business of yours?"

"It could be."

"The hypodermic needle contained a powerful stimulant. Any horse injected with it before a race would have a good chance of winning. However, the most routine urine test for drugs would have revealed it."

Michael Vlado nodded. "Could I speak with you in private?"

"About what?"

"My theory on the case."

They walked away together while Segar watched. Michael was talking, explaining, and after some moments Nevsky started talking too. They might have been having an argument. Finally they returned and it was Nevsky who spoke. "Mr. Vlado has some interesting theories on the case."

"Could we all go someplace and talk?" Michael asked.

Tanti suggested a room where the jockeys relaxed before their races. With the last race about to be run, it was empty now except for Fritz Leiden who was busy cleaning up. Nevsky led Michael, Tanti, Segar, Konrad, and Alexis inside. "Now tell them your theory."

"Yes," Michael said. "I thought of it when someone said they'd seen a stable boy by the place where Kosok's body was found. Why would he have been there? To clean the stables? But this is Wednesday morning and Ivanov had shipped off the horses that used those stables after Sunday's races. They would have been cleaned on Monday – or yesterday at the latest. Isn't that right, Fritz?"

"You're correct," Leiden agreed. "No stable boy should have been in that area this morning."

"But if it wasn't a real stable boy, who was it? The hypodermic needle tells us that. It was someone posing as a stable boy to get near the horses, to inject one of them with a powerful stimulant. As bad luck would have it, Kosok ran into him, probably recognized him as a fellow gambler and got himself killed. I think if Investigator Nevsky checks on known gamblers with special interest in this evenings horses, he may find the killer."

Surprisingly, the Russian detective agreed. "You will all be leaving in the morning, going back to Romania?"

"I think it's best," Michael said over young Tanti's objections. "We've raced at the Hippodrome and won. Why press our luck?"

"Why indeed?" the Russian said.

After he'd gone, Segar took Michael aside. "What sort of story did you feed him earlier?"

"What I just said, as far as it went. I also told him that Kosok and Ivanov were gambling partners. And I told him about the scheme to bribe one of the cashiers."

"What about my brother?"

"He'll be all right as long as we don't race again. He made some big bets too, didn't he?"

"I suppose so," Segar admitted. "I saw Alexis collecting some winnings after Rom Way won."

"You and I, we're better off back in Romania," Michael said.

Konrad saw them off in the morning. They stopped at the Hippodrome to pick up the horse trailer with Rom Way and said goodbye to Fritz Leiden. Then they headed south the way they had come. A summer mist hung over the valleys and the sun was only starting to break through and warm the air.

"That was quite a trip," Tanti said. "Something I'll remember a long time."

"I should think so," Segar agreed. "Racing at the Hippodrome is something that happens once in a lifetime."

Michael was at the wheel guiding the car and trailer along the divided highway. It wasn't until they left the main road that he relaxed and spoke. "In a way I'm sorry we went."

"Because of the murder?" Segar asked.

"Yes."

"You think my brother killed him don't you?"

"No. In fact I knew from the start that he was innocent. You see, the killer posed as a stable boy and Konrad couldn't have fit into those overalls. You'll remember the pant legs were turned up for a short person."

"Maybe it was one of the stable boys."

"No. He wouldn't have risked abandoning his overalls. Kosok's head wound left virtually no blood in the stable where we found him – that indicates he was killed elsewhere and dumped there."

"Someone carried the body in broad daylight?"

"Wheeled it would be more accurate. Kosok was a small man – his body would have fit into one of those big wheelbarrows the stable boys use. Covered with a tarp and a bit of straw, no one would see it. Remember, someone did notice a stable boy with a wheelbarrow near those stables. And I asked myself something else. Why was the a stable boy's costume needed at all? Anyone could have pushed that wheelbarrow without attracting attention. Unless their regular clothes were distinctive enough to catch the eye."

Captain Segar felt uneasy. "What are you trying to say, Michael?"

"That the killer of Vladimir Kosok had to be a small person, like a jockey. That he had to be wearing eye-catching clothing, like a Gypsy. That he had to have murdered Kosok in our stable where fresh straw covered the bloodstains. Tanti, why did you kill him?"

They stopped the car at the side of the road while Tanti Slatina went off to the woods and was sick. Presently Michael and Segar followed him, and sat with him.

"I found him in the stable with that needle," Tanti said, sobbing it out with an emotion that shook his whole body. "He tried to bribe me to inject the stimulant into Rom Way. He said if I did it just before the race Rom Way would win. What he really wanted was a disqualification so the horse he backed – Ivanov's horse – would win. When I refused, he said he'd inject Rom Way himself. We struggled and I hit him with a horseshoe. I didn't mean to kill him."

"Why didn't you tell us?" Segar asked. "Why did you move the body?"

"I – I wanted to race at the Hippodrome. I wanted it more than anything else on earth. If I admitted killing him even by accident, I knew they'd put me in jail and I wouldn't race. So I put on the overalls and shirt and moved his body in a wheelbarrow to an empty stable. The hypodermic needle must have fallen into the wheelbarrow and I missed it."

Michael nodded. "You said it was Kosok before we turned over the body, though you barely knew him. That made me suspicious, and when I saw the fresh straw in our stable I searched the floor for bloodstains and found them. But I had to let you ride."

"What if my brother had been arrested?" Segar asked Tanti quietly. "What about that box of matches in Kosok's hand?"

"I picked them up at his apartment for a souvenir. Kosok must have ripped them from my pocket during our struggle without me realizing it. Believe me Captain, I would have confessed if Konrad was arrested. I still will."

Michael stood up, helping Tanti to his feet. "You just have, to a captain in the Romanian police."

Segar nodded and followed them back to the car. He stood for a moment looking at Rom Way in the trailer and then he got into the car with them. "It's out of my jurisdiction," he said at last. "Let's go home."

BLOOD OF A GYPSY

It had been some weeks since Captain Segar had last driven into the foothills of the Transylvanian Alps to visit his Gypsy friend Michael Vlado in the little village of Gravita. He never imagined that his next trip would come at the instigation of his commanding officer.

Inspector Krisana sat at his cluttered desk beneath the tricolor Romanian flag with its coat of arms centered directly over his head. "I believe you have some close contacts among the hill Gypsies, Captain Segar."

"Some are friends of mine," Segar admitted. "I speak the Romany tongue quite well."

"You know their leader?"

"I know Michael Vlado. The hill Gypsies are not nomadic. For the most part they live in settlements or villages under separate Gypsy kings. In Gravita, the village I know best, the king is ill and elderly. For practical purposes, authority has passed to a younger man, Michael Vlado. One day he will be king."

"What is their feeling about the Socialist state?"

Segar shrugged. "They live their own lives, by Gypsy law. For minor offenses, they hold court among themselves. On the few occasions when violence has occurred, we have been summoned."

"We need a Gypsy leader to represent his people at a state function in Bucharest next month. Do you think Michael Vlado might be the man?"

"He is very independent, as are all Gypsies. I would have to ask him."

Inspector Krisana nodded. "Drive up to Gravita tomorrow and speak with him. I'll give you the details of the event we wish him to attend."

"I was preparing my reports for the inspector-general's visit – "

"This takes precedence. I have been ordered to choose a Gypsy representative."

"Very well," Segar agreed. "I will drive up there in the morning."

The journey up to the village took more than two hours, but Segar enjoyed the opportunity to get away from the office. Paperwork had never been one of his favorite activities and the drive through the October landscape, filled with unexpected bursts of color, was a welcome relief from his desk.

Michael Vlado, a tall, dark-eyed man with a weathered Gypsy face, was in the field with his horses, as Segar had expected he would be. The crops had been harvested for another year and the Gypsy leader could devote time to his true love.

Seeing Segar emerge from his car, Vlado galloped over on a fine bay colt to greet him. "It is an honor to see you again, Captain. Is your visit one of duty or pleasure?"

"Both, I suppose," Segar said, quickly outlining the reason for his call. As he spoke, Michael merely smiled, then finally said, "This sort of event is not for me, old friend. The Socialist state tolerates us, but the less we are seen the better."

"Is there anyone else who could go as a representative? The inspector needs a Gypsy." He paused and added, "We must all look after one another in this life, you know. I do you a favor, you do me one in return." Segar knew that Michael would understand the reference to their Moscow trip earlier that year, when the captain had arranged for Michael's horse to race at the Hippodrome.

"I understand that," Michael Vlado answered seriously. "But who would I send?"

"How is King Carranza these days?"

"Still confined to his wheelchair. He could not make the journey." Suddenly Michael spotted a red tractor lumbering along the dirt road. "Let me speak with Arges Gallipeau."

Captain Segar knew most of the village's Gypsy families, at least by sight, and he'd met Gallipeau once or twice. He was a slim man with a wisp of beard clinging to his chin. Like Michael, he was in his early forties, but there all resemblance ceased. His manner was almost timid at times, and he lacked the driving force with which Michael shepherded his people.

"Arges!" Michael called to him. "Wait there so we can talk!" He ran over to the tractor and asked, "Is your brother at his house?"

"He is there," Arges answered somewhat disagreeably. "Probably with Krista."

"Are you headed there now?"

Arges shook his head. "I want to get the tractor into the shed. They say we might get a little snow later."

Segar glanced up at the gathering clouds. With the temperature well into the forties, snow in late October seemed unlikely, though he knew they sometimes had traces in the higher elevations.

Michael allowed the tractor to continue on its way and said to Segar, "We could drive over to see Nicolae. He might be the man you need."

"If you won't do it, I suppose he would be a possibility." Nicolae Gallipeau was a respected member of the Gypsy community, a learned man who had even attended school in Bucharest. Following the death of his wife, he had taken a young Gypsy girl named Krista as a lover, and she was at his house much of the time. This had caused some comment in the community, and even his own brother Arges had turned against him on the matter. To Captain Segar it seemed an affair of little consequence but he knew that Krista's parents had petitioned Michael to bring the matter before the Gypsy court, or kris. Though an informal tribunal, all kris rulings carried great weight in the community.

Nicolae's house was one of the village's better homes, a two story structure with an attached woodshed and a wellhouse. The man himself met them at the door, welcoming Michael with a hug and shaking hands with Captain Segar. Though he did not look that much different from his brother, there was a world of difference in their personalities. Nicolae was clean shaven and smiling, perhaps a bit heavier than Arges, and he wore a gold ring in his right ear. He remembered Segar from their prior meetings and immediately began questioning him about recent events in the city. When they finally sat down, Segar quickly brought up the subject of his visit. "What?" Nicolae asked with a chuckle. "You want me to represent the Gypsies? At what – a firing squad?"

"A Socialist anniversary," Segar said, filling in the details.

"The Romanian Gypsy is rarely so honored," Nicolae observed. "Did you ever read Bram Stoker's *Dracula*, Captain?"

"I expect every literate citizen has," Segar answered stiffly.

"At the end of the novel, Count Dracula's coffin is being transported through a snowstorm on the back of a Gypsy wagon. Jonathan Harker and the others overtake it, fight off the Gypsy knives and drive a knife through Dracula's heart. I think that is still the image some Romanians have of the Transylvanian Gypsy – the knife-wielding cohort of vampires."

"I doubt it's as bad as all that."

"At the very least they view us as flouting their stupid tax laws."

"We are guilty of that," Michael agreed. Romania imposed a tax on unmarried people over the age of twenty-five, and on childless couples, in an effort to spur the country's sagging population. Gypsies believed their traditional tribal laws took precedence over such government interference.

Nicolae took a pipe from the pocket of his fringed leather coat. "Then why do they want us represented at their anniversary?"

"They want better relations," Segar told him with a sigh. "Is that so difficult to understand?"

"It is for me," Nicolae retorted but his reply was cut short by the entrance of Krista into the room. She was dark-eyed and lovely, the sort of awesome Gypsy beauty famed in song and story but rarely encountered in real life. Segar knew she'd been listening to their conversation even before she spoke.

"Nicolae, I think you should go," she announced, sweeping across the room in a colorful skirt that almost touched the floor. Her low cut blouse did little to hide her voluptuous figure and her raven black hair glistened in the light. "You will be representing all of us."

The sight of her coming to the aid of his argument spurred Segar to renewed efforts. Michael joined in, too, urging with greater vigor than before. Finally, Nicolae threw up his hands with a rueful smile. "All right, I'll consider it. At least give me an hour or so to get used to the idea. Come back after lunch and I'll give you my decision."

Krista was going down to the main street of the village to shop for fresh vegetables and Vlado and Segar accompanied her. "Do you think we convinced him?" Michael asked.

"After all these years, you know him better than I do," she replied. "But I think so."

While she shopped, Michael suggested a bit of lunch. Captain Segar followed him into a little café next to the vegetable stalls. The wind had turned sharply colder and he was beginning to believe the warnings of snow. The café consisted of a few tables and a bare wooden counter, behind which the food and drinks were prepared. It was nothing like the wine shops and restaurants one found in the city, and for a moment it seemed like a foreign country to Segar. Michael Vlado spoke to the young man behind the counter in the Romany tongue and ordered a light lunch for them both. When the man disappeared into the back, Michael said in a low voice, "That's Trey Zuday. He used to be Krista's lover. I didn't realize he was working here."

Presently the young man returned with their food and Captain Segar studied him with more than passing interest. He was certainly younger than Nicolae Gallipeau and handsomer, but apparently Krista had chosen the security of an older, successful man. From what Michael had said earlier, even the opposition of her parents had failed to sway her.

It was at this point that Krista herself entered the café with a bag of vegetables ready to join them as planned. It was immediately apparent that her former lover's presence in the place was as much a surprise to her as it had been to Michael.

"Krista!" Trey Zuday exclaimed, his face a mixture of emotions. "What brings you in here?"

"I was shopping. I came to join Michael and the Captain."

He gave her a sardonic smile. "I hoped you might have come to see me."

"I thought you still worked on the farm."

"The harvest is finished for the year. I needed work."

"Oh." Her face was flushed and she looked away, not knowing whether to sit down or run out the door.

"How are your parents?"

"They are well, thank you."

"And Nicolae?"

"I – " The words caught in her throat and she was unable to answer.

"More vigorous than ever, I imagine, with a fine bedmate like you!"

"Trey, don't – "

He used some Romany phrase that Segar couldn't catch, and she burst into tears. Michael got to his feet. "She doesn't deserve obscenities," he told Trey quietly.

"Are you taking care of her now?"

Michael barked a few words in Romany and the young man fell grudgingly silent. "Let's get out of here," Krista said.

They followed her out, the food uneaten. "I thought I knew the language," Segar told Michael, "but I still have a few words to learn."

"Better you don't know those. They could bring you a Gypsy knife in the gut under the wrong circumstances." He called out, "Krista! Wait up !"

"I'm sorry," she said, and turned a tear-streaked face to them. "I shouldn't involve you. Go back and finish your lunch."

"When my people are involved, I am involved," Michael Vlado said. "Let us walk back to the house with you."

"There are a few flurries," Segar pointed out. "The snow is starting."

It was a ten minute walk back to Nicolae's house, but it was still warm enough to melt the snowflakes as they fell. Nicolae saw them approaching and came out to take the bag of vegetables from Krista. Behind him they saw his brother Arges, scratching his wispy beard. "I must be going now," Arges said. "Good to see you Krista."

"Can you not stay a bit?" she asked.

"No, no – Nicolae has agreed to what you asked Michael. He will tell you."

They turned toward Nicolae and he nodded. "I will represent the Gypsy community. My brother agrees that I should do it."

"That is good news," Captain Segar said, shaking his hand.

Arges gave a wave and headed across the field to his waiting tractor. Segar watched him for a moment, but his attention was distracted by the sudden appearance of Trey Zuday, running up the road from the center of the village. "What does he want?" Nicolae asked. "I thought you were finished with him, Krista."

"I am! We ran into him at the café. Be careful, Nicolae."

"I came to settle this, Nicolae!" the young man shouted, still twenty feet away. His hand moved quickly to the back of his belt and appeared holding a hunting knife.

"*Trey!*" Krista shouted, "Don't be crazy!"

Segar stepped quickly between the two men, holding out his hand with a gesture of authority. Perhaps it was the sight of his uniform that made Zuday hesitate. "Let him come!" Nicolae shouted. "I'm still man enough to beat him with my bare hands!"

"No, no!" Krista ran from one to the other, first pushing the older man back toward his house and then urging the young one to turn away from his foolhardy mission.

"You'd better go in," Michael told Nicolae. "We'll talk later about the Bucharest trip."

Krista had finally persuaded Trey to return the knife to his belt. This was the moment for which Nicolae had been waiting. He broke free of Michael's half-hearted grasp and ran at the younger man, striking him a glancing blow off the jaw. Trey staggered but did not go down. Instead his hand went back to the knife and it took both Segar and Michael to keep the two men apart.

Even Krista seemed disgusted by the action. "Nicolae – my God, you're worse than he is!"

The snow was falling harder now, and Kirsta led Trey away. Segar watched them part a little way down the road. The young man said something that made her throw up her hands and go off in the opposite direction. He continued back the way he had come.

"Go inside now," Michael commanded. "We're all getting wet."

Nicolae spat on the ground. "That young bull thinks he can win her back, but I can best him any day – with a knife or in the bed!"

"Go inside!" Michael repeated. "We all need to cool off."

Nicolae reentered the house, closing the door behind him. Now the grass was beginning to trap the wet flakes and Segar saw the trail his footprints had made.

"They'll calm down," Michael told him with perhaps more hope than assurance. "Gypsy blood is hot, and passion is always near the surface."

Segar's car was parked a little way down the road and they turned toward it.

"You're sure Nicolae won't change his mind about going to Bucharest?"

"If he gives his word, he keeps it," Michael assured him.

Suddenly there was a muffled shout from the direction of the house and both men turned. Through the falling snow they saw the front door begin to open. They had a glimpse of Nicolae Gallipeau, his face and chest covered with blood.

"Come on!" Michael shouted running toward the house through the light dusting of snow. Segar turned to summon Krista, but neither she nor Trey was in sight.

The door had swung shut by the time they reached it, but it hadn't latched. Michael pushed it open and went at once to Nicolae, who had staggered back and collapsed face down near the big wood stove. Michael started to turn him over and then took his hands away, staring up at Segar in disbelief. "He's dead. His throat's been cut!"

Segar knelt by the body and confirmed the fact that Nicolae Gallipeau was indeed dead. The blood had come from a terrible gash across his throat. The sight almost sickened him. "After his throat was cut, he managed to stagger from the parlor to the front door. See the trail of blood?"

"Where is the killer?" Michael asked, looking carefully about the room.

Segar drew a 9 mm pistol from his holster and stepped into the kitchen. Like most houses in Gravita, the place was equipped with telephone and electricity but no running water. A pump brought water to the kitchen sink, and an open well beyond the woodshed was available for hauling it up by the bucket. Segar moved carefully through the kitchen and woodshed to the wellhouse, checking cupboards and wood piles without success. A heavy door leading to the basement was bolted on the kitchen side, and though the back door of the wellhouse was unlatched the snow outside was unmarked. A small anvil stood near the door, apparently to hold it open when need be.

Segar returned to the front room where Michael had remained with the body. "He must be hiding upstairs." He started up more cautious than before, his pistol extended in front of him. He checked the bedrooms one at a time, looking in closets, under beds, and even in some of the larger drawers. At one end of the second floor he checked the storeroom, which served as a sort of attic. A large trunk yielded nothing but blankets and shawls. He tried the windows, seeking access to the roof, but they were all latched tight from the inside. There was no place even a child could have hidden.

Back downstairs, Michael Vlado stared at him as he returned. "Nothing?"

"Nothing. It makes one believe in Gypsy curses."

"The snow is unmarked at the back of the house?"

Segar nodded. "Stay here while I walk around the outside." Only a few flurries were drifting down, but the light coating on the ground provided an effective shield for the house. No one had entered or left since the snow fell, except by the front door. Segar even checked the outhouse, though the unmarked snow told him it would be empty.

He returned to the front of the house and told Michael. "The killer is still inside, if there ever was a killer."

"What other possibility is there?"

"He might have committed suicide."

"Cutting his own throat?" Michael Vlado shook his head. "Then where is the weapon? It's nowhere in the room."

"He might have thrown it as he opened the front door."

"We would have seen it. The snow's not deep enough to hide anything."

Nevertheless, Segar inspected the ground near the front door. Not even a razor blade could have escaped his scrutiny. There was nothing in the snow. "You're right," he finally agreed, straightening up.

"I must tell his brother," Michael said, "and Krista, if I can find her. Will you stay here with the body?"

Captain Segar nodded. "I'll phone my office and have them send a team of investigators up here. And an ambulance for the body."

Michael Vlado frowned. "He must be buried here, on Gypsy land."

"Not until we do an autopsy. I want a full report on that wound. We might get some idea as to what caused it. Perhaps a booby trap of some sort that did not require the murderer's presence – "

"It was his own house. He'd been in it only moments before. And what sort of booby trap would leave no traces?"

Vlado left Segar and went off across the fields toward Arge's house. Segar went back inside and used the telephone near the front door, trying not to look at the body on the floor. He spoke directly to Inspector Krisana, who promised to have people there from a district substation within thirty minutes. Segar didn't bother to tell him that the victim had been the would-be representative at the forthcoming state function.

Michael Vlado returned in twenty minutes, looking frustrated. "Arges isn't at home and I can't find Krista. Trey Zuday isn't in sight either."

"It's still snowing a little. Not exactly the sort of weather for working outside, or taking an autumn stroll."

"Did you phone your headquarters?"

Segar nodded. "They should be here shortly. They're coming from Racari."

He had another thought. "What about the basement? The door was bolted, but I should check down there anyway. How far does it run?"

"Under the main part only. It's more for food storage than anything else."

"Stay here. I'll take a look."

He used his flashlight to inspect the dirt-floored basement, finding only a thick festoon of spiderwebs that covered the ceiling. No one was hidden there and it seemed unlikely that anyone had ventured into the place in many months.

By the time he returned upstairs, a state militia car and a government ambulance were pulling up before the house. Captain Segar spoke quickly to the new arrivals and watched while they went about their tasks. The medical intern on the ambulance pronounced Nicolae dead, noting the date and time on his records. Then the technician from the Ricari substation took some pictures and dusted halfheartedly for fingerprints. "Where's the weapon?" one of them asked.

"No weapon," Segar told them.

"These Gypsies are nothing but trouble. Why do we drive all this distance for a Gypsy killing? Let them cut throats all they want."

Michael Vlado was close enough to hear and Segar saw the line of his jaw tighten. Perhaps he was remembering the Gypsies who had died in Hitler's concentration camps alongside the Jews. "Come outside," Segar told him quietly, placing a hand on his shoulder.

"Is that the government position?"

"Of course not." They went into the brisk afternoon air, still white with drifting snowflakes.

The ambulance attendants came out to their vehicle for a large plastic body bag. The technicians, finished with their work, were leaving. "Where are the suspects?" one of them asked Segar. Even the sight of the official vehicles had attracted no curious neighbors. It was as if the village and the countryside were suddenly deserted.

"There aren't any," the captain replied, turning helplessly to Michael Vlado.

"The sight of government officials keeps villagers away," Michael explained. "They will mourn Nicolae's death at the proper time and in the proper Gypsy manner – when outsiders have gone."

The intern and ambulance driver were having a cigarette before returning to their task. Segar stood in the snow, staring up at the house and wondering what its secret was. "He's in there someplace," he told Michael. "That's the only possibility. There has to be a secret panel somewhere."

But Michael shook his head. "I helped Nicolae build that house. It has no secret panels or hidden rooms."

"You agree that the killer was waiting inside?"

"It would seem so."

"He was inside when we returned to the house."

Michael nodded. "Or else he slipped around the back and entered through the woodshed while we talked out front, before the snow had accumulated enough to show his tracks."

"It could have been Trey Zuday."

"Or anyone else."

"Someone small enough to hide – where?" He remembered how carefully he'd searched the house. "That big wood stove inside the door?"

"Surely it is in use on such a cold day."

The intern and driver finished their cigarettes and returned to the house, pushing open the front door as they unfolded the body bag. Gallipeau's head hung down as they lifted his leather jacketed body and half slid, half rolled it into the bag, zipping shut the side opening. The dead man's right ear seemed to be listening, and in that moment it was as soft and unadorned as a baby's at birth. Perhaps we all die that way, Segar mused – listening like babies to some distant trumpet. He wondered what his Socialist master would think of such spiritual meditations. Surely in Russia men had been shot for less.

"The well!" Michael said suddenly, as the body was being slid into the back of the ambulance.

"What?"

"The well! When you searched the house, did you look in the well?"

"No," Segar admitted. "I looked at it, but not into it."

"Come on!" Michael turned to the driver. "You men stay here until we return."

Segar repeated the order so it would be obeyed, then followed Michael inside. "How could anyone be hidden in the well? Wouldn't they drown?"

"There are iron rungs in the side for climbing up or down. Nicolae was always afraid someone would fall in and drown before they could be pulled out."

It was a good idea but the flashlight revealed that the well was empty. The rungs led down to the water, but no one was standing on them. They watched long enough to establish that no one was holding his breath just beneath the water's surface. "That's all right," Segar assured Michael. "We all have our ideas."

Michael walked over to the wellhouse door and opened it. "There are footprints by the outhouse."

"Those are mine," Segar told him. "I checked it earlier." He glanced around for something to prop the door open, finally settling on a block of wood. "I think we should search the house together while the ambulance people watch the front door."

Michael agreed, and they quickly went through the place. No one was hidden there, and no one had run out the back door across the snow. The house was empty as on the previous search. Segar reluctantly told the driver to proceed to Ricari with the body.

"A wire might have been pulled across his throat," Michael speculated.

"By whom?" Segar demanded. "Where did it go?"

"Perhaps a knife was thrown."

"Then where is it? Who threw it? The thing is impossible. If Trey Zuday killed him, he was invisible."

Michael Vlado watched the ambulance pull away. "Impossible. And yet it happened. Nicolae is certainly dead."

Segar could see Gypsies emerging from their homes now that the police and ambulance had departed. Only he remained and they trusted him. Krista was one of the first to reach the house, and she sobbed as Michael told her what had happened. She entered the house and stared bleakly at the floor where blood still marked the place of Nicolae's death. "Where is the little rug?" she asked.

"It was bloody," Michael answered. "Perhaps the ambulance attendants threw it out."

"Something else is missing," Segar said suddenly. "When I searched earlier, there was a small anvil in the wellhouse. Just now I couldn't find it. I used a block of wood to prop open the door."

"Anvil," Michael repeated. Then, "Quickly! To your car!"

"What?"

"We have to go after that ambulance!"

It was a nightmare ride, speeding over back roads, once taking a wrong turn. What did the missing anvil have to do with catching the ambulance? Segar kept asking Michael the question, but the Gypsy was not yet ready to answer. He only urged Segar to drive faster, to use his siren.

Finally they saw the vehicle ahead through the falling snow. Siren pulsating, Segar's car passed it and forced it to stop. Then Michael was out of the car, running like a madman to the back of the ambulance, opening the door, yanking the plastic body bag onto the snowy road. It was the final scene of *Dracula* again, Segar thought. His friend had surely gone mad, coming here to plunge a stake through the heart of a dead man.

But Michael was more interested in raising the dead than in killing them again. "Come out of there, you murderer! Just as Cain slew Abel, you have killed your brother!"

And Segar saw that the man inside was not dead, and it was not Nicolae Gallipeau. It was his brother Arges.

Michael accompanied Segar and the others into the substation at Racari, and while he drank a cup of coffee he answered Segar's questions about the amazing case. "What did Arges plan to do? Why had he taken his brother's place in that body bag and how did he accomplish it?"

The Gypsy leaned back in his chair. They were in a plain, drab office where a large blue, yellow, and red Romanian flag on the wall was the only decoration. It reminded Segar glumly of Inspector Krisana's office back at headquarters. "Oh, I have no doubt Arges would have cut his way out of the bag and leaped from the ambulance when it arrived here," Michael Vlado said. "He still had the murder knife with him."

"How did he do it?"

"Simple. He left us in front of his brother's house, made a wide circle and reentered through the rear wellhouse door just as the snow was beginning to stick to the ground. He planned to kill his brother and exit in the same manner, but by the time he returned to the back door the snow had accumulated enough to show footprints. He was trapped inside the house."

"But where did he hide? I searched the house twice."

"The first time he was in the well, clinging to those iron rungs. Later, when the technicians departed and the intern and driver went outside for the body bag, he saw his opportunity. He changed places with his victim. You must have noticed that they look something alike, as brothers would. Hacking off his wispy beard with his knife or a handy scissors, he removed Nicolae's distinctive jacket and put it on over his own clothes. He smeared blood over his face and neck to cover the stubs of his beard, and lay down in his brother's place. The body had been examined already,so the ambulance people merely placed it in the body bag without a second thought."

But Captain Segar was not satisfied. "What did he do with the real body? We searched the house a second time remember? A dead body would have been as impossible to hide as a living one."

"You solved that mystery yourself when you mentioned the missing anvil. Nicolae's body was dropped down the well, weighted with that anvil. And the rug Krista noticed was missing – that was probably used to pull the body out to the wellhouse so there wouldn't be more blood spread through the place. The body was probably wrapped in it before he dropped it down the well."

"How did you know all this?"

"It came to me when you mentioned the missing anvil. I also remembered something odd about the body as they placed it in the bag. Perhaps you noticed it too. The right ear was bare, though Nicolae wore an earring in his ear. If Nicolae's body had gone down that well and the killer was escaping in that ambulance, I knew it must be Arges. No one else looked enough like Nicolae to get away with it."

"Why did he do it?"

"I asked him that. His motive was Cain's motive – jealousy of his brother's achievement. Choosing Nicolae for that honorary appearance in Bucharest was the last straw. He'd always loved Krista from afar and that played a part too. Nicolae had the better house, the better woman, and now the honor of representing all the Gypsies. Arges could take it no longer."

"I only went to him because you turned it down."

"Yes," Michael said. Clearly, he had considered that.

"What will I do now?"

"I will go to Bucharest," Michael Vlado decided. "I owe Nicolae and Arges that much."

THE GYPSY TREASURE

Captain Segar's usual job was law enforcement in the cities and towns that bordered the Transylvanian Alps in central Romania. He disliked the Communist politicians one encountered all too frequently in Bucharest and for that reason he usually managed to steer clear of his nation's capital. However, the November conciliation meeting required the presence of a Gypsy leader, along with representatives of other ethnic groups and so Segar accompanied his friend Michael Vlado to the gathering.

Michael was even more ill at ease than Segar in the streets of the city, longing for the quiet of his little village of Gravita. He wasn't a nomadic Gypsy by nature but a settled one, descended from a line of cattle drovers who had made Romania their home for more than a century. He had a wife and family back in Gravita and he was anxious to return to them.

It was on the second day of the two-day meeting that Captain Segar saw a Gypsy woman approach Michael in the hotel lobby and hand him a message. He seemed startled to see her and tried to say something, but she retreated as quickly as she had come.

"Who was that?" Segar asked as Michael stood reading the message he had been handed.

"The daughter of an old Gypsy king," Michael replied. "She brings me news of the death of her uncle."

"I'm sorry."

Michael nodded acknowledgement. "There is a Gypsy festival in Oradea this weekend and tribes from all over Europe will be there. I had hoped to see Greystone at it." He pondered the message for a moment and then folded it into his pocket.

"You will not be returning to Gravita then ?" Segar asked.

"No, I must go to Oradea for the festival."

"That's almost to the Hungarian border!"

"It must be," Michael answered simply.

He seemed troubled and distant for the remainder of the day. In the late afternoon when the time came to depart, Segar found him alone in the lobby. "How will you get to Oradea?" he asked. They'd made the trip to Bucharest in Segar's official car.

"I can go by train," Michael answered. After a moment he added, "unless you would be able to accompany me."

"Me? I must be back to work on Monday."

"But your weekend is free?"

"Well, I suppose so," Segar admitted.

"I would appreciate it if you could accompany me. There may be a need for your services."

"My official services? Oradea is outside my district."

"But as a captain of the security forces you would have authority to act in the absence of the local police."

"What is it that troubles you so, Michael?"

"Greystone, the Gypsy who died, was murdered. It happened just a few miles from the festival site at Oradea. There could be further violence at the festival."

"I will accompany you," Segar decided reluctantly. "But I need more details."

"There will be plenty of time to talk on the way," Michael said.

The journey was a long one, some three hundred miles by road through the mountains. The border city was in a valley given over to fields of wheat and corn. It was in a meadow south of the city that the Gypsy festival would be held.

"Oradea is much smaller than Bucharest," Segar noted at they drove through the night on the last leg of the journey. "There are few of the modern buildings one sees in the capital."

"We will not be going to the city itself."

"Tell me about the man who died."

"Though he was called Greystone his real name was Zuloaga. His brother Konrad Zuloaga is a Gypsy king – it was Konrad's daughter Livia who brought me the message at the hotel."

"How did Greystone die?"

"Stabbed to death as soon as he arrived in Oradea. It was made to look like a knife fight, but his brother is convinced it was a carefully planned killing."

"Why do you believe there may be more violence? Is it a feud between rival Gypsy tribes?"

"No, not in the way you mean. To explain it, I must tell you about the Second World War and about the treasure of the Gypsies."

"Don't all Gypsies have a hidden treasure?" Segar asked remembering old legends.

"This is treasure of a more modern sort. As you know, many Gypsies died in Nazi concentration camps along with the Jews. In some cases, entire tribes were wiped out. The Gypsies of Hungary and Romania, realizing they were doomed, banded together to keep their gold and jewelry from falling into the hands of the Nazis. This so-called treasure was hidden somewhere in the area of Oradea and its whereabouts was entrusted to five men, each of whom was given a portion of the secret.

"But the war has been over for forty years!"

"What is forty years when measured as part of eternity? The original owners of the treasure died in the camps. Others didn't know quite what should be done with it. Finally, the cards were consulted, and the other oracles that my people rely upon. It was decided that the treasure should be recovered this year on this first November weekend, and so the festival was planned."

"It's getting a bit chilly for an outdoor festival. You'll remember there was snow in Gravita two weeks ago."

"Only a flurry. And this area is warmer being in a valley."

"What of the five who know the treasure's location? Are you one of them?"

"Hardly. I wasn't even born until after the war had started. As you know, I was named for the young King Michael who ruled from 1940 until the Communists forced him to abdicate in nineteen forty-seven."

Segar nodded. "A good man even though his father was a Fascist."

"No, I wasn't one of the five," Michael continued, "but I have known them all. Two are dead now."

"Greystone is one of them?"

"Yes. And whoever killed him may have taken his portion of the secret."

"What is it – a map divided into five pieces?"

"No one knows . Except the five."

"What about the other one who died ?"

"A natural death, some years ago. The secret passed to his son."

Captain Segar pondered the information as he drove. "Why do you expect more violence?"

"The so-called treasure, if it really exists at all, must be worth a large fortune. Even my fellow Gypsies are not above killing for money, and now that blood has been spilled more may follow. The idea of the festival bothered me from the beginning. Why not assemble only the five? Why bring in five hundred?"

They'd driven through most of the night stopping only to sleep for a few hours along the road. Now, as the first gentle streaks of dawn appeared in the east, Segar rounded a bend in the road and saw in the distance the first wagons of the Gypsy encampment. "We're here," he told Michael.

Many of the Gypsies had come in campers and house trailers but a surprising number of traditional horse drawn wagons were in evidence too. Though it was barely dawn there was evidence of activity at the camp. Fires were going and breakfast was being prepared.

"They're setting up the fortune-telling booths already," Segar observed.

"It is their livelihood after all," said Michael.

They parked the car off the road and strolled among the campers, several of whom shouted greetings to Michael. Even over breakfast some of the men were playing cards, betting small amounts of money on Austrian tarot or American poker, sometimes mixing English phrases with their Romany speech. Near one of the wagons a young Gypsy was practicing on his violin.

"There will be music and dancing," Michael said, "and card games and fortune telling – all designed to separate the local people from their money in one way or another." He led the way to a large mobile home at the back of the encampment. A woman opened the door as they approached and Captain Segar recognized the Gypsy who'd delivered the message to Michael in Bucharest. She was more attractive close up than he'd first supposed. A single golden earring through her left lobe balanced a cascade of black hair on the right side of her head.

"Ah, Livia! You're done up in fine style for the townsfolk."

"Thank you," she told Michael with a smile. "Will you stay to see my dance?"

"That depends on your father."

She escorted them into the vehicle where a grey-haired Gypsy sat across the table from a younger man in traditional farmer's overalls. The Gypsy rose, smiling, to welcome Michael. "I was afraid you would not come, Michael. We need your sage advice. But you have brought someone with you."

"Konrad, this is Captain Segar, a friend and traveling companion."

"A captain of police?"

"He is on holiday. Captain, this is Konrad Zuloaga, a king much beloved by his people."

Zuloaga in turn introduced his guest. "Rudolph Fuhl who has the farm across the road."

Fuhl, a man in his thirties, shook hands with a powerful grip. "I was surprised to see so many vehicles arriving during the night. When King Zuloaga wrote me of this gathering, I understood only five Gypsies and their families would attend."

"It has turned into a festival," Zuloaga acknowledged. "We will be gone by Monday and the countryside will be peaceful once more. In the meantime, bring your family and enjoy it."

"Is this your property?" Michael asked the farmer.

"It's state property. All this area belonged to a great uncle named Prando during the war. He was killed in a bombing raid and the state seized it. My father was allowed to keep farming his portion across the road. Of course, all arable land was nationalized in nineteen sixty-two, so now I have only a half acre plot for private use."

Michael nodded. "Such is the case in Gravita as well. But if this is state property why are you concerned?"

"There will be trouble and the authorities will come. There is always trouble when there are Gypsies."

"There will be no trouble," Konrad Zuloaga assured him. "You have my word for it. Livia, escort Mr. Fuhl to the road." Then, perhaps aware of the suddenness of the dismissal, he repeated, "Bring your family over later for the festival, Mr. Fuhl. I'm sure they will enjoy it."

"Thank you," the farmer said. "I might do that."

When they were alone, Zuloaga relaxed a bit and turned to Michael. "I feel better with you here. The four are meeting this afternoon to compare clues to the treasure's location. After the killing of Greystone, I fear what might happen."

"Was his clue to the treasure taken from him?"

"Yes."

"You still have yours ?"

"Of course. For more than forty years I have guarded it."

"You and your brother. A third keeper of the secret, the crippled Gypsy, one-eyed Heron, died of natural causes more than a decade ago."

Zuloaga nodded. "His son Radu is here with that portion of the secret."

"And the other two?"

"Kings in their own right – old Cuza of the Wanderers and a man who should be king, the English Gypsy, Reynard."

"I have heard of Reynard but never met him," Michael said.

"Some find him too sly, too disdainful of the old Gypsy customs but he has kept the secret for all these years along with the others. We were only five boys at the time, some of us still in our teens, and the secret given to us changed our lives. I would say that old Cuza is a king today because he was one of the treasure's guardians. Perhaps that is true of me as well."

"The five of you were chosen at random?"

"Young men were picked who might have a chance of escaping the Nazi roundup by fleeing cross country. It was a wise choice, obviously, since four of us made good our escape. Heron was caught by the Nazis near the Swiss border and brutally treated. His experience in the camps left him a one-eyed cripple, but he survived. After the war, he married a Gypsy woman he'd met in the camp and fathered Radu. The treasure clue passed to Radu when his father died."

"He was able to keep the clue with him all through the camps?"

"By its very nature it is easily hidden," Konrad Zuloaga said. "You will see soon enough. I want you to be here this afternoon at two o'clock." He glanced at Captain Segar. "Your friend too, if you wish."

Michael nodded. "I do wish. Captain Segar is a man of the law, but one who respects the way of the Gypsy."

"Bring him then."

"You believe the killer of your brother will be among those present?"

"It is possible."

Livia returned from escorting Fuhl out of the encampment. She was laughing and full of high spirits. "Everything is ready for the festival."

"The farmer is gone?"

She nodded. "He is so frightened of our people! He thought one of Cuza's daughters gave him the evil eye." The thought made her laugh anew.

"Captain Segar and I will be leaving now," Michael said. "We will return at two o'clock."

Some people from the city had already driven out for the festival, though the hour was early. The fortune-telling booths were attracting the largest crowd but some of the men had already strolled over to watch the Gypsy dancers. "King Zuloaga seems so stern and dignified," Segar observed, "yet we step out of his trailer and see all this."

"There are many tribes represented here. Some still relish the old Gypsy ways. We should enjoy it while it lasts – the tide of history is running against the wanderer."

They strolled past dark-skinned women in colorful scarves, past gambling games and tarot readings. The music of the Gypsy violins grew louder and seemed to drive the last morning clouds from the sky. With the sun came a warmth more like August than November. "A beautiful day, Michael," said Segar.

"It is." He paused at the edge of the encampment to study a weathered barn some hundred yards away. "That barn is all that remains of the original Prando farm. You can see the remains of the house foundation nearby. When the

Gypsies met here in the early days of the war, it would have been a thriving farm."

"How do you know the Nazis never found the treasure?"

"Someone would have known. It wasn't the sort of thing the Nazis would keep secret. More likely, they would have announced it as a great triumph over our people."

"More to the point, how are you so certain there ever was a treasure?"

Michael shook his head. "When a Gypsy tells another Gypsy there is a treasure you can be sure of it. We may lie to outsiders, but not among ourselves. The Gypsy code is very strict. Livia, the king's daughter, was married once. Her husband divorced her for sleeping with another man. Under Gypsy law, he could have killed her. Yet if she had taken money from her lover it would not have been considered adultery."

"Amazing."

"Another example – Gypsy children are never beaten by their parents. It is considered a greater crime to beat one's children than to beat one's parents – "

Someone called Michaels name and they were joined by a rough-looking man in his thirties. He had a knife scar on one cheek and an insolent manner that Segar disliked at once. "Michael, you have surely lowered yourself to attend our festival! What bring you all the way from Gravita?"

"Hello, Radu. This is Captain Segar, my friend."

"You travel with the police these days?"

"When necessary. You are here to do your father's duty?"

The man's face twisted into a humorless grin. "I am here to claim his share of the treasure."

"The treasure came from all of us. It belongs to all of us."

"Oh no – not my father's share. He was tortured by the Nazis and managed to survive. But his life was crippled and shortened by the experience. I am owed his share of this treasure and Konrad Zuloaga will not keep it from me."

"We have to find it first," Michael reminded him.

"It will be found." Radu started away.

"This afternoon will tell," Michael said.

When they'd walked on, Segar commented. "A disagreeable man. He is Radu Heron, possessor of his father's share of the secret?"

"Correct. Of the secret, not of the treasure."

Captain Segar spotted Livia running through the crowd, pausing to joke with one of the violin players. "You said her husband divorced her for adultery. Is he here today?"

"You have just met him," Michael replied. "She was married to Radu

Heron. It was her lover who gave Radu that scar, before Radu killed him."

Toward noon, they decided to eat and Segar followed Michael to a modern camping vehicle of British manufacture. The man they met there was unlike any of the other Gypsies Segar knew. Tall and slim, he had the look of a handsome, suntanned Englishman, the sort Segar imagined one met at polo matches. It was only when Reynard spoke that a trace of his Gypsy heritage surfaced.

"Captain Segar – so pleased to meet you! Back in England some of my best friends are members of the police. I look forward to chatting with you after the day's business is completed."

He had traveled to Oradea with a blonde Englishwoman somewhat younger than his sixty-odd years. Her name was Charlotte and she kept to the background, casting occasional apprehensive looks in Segar's direction. Michael had never met Reynard before but each of them knew the other. Unlike Zuloaga and old Cuza, Reynard had not aspired to a kingship among the Gypsies. He had become another person, of another tribe, and he made it clear that this visit back to his past was not pleasant for him.

"Have you seen Cuza?" Michael asked. "Or Konrad Zuloaga? The son of Heron is here, too."

"These are but names from the past to me, Michael. Charlotte and I have a different life in England. I do not live as a Gypsy there." He smiled a bit. "Except perhaps for a weekend's camping."

Charlotte served a light lunch of food they'd brought with them. There was no trace of Gypsy cuisine here, only traditional British dishes. Segar found the lunch appetizing enough, if a trifle bland for his taste. After they'd finished, Michael took his leave. "You'll be at Zuloaga's at two?"

"I'll be there," Reynard assured them. "And once I'm rid of my part in this confounded secret, the rest of you can keep the treasure or do whatever you want with it."

They left the camper and continued on across the encampment toward Zuloaga's mobile home. There were more townspeople now, strolling among the trucks and wagons, stopping to admire a horse or buy a scarf or wager a few lei on a game of chance. Segar could merely shake is head. "The local police should be here. There's thievery all around us."

"Remember you're on a holiday," Michael chided him.

"Are we going to see the other one now? Old Cuza?"

"It's getting close to two o'clock. We'll see him at the meeting."

Livia poured six globets of wine for the group and then vanished into a bedroom as Radu Heron and Reynard arrived. They sat at a round table with Konrad Zuloaga while Michael and Segar took seats to one side. "What is the policeman doing here?" Radu wanted to know, scowling at Segar across the table.

"He's here at my request," Zuloaga said. "My brother is dead, possibly because of the treasure. I want no more killing here."

"A body guard for a Gypsy king!" Radu scoffed. "When I am king, I will defend *myself*."

"I forgive your tongue," Zuloaga told him, "because your father suffered for his people."

Reynard was restless. "Where is old Cuza?" he asked. "Let's get this business behind us."

"Cuza is an ill man," Zuloaga said. "He was the oldest of us back then, you'll remember. The oldest of the five. I visited him for lunch and he gave me his share of the secret, in this envelope, in case he is not able to attend. His daughters are caring for him."

Their eyes went to the envelope Konrad Zuloaga held in his hand. "Let's get on with it, then," Reynard insisted, reaching into his own pocket. "Here's my portion." He tossed a worn playing card onto the table. It was the eight of hearts, and across the face of it was written in faded ink the words *Prando Farm, Oradea*.

"Interesting," Zuloaga commented. "It is the card for thoughts of marriage in fortune telling." He opened the envelope by ripping one end of it. "Here is Cuza's contribution."

It was another playing card, the eight of clubs.

"An accident," Michael said softly from the sidelines giving the Gypsy meaning.

Konrad Zuloaga nodded. "And my card – the eight of diamonds. It suggests a jewel."

They sat staring at the three eights. All the cards were from the same deck, with a faded Albanian flag on the back, its black two-headed eagle poised against a red background. And all had the words *Prando Farm, Oradea* scrawled across the face of the card in the same handwriting.

"That was our father," Konrad said, noting Michael's perusal of the cards. "It was a deck he always carried with him. We sat in this very field as he chose my brother and me and Reynard and Heron and Cuza. He wrote that on each of the cards he chose without letting any of us see the other's cards. He told us to travel far and always keep the card with us because when we were reunited they would tell us the location of the Gypsy treasure."

All eyes were on Radu Heron now, and Michael said, "Show us your father's card, Radu. Show us the fourth eight."

Radu spit on the floor and tossed his card onto the table. It had been folded twice, apparently so it could be hidden in a small space. But it was not the eight of spades everyone expected.

It was the six of diamonds.

"Beware of speculation," Konrad Zuloaga said with a chuckle. "A card with a special meaning to a speculator like Michael."

"I guessed wrong," Michael admitted.

"Three eights and a six," Reynard said. "Most interesting. But what about the fifth card?"

"My brother had it with him when he was killed," Konrad replied. "His murderer took it."

"It might not be three eights and a six at all," Michael pointed out. "It could be two diamonds, a heart and a club."

"Do you wish to deduce its meaning?" Konrad challenged.

"That's difficult without the fifth card, especially since the geographic features of the farm might have changed in forty years. But two of you were here then. Tell me about this place, Reynard and Konrad."

It was Reynard who answered first. "I remember a big farm, well equipped for its time. You can still see the foundation where the main house stood. There was the barn, and a horse barn, and some other buildings. A silo. I remember especially a huge old oak tree that stood in a far corner of the field marking one corner of the boundary. The farm was bigger then, on both sides of the road, and more than a dozen Gypsies worked here. Even then, they settled down and stopped wandering like many Gypsies of Eastern Europe."

Konrad Zuloaga took up the story. "It was my father who gathered up the gold and jewelry when we saw what was happening to the Gypsies. There was a great deal of it. I remember it filling half the back of a truck. We never saw what they did with it, but it was hidden somewhere on this farm. And the clues were given to the five of us. We were never to show each other our cards until all of us had gathered here again. That was to take more than forty years for a variety of reasons."

"Your father must have felt that the hiding place of the treasure would become obvious once the five playing cards were seen together," Michael said.

"But we need the fifth card," Radu insisted. "These four mean nothing by themselves."

Reynard cleared his throat. "They may mean less than nothing. Have you considered the possibility that one of us may have substituted a fake card for the real one?"

"What would that gain?" Michael asked.

"One of us would know the true location of the treasure while the others were kept in the dark. One of us could come and steal it away."

"The treasure is for the common good of all Rom peoples," Konrad Zuloaga insisted.

"The hell it is!" Radu growled, his anger building once more. "It belongs to the five and one fifth of it is mine, as my father's son. You are so noble sounding about the Rom people, but it is you who had the best opportunity to switch one of the playing cards – or even two! How do we know that eight of clubs is really old Cuza's card?"

"You can ask him," Konrad answered simply. He raised his voice and called out, "Livia! Please come here."

His daughter came out of the bedroom to join them. Segar saw her eyes go to the four playing cards in the center of the table. "What is it, Father?"

"Go to Cuza's camper and ask if he is well enough to join us now. If he is not, ask if we might visit him."

She nodded. "I'll go at once."

Segar watched through the window as she cut across the campground weaving through the crowds of townspeople. "You will have your answer very shortly," Konrad told Radu.

Michael had reached out to pick up the four worn playing cards and was turning them over in his hands. He studied the identical Albanian flags on the back and asked, "Did your father come from Albania, Konrad?"

"He acquired the cards once when passing through there, in the late nineteen thirties."

"And he kept the rest of the deck?"

"No. He threw it into the campfire."

"That's right," Reynard confirmed. "I remember that part."

"The black eagle is similar to the one on the old Austrian flag, except it has two heads."

"Albania is called the Land of the Eagle," Konrad explained. "The two-headed black eagle on the red background is the flag Scanderberg used in his revolt against the Turks five hundred years ago. It is very dear to the Albanian people."

"Have you been there recently?"

"Not since the Communists took over in nineteen forty-four. Romania is bad enough but at least there is some freedom here."

Segar started to say something in defense of the present government, but his words were cut short by the sudden return of Livia. She was out of breath from running and her face was ashen.

"What is it?" her father asked, rising to his feet.

"Cuza is dead! He's been murdered."

Cuza had come to the festival grounds in a small camping vehicle. A canvas covering at the back gave it the look of a tent, and Captain Segar thought it more in keeping with the Gypsy spirit than the more modern trailers and camping vehicles. Livia led the way under the canvas flap and then held open the door of the vehicle so Segar and Michael could enter first.

The inside was more spacious and modern than one would have guessed from the exterior, with bunk beds, a bottled-gas stove and a working refrigerator. There was even running water, apparently from a tank carried at the front of the vehicle. Cuza was in the lower of the bunk beds. Blankets covered his body to the neck but even so it was easy to see the blood from the deep throat wound.

"A knife," Segar guessed. "A single slash while he slept."

Konrad Zuloaga entered then, trying to keep Radu and Reynard from following him through the doorway. "Like my brother," he said his voice full of sadness.

"It means the killer is here," Michael told them, "on the festival grounds."

"It means more than that," Radu Heron argued. "Zuloaga killed old Cuza himself when he saw him at lunch. That's how he got his clue to the treasure."

"It does appear that the camper has been searched," Segar pointed out indicating a half-open drawer and some papers on the floor. He bent to pick up a road map of the area that had been carelessly refolded in the wrong way.

"As I told you," Radu persisted. "Zuloaga killed him, found the playing card and took it."

Michael turned to stare at him. "For what purpose? To reveal it to us, as Cuza himself would have done?"

"No, to substitute another card and keep the location of the treasure to himself."

Konrad could take no more. "I loved and respected your father, Radu, but I can tolerate these charges no longer. Outside, we will settle this with knives!"

"No!" Livia screamed, grabbing her father's arm. "You're doing this for me. Stop it, both of you!"

"Not for you," Konrad told her. "For my honor."

Radu glared at Livia and spat on the floor. "I will wait outside with my knife."

"I want to see that knife," Segar said. "Give it here."

"By whose order?"

Segar showed his badge and identification. "I have jurisdiction here until the arrival of the local police." He took the knife that Radu grudgingly surrendered and looked carefully at the blade. He could see no traces of dried blood but decided to keep possession of it for a while.

Michael was sniffing the air around the stove. He stopped to peer carefully at one of the burners. "Segar, I can see some charred remains here. Something was burned recently. You can still catch a whiff of it in the air."

Segar glanced at the burner. "Nothing but charred remains, whatever it was."

He turned back to the others, going through the investigative routine he knew so well. "What time did you last see Cuza alive, Mr. Zuloaga?"

"About one-fifteen. That is when he gave me the card."

"I'd guess he's been dead over an hour, so he was probably killed before the start of the two o'clock meeting. If the motive was that playing card, it was important for the killer to strike before the meeting."

"Of course," Raynard agreed. "But Konrad already had the card."

"The killer had no way of knowing that," Segar said.

Radu glared at him.

"You're saying it was Reynard or me?"

Before Segar could answer, Michael gave a cry of triumph. Still bent over the stove he lifted a portion of the burner and produced a tiny bit of stiff paper charred on one side. "What is it, Michael?" Konrad asked.

"The corner of a playing card. See the red back?"

"The missing card!"

"Can you tell which card it is?" Segar asked.

"I can, but it only confirms what I already knew. The card is the six of spades."

"The six of spades," Konrad Zuloaga repeated. "And whose card is it?"

"Your dead brother's, I think."

Segar ran over them from memory. "The six of spades, the six and eight of diamonds, the eight of clubs and hearts. How can that tell anyone where the Gypsy treasure is hidden?"

"It tells us that," Michael insisted, "and it also tells us who killed Greystone and old Cuza."

While they waited for the Oradea police to arrive, Michael herded everyone back to Zuloaga's mobile home. In addition to Konrad and Reynard and

Radu, Livia joined them, along with Charlotte, the woman traveling with Reynard. As they settled down around the table, Livia averted her eyes from Radu. She had not spoken to her former husband all day so far as Michael and Segar could tell.

"I'll try to keep this as brief as possible," Michael explained, "so we can wrap it all up before the local police become involved. There are really only two logical possibilities regarding that burnt six of spades. One, it was Cuza's card and Konrad burned it after killing him so he could substitute the eight of clubs he showed us earlier. But I think I can show that it's highly unlikely any of the cards were substitutions.

"We've heard that Konrad and Greystone's father burned the rest of the original deck after passing out those five cards years ago. Since a deck with an Albanian flag on the back would be difficult to obtain in Romania, especially during the war, I think we can safely assume that none of you had a duplicate card or deck at the time. Did one of the five obtain a duplicate deck years later with the purpose of hiding the treasure's location from all but himself? No, again, because all four of those cards came from a deck printed prior to nineteen forty-four."

"How do you know that?" Livia asked.

"Look again at the Albanian flag. A two-headed black eagle against the red background. Is that same flag in use by Albania today?"

"Of course it is," Konrad insisted.

Michael Vlado smiled and shook his head. "A minor but important change was made in 1944 by the new Communist government. A gold-edged red star, a symbol of Communism, was added just above the eagle's twin heads. So we can safely say the playing cards are the genuine article, because we can prove that they predate nineteen forty-four. Now if these four are genuine what about the fifth one? There would be no purpose served in burning a fake card. Yet if the fifth one is genuine it could only have come from Greystone. It must be the missing fifth card, and we can reasonably assume it was brought to Cuza's trailer by Greystone's killer, who then killed Cuza."

"Wait a minute," Konrad interrupted. "Why would he keep my brother's card for a few days and then burn it?"

"He kept it as a possible match to Cuza's or others that he found. But after killing Cuza he must have realized that if the card was found on him it would link him with this latest murder. So he burned it before leaving the trailer."

Konrad shook his head. "I would think he would keep the cards if he was seeking the treasure. Why kill us just to destroy them?"

"Exactly," Michael agreed. "Just to destroy them. The most likely reason is that the killer already knew the location of the treasure. He killed to keep the rest of you from finding out the location and discovering that the treasure is no longer there."

"Not there?" Radu gasped. "Where is it?"

"Remember the cards. Forget the suits – they're not important. The cards were three eights and two sixes. And what is that combination of cards called?" The others around the table looked blank. "The American game of poker is played throughout the world – even among Gypsies, as we saw when we arrived here today. And English-language phrases are often used. This combination of the three of a kind and two of a kind is called a *full house*."

"A full house," Konrad repeated.

"The house of Rudolph Fuhl, that farmer from across the road. We heard that the Prando farm was formerly on both sides of the road, and when the treasure was hidden the Fuhl house was part of it. In the intervening years, Fuhl found the treasure, perhaps from a clue left by his father. Then you wrote to say the Gypsies would gather to uncover the hiding place and he knew he had to act. He killed Greystone and Cuza in the hope of stealing their cards and keeping the hiding place a secret forever. It would be a simple task for him to return here this afternoon with the crowds and sneak into Cuza's trailer."

Radu Heron was on his feet. "Let's get him!" he shouted and ran for the door. Segar made a grab for him but missed.

They hurried after him with Michael and Segar in the lead. To Rudolph Fuhl, watching from his house, it must have seemed as if the entire Gypsy encampment might be storming the place. He appeared at the front door, rifle in hand and killed Radu with a single shot. Before he could fire again, Captain Segar brought him down with two bullets from his pistol.

Fuhl confessed to the killings before he died, and in the basement of his house they found what little was left of the Gypsy treasure. "There's something, at least," Konrad Zuloaga said. "It'll feed a few families."

Michael nodded. Then he said, "I must be getting back to Gravita. The only treasure there is the beauty of the hills, but perhaps that is all we really need."

PUNISHMENT FOR A GYPSY

There are places in the mountains of Romania where the old customs die hard, where even the country's Communist government has had little impact on changing the way people have lived and worked and died for centuries. It is a land of superstition compounded by Gypsy lore and vampire myth, a land where one sometimes hopes and prays that things are not what they seem.

The following happened in the village of Bistritz, where people believed that the old superstitions could only be fought by the old laws. Michael Vlado told it to his friend, Captain Segar, one summer's day in Gravita as they watched Gypsy children playing on a freshly made haystack.

Michael had driven down the mountain for supplies and it was only by chance that he decided to take the rougher but shorter road that led through the village of Bistritz. Unlike Michael's own home at Gravita, Bistritz was not a Gypsy settlement, although a few of his people were known to travel in the area.

There was a small crowd of people in the center of the village, at the crossroads, and rather than try driving around them Michael brought his pickup truck to a halt. That was a mistake. A tall man wearing a black suit and a necktie spotted him at once and pointed a finger. "A Gypsy! We have us a Gypsy!"

At once the truck was surrounded by a half dozen men and Michael was dragged out of the cab. "What is this?" he shouted. "Let me go! I am Michael Vlado from Gravita – "

But if they recognized him as a Gypsy leader, it meant nothing to them. "We don't care who you are," the tall man growled. "There's a job to be done and you're the one to do it."

"What job?" Michael managed to ask with growing alarm.

"The Gypsy, Arad Bercovia, is to be executed for murder at high noon. We are following the ancient law that says the first Gypsy met on the road is to serve as his executioner."

"That's insane!" Michael protested. "Even in Romania that custom has not been practiced for a hundred years."

"His crime is an old one," the tall man said. "So we have chosen a punishment just as old."

"You spoke of murder."

"So I did. I am Konrad Kanici, the magistrate of Bistritz. It is I who passed sentence on the Gypsy, Bercovia, for the murder of our shopkeeper, Marco Rapnell, in his own home."

"I am no executioner," Michael insisted. "I was simply driving through your village."

"Hang them both!" someone shouted from the crowd.

The others surged around him and Michael was outnumbered, at their mercy. He couldn't save the condemned man or himself by continuing to resist. He had an hour before the appointed time of execution and a great deal could change in an hour's time. "All right," he told the black-clad magistrate. "Show me the man I must execute."

They led him inside a wooden building that served as a meeting hall, to a table where he stood facing a weeping, terrified young man wearing a colorful Gypsy shirt and bandanna and a single gold earring.

"Are you Arad Bercovia?" Michael asked.

"I am Arad."

"This Gypsy is to be your executioner," the magistrate announced, "according to the old law. You will hang from that pine tree in one hour's time."

"No !" the young man cried. "I swear I did not throw the knife which killed Rapnell!"

"Let me spend some time alone with my Gypsy brother," Michael pleaded. "I must hear his story."

"His story is simple enough. He was traveling with a carnival when he met and seduced Rapnell's daughter Myra. The father threatened to kill him and there was bad blood between them. Two nights ago, the Gypsy came to Rapnell's door and was seen to hurl a knife inside. Rapnell was found with the knife in his chest, dead in his kitchen."

"Who else was in the house at the time?" Michael asked Kanici.

"No one. His daughter had fled the place after they argued."

"He beat her!" the Gypsy insisted. "I went there to warn him to stop treating her like that. I never entered the house!"

"But you threw your knife," Michael said.

"I admit that. Several people saw it."

"And like all Gypsies you are skilled at knife throwing," said Kanici. "That is all the evidence we need."

"I didn't kill him! He was nowhere in sight when I threw the knife."

Michael was weighing the possibilities. "Could I speak with the dead man's daughter? He asked. "Could I see the house where the crime was committed?"

"You are neither judge nor jury but only the executioner," Konrad Kanici reminded him. "Bercovia has already been convicted."

"I only want to help a brother Gypsy if I can."

"Your help will be to slip the noose around his neck."

Arad Bercovia wailed at the words and buried his face in his hands. "Come – " Michael turned to Kanici " – show me the scene of the murder. We have nearly an hour before the execution."

" I will take you there," the magistrate decided. "But it will do you no good. The Gypsy will die at noon, and you will be his executioner. It is already written in my book of judgment."

They left Bercovia sobbing at his table in the meeting hall, guarded by one of the villagers. Outside, the crowd still waited. Michael couldn't help noticing the table which now stood beneath the pine tree and the coil of rope resting on it. Kanici led him down the street away from his parked truck, where another guard now stood. Escape seemed as impossible for Michael as it did for the condemned man.

"Here is the house," Kanici announced pausing before the two-storey wooden dwelling badly in need of paint. "Rapnell was buried this morning. Here is his daughter Myra."

A young woman dressed in black saw them and came forward. Her pale face seemed a reflection of her grief. A bearded man by her side looked equally grief-stricken as he asked, "Has justice been done?"

"He will hang at noon," Konrad Kanici told them. "We have found a passing Gypsy to perform the execution according to the old laws." The bearded man stared hard at Michael, as if he might know him, "You are from near here?"

"From Gravita, farther up the mountain. I am Michael Vlado."

"My name is Hans Becker. I am a cattle buyer from Leipzig. You may remember I called at your village once last summer but we could come to no agreement."

Michael did remember him. "Are you buying cattle?"

"I am a friend of the Rapnells. I was visiting them when this terrible thing happened."

"Arad Bercovia claims he did not kill your father," Michael told the young woman.

"I want to believe him but I cannot. Hans and others saw him throw the knife."

"Where was he standing when this happened?"

"Over here," the magistrate said, taking several long strides toward the door. Myra Rapnell unlocked the door and Michael peered down a dim hallway perhaps twenty feet in length. He followed Myra and the magistrate into the house, with Becker behind him. The hallway ended at a blank wall and they turned right to enter the kitchen.

"We ran in the front door, down the hall and in here," Becker explained, "right after he threw the knife. Myra's father was in the kitchen slumped at the table where he'd been eating dinner. The knife had struck him right through the heart. It must have killed him instantly."

"This table?" Michael asked, studying the kitchen.

"Yes. He was facing the door."

"But – "Michael shook his head not comprehending " – I don't understand this. If he was seated at the table, a knife thrown from the front door couldn't have hit him. It would have had to make a right turn at the doorway just as we did."

"Now perhaps you see the reason for my actions," the magistrate said. "The reason why I have returned to the old laws. Arad Bercovia must be executed by another Gypsy, the first one encountered along the road, because Bercovia killed Marco Rapnell with a Gypsy curse that guided his knife around a corner to its target."

Black thunderheads had appeared over the top of the mountains blotting out the sun and casting a brief pall over the village. Michael heard murmurings from the crowd in the street and knew they had taken this as a sign that the hour of the execution was drawing near. He stood in the doorway for a moment studying the clouds and then turned back to face Konrad Kanici.

"I do not believe in Gypsy curses," he said quietly. "This man is innocent."

"There are witnesses – "

"Witnesses who saw him throw a knife." Michael strode back down the corridor and stood in front of the blank wall. "There is not a mark on this wall not a dig from a thrown knife. What happened to it?"

"The knife lodged in the chest of Marco Rapnell."

"After turning a corner and entering the kitchen."

"Yes."

Rapnell's daughter Myra said, "The Gypsy killed my father. There was no one else in the house."

"Do you believe in curses too?" Michael asked staring down into her dark eyes.

"My father might have been hit by the knife in the hallway and staggered into the kitchen to die."

The magistrate shook his head. "I saw the body. The knife penetrated the heart. Your father could not have taken more than one or two steps before he died. He certainly could not have crossed the kitchen and seated himself behind the table. And there was no blood on the floor."

"The knife in the wound might have prevented much external bleeding," Michael speculated. "Still if the dead man was actually seated at the table it's doubtful he could have been stabbed in the doorway." He turned back to Myra. "How do you know the house was empty?"

"We searched it," Hans Becker said. "As soon as we found Marco. There was no one here but the dead man."

Michael stepped to the kitchen door which led to a back porch and a small yard with a garden. "That door was locked," Kanici told him. "I checked it myself."

"Locked from the inside?"

"Yes. The key was turned and the bolt was thrown."

"And the windows?"

"All these downstairs were locked. There was a breeze coming in through several upstairs." He stared hard at Michael. "But why do you ask these questions? The case has been decided. You prowl and pry like a detective but there is no mystery to solve."

"Bercovia says he is innocent."

"Did not Cain say he was innocent in the Garden of Eden?"

"The man is beside himself with fear, crying and carrying on like a doomed soul. Is that the attitude of a cold-blooded murderer?"

"I have seen all sorts in my time," the magistrate said.

"What of motive?"

"Talk to Myra Rapnell. She will tell you the motive."

Myra had slipped away while they talked and Michael found her in the back garden pulling a few weeds with her dainty hands. "That is a dirty job," he observed.

"Someone must do it now that my father is dead."

"Did you live here with him?"

"Yes."

"Your mother – ?"

"She ran away years ago with a carnival man who was passing through the mountains. That was when I was very young. My father never forgot it. I think that was one reason he hated Arad so much."

Michael looked at the sky. The thunderheads were passing to the south and the storm seemed to have avoided them. "Why?" he asked. "What was the reason he hated Arad?"

"Because of the carnival. When I met Arad he was a knife-thrower in a traveling carnival. He left the show and stayed here because he was in love with me. For my father it was history repeating itself. That's why he asked Hans Becker to visit us. He wanted Hans to win me over, make me forget about Arad."

"Was he succeeding?"

"All too well. And my father didn't stop Hans and me." She brushed some garden dirt from her hands. "He had Hans track down the carnival where it was playing in Bucharest and bring the woman here who had worked with Arad in his act."

"She's here now?" Michael asked.

Myra nodded. "She's here. Hans knows where, but he won't tell me."

The magistrate came to the kitchen door. "In thirty minutes you must do your duty, Gypsy," he called out. "Do not try to escape or you will join your brother with a noose around your neck."

"I will be there to see justice done," Michael promised.

He found Hans Becker, the Leipzig cattle buyer, on the road in front of the house. "Are you satisfied we tell the truth?" the bearded man asked Michael.

"I am satisfied of nothing. I must hear the story once more, of what happened when Myra's father died."

"I was coming to the house with a visitor. As I approached, I saw that the Gypsy was standing by the open front door."

"You're certain the door was open?"

"Yes. People sometimes leave them open in this warm weather."

"Go on," Michael urged.

"He shouted for Myra's father to come out, to face him. He was wearing his bright Gypsy carnival shirt as if to taunt the man. Myra told you about her mother?"

"Yes."

"Then he brought his arm back in a throwing position and I saw the knife in it."

"What sort of knife?"

"A slim balanced throwing knife without the guard or crosspiece. The sort used in knife-throwing acts. The sort that killed Rapnell."

"Go on."

"He hurled it into the house with a shout as we came running up."

"Who was with you?"

"I – a visitor."

"Myra has already told me you located the woman who worked with

Bercovia in his knife-throwing act."

"Yes," Becker admitted. "She was with me. Her name is Dora Gitano – I found her with the carnival in our nation's capital. We were coming to see Rapnell. The magistrate was with us."

"Kanici?" This news surprised Michael. "He was with you at the time of the murder?"

"Yes. We entered the house together."

"And who was the first into the kitchen? Who reached the body first?"

"Kanici and I entered together. I kept Dora back so she wouldn't see Rapnell. We could tell from the doorway that he was dead."

"Where is Dora Gitano now?"

"At the inn by the crossroads. She wants to see Bercovia again before the hanging."

"And I want to see her," Michael said. "Take me to her."

"Only if the magistrate approves," Becker answered uneasily.

Michael saw Konrad Kanici waiting for him down the road. "It is time to get back," the magistrate said as Michael approached. "It is almost noon."

"One last thing, sir" Michael said. "I must speak with Dora Gitano, the woman who knew the Gypsy at the carnival."

"That is impossible. There is not enough time remaining."

Michael stepped very close facing the man in black. "Listen to me. You found me by chance on the road, driving through your village. Perhaps you have heard of King Carranza who rules us."

"I have heard the name," Kanici admitted. "But he is crippled."

"Exactly. And so I carry out the orders in his place. I conduct the Gypsy courts, and I pass judgment among my people just as you do here."

"Then you know you must respect our laws."

"I do respect them. But I will never respect a belief in superstition, not even Gypsy superstition. Knives cannot be thrown around corners, even by the most skilled performers."

"I agree, but Arad Bercovia was not performing when he hurled that knife. He was bent on murder and he brought all his Gypsy powers to bear. He willed that knife to seek out his victim. Call it a curse, call it what you wish."

"If you believe such Gypsy powers you must believe he could escape from your noose if he wished."

"Not if another Gypsy tightens the knot."

Michael sighed. "Allow me to speak with this woman, Dora Gitano."

Kanici took out his pocket watch. "It is ten minutes to twelve. You will find her with the condemned man."

Dora Gitano was a lithe, sensuous woman who moved like a cat about the large meeting room never taking her eyes from Bercovia's face. She treated Michael as an unneeded intruder and precious minutes slipped away before he finally managed to get through to her. "I was stopped on the road an hour ago and pressed into service as Arad's executioner," he said.

"You would kill a fellow Gypsy?"

"I seem to have no choice unless you can help me."

She slowed in her prowling. "I am not a Gypsy, if that is what you think. Arad and I only worked together in this carnival."

Michael glanced at Bercovia who now seemed paralyzed with fright. "He threw knives at you?"

She nodded, wetting her lips with a darting nervous tongue. "I stood against a board and he outlined my body with knives. It was a trick, of course. He didn't really throw them. The knives shot out of the back of the board around my body. We were very good at it – until he met her."

"Myra?"

"Yes. The carnival was playing in a nearby town a few weeks back. He left it to stay near her."

Michael glanced over at Arad. "Do you love him?"

She hesitated for an instant. "No, no I don't love him. But I feel sorry for him. We were very close."

"You were there when the murder was committed. Do you think Arad killed that man with his knife?"

"No, of course not. He had dozens of those throwing knives. Anyone could have stolen one to frame him for the crime."

"But if I cannot prove it within the next five minutes, I am the one who must tighten the noose around his throat."

"There is another way," she said her, voice barely a whisper so that the guard wouldn't overhear.

"What?"

She turned her back to the guard and slipped a hand into her purse. It came out holding a tiny American made pistol. "Only two shots," she whispered, "but it would be enough for you to escape with him."

Michael reached out to take the weapon and slip it in his pants pocket, wondering if he could bring himself to use it, even to spare the life of an innocent man.

The door of the meeting room swung open and Konrad Kanici stood outlined against the leaden sky. "It is time, Gypsy," he intoned.

The guard tugged Bercovia to his feet. "It's not fair," the doomed man complained. "I never threw the knife that killed Marco Rapnell."

They led him outside and Michael followed along with Dora Gitano. He saw Myra standing in the crowd of spectators along with Hans Becker. As Michael reached the road, he glimpsed the noose hanging from the pine tree and stopped frozen in his tracks until the magistrate poked a finger in the small of his back.

"Do your duty, Gypsy, or you will join him up there."

Michael climbed onto the table and helped the condemned man up. The crowd moved a little closer, hemming them in. He felt the weapon in his pocket and wondered what use it could be to him now. The two bullets might do more to infuriate the crowd than to scatter it. For all he knew the gun might not even be loaded. An unloaded pistol might be the perfect weapon for a Gypsy who didn't throw knives.

Didn't throw knives –

Michael asked the condemned man a single question, making himself heard above the increasing roar of the crowd.

Arad Bercovia turned his sad eyes to Michael's and answered. The fight had suddenly gone out of him. "It isn't fair," he insisted. "It isn't fair to hang me because of a foolish superstition. I have no magical powers."

"The verdict wasn't fair," Michael agreed, tightening the noose around the Gypsy's neck. "But it was just."

Captain Segar sat up staring at Michael as he finished his story. Do you mean you hanged the man Michael? A fellow Gypsy?"

"I hanged him because he was guilty. If I had rescued him from that mob it would only have been to deliver him to the State executioners. One could hardly expect a Gypsy to be spared in a murder case."

"But he swore he was innocent. You told me the man was sobbing with fear, saying it wasn't fair."

"He never said he was innocent of the murder. He said he had not thrown the knife that killed Rapnell and he didn't. The question I asked him on the gallows was whether he had stabbed Rapnell. And he had. He stabbed him at the kitchen table."

"But he never entered the house," Segar objected.

"We only had his word for that. The house was empty except for Rapnell, and he was dead. I believe Bercovia went to the house to argue with Rapnell over his daughter. Rapnell had recently brought Hans Becker to the village to induce his daughter away from the Gypsy, and this must have infuriated Bercovia. They had words, and he stabbed Myra's father at the table. Then as he was leaving the house he spotted Becker and Dora approaching with the magistrate. He was caught in the act, unless he could make them believe he'd never entered."

"Then all that business of hurling the knife through the open door was only pretense?"

"Yes. When I noticed how securely locked the back door and windows were, it seemed strange that the front door would be standing open alone. If it had been open for ventilation, Rapnell would have opened a window or the back door as well. When Bercovia was spotted at the open door he pretended he'd found it that way and acted out his stunt of hurling a knife into the house. But as Dora Gitano told me he didn't really throw the knives in his carnival act. They sprang out of the board behind her, giving the illusion they were thrown with great skill. Bercovia didn't really throw the knife through that doorway either – he palmed it and slipped it into the sleeve of the fancy Gypsy shirt he was wearing. He knew Rapnell would be found with the knife in his chest but he also knew there was no way the knife seen to be thrown by him could have traveled around the corner to reach his victim. By presenting them with impossibility he hoped to shroud the real circumstances of the killing and gain freedom for himself.

"When I remembered that Bercovia only pretended to throw knives in the carnival act, it tied in with the fact that no knife or mark of a knife had been found in the wall opposite the front doorway. The knife never hit the wall because Bercovia never threw it. Yet the vanishing of that knife plus the knife in Rapnell's chest was too much of a coincidence. Bercovia must have known the dead man and the method of murder. He could only have known if he'd already been in the house to kill Rapnell."

Captain Segar nodded. "In the city he might have gotten away with it. The police would agree that the knife could not have turned a corner and they would have concluded that Rapnell must have been killed by someone else. But in these superstitious mountains where Gypsies are still thought to possess magical powers, the magistrate simply concluded that the Gypsy magic had directed the path of the knife. No wonder Bercovia cried and carried on so, insisting that it wasn't fair. He'd presented them with an impossibility which they simply ignored because he was a Gypsy."

"He was right," Michael Vlado said, "It wasn't fair."

"If I had been with you, this never would have happened. I would have taken charge of the prisoner and forbidden the execution."

"But then justice would not have been done. Perhaps it's better the way it happened – better for everyone except Arad Bercovia."

THE GYPSY WIZARD

Michael Vlado had traveled some seven hundred miles across southern Europe to reach Milan, having left his wife and Captain Segar and the people of Gravita with only a few days' warning of his impending journey. Crossing from Romania to the west was not an easy task, even for a Gypsy. He'd gone by way of Yugoslavia rather than Hungary because the border crossing was a bit easier. Perched between east and west, the Slavs asked fewer questions and their gates were open to wanderers.

The few who questioned him along the way saw nothing unusual in a Gypsy like Michael traveling to Milan. After all, Gypsies were born to move about. He felt no obligation to correct their false impression. The Gypsies of Michael's tribe traveled little, content to farm the land and breed horses in the Romanian hills, as they had for a hundred years.

But Josef Patronne was different. He'd left the region of the Carpathian Mountains in his youth to settle in northern Italy shortly after the end of the war. And become a wizard.

Michael found him at a table in a little outdoor cafe near the Galleria Vittoria Emanuele. He was easily recognizable with his bristling black moustache and the gold chains and rings he wore. When Michael joined him at the table, he said simply, "You are a Gypsy."

"I am," Michael conceded, taking a seat without being asked. "Your brother back in Gravita asked me to come find you. He saw your picture in the newspaper. FIFTY WIZARDS KEPT FROM THE POPE, the headline said, and one of them was you."

"That was last month," Josef Patronne said with a wave of his hand, as if it had been a lifetime ago. "We went to Rome, but the Swiss Guards kept us from seeing the Pope."

"Your brother worries about you. What is this wizard business? You are a Gypsy, not a wizard."

"Cannot a man be both?" Patronne finished his glass of wine and said, "Tell me your name."

"I am Michael Vlado. I lead your brother's people in Gravita."

"You are too young to be a Gypsy king."

"The old king is crippled and unable to rule. I do the job."

"And they have sent you to find me? What for? To return me to Gravita after forty years?"

"Your brother is worried. The newspaper article said you lived here in Milan and claimed to have the power to fly unaided."

Josef Patronne smiled for the first time, almost like a schoolboy taking special pride in some accomplishment. "He is worried that I will fall?"

"He is worried that you delude yourself, Josef."

A slender man of about Josef's age suddenly joined them at the table, pulling up a chair and extending a hand to Michael. "I am Axel Tortero, a friend of Josef's. Go on talking, you two. I only want a cup of espresso."

"Axel is also a wizard," Josef explained, "but not a Gypsy. He was with us in Rome. Axel, this is Michael Vlado, from Romania."

"I'm an herbalist," the newcomer explained. "I don't fly like my friend Josef."

"Forget the flying," Michael said, feeling that somehow he had stepped into another world. "Why were you in Rome?"

"Ah!" Axel Tortero held up a finger. "We wanted to see the Pope at his weekly audience. We wanted him to acknowledge that the occult sciences are compatible with Christianity. You know, a Pope in the sixteenth century once described this area of northern Italy as a hotbed of witchcraft, and many still believe it to be so. Certainly there are superstitions here – "

"And wizards."

"And wizards. But they are everywhere. If a priest heals a sick man, it is a miracle. If a wizard does the same thing, it is superstition."

"We are poor, ignorant people back in Gravita," Michael tried to explain. "When we read of someone who can fly through the air, we do not think of miracles or superstition. We think the person is merely sick in the head. That is why your brother asked me to come here, Josef."

The black-haired man hit the table with his fist. "Henrik always worried too much about me, even when we were children. Go back and tell him I'm all right. Tell him I really can fly."

"Where do you do your flying?" Michael asked.

"Next I will try the huge Galleria across the square. Have you been there yet?"

"No."

"Come, then – Axel and I will show it to you."

Milan's main square itself was a magnificent open space, dominated by a vast cathedral built entirely of pearly white marble. "It took forty architects four centuries to complete it," Axel said as they passed it. "There is not another cathedral like it in all of Europe."

"It's quite impressive," Michael admitted, though he'd seen few cathedrals in Europe or anywhere else.

"They have always built big in Milan. It is Italy's commercial center and second-largest city. For a decade in the 'sixties, the thirty-two-storey Pirelli Tower was the tallest office building in Europe."

They crossed the square and entered the Galleria Vittoria Emanuele. It was a huge place with intricate mosaic floors and a curved glass roof some sixty or seventy feet above their heads. There were shops and cafes along the main floor, many with green awnings covering tables and concessions to lend an outdoor appearance to the sunlit activities. The Galleria was open to the surrounding streets and the square through its four roof-high entrances, and Michael could see a confused bird or two flapping their wings against the vaulted glass ceiling.

"Here is where I will fly," Patronne said. "The Galleria's architect, Giuseppe Mongoni, fell to his death from the glass roof just days before the opening in 1878. Perhaps he was trying to fly, too."

His friend Axel, who might have been a booster of the Milan Chamber of Commerce, continued, "It is still the largest shopping arcade in Italy."

Michael stared up at the three floors of windows above the shops and at the wrought-iron balcony that circled the arcade at the third level. "What's up there?" he asked. "More shops?"

"And offices. Some places have been here since before the war."

A burly man smoking a thin cigar approached them. "No Gypsies or peddlers allowed here," he announced. "Keep moving."

Josef Patronne's face brightened. "My old friend Inspector Storia! You think we are shoplifters, perhaps?"

"I don't care what you are. Just keep moving."

"Inspector, this is Michael Vlado, come to visit me from my home in Romania."

"Another Gypsy," the detective grumbled. He took another puff on his cigar.

The detective's presence seemed to disturb Axel more than Josef. He tugged at his friend's coat, saying, "We must be going, Josef. You will fly another day. It is nearly time for your class."

Inspector Storia caught this last exchange. "I have had more complaints about you from the mothers, Patronne. What you teach their children has nothing to do with reading and writing. Be careful or you will have to fly from a prison cell."

"I teach religion."

"You teach the black arts. Three hundred years ago you would have been put to death by the Inquisition."

"Then it is good that I live in the twentieth century," Patronne replied with a trace of a smile.

He and Axel moved on, not waiting for Michael, and it seemed that his seven-hundred-mile journey was at an end. He turned back to the inspector. "I'm sorry you scared them away. I came here to see Josef Patronne."

"You saw him. Now be on your way, Gypsy."

Crowds of shoppers and strollers were moving all about them, but Michael barely noticed. He'd rarely encountered such an open hatred directed toward him because he was a Gypsy. It was a new experience, and an unpleasant one. "I have traveled far on my mission. I would like your help."

The inspector paused, eyeing him critically. "Say what you have to."

"Josef's brother read about his visit to Rome to see the Pope."

Storia laughed – a short sharp noise that was hardly amused. "Foolish people, thinking the Pope would see them, much less condone what they were doing."

"What *do* wizards do?"

"In their more harmless moments they practice faith healing and herbalism. At other times they've been known to act as the high priest for a coven of witches."

"And witches fly on broomsticks."

"No one flies, Mr. Vlado, except in airplanes. Medieval witches who confessed to flying were probably high on some early version of opium or belladonna."

"Then you don't believe Josef's claims?"

"I don't believe him, but I fear there are a great many children who might. That is why the man is a menace. Stay away from him. Go back where you came from."

"I must see him once more," Michael decided. "I must have something more positive to tell his brother."

"Talk to the women. Find Elsa Mancini and Ida Fileno. Ask them what they think of your friend."

"Where do I find them?"

"Ida is a nurse at Children's Hospital. Elsa would be at home with her children. There are others as well."

Michael nodded. "Thank you."

As he left the Galleria, he saw Inspector Storia standing in its very center, staring up at the glass-enclosed sky.

Elsa Mancini lived in a middle-class block of apartments not far from Sempione Park near the center of the city. She was a handsome, shapely woman in her mid–thirties and her first reaction to Michael's visit was one of apprehension. "My husband is not at home. I do not allow visitors or salesmen inside."

"Then we'll talk at the door," Michael answered agreeably. "It's about Josef Patronne. His brother – "

"Patronne, the wizard! He should be in jail!"

"His brother is worried about him. He believes he may have mental problems. He talks of flying – "

"Always the flying! And he tells this to my son! Already one boy has tried to fly and broke his leg."

"I'm sorry about that."

"Are you a relative? Do you have any control over him?"

"No, I only come at the wish of his brother."

"Take him away. Take him out of here."

"I'm afraid I can't do that."

"Then we have nothing more to talk about."

Michael tried to catch the door but she closed it in his face.

He thought about going to the hospital next, to talk with Ida Fileno, but decided that could wait until tomorrow. Instead he had an early dinner and then tried to locate Axel Tortero. But Josef's friend had vanished from his neighborhood, at least for that night. Perhaps they were together somewhere.

Michael had taken a room at a low-cost tourist hotel on the Via Tunisia. It was there Inspector Storia found him shortly after midnight. "Get up and get dressed," he shouted through the closed door.

"What is it?"

"Your friend Patronne tried to fly tonight at the Galleria. He's dead."

Michael Vlado had barely known the man in life, yet he was sorry to see him dead, crumpled and broken on the mosaic tile floor, his blood making a pattern of its own. He lay near one of the green awnings, but not quite close enough that it could have broken his fall.

"A security guard found him shortly before midnight," Storia told Michael. "The Galleria has no doors, as you can see, but those gates limit access at night. Still, it would have been quite easy for him to get in and reach the upper floors. It looks as if he dove off the balcony up there or else one of the windows above it."

Michael shook his head sadly. "He couldn't fly after all."

There was a commotion at the nearest gate and they saw Axel Tortero bearing down on them. "Let him through," Storia called out to his men.

When Axel saw Josef, he was beside himself with grief at the death of his friend. "The fool, the stupid fool! Those women put him up to this. He wanted to fly, to be some sort of real wizard."

"Did he tell you he was coming here?" Storia asked.

"Not tonight, no. But he'd told me many times that he wanted to fly here soon."

The detective nodded. "And where were you this evening, Axel?"

"Where? At the cafe, where I always am."

"All evening?"

"I strolled a bit in the square, stopped in the Cathedral to visit."

"You, in the Cathedral?"

Axel shrugged. "Even a sinner must speak to the Lord at times."

"You're sure you weren't with Josef? I don't think he would have tried this alone, without witnesses."

"I would have stopped him if I'd been along." He dropped to his knees beside the body, unmindful of the blood that quickly soaked into his pants.

"Don't touch the body!" Inspector Storia cautioned in a commanding voice. "This is still a criminal investigation."

Michael frowned. "Is flying against the law?"

"No, but witchcraft is. Whatever went on here tonight, I mean to get to the bottom of it." He stooped to pry something – a torn piece of paper – from the dead man's fist.

"What's that?" Michael asked.

"A paper with the word 'pevole' printed on it."

While the photographers and police technicians labored, Michael followed Axel out of the building. He caught up with the slender man halfway across the square. "I have some things to ask you," he said.

"About herbs and healing, that I know. About flying and falling, those subjects are foreign to me."

"What did you mean when you said the women put him up to it?"

"The women. Elsa, and that Fileno woman, and the Petrie sisters and the rest. He spent too much time with them. I think he was with them tonight."

"Oh? Did they encourage him in his fancied flights?"

"I don't know. I stay away from them. Ask Elsa Mancini."

"I will."

Michael sent a message back to his friend Captain Segar, asking him to deliver word of Josef Patronne's death to his brother Henrik in Gravita. There was little chance Henrik would claim the body or journey to Milan for the funeral. Josef had long ago cut his ties with the Gypsy family back home. He was a wizard now and perhaps he would be buried as one, with his friend Axel sprinkling life-giving herbs across the lid of the coffin.

In the morning, Michael went to see Elsa Mancini at her apartment. At the door she hesitated, remembering him from the previous day, but now her husband was at home and she allowed Michael to enter. Davide Mancini was lounging at the kitchen table in his undershirt, a middle-aged man beginning to run to fat. He glanced curiously at Michael, noting the gold earring, and said, "This another of your Gypsy friends, Elsa?"

"I don't know him. He came here yesterday with questions about Josef Patronne." She turned back to Michael. "What is it now?"

"Patronne is dead. He fell from the top of the Galleria last night."

The woman crossed herself at the news, while her husband merely took another sip of his morning coffee. "Was he trying to fly?" she asked. "He talked of it sometimes."

"The police don't know. It's a possibility. Someone told me he might have been with you earlier last evening."

"I did not see him. I had some women friends in for a game of cards." She motioned toward the living room, where Michael could see three card tables still set up with chairs around them. There were half-finished drinks and ashtrays still about.

"A large group," he commented.

"A dozen of us. We get together for cards once a month."

"And drive me out of the house," her husband complained. "I come back at midnight and the place isn't even cleaned up."

"We played late," Elsa explained.

Michael remembered some of the other names Axel had mentioned. "Was Ida Fileno here?"

"She came late, after she finished at the hospital."

"And the Petrie sisters?"

"Yes, they were here. Why do you ask?"

Michael had strolled into the room to look at the card tables. On one, a deck of cards still rested on an unused score pad. "I was only wondering. They are names I've heard."

"We are all friends."

Michael nodded, preparing to leave. "But you saw nothing of Patronne last night?"

"Nothing."

Michael reached out and cut the deck of cards, turning over the top half. He almost expected to see one of the death cards, perhaps the queen of spades.

Instead he saw the ten of swords. It was a tarot deck.

Michael lingered in a cafe down the street that afforded a good view of Elsa Mancini's apartment building. About an hour after his visit, he saw Elsa's husband come out the front door and start up the block with one of their children, a boy of nine or ten. He followed them to a playground some two blocks away. The boy joined in a game with some friends while Davide unfolded the morning news paper and sat down on a bench to read it. Michael went up and sat next to him. Davide did not notice him at first, then said, "You again!"

"I saw you here and thought we might talk for a bit."

"I have no time for Gypsies," Mancini replied.

"It's about your wife and Josef Patronne."

"Why should I talk to you? Are you the police?"

"No, only a friend of Josef's brother. When I go back home to Romania, I want to be able to tell Henrik how Josef died."

"Ask the police, don't ask me."

"I want to know about your wife's card games. What happens at them?"

Davide shrugged. "They play cards – and gossip, I suppose. How should I know, when they send me away?"

"There were tarot cards on the table. Those are used for fortune telling and the black arts."

"You credit my wife with powers well beyond her. Tarot cards are also used for Austrian tarock, a popular game in the north of Italy and other parts of Europe. It's a game for three players but it can be adapted for four. Elsa and her friends have three tables so that a dozen of them can play at once."

Michael shook his head. "I know tarock. It's played with a fifty-four-card mixed deck of tarot and regular playing cards. The deck on the table was a full seventy-eight-card tarot deck. They weren't playing tarock."

"Well, then, perhaps it was tarocco. That's played with a full tarot deck."

"But by only three players."

"You know your cards, Gypsy."

"What were Elsa and her friends doing last night? Was Patronne with them?"

"How should I know? Ask her, not me."

"You are a superstitious people in this region. Witchcraft flourished here once. I'm sure you know what a coven is."

Davide's eyes narrowed as he studied Michael's face. "A group of witches led by a high priest or wizard. The traditional number is thirteen. Twelve witches and – "

"And Josef Patronne?"

Davide jumped to his feet, anger written across his face. "What are you saying about Elsa? Why do you make up these lies?" He called out to the child at play, "Come, Arturo – it is time to go home!"

There was no point in pursuing them. Michael decided he'd already said enough – or too much.

He found Inspector Storia at the Galleria. The detective was smoking another thin cigar, studying the glass roof and the sky beyond. "They tell me, Gypsy, that there is a Galleria in Toronto, in Canada, that is patterned after this one."

"It's an impressive place here," Michael agreed.

"We have the autopsy report on your friend Patronne."

"Oh?"

"There was some sort of drug in his system. A sedative."

"Something to calm his nerves before he tried to fly?"

"According to the autopsy, he couldn't have walked, much less flown."

Michael shook his head. "I don't understand. How did he climb up to the roof?"

"He didn't. He was already unconscious when somebody carried him up there and pushed him over the railing."

"You're saying he was murdered?"

"Yes."

Michael Vlado was not as certain about it as the inspector seemed to be. He'd known Gypsies to perform amazing feats of strength and endurance while under the influence of alcohol or drugs. He could imagine Josef Patronne swallowing the sedative as a preliminary part of some bizarre ceremony and then launching himself from the Galleria's glass ceiling while his coven watched. Or was he conjuring up demons where none existed? Was there a simpler explanation for what had happened?

He found Axel Tortero on the street near the cafe, in animated conversation with a dark-haired young woman. Watching as Axel gestured and waved his hands, Michael found it hard to believe that Axel and Josef could have been close friends. Why, he wasn't sure. They came from different cultures, after all, and there was only the nebulous fraternity of wizardry to unite them. But perhaps that was enough.

When he approached the couple, the woman immediately backed off a few feet, frowning. "Who are you?" she asked. "I saw you at the playground with Elsa's husband."

"I'm Michael Vlado, a friend of Josef Patronne's brother in Romania."

She nodded. "I am Elsa's friend, Ida Fileno."

"I was going to come by and speak with you at the hospital."

She shrugged uncertainly. "This is my day off. What did you want to talk to me about?"

"Actually, it was before Josef's death that I wanted to talk. His brother back home had read about his trip to Rome with the other wizards. He feared Josef might be having mental problems."

"He may have been right," Ida said, nervously twisting the wedding ring on her finger. "Josef often acted strange."

"You knew him well?"

"I – my daughter was friendly with him. She's just at an age where all this supernatural business intrigues her. Ghosts and witches – and wizards."

"He came to your house?"

"The children knew him from the playground. And the Galleria. He taught an informal class at his apartment, filling their minds with wild ideas. Axel here was nearly as bad with his herbs."

Axel scowled, still angry with her. "You and Elsa tried to get him arrested! He was only teaching religion!"

"Not the religion of our churches." She turned away, ending the discussion. "He is dead now. It is past arguing about."

"Did you play cards with Elsa Mancini last night?" Michael asked her.

"Cards? Yes, we played. We play every other week at someone's home." Her mind seemed to be far away.

"With a tarot deck?"

"What?"

"I saw a tarot deck at the Mancini apartment."

"Oh, that." She waved it away. "One of the Petrie sisters was telling fortunes after the game. You know – the sort of things Gypsies do," she said pointedly. "How many babies we can expect and whether or not our husbands really love us."

Michael nodded. "Yes, I know about fortune-telling with tarot cards. Patronne wasn't there, too, was he?"

She turned her deep-brown eyes toward him. "Why should he have been there?"

"Perhaps to instruct you, to lead you as he did the children."

"No." She shook her head. "You are wrong, Mr. Vlado." She walked away from them and Axel watched until she rounded the next corner. "There's a cool one," he said. "She knows more than she tells."

"Was Josef part of it?" Michael asked. "You know, don't you? Was it a coven? Twelve witches and a wizard?"

Axel backed away from him. "What gave you that terrible idea? Josef never practiced black magic or Satanic rites!"

"Are you certain?"

Axel turned and broke into a run. Michael started after him and then let him go. He went looking for Inspector Storia again and finally located him at the police station on the Corso Magenta. Storia had his necktie off and was drinking a cup of hot coffee as he read through some reports. "What is it now, Gypsy?" he asked.

"That piece of paper you found in Josef's hand – could I see it?"

"It's in the file. I have too much else on my desk to worry about that." But he rose from the desk with some reluctance and pulled open a file drawer. "Here it is."

Michael took the plastic envelope and studied the slip of paper with 'pevole' printed on it. "It might be someone's name," he suggested. He noticed that though three sides of the paper were sharply cut as if by a scissors, the fourth side by the letter 'p' was torn jaggedly.

"No, we checked the telephone directory," Storia told him. "It's not a name."

"What, then?"

"Who knows?" The inspector took the envelope from Michael and returned it to the file. "I have to leave now. They need my testimony in a trial."

Michael stared at the detective. Something –

"Come on, you have to go now," Storia insisted.

"An idea's just come to me, Inspector."

"Ideas we get all the time. Bring me some evidence and I'll listen."

He disappeared into the elevator and Michael watched the doors slide shut behind him.

Michael found Elsa Mancini shopping at the open–air vegetable market near her apartment. "It's you again," she said, not unkindly. "I thought you'd have left for home by this time."

"I will be leaving soon," he confirmed. "I had to see you once more, to tell you I made a bad mistake about you. I told a couple of people I thought you were a witch."

"A witch?" The statement seemed to take her by surprise. "Where on earth could you have gotten that idea?"

"There were twelve of you at your apartment last night, supposedly for a card game, but I knew you didn't play cards."

Elsa picked up a head of lettuce, weighing it speculatively. "How did you know that?"

"Because of the tarot deck on the table. The most common tarot games are three-handed, or else they're played with a mixture of tarot and regular cards. Also, you told me the group met once a month. Your friend Ida said it was every other week. It's an odd card club when the members can't agree on how often they play."

"So you thought we were witches?"

Michael nodded. "The Gypsy mind runs to superstition too easily, I suppose. A coven of witches led by the wizard Josef Patronne. It made perfect sense, except – "

"Yes?"

"Except that I was wrong. There is one other thing that twelve women might do besides playing cards and engaging in witchcraft."

She put down the lettuce and stared at him. "What would that be?"

"Serve as a jury."

"You're very clever, Mr. Vlado."

"Josef Patronne was tried and convicted by the twelve of you, and then he was executed for his crime. You injected him with a sedative, no doubt obtained by Ida Fileno from the hospital where she works, and then you carried him to the top of the Galleria and shoved him over the railing to his death. Everyone knew he'd talked of flying. It was a perfect way to kill him."

Elsa walked away from the vegetables, her face drained of color. "You're guessing. You have no proof."

"*I* haven't, but the police do. You wrote your verdicts on slips of paper. A torn portion of one slip was clutched in Josef's fist. It said 'pevole.' The entire slip would have read 'colpevole' – the Italian word for 'guilty'."

"He *was* guilty!" she flared out. "Guilty of the worst of crimes! And the police would do nothing!"

"You went to them?"

"Time and again! We told Inspector Storia what he was doing to our children, twisting their minds with his tales of wizardry. He only laughed and promised to speak to Patronne. Then it became more serious. Two of our children were physically molested by him. Still the police did nothing. They thought we were lying, getting our children to invent stories merely to harass

Patronne. That was when we decided on our own brand of justice. We held a trial, and even gave him a chance to defend himself. He was found guilty."

"I can't believe he did those things."

"He did them, all right. He admitted everything as he tried to storm out of my apartment last night. Ida used a hypodermic on him, as you guessed. We wrapped him in a rug and carried him to the Galleria. There we took the elevator to the top floor where one of the women worked. We pushed him out a window."

"I'll have to tell the police about this," Michael warned.

"Tell them. I'm not sorry for what we did. We'd do it again to protect our children."

Michael slowed his pace and watched her walk on alone. He wondered what he should do, and what he should tell Patronne's brother back home.

In the morning, he stopped at the police station before leaving Milan. Inspector Storia was busy. There'd been a shooting overnight, and a jewelry-store robbery. "Go away, Gypsy," he told Michael. "I have no time for you now."

"It's about Patronne's death."

The inspector reached for a ringing telephone. "That case is closed."

"Closed?"

"We don't have the manpower to pursue every unexplained death. My superiors have ruled it accidental."

"But – "

Storia waved Michael away. "After all, he was only a Gypsy. And a wizard besides."

MURDER OF A GYPSY KING

On the long, lonely highway into Bucharest that sunny August afternoon, Jennifer Beatty suddenly changed her mind. She ignored the arrow that read BUCURESTI 50 KM and took a left fork that ran up the side of a hill toward the dense forest beyond. She hadn't really been going to Bucharest, anyway. She was running away, and she had a feeling Peter would come looking for her before too long – if for no reason than that she'd stolen his motorcycle when she took off the previous night from a resort town on the Black Sea.

Now, feeling the heat of its engine between her legs, she remembered the good times they'd had touring the Balkans all summer, moving from the Greek Islands up through Macedonia and the western tip of Turkey, then up the coastline through Bulgaria and into Romania. Travel in the Eastern Bloc countries had eased considerably, even for Americans, and Jennifer had ridden the back of Peter's motorcycle for so long that when the inevitable finish came it seemed natural for her to take it. She had no other transportation and very little money.

The road ahead seemed to climb relentlessly and for the first time she wondered if she'd made the right choice in leaving the highway. She slowed the motorcycle to stop by the side of the road just as a black military staff car appeared ahead at the crest of the hill. It paused next to her and a man in military uniform rolled down the window. "Are you lost?" he asked, using some of the first words she'd learned from her Romanian phrase book.

There was a time just a few weeks back when she wouldn't have been able to respond without consulting the book, but now she was becoming quite proficient in the language. "I'm only traveling through," she told him.

"An American?"

"Yes."

He was a handsome man in his forties, who reminded her a bit of her Uncle George back home. "I am Captain Segar of the district police," he told her. "This road leads into the foothills of the Transylvanian Alps. There is nothing ahead but a few farming communities and Gypsy villages."

"Gypsies!" Jennifer was an incurable romantic. "Do they travel in caravans and tell fortunes?"

He looked at her. "These Gypsies farm the land and raise horses. They will not harm you, but still it is not safe for a young woman to travel these back roads by herself. Do you have a passport?"

She removed it from her saddle bag and handed it over to him, wondering if Peter might have reported the stolen motorcycle to the local police. "You'll find it in order."

He flipped quickly through the pages. "It is a good picture of you. Only twenty-two? So young to be traveling alone."

"I graduated from college in May," she replied. "I'm on my own now."

"I see." He hesitated for a moment and then returned the passport. "If you insist on continuing up this road, look for a village named Gravita and ask for Michael Vlado. He is the leader of the Gypsies there. He and his wife will take you in for the night."

"Thank you," she said.

He waved as he pulled away and continued down the hill.

Toward evening, Jennifer reached the village of Gravita. She'd been uncertain about whether to stop, but with the coming of the twilight a pause for the night seemed best.

A Gypsy working in a field directed her to Michael Vlado's farm, not without some difficulty. It hadn't occurred to her that the residents of Gravita would speak the Romany Gypsy tongue rather than the nation's official language. When she reached the Vlado farm, she was relieved to find them willing and able to converse in the language she knew.

It was a pleasant-looking woman who responded to her knock, surprised to find a late caller on the doorstep.

"I'm touring through here on my motorcycle," Jennifer quickly explained. "I met a police officer named Segar on the road and he told me I might find a night's lodging with Michael Vlado."

"I am Rosanna, Michael's wife," the woman said. "He's putting the horses away. Please come in."

"I'm an American," Jennifer explained. "I've been traveling through the Balkans this summer. My name is Jennifer Beatty."

"Alone? On a motorcycle? Come sit down. You must be hungry. We have food left from dinner."

The house was neat and homey, with colorful Gypsy good-luck symbols decorating the walls – otherwise the residents could have been any European nationality. Jennifer noticed a work table with carefully carved wooden animals in various stages of completion. "Did you do these?" she asked. "They're lovely."

Rosanna beamed. "I carved them to sell at the shops in the village."

A few minutes later the back door swung open and a tall Gypsy with a weathered complexion entered. "I saw a motorcycle outside," he said. "We have a visitor." Jennifer noticed the single earring in his left ear.

"My husband, Michael," Rosanna announced. "This is a young American named Jennifer Beatty. She's been touring the Balkans on her motorcycle and met Captain Segar on the road."

"He was such a nice man," Jennifer said. "He advised me to stop here overnight. But I'd hate to be a burden – "

"You are no burden," Michael assured her. "Perhaps Rosanna and I will learn something of America."

She accepted their offer of food, realizing for the first time how hungry she was. She told them of her life back home and of her summer in the Balkans, omitting any mention of Peter. Finally, as the hour grew late, Rosanna showed her to an upstairs bedroom where a four-poster bed with a down comforter put her to sleep within minutes.

She awakened to the sound of horses beneath her window. It was daylight and her watch showed the time to be well after eight. She hadn't slept so late all summer. Stretching, she slid out of bed and made her way to the bathroom down the hall.

Hearing her shut the door, Rosanna climbed the stairs and called, "Did you sleep well?"

"Fine, thank you!"

"We're eating breakfast now if you want to join us."

Throwing on her jeans and T-shirt, Jennifer went downstairs and found Michael at the table, finishing a plate of ham and eggs. "Everything about this place surprises me," she told him as Rosanna brought a plate for her. "You eat American food for breakfast, you have flush toilets, you're not up at dawn like other farmers – "

Michael and Rosanna laughed. "The American breakfast is for you," Rosanna said. "Michael has been up and working since dawn. And only our house and that of King Carranza have flush toilets and septic tanks. The rest of the villagers still use outhouses. Of course, we all depend on well water."

"Who is King Carranza?"

"The leader of our particular tribe of Gypsies," Michael explained. "Although these days he's too ill to do much leading. Until a runaway horse crippled him, he was a blacksmith with the strength of ten men."

"I'd like to meet him. A Gypsy leader!" Then she remembered what Captain Segar had said. "But you're the leader, aren't you?"

"I preside over the Gypsy court with King Carranza on all important matters." He made a sudden decision. "If you really would like to meet him, you can do so before you leave. I'll be going over there later this morning."

"You'd take me with you?"

Michael exchanged a look with his wife. "Yes. It would be all right. King Carranza likes to greet visitors to our village."

After breakfast, Jennifer followed Michael outside. "I should move the motorcycle out of the way."

"Put it in the shed," Michael suggested, motioning toward an outbuilding some hundred feet away.

Jennifer climbed onto the motorcycle and started it, only to have it stall. Embarrassed, she gunned it a second time and rode it to the shed. Michael followed along on foot.

"Did you raise all these horses?" she asked, watching a pair of colts frolicking in the pasture after she parked the motorcycle.

"Most of them. Some I keep here to train for others. We race them at fairs and such."

"It sounds exciting."

"Its very dull. Once, though, we took a racehorse to Moscow to their big track at the Hippodrome. That was exciting. Captain Segar came with us."

"Moscow!" She shook her head. "I have such a dull life back home."

"But over here it is exciting, no?"

She turned quickly, detecting some change in his voice. "What do you mean?"

"Stealing your boyfriend's motorcycle is exciting?"

"How did you – ? What are you talking about?"

He smiled slightly at her surprise. "It is is not difficult to surmise. The saddlebags have the initials *P.F.* Hardly the initials of Jennifer Beatty. I assume that's your real name because Captain Segar certainly would have checked your passport if he stopped you along the road, and you wouldn't give one name to him and another to me. You had difficulty starting the cold engine just now, showing some unfamiliarity with the machine, hardly as if you've been driving it across the Balkans for two months. Would you be traveling all over with a woman friend who happened to own a motorcycle? Very doubtful. A male, a boyfriend, is most likely. It's his motorcycle, but you have it. Did he sell or give it to you, or did you steal it? I'd say the latter as the most likely possibility, especially since the key you used to start it seems to be still attached to a very masculine key ring."

She glanced down at the keys still in her hand and blushed when she saw Peter's tiny nude in pink plastic dangling from it. "You sound like Sherlock

Holmes."

He laughed. "Better than being compared to Dracula, I suppose. In these mountains, the Count is more popular than Holmes – they've even made a tourist attraction out of him."

"What else do you know about me?"

"Well, you speak the language well enough so I know you didn't cross the border yesterday. You and your boyfriend must have been living here at least for a few months."

"Three weeks," she told him. "I'm a fast learner."

"You are indeed, Jennifer. Do you want to tell me why you left him?"

"It didn't work out. He got so he was shooting dope every night and that's not my scene. I left him in Vasile on the Black Sea."

"A charming place. And the motorcycle?"

"I had no transportation and virtually no money. It was my only way out. I left him a note yesterday morning and took off."

"Will he come looking for you?"

"I don't know."

They walked across the fields to the only house in sight that was larger than Michael's. On the porch they found King Carranza seated in his wheelchair. Jennifer stared at his powerful arms and shoulders and the iron grey hair that twined around his head like a crown. It was a full minute before her eyes strayed to his crippled legs, hidden by a faded horse blanket.

"It's a pleasure to meet you," she said, but he only smiled and nodded in response.

"King Carranza speaks Romany," Michael explained. "He has never found it necessary to learn the local language."

"Does he live here alone?"

"Yes. His sister comes in and cooks for him. He still works in the blacksmith shop around the back of the house. He had a wife, but she is gone now."

"Dead?"

"Gone," Michael repeated. He said a few words to the king, conveying Jennifer's greeting from America. Then he translated the response for her. She liked the king and the kindly way he studied her and felt regret that he was confined to a wheelchair.

A few minutes later, as they watched him at work in his blacksmith shop, she tempered her initial feeling a bit. With his powerful arms, he could do more than most able-bodied men she knew, including Peter, who was virtually helpless in the real world.

Michael took her around to meet others in the village. A couple named

Steven and Maria Fetesti, married only a year and working together on their tiny farm especially impressed her. They spoke Romanian as did many of the younger Gypsies and she was pleased to be able to converse with them directly.

"One more stop," Michael said as they left the Fetesti's. "I want you to see a shop in the village. It's where my wife's carved animals are sold."

The shop was run by a thin, bearded man named Ivan Raski. Somehow he seemed different from the others, and the Romanian he spoke was not as clear or as intelligible. But his shop was a delight. Jennifer wandered around, studying the mostly handmade crafts, wishing she had the money to buy something.

"Are they all made in the village?" she asked Michael as they were leaving.

"Almost all. Some come from a neighboring village."

"But do enough tourists come through here to buy them?"

"A few travel this road, but we buy many of these things ourselves. Blankets to keep us warm in winter, Gypsy skirts and blouses, wooden toys for the children. We are almost self sufficient here."

"This is free enterprise – doesn't the Communist government object?"

"Not on this small a scale. The Gypsies in the cities have some degree of regulation. Up here they rarely bother us. Captain Segar looks after our interests."

They strolled back toward Michael's farm, Jennifer all too aware that she'd soon be leaving this idyllic place with no firm destination in mind.

"Ivan Raski didn't seem like the others," she observed. "Is he a Gypsy?"

"No, he's Russian. He came here some years ago and we took him in. This is not a closed community."

"Could I stay here for some time?"

"I don't know. Would you be happy here? You would have to do some work on my farm or elsewhere."

"I might like that."

Michael stopped and studied her. "Suppose you stay for another night and we'll both think it over."

She was pleased at his reply and was about to accept the offer when they heard a woman scream. Michael froze, then turned toward the sound. A middle-aged Gypsy woman was running toward them across the field from the direction of King Carranza's house.

"Its Carranza's sister Theresa," Michael said. "Something's wrong!"

They ran to meet her and she fell to the ground at Michael's feet, gasping for breath. "He's dead!" she screamed. "My brother has been murdered … !"

It was true. King Carranza was dead. He lay in a pool of blood on the living room floor next to his overturned wheelchair. The apparent murder weapon, a heavy blacksmith's hammer, was on the floor nearby. Jennifer took one look and buried her face in her hands.

"Stay outside," Michael told her. "Don't look."

He turned to Theresa Carranza, who was stiff with terror. "Try to tell me what happened."

"I came over to see him as I do every morning. I was later than usual today because my son has a little fever. I found him – like this!"

"No one else was here?"

"No one!"

For the first time, he seemed to notice drawers that had been pulled open, papers strewn about. "It looks like a robbery." He turned to Jennifer. "Run back to my house and tell Rosanna what has happened. Tell her we need people here – Festesti, Raski, she'll know who else."

"All right."

She ran across the fields, glad to be away from the dead king and his grieving sister. When she broke the news to Michael's wife, the blood seemed to drain from Rosanna's face. Then she steadied herself and said, "It's like losing a father. What did Michael tell me to do?"

"He needs people to help. He mentioned Fetesti and Raski. He said you'd know others."

Rosanna nodded, wrapping a shawl around her though the morning was warming nicely. "Tell him I'll get help and come quickly. Everyone will be there."

The word spread quickly and soon after Jennifer returned to the Carranza house the crowd began to gather. She hadn't imagined so many people lived in the village. Every man, woman and child seemed to be there. Michael went out on the porch and spoke to them. Though she couldn't understand the words, she knew by the crowd's reaction that he was telling them what they already knew – that their king had been killed by someone unknown. Their reaction was a mixture of grief and anger.

"What are they saying?" she asked Steven Fetesti.

"They must find the killer. No one can believe it was one of us. Only an outsider could have done something so terrible."

Rosanna was comforting the dead man's sister while others went about the work of removing King Carranza's body. After a brief conversation with some of the others, Michael placed a telephone call to Captain Segar. He promised to come at once, though it was a two-hour drive from his office in town.

As the body was removed Michael examined the house. "Can you tell if anything has been stolen?" he asked Theresa.

She went through the downstairs rooms, including the bedroom and bathroom. "He had some money he kept here – gold jewellery and coins, as well as paper money he earned from smithing. It seems to be gone."

"Could it be upstairs?"

"He hasn't used the upstairs since his accident years ago. He had some things stored up there, that's all." But she went up to inspect it anyway, with Rosanna, and they reported back that the upstairs storage area appeared untouched. The thief and murderer had apparently confined his activities to the ground floor.

In the crowd outside, with tensions running high, a fight had broken out. A big Gypsy Jennifer didn't know had started tussling with Ivan Raski, the little Russian shopkeeper. Michael sprang out the door and leaped off the porch, landing on the combatants and carrying them both to the ground. Then he yanked them apart by sheer force. "What's this about?" he shouted at them in Romanian.

The Gypsy said something Jennifer could not catch, but his meaning was all too clear when Michael responded angrily, "Why? Is Ivan to be suspected merely because he is not one of us? This girl and I were in his shop very near the time the killing must have taken place – he is not the one we seek!"

It was less than five minutes later when Rosanna spotted the drops of blood near the back door and called Michael. "Perhaps King Carranza managed to wound his attacker," she suggested.

"It is a possibility," he admitted. "It couldn't be Carranza's blood this far from where Theresa found him."

"Why not?" Jennifer asked. "His blood might have splattered on his killer."

"These drops are perfectly shaped and not yet dry. They dripped from an open wound. See – here's another on the back steps." When Fetesti came to observe, Michael told him, "Go get your dogs. They are good trackers. They will lead us in the right direction."

The young Gypsy returned in minutes with two shaggy beagles. At first they seemed uninterested in the bloodstains, caught up instead by the odors in the kitchen, but Steven yanked on their leashes and finally managed to direct their attention. The dogs went out the back door and headed across the field toward the woods, pulling their master behind them.

"Come along," Michael said to Jennifer.

"Don't you need a gun?"

"If he's still there, it means he's too badly wounded to put up a fight. He used Carranza's hammer for the killing, remember – that implies he has no other weapons."

They followed the dogs into the woods and then out the other side. There was another dirt road. The dogs hesitated a bit here, but finally picked up the scent again. Michael and Steven followed them to a narrow culvert along the side of the road.

"There his is," Michael said pointing. "Stand back, Jennifer."

A sandy-haired man in jeans and a striped T-shirt lay in the culvert. Michael bent over him and went rapidly through his pockets. "German passport in the name of Hans Funken. Probably died from loss of blood. The body's still warm.

Jennifer could see the bloody wound in the young stranger's side as she edged closer to the culvert. "Was he shot?" she asked.

"It looks more like a knife wound," Michael said, continuing to search the body. In one pocket he found two gold coins. "These were Carranza's. No one else would have had coins this old."

"But why would he kill him?" she asked.

"It was probably a simple burglary that went bad. Carranza was an expert at knife-throwing. He hit this fellow with a blade and the man stopped to beat his head in before he fled. I suppose he had been wandering across the country-side and picked Carranza's house because it was the largest in the village." Michael stared off at the horizon.

"You were very close to him, weren't you?"

"He was like a father to me." Michael turned back to Steven. "Stay with the body. I'll send a truck around to carry him back."

As they returned to the Carranza house the way they had come, Jennifer asked, "Will you be the new king?"

"Usually the old king passes on his medallion and ring – the symbols of his office – to a chosen successor. King Carranza had no children, and though I acted in his place on the Council of Elders many times he never chose me to succeed him. It will be up to the Council to name a new king. But that won't come until after his funeral ceremony. When a king of a Gypsy clan dies, there is often a gathering of other clans in the area. It is a mournful occasion but a festive one too."

At the Carranza house Michael dispatched two of the men to help Steven Fetesti with the body. Ivan Raski listened to Michael's account of the discovery. "A stab wound, you say?"

"It appeared so. We must search for a second weapon. You remember how skilled Carranza was with a thrown knife."

"As are many Roms," Raski agreed.

Jennifer watched them search beneath the chairs and tables in the sitting room, then wandered out to the kitchen and began searching there, as much to remove her from the death room as for any other reason. The body was gone now, but the terrible bloodstains still soiled the carpet. Out here at least there were no bloodstains except those by the stove and the back door.

She spotted the knife almost at once by the woodpile next to the stove. "Michael!" she called. "Here it is!"

He hurried into the kitchen, with Raski close behind. "Yes, I recognize it," he told her, picking it up carefully. "It was his favorite throwing knife. He wore it beneath the sash around his waist."

Raski turned to look in at the overturned wheelchair. It was in the direct line with the stove. "He hurled the knife and caught the killer as he was going out the door."

"Perhaps," Michael said.

Jennifer watched him as he studied the carpet in the short hallway between the living room and the kitchen. He opened a door and glanced in at the bathroom. "Anything?" she asked him.

"No," he said shutting the door.

He was interrupted by the arrival of a car outside. Jennifer could see by his face that he recognized the sound of the motor, and he hurried to greet the new arrival. "It's Captain Segar," Ivan Raski explained.

She saw the uniformed man climb out from behind the wheel. There was someone with him in the car and Jennifer assumed it was one of his deputies. Segar shook hands with Michael as they met in front of the house. "My dear friend," he said, "I know how much Carranza meant to you."

"He was our king," Michael said simply. "There will never be another like him."

Then Segar's gaze swept the crowd in front of Carranza's house and settled on Jennifer. "I've brought someone who is looking for you," he announced. The other man had emerged from the car and was walking towards her. She saw with a shock of fear that it was Peter Fry.

"So this is where I find you," he growled. "In a Gypsy camp!"

"Peter, you – "

He towered above her, his fists clenched as if he might strike her at any moment. "You deserted me and stole my motorcycle! Where is it?"

"It's safe , in Michael's shed."

"Michael, is it? You didn't waste any time, did you?"

"Peter, stop acting childish." She was aware that several of the villagers were close enough to overhear them.

"Why did you leave me?"

"I thought the note I left made everything clear. How did you find me?"

"I borrowed a car from a friend and kept asking people along the way. A girl like you alone on a motorcycle attracts attention. Finally I saw this government car down the hill and asked Captain Segar if he'd seen anyone answering your description. He told me he'd met you on the road yesterday and directed you here. He was on his way here to investigate a killing, so I left the car and rode along with him."

"I'll return your motorcycle and you can go," she told him, turning to walk away. He grabbed her arm and spun her around.

Suddenly Michael was at her side and pulling Peter's hand away. "Is there some problem here?"

"She's going back with me," Peter said.

"Not unless she wants to." Michael turned to Jennifer. "What do you want to do?"

"I don't know. I want to stay here with you, I think. At least for a while."

Michael sighted. "Lets go inside and talk it over."

They'd brought back the dead man, and Steven Fetesti helped to unload him from the truck and lay him on the ground. When one of the Gypsies tried to kick the body, Segar quickly intervened. "Keep back everyone. Was there any identification on him?"

Michael handed over the German passport he'd found. "His name is Hans Funken. He must have been passing through the area and picked the Carranza house to rob because it was the largest in the village. We found these two coins in this pocket but nothing else."

"Does anyone remember seeing him around?" Segar asked the Gypsies. Several shook their heads. No one seemed to have known or seen him before.

Jennifer and Peter followed the others into the house, where Theresa sat in grieving silence in a corner of the room. "There must be preparation for the funeral," Maria Fetesti said softly.

Michael nodded. "Of course. Notify those from the nearby tribes who might want to attend and have some of the men begin to erect tents."

Peter sat down next to Jennifer while the others made plans. "I'm sorry I grabbed you like that, but I want you to come back with me."

"I don't think so, Peter."

"I thought we had a pretty good thing going."

"Better for you than for me, I think."

"If it's the junk, I'll try to lay off it."

"You've tried before, Peter," she said with a sigh. "If you really want to kick the habit, you need medical help."

He stared off for a few minutes, then shook his head. "At least drive the car back and I'll ride the motorcycle. I can't handle both of them."

"That's your problem." Jennifer said.

Michael was telling Captain Segar what little they knew about the killing as Segar studied the knife and the bloodstains in the kitchen. Peter, looking dark, got up and went into the bathroom. Jennifer feared he might shoot up while he was in there, but he returned after a minute and sat back down next to her. She sighed. Perhaps she was being unreasonable. She had stolen his motorcycle, after all, and it was her responsibility to help him get it back. After that, she could decide what to do next.

Finally, she went over to Michael to tell him her decision.

"Wait a bit," he said after hearing her out. "Stay for the funeral. Peter can stay, too. You needn't decide anything yet."

"When will that be?"

"The ceremonies will start tomorrow."

"I'll talk to him," Jennifer said, and went back to Peter. She told him what Michael had proposed and he listened in silence.

"Will you stay?" she asked.

"No," he said. "I'll have to get the car back. I'll take the motorcycle and see if I can find a hitch for towing it. There's probably not much chance of that around here, though."

Feeling guilty again, she turned away, wondering what to do next.

"I want everyone to sit down," Michael was saying. "I have something I want to tell you about the murder of King Carranza. I wanted to wait until later, but I can see there may be no time to wait."

"What is there to say?" Segar wanted to know. "The king himself saved us the trouble and expense of a trial with his throwing knife."

"But you see," Michael said, "of all the people in the village at the time of King Carranza's death, this German youth, Hans Funken is the one person who could not have murdered him."

It was Maria Fetesti who spoke first. "Are you saying that one of us killed him? That is impossible!"

"Consider the evidence," Michael said. "It's plain to see that Hans Funken entered this house to rob Carranza. Perhaps he peered through the window and saw him in a wheelchair and considered him an easy victim. After searching the downstairs, he was in the kitchen near the back door when the king managed to pull out his knife and hurl it at him. Funken was hit in the side but pulled the knife free of the wound and let it drop to the floor. Then what happened?"

"He went back to the living room and beat Carranza to death with the blacksmith's hammer," Ivan Raski said.

"No," Michael told him. "Because there's not a trace of blood on the floor or rug between the kitchen and the living room. I looked very carefully. And once the knife was removed, the wound bled freely. There were drops of blood on the back steps and Steven's dogs were able to follow the trail all the way through the trees to the road."

"All right," Raski agreed. "Then he must have bludgeoned the king *before* he received the knife wound."

"Equally impossible. The wounds with that hammer would have been fatal almost instantly. Even if King Carranza could have lifted himself from the floor with his dying breath he could hardly have thrown that knife through the hall and into the kitchen with such accuracy. Carranza couldn't have killed Funken after he was bludgeoned and Funken couldn't have killed Carranza after he was knifed – the two attacks couldn't even have happened simultaneously because they were too far away from each other."

"Then who did kill my brother?" Theresa asked coming out of her silence.

"There are two possibilities," Michael said gently. "One is that someone from the is village entered the house after the robbery and killed the king, assuming it would be blamed on the thief. The other possibility is that two thieves took part in the robbery and Funken's accomplice killed Carranza after the king threw his knife. Again, let us examine the evidence. Which way did the mortally wounded Funken head after he fled from the house? Toward the road beyond the trees. Certainly that suggests a car was waiting there. But we found no car. Nor did we find most of the gold jewellery and coins you told us were missing from the house.

"There can be little doubt it was an accomplice who murdered Carranza and then helped the dying Funken through the woods and back to his car. He left the body by the road, took the loot from the robbery, and fled in that car."

"Where do we find this accomplice," Segar asked.

"Here," Michael said pointing an accusing finger. "Peter Fry killed our King."

Peter made a grab for Jennifer – perhaps to take her with him or to use her as a shield, she was never sure which – but then Steven Fetesti and Ivan Raski were on top of him, pulling him to the floor.

Michael said, "He knew where the bathroom was. He stepped into a strange house in a foreign land and walked directly to the bathroom without asking anyone where it was, or if one even existed. Only two houses in the entire village have indoor bathrooms. One might argue that a young man from America where indoor plumbing is common might simply assume we all have it too. But for him to approach the bathroom here with such assurance he had to have been in this house before. The door was closed. I'd opened it earlier to check inside and then closed it again."

Later, as the clans began to arrive for the funeral of the Gypsy king, Jennifer stood alone in front of Michael's house. When he came out to join her, she asked, "What will become of me, Michael?"

"You will go back to Bucharest after the funeral. I've already arranged for Captain Segar to take you. He will get you a flight back home. Peter Fry will be staying here for a long time."

"You can keep the motorcycle. I won't need it now."

"Neither will Peter. Segar found the jewelry and coins hidden in his car. Or I should say, Funken's car. Segar confirmed that it had German license plates. Peter must have encountered Segar's official car on the road after the murder and decided it would be less suspicious to stop and ask about you. When Segar brought him along, he probably didn't realize until too late that he was returning to the murder scene. I suppose the two of them were searching for you, following your trail, when they happened upon this village and decided on a robbery for drug money."

"I brought all this on you and your people," Jennifer said.

"King Carranza lived a long life," Michael told the lost girl as a cheer went up. Another Gypsy clan had arrived for the funeral.

GYPSY AT SEA

The letter arrived in a plain white envelope addressed to Michael Vlado, Gravita, Romania. No other address was needed because everyone in Gravita knew Michael. Since the death of their Gypsy king, Michael had been elevated to the title, though still a relatively young man in his early forties. The news had reached the outside world somehow, picked up by some of the larger metropolitan papers as a filler on an inside page. One such paper had been in Athens, and the first thing Michael saw upon opening the envelope was a clipping with half remembered Greek letters headlined : NEW GYPSY KING FOR REMOTE VILLAGE.

It was the first time he had read Greek in years, and it brought back memories of the period in his youth, a quarter century ago, when he had traveled with a band of Gypsies one summer, harvesting crops up and down the coasts of Greece. That was where he'd met a stunning nineteen-year-old girl named Nita Delvado, a Spanish Gypsy with the pure features of a goddess.

The letter in the plain white envelope was from Nita Delvado.

"What is so important there?" Michael's wife Rosanna asked, watching as he read the letter.

"It's from a woman I knew long ago in Greece." He read on a bit. "She wants to see me. She wants me to come to Athens."

"Were you lovers?"

"No. She was a year older than I and there were enough older men in the tribe to keep her interested. We were good friends, though. Close friends."

"You're not going, are you?"

"I think I must."

"Why, Michael?"

"Nita drowned in the Aegean Sea twenty-five years ago. I identified her body."

Had it not been for the eternal vision of the Parthenon looking down from the Acropolis in the middle of the city, Michael might have had difficulty in connecting this modern Athens with the place of his youth. Office buildings sprawled in every direction, and the air was grey with chemical pollution. Now, waiting for the next harvest season, the city's Gypsies lived in old army platoon tents erected in vacant lots. Michael went there first when he arrived.

One of the older Gypsy men recognized him at once. "Michael Vlado! You've come back to us!"

Michael studied the deep brown eyes beneath the fringe of graying hair and then he remembered. "Hello, Sasha. How have you been?"

"Fine. Michael. You've changed little."

"As have you, my friend," Michael lied. He barely recognized the weathered face before him. A quarter century of harvesting crops beneath the Grecian sun had taken its toll. "How are the others?"

"The ones you knew? Dead, mostly, or wandering again. I have settled down with a wife and children. Three fine boys."

Michael slapped his old friend on the back. He was remembering a day when they were both eighteen, and Sasha had told him his name meant Alexander, the conqueror. And Sasha had wanted to be a conqueror in those days. He had apparently settled for something less.

"Are you married, too, Michael?"

"Yes. My wife Rosanna is back in Romania."

"But no children?"

"Not yet."

"What brings you to Athens, old friend?"

Sasha would probably not have seen the newspaper account of his election as king of the tribe, and Michael saw no point in mentioning it. "I heard recently that Nita Delvado is still alive. Do you remember her?"

"Who could forget her?"

"We thought she'd drowned."

"It was a case of mistaken identity, old friend."

"I saw the body myself, Sasha."

The greying man shrugged. "It's best not to ask questions."

"Have you seen her since her return among the living?"

Sasha glanced away. "Yes, once."

"And?"

"And I asked no questions."

Michael patted his shoulder. "Thank you, Sasha. I'll see you again before I leave Athens."

"Where are you going now? To see her?"

"Yes."

"Be careful, Michael."

As he moved away from the little village of tents, Michael was aware that a Gypsy youth wearing a red scarf was following him. He followed for some time before Michael finally lost him in the city's traffic.

The address on Nita Delvado's letter was a walk-up apartment in an old building in the Vathi section of the city, a few blocks from the Archeological Museum. Michael rang the bell and a woman's voice came through the speaking tube. "Who's there?"

"Michael Vlado. Is this Nita?"

"Michael! You're here, in Athens?"

"Right downstairs."

"Come up. It will be good to see your face."

The door on the third floor was unlocked, and he found Nita waiting for him. "I thought you were dead," he told her.

She kissed him sweetly on the cheek, as a sister might. In her forties, she was still a lovely woman, and it wasn't until she turned from him that he glimpsed the jagged red scar across her left cheek. "Not dead, no. That was a mistake." She laughed harshly. "Sometimes I think my entire life has been a mistake." A faint scent of perfume clung to her, like the past.

"Tell me about it."

"I didn't mean to involve you, Michael. When I read of your good fortune – the king of your own tribe at such a young age – I had to write."

"I'm happy you did, though your letter was a shock. Who was it that died that day? Whose body did I identify as yours?"

"Remember Mosha, the Greek girl who worked on the boat with her brother? I'd gone out that day with some others who'd chartered her brother's boat. We were heading for one of the islands for a few days stay – the island of Kea, not far from the mainland. On the way back, the boat ran into a sudden storm and was wrecked. All five aboard were drowned. After a battering in the sea, Mosha's body was taken for mine. Her brother died too, so there was no one alive to correct the mistake."

"Except you."

"Except me," she agreed. "I'd stayed behind on Kea."

"Alone?"

"I'd met a man staying at the hotel there. We were having a good time and he persuaded me to remain on the island with him for a few extra days. Then the boat went down and I was reported dead. He said that was perfect for his plans. He was in a line of work where a beautiful woman without a past could earn a great deal of money."

"As a prostitute?" Michael asked cynically.

"No, as a spy."

"Nita, you must be kidding me."

"It seems like a bad joke now, but I was nineteen years old at the time, remember. I had little education and all I had to look forward to was a lifetime of traveling the harvest circuit with the others, in beat-up trucks, living in those awful tents you still see around the city."

"But a spy? For whom?"

She shrugged. "Let me get you a drink."

He asked for some ouzo, remembering the pleasing anise flavor from his youth. Her apartment was modestly decorated, and while she busied herself in the kitchen he allowed his eyes to wander about. If spying had been a profitable trade for Nita, there was little sign of it here. Even the television set was a dozen years old. He'd seen newer ones in the villages back home.

When she returned with the drinks, Michael asked, "How long have you lived here?"

"I've been back about four months. Ever since this." She touched the scar on her face.

"How did it happen?"

"A Gypsy cut me. He said I'd betrayed my people."

"Had you?"

"Not in the way he meant. I suppose I've betrayed a great many groups in the past twenty-five years, but I never consciously hurt or betrayed a Gypsy. If you mean did I turn my back on my own people and try to make a life for myself away from them, I suppose I betrayed them in that way. But I was dead after that boat went down. Nita Delvado, the beautiful Gypsy girl, no longer existed. I was a new person."

"Who did you work for?" he asked again.

"Only one person – Alec Grimsby, the man who recruited me."

Michael's eyebrows went up. "British?"

"A British citizen, yes. He hasn't been home in twenty years. He runs a free-lance intelligence network in the Middle East. When I met him on Kea he was working for Israel. Now much of his work is for the other side, the Palestinians."

"And you've devoted your life to this sort of foolhardiness?" Michael couldn't believe it. "It's a wonder you haven't been killed."

"I'm out of it now," she said. "That Gypsy's knife ended my career."

"Surely you can have plastic surgery."

"I will have it, but it means several operations and skin grafts over a period of three years. I'm forty-four now. In three years Alec will have replaced me with someone younger."

"Has he given you money?"

She nodded. "Enough for a modest living. And he promises to pay for the operations."

"You could write a book about your experiences. It might bring big money."

"I have never written anything longer than a letter."

"A publisher could arrange for a collaborator."

"It would mean exposing Alec. I couldn't do that."

"Is he your lover?"

"He was, for all those years."

Michael finished his drink in anger. "He used you, Nita, and now he's throwing you aside."

"Maybe I wanted to be used. I was nineteen and without a friend."

"I was always your friend," Michael said softly.

She glanced at her watch. "Thank you for saying that, Michael. Now you must go. I have an appointment soon and I must change for it."

"You asked me to come all this way to see you Nita, to welcome you back among the living."

She smiled sadly. "I should never have written you. I was better off in your memory."

"No," he protested, but she had gotten to her feet and was moving toward the door.

"Goodbye, Michael. We will not see each other again."

He paused at the door. "The Gypsy who cut you – he must have recognized you from the past."

"Yes."

"Who was he?"

"An old friend of both of us. Remember Sasha?"

After he left the apartment, Michael circled the block and returned to wait in a doorway across the street, curious to see who Nita's visitor might be.

Within twenty minutes, a French made limousine pulled up to the curb and a tall white-haired man got out. He appeared to be in his fifties, and when he told the driver to wait for him he spoke in English. Michael had little doubt it was Alec Grimsby.

He waited in the doorway, but after a half hour passed he grew tired of it. Whatever they were doing up there was none of his business. He walked back through the narrow streets to the little hotel where he was staying. It had been an afternoon of conjuring up memories of other days, of feeling emotions he didn't fully understand. There was Nita, whom he might have loved years ago, and Sasha, a friend from the same past. But what was their relationship to each other, and what had caused Sasha to cut her face like that?

Michael was just crossing the street in front of his hotel when he again saw the Gypsy boy with the red scarf who had followed him from Sasha's encampment. Michael entered the lobby and walked quickly to a side door. Slipping out into the late afternoon crowd, he circled back to the front of the hotel in time to see the youth pause in front of the building. Michael walked quickly up to him and fastened a steely grip on his shoulder.

"Let go!" the boy cried, trying to break free, but Michael hung on. "I want to talk to you." The youth was in his early teens and close up there was little doubt who he was. Michael had seen that same crafty expression too many times before. "You're one of Sasha's sons, aren't you?"

"So what if I am? I was just walking on the street!"

"You were following me. You followed me when I left your father's tent."

The boy struggled to get loose, but Michael forced him against the building. A few passersby glanced at them curiously and hurried on perhaps concluding that Michael had caught the Gypsy boy in the act of picking his pocket.

"I didn't do anything wrong!" the youth insisted.

"Your father and I were boys together. What is your name?"

"Alberto," he replied after some hesitation.

"Well, Alberto – " Michael adopted a more friendly tone of voice " – you are quite clever at trailing people. Your red scarf is too easy to spot in a crowd, but otherwise you have developed all the right skills. I was certain I'd lost you once, before I reached that apartment in the Vathi district. How were you able to stick with me without my knowing it?"

The boy looked down at the sidewalk then apparently decided to share his secret. "There was a man following you, too – a man I've noticed hanging around our tents. When I saw him follow you, I followed him – "

"What does he look like?"

"He has dark hair and a beard. Sometimes he carries an artist's easel and rolled up canvas like a painter."

"All right," Michael said, relaxing his grip on the boy's shoulder. "Run along now and report to your father. Tell him I'll be seeing him soon."

Michael spent a restless night. He had seen Nita Delvado and heard at least the broad outlines of her story. By rights he should be getting the train back home to Romania. But should Nita be warned about this man who had followed him to her apartment? In her line of work, one could collect a great many enemies in twenty-five years.

By morning he had decided. He would visit her one more time before he left. And he would visit Sasha too, as he had promised. The morning air was warm so he decided to walk to Nita's apartment as he had the previous day. Traffic seemed heavy for a Saturday morning but he reminded himself that he knew nothing of this city as it was today.

There was a car in front of Nita's building, and for a moment Michael thought it might be Alec Grimsby's limousine again. Then he realized it was an official car with a police seal on the door. A uniformed officer stood guard.

"What's the trouble?" Michael asked. "I'm a friend of Nita Delvado, who lives here."

The officer spoke quickly to a man inside the entranceway, his Greek too fast for Michael to understand. The second man motioned Michael inside and led him upstairs to Nita's apartment. A man in a braided uniform, obviously in charge, stood just inside her door.

"Did you know the dead woman?" he asked.

Michael looked down at the body in the center of the floor, the scarred cheek turned toward him. She was wearing the same dress as the day before. "Yes," he managed to say. "Her name was Nita Delvado."

She had been shot once in the chest at close range, the officer told Michael. Since none of the neighbors heard a shot, the killer may have used a silencer. It had happened sometime during the night, probably after midnight. "Did she have any enemies?" the officer asked.

"I saw her yesterday for the first time in twenty-five years," Michael explained. "She wrote to me recently saying she'd like to see me again. I came here to visit her. She told me a little of her past life. She may have had enemies but she mentioned no one by name."

They questioned him further and took his name and address. "Do you know where she got the scar?" one of them asked.

"No," Michael answered thinking of Sasha. Likewise there was no point in mentioning Alec Grimsby or the mysterious bearded man. If any of them had had a hand in her death, he'd need evidence to prove it.

Finally they let him go. He wandered the streets aimlessly for an hour, to be certain the police weren't following him, then he headed for the Gypsy encampment in the vacant lot near the markets.

For the weekend tourists, the Gypsy women had set out card tables and folding chairs, and were telling fortunes – reading palms and interpreting the fall of the Tarot cards in exchange for a few coins. Michael found Sasha far away from this activity, talking with some of the men of the tribe. His son Alberto hovered nearby playing with a jackknife.

"May I speak with you?" Michael asked.

Sasha nodded. "Of course, Michael. Alberto told me about yesterday. I hope you don't think I sent him to spy on you. He's a good boy but he goes off on his own too much. I had no need of Nita's address, and if I did I would have asked you for it."

"Nita is dead, Sasha. Someone murdered her during the night."

"What are you saying!" He seemed truly surprised.

"Someone shot her in her apartment. This morning a neighbor noticed the door was ajar and found the body."

"I can't believe it." Sasha seemed to sag noticeably at the news. "Was she robbed?"

"Apparently not, and there was no sign of forced entry. She seemed to have known her killer."

"Alberto said a bearded man followed her. Perhaps it was someone from her past life."

"Perhaps," Michael agreed. "You said you saw her once. How much did she tell you of that past life?"

"She mentioned a man named Grimsby. She'd been shopping at the market and I came upon her accidentally. I'd heard rumors she was alive but the meeting was still a shock for us both. I couldn't believe my eyes."

"When was this?"

Sasha thought. "Probably three or four months ago now. I remember it was the beginning of the good weather before we went off on the circuit to help with the planting."

"Did you argue?"

Sasha looked away. "Why would we argue?"

"She said you did."

"It was foolish. At first I couldn't believe it was really Nita. I kept telling her she was dead. Finally, when she convinced me, I welcomed her back. I thought she had come to live with us, but she was only passing through. She said she would never come back to this sort of life, the Gypsy life was what she'd escaped from. The way she said it – I'm afraid I slapped her, Michael. I think you would have done the same."

"Sasha – "

"She'd fallen in with bad people."

"People like Alec Grimsby? Were you upset because she'd been living with that man? Because she rejected her Gypsy heritage?"

"Yes." His voice was soft and ashamed.

"One more question, Sasha. Did you cut her face with a knife?"

"*Cut* her? Certainly not. I only slapped her."

"Did she have a scar on her cheek?"

"Not then. Alberto told me later that he saw her on the street and she was scarred."

"She said you did it."

That was a lie!"

"Alberto seems to know everything," Michael commented. "Come here, boy!" he called out to Sasha's son, who was still playing with his knife.

"What do you want?" Alberto asked suspiciously.

"You seem to know what's going on. Where would I find this Englishman Grimsby, the one who was with Nita Delvado that day?"

"The one who came to her apartment after you left yesterday?"

"That's the one."

"Is it worth any money?" the boy asked slyly.

Michael laughed. "He learns well from his father." He took a gold coin from his pocket and handed it over. "Now tell me."

"On his boat in the harbor. The motor yacht, *Quincade*. I followed him there one day. He only returned to Athens recently."

Michael nodded his thanks and turned to take his leave of Sasha. "Are you going there?" Sasha asked.

"I am. I think Grimsby can tell me who killed Nita."

The *Quincade* was an impressive ship more than sixty feet long, the sort frequently encountered in the Mediterranean waters. Michael remembered them from his boyhood in the early 1960s and he knew that any man who owned such a craft would not be an easy person to reach. He'd taken a taxi to the thriving port area of Piraeus, a suburb of Athens some five miles from the center of the city. The ship lay peacefully at anchor, its gangplank guarded by a burly-looking crewman.

"I'd like to see Mr. Grimsby if he's aboard," Michael said.

The crewman almost smiled. "The cap'n don't receive visitors."

"Tell him it's about Nita Delvado. I think he'll see me."

The crewman shrugged and disappeared up the gangway. While Michael waited he watched a boat at the next dock unloading nets full of sponges taken from the nearby water. Presently the man returned and said, "Follow me."

Alec Grimsby, the white-haired man Michael had first seen entering Nita's apartment the previous day was seated on a roofed deck in the stern of the yacht sipping a tall glass of iced tea. He rose and offered his hand as Michael joined him. "Nita mentioned you," he said. "It is a terrible thing about her."

"You learned about it quickly."

The Englishman smiled and sat down again, offering Michael a chair. Up close he seemed younger, and there was something a bit debonair about him. Michael caught a whiff of the aftershave or cologne he'd first smelled at Nita's apartment. "The police have already been here," Grimsby told him. "A neighbor told them about my visits."

"Were you with her last night?"

Grimsby shook his head. "I saw her earlier to say goodbye. I'm leaving port today. I have business matters elsewhere."

"Nita told me you'd been friends for twenty-five years."

"A long time, yes."

"She told me the sort of thing she did for you."

Alec Grimsby squinted at Michael. After a moment, he suggested a glass of tea. "Gyspies drink tea, don't they?"

"Not this early in the day," Michael answered. "I came here to ask you about Nita, and who would have wanted to kill her. I've been followed by a bearded man who sometimes carries artist's materials. Would he have had reason to kill her?"

Grimsby smiled. "I have no idea what sort of life Nita has had here in Athens. She left my employ some months ago."

"How many people like her do you have, risking their lives to line your pockets?"

The smile froze on his face. "Whatever she did was of her own free will."

"Why did she return to Athens?"

"For plastic surgery on her face. She came back four months ago."

Michael took a deep breath. "In the Romanian newspapers I read about the prostitutes in New York. They have pimps who keep watch over them. The pimps drive around in big fancy cars. In a way, the Mediterranean isn't so different from New York, except that here the stakes are higher."

"I will not be lectured to by a Gypsy," Grimsby told him, his face frozen with controlled rage. "Go back to Romania or wherever you came from."

"Did you cut her face?"

"That's a Gypsy trick. You are wearing a knife on your belt right now."

"*Did* you?" Michael repeated.

Grimsby must have pressed some hidden button – suddenly the burly sailor was lifting Michael from his chair, gripping him in a bear hug. "Time to go, mate!"

Michael doubled over, lifting the man's feet from the floor and then quickly shifting his weight to roll him off his hip. The sailor went down hard, then came back up with a knife in his hand. Michael quickly drew his own weapon.

Grimsby barked an order to his man in a language Michael didn't know. "I want no blood on my deck," he said in English. "Get out of here, Gypsy!"

"If you killed her, I'll be back for you!" Michael said over his shoulder as he walked toward the gangplank.

Somehow Nita Delvado, a woman who had been dead for him for twenty-five years, had become very important during her brief rebirth.

Michael found Sasha at the fish market, looking over the day's catch while the women of the tribe used their fortune-telling money to buy food for the table. "We'll be on the road again in two weeks," he told Michael. "Sometimes I think it's not so bad. At least we get out in the fresh air, away from the city's pollution."

"Sasha, I have to ask you something."

"What is it my friend?"

"That day four months ago when you saw Nita. You told me you didn't cut her."

"I didn't. My God, Michael, I would never use a knife on any woman!"

"And you said she had no scar that you noticed."

"I told you that."

"On which cheek did you slap her?"

"Which cheek? Michael, what difference does it make? I am right-handed. I was facing her, so I must have hit her on the left cheek."

Michael nodded. "The one with the scar. Isn't it possible that your nail caught her flesh and tore it without your realizing it?"

"No, it is not. I felt bad as soon as I did it and I looked at her cheek. It was red from the slap, but the skin wasn't broken. She was crying, her face already wet from the rain – "

"What?"

"She was crying – "

"You didn't mention the rain before."

"Michael, do I have to give you a report on the weather conditions? It was raining. What difference does that make?"

"All the difference in the world – " Michael turned and ran for a taxi hoping he was not too late.

But the Saturday afternoon traffic had moved in, and his second journey to the docks at Piraeus took longer. By the time he reached the berth of the

Quincade, there was no sign of the motor yacht.

Michael ran to the sponge fisherman at the next dock. "I'm looking for the *Quincade*. It was anchored there a few hours ago."

The fisherman shrugged. "Gone. Sailed with the tide."

"Where to?"

"Who knows? Perhaps to one of the islands. Everyone goes to the islands in the summer."

Michael felt defeated. He stared out at the horizon, hoping for a sign.

The islands –

"Is there a ferry to Kea?"

"Yes, but it takes three hours."

"Where does it dock?" The fisherman pointed and Michael waved his thanks and ran, catching the Kea ferry as it was about to depart. For the entire time of the crossing, he stood in the bow, feeling the warm salt air against his face. Finally, when the rocky shorelines of Kea came into view, he saw that the fates were with him. The motor yacht *Quincade* was riding at anchor.

When he left the ferry he started toward it, then changed his mind. Not the yacht. A hotel.

At the taxi-service stand, he asked a driver, "Where is your best hotel?"

"Straight ahead," the man answered indicating a building of glass and chrome.

"No, I want something that would have been here twenty-five years ago."

"You mean the Kythnos. I can take you there."

It was an older white-stone building that showed signs of aging. At the dinner hour a rear terrace had a few diners, and Michael saw that he'd guessed correctly. Alec Grimsby was seated at a table off to one side with a woman companion. He half rose from his chair as he saw Michael approaching.

Michael barely glanced at him. It was the woman he'd come to find. She was blonde now and there was no scar on her cheek, but he would have known her anywhere. "Hello, Nita" he said.

She stared up at him coolly, without surprise. "Hello Michael. Will you join us for dessert?"

"Only for talk," he said pulling up a chair. He hadn't eaten since breakfast, but just then he had no appetite.

"Don't try any funny business," Alec Grimsby warned. "My crewmen are armed, and only minutes away."

"My mind doesn't run to funny business, certainly not to anything as devious as the two of you."

"I had to do it, Michael," Nita said. "An Israeli assassin has been on my trail."

"So you decided to die again. It worked so well the first time, you figured it might give you another twenty-five years. And you brought me back because I was the one who misidentified you the first time."

"It wasn't like that at all," she tried to explain. "When I wrote and said I wanted to see you again, I meant it. But I had no certainty you'd come before I had to disappear again, no certainty the police would show you the body."

"Who was it by the way? Who died for you this time?"

"Mosha's death twenty-five years ago was an accident. Alec didn't recruit me until after it happened, when it appeared my supposed death could be put to some real use. We had a good living, but four months ago we learned there was a price on our heads. Alec had seen a woman on Majorca who looked amazingly like me, except that she had a bad scar on her left cheek. She was a prostitute. I returned to Athens and let myself be seen by neighbors and a few old friends with a paste scar. I applied it with makeup every morning and touched it up when necessary. The assassin had tracked me to Athens by this time, but he waited to see if Alec would show, so he could kill us both. When Alec did come, he had the Majorca woman with him on the yacht. We exchanged places."

"And you killed her?"

"She died," Grimsby said. "But how did you know Nita was alive? How did you know where to find us?"

Michael shook his head, unable to accept their cool dispassion. "Is that all a human life means to you?"

"How did you know?" Grimsby repeated. "If we slipped up somewhere – "

"The makeup was good, and you arranged the body perfectly. When the neighbor found it, and when I saw it later, the first thing we saw was the scar. You even dressed her in the same clothes Nita wore yesterday. So I saw the scar and the clothes – your scar, your clothes, your apartment, Nita – and I didn't need to study the face. But there was one thing that bothered me. You said you'd come to Athens for plastic surgery on your scar, but you also said a Gypsy cut you. When pressed, you said it was Sasha."

"But both things couldn't be true. If you came to Athens for surgery then you had the scar before you met Sasha again. He said you didn't have it when he met you, and that stumped me for a while. But then he told me it was raining that day. I decided you'd gone out on some quick errand and hadn't bothered with the fake scar, fearful the rain would expose it for what it was. My suspicion of a false scar made me remember two other things. When I left you yesterday, you said you had to change your clothes for an appointment, yet the dead woman was wearing the dress you'd had on. You might have changed back into it, of course, but there was something else – the scent of your perfume in the apartment. I smelled it today on board the *Quincade*. At first I thought it was Grimsby's cologne. But Grimsby didn't come to your apartment until after I'd left, and cologne wouldn't have lingered from his last visit. It was your perfume I smelled, Nita, and I smelled it again on the yacht because you were there. You were probably listening to our conversation from behind the cabin door."

"And so you followed us here to Kea" she said.

"Its where you both were twenty-five years ago. I thought you might be sentimental enough to come back to the same place for your second funeral."

"What do you plan to do", Grimsby asked. "We're beyond the jurisdiction of the Athens police."

"I plan to do nothing," Michael said, and stood up. "Nothing."

"Michael – " Nita called as he walked away, but she did not come after him.

As he boarded the ferry, he saw a bearded man getting off, carrying an easel and a roll of canvas. All the way back to Athens, he tried not to think of what might have been inside that canvas ...

He took the morning train to Romania and seated in the coach with the Sunday paper he found the story on page 2, under a headline that read: TWO SLAIN ON KEA. It was brief a story, with more details promised in later editions: "A wealthy British businessman and a woman companion were slain Saturday as they finished dinner on the terrace of their hotel on the island of Kea. A lone assassin opened fire with a submachine gun and escaped in the ensuing panic. The dead man was identified as Alec Grimsby, in his fifties, said to have close ties to various Middle Eastern factions. The woman killed with him has not been identified."

THE GYPSY DELEGATE

Michael Vlado was working back in the field on the day that Captain Segar of the government militia drove up through the hills to seek him out. It was January and there was little farming to be done, but the horses Michael raised always needed tending to. His wife Rosanna was in the house and she rang the dinner bell to summon him.

Word had reached the Gypsy village of Gravita of the stark events of previous weeks, when the uprising of the Romanian people had ousted the country's leaders and led to the Christmas Day execution of the former President and his wife. Trudging back across the frozen earth, Michael caught a glimpse of Captain Segar standing in the doorway with Rosanna and his first thought was that his old friend had been dismissed by the new government. The familiar militia uniform was missing and Michael could see that under his dark blue overcoat Segar wore a conservative business suit like those he'd seen worn by government officials.

"Are you out of a job?" he asked, shaking hands with his friend.

Segar smiled. "I'm out of the militia, but into a better job with the new government. I'm an official in charge of this region. I may have to run for election, depending upon the working of the new constitution, but for now – "

"Congratulations!" Michael said, meaning it. "You're exactly the sort of official our new government needs."

"If I can get through my first month without being shot, perhaps there's some hope." Segar's face turned serious. "But I didn't drive up here for your congratulations, Michael. The new government has a mission for you."

"For me – a Gypsy? The former President never looked on us with any great favor."

"Things have changed, believe me. Remember King Michael?"

"I was only a baby at the time, but I was named after him."

"You know he was forced to abdicate at the end of nineteen forty-seven when the Communists took over the government. But did you know he was still alive?"

"Michael, alive?" Somehow the idea surprised him. "He'd be – what? almost seventy years old now. Where has he been?"

"Living in exile in Geneva. He has offered to return if the Romanian people want him."

"As a king? Do the people really want that?"

"Of course not. They want their freedom, along with the rest of Eastern Europe. But the new government feels it might be wise to send a delegation to Geneva. It would be an unofficial delegation, of course, without notice to the press. Because of my familiarity with the Gypsy villages in this area, I was asked to nominate a Gypsy delegate. I suggested you."

"Me!"

"They want a five-man delegation representing various groups. When it was decided one representative should be a Gypsy, I immediately thought of you, Michael. Naturally the chosen one should be a Gypsy king, to meet with our deposed king, and you know yourself that many of the others are elderly and unable to travel. You are a vigorous man only in your mid-forties."

"What would this involve?" Michael asked with some misgivings.

"You would meet your companions at an orientation session in Bucharest next Monday and then proceed by train to Geneva."

"Wouldn't flying be faster?"

Segar shrugged. "Dr. Vincenti, chairman of the delegation, does not fly."

"How long would I be away?"

"You would be back here by Friday."

Even before discussing it with Rosanna, Michael knew he would go. It wasn't every day one got to meet a deposed king and one's own namesake.

On Monday morning Michael met the other four delegates in an ornate high-ceilinged room at the Palace of Culture. It was the minister of culture who spoke to them, explaining first that the President was otherwise occupied. "We must realize that these are trying times for our nation, and for all of Eastern Europe. You five have been chosen to make a delicate, unofficial visit to our deposed king. Of course, to reinstate him in his former position is out of the question, but with demonstrators still in the streets we must investigate every avenue that could lead to stability. Perhaps a conciliatory statement from him might help our situation."

Michael found his thoughts wandering to the other four seated with him. They would be his companions for the next few days. All were dressed conservatively, though he wore a red high-necked tunic under a dark blue suit coat. Dr. Vincenti, a tall man with a silvery white beard, had been the first to introduce himself. He was the official spokesman for the group and had known King Michael in his youth. Now, at seventy, he was a distinguished educator who'd managed to stay clear of government involvement for much of his life.

Michael's main attention was directed toward the lone female in their group. Slava Botosana's conservative grey suit and white blouse couldn't hide the fact that she was an exceptionally attractive woman in her thirties. Her dark hair was nicely styled and her makeup carefully applied – something one rarely saw in the villages of Michael's area. As if to counteract the plainness of her suit and blouse, she wore fashionable shoes with three-inch heels, and an expensive leather briefcase, probably purchased in the west, leaned against the leg of her chair. As the cultural minister spoke, she made notes with a slim gold pencil.

The younger of the other two men, a representative of the Romanian Workers' Alliance, was quite outspoken. His name was Petru Grazu, and Michael guessed his age to be about thirty. He was blond and handsome with Germanic features that marked him as one of the nation's two percent minority from the Banat region.

"What route will be we be taking to Geneva?" he wanted to know.

The minister didn't seem pleased at the interruption. "You leave this afternoon by train to Belgrade. There you change to the Direct Orient Express, which will carry you to Geneva with stops at Trieste, Venice and Milan. The train actually stops at Lausanne, but that's only sixty miles along Lake Leman from Geneva – a very scenic bus ride."

"Is Michael expecting us?"

"Of course. We have been in communication with him. It is best to avoid the media, however – we do not want it known that a delegation has gone off to see the deposed king, even on an informal basis."

It was the fifth member of the group, a balding man about Michael's age, who broke in to say, "Referring to two Michaels is confusing. It may help our new friend Michael Vlado if we refer to the other as King Michael, though we realize he will never hold that title again."

Michael smiled at that man and shook his hand. "I'm sorry I didn't catch your name."

"Constantine Aman. I was director of the Art Museum of Romania until the former President dismissed me for deviation from the strict party line. Now I am back in the government's good graces – as long as there is a government."

As the meeting was breaking, Michael sought out Slava Botosana. "Did I hear someone say you were an actress?"

She laughed softly, and he found it a pleasant sound. "Once I was. Now I am on the governing board of the national theater. I believe they chose to include me only because I am a woman. They wish to charm King Michael into making a statement on behalf of the new government, and I have a reputation for charming men, even those nearing seventy."

Michael reflected. "We're a mixed group. An educator, an actress, a workers' representative, a former museum director – "

"And a Gypsy king." She said it with a smile. "I thought you would be a bearded old man with a limp."

"Our old king was too old, with too much of a limp. He was confined to a wheelchair and I was pretty much running things, conducting the Gypsy court, deciding issues that affected our people. Then someone killed the old king in a robbery and the title passed to me. I was surprised the people chose me, but I am grateful for it."

"Why don't you travel around in caravans like other Gypsies?" she wanted to know.

"Some of my people do, but Romanian Gypsies have never been as nomadic for some reason. We have settled here in the hills, farming the land and raising horses."

"So now you are a statesman!"

Michael held up his hands in protest. "No, no – only a poor Gypsy. I hope you will put up with me for the next few days."

They were in Belgrade that evening, changing trains while the last of the daylight faded. As the train pulled out of the station, Michael saw leafless trees outlined against he dark blue sky and, for a time, a pack of wild dogs chasing alongside.

"What is it, Gypsy?" Dr. Vincenti asked watching the dogs. "An omen?"

"Only if you believe in omens. I am one Gypsy who does not."

"But if something bad happens – "

Michael shrugged. "It will be a coincidence." He looked at Vincenti. "What is it that bothers you about our trip?"

"This is a time of great uncertainty for the Romanian people, Michael. The government situation is still fluid, with several factions fighting for control. Some think the old government hardliners might even try for a comeback. If that were the case, they might begin by assassinating the deposed King Michael."

"Why do that? There's no chance he'll return as our ruler."

"No, but he could become a symbol. Sometimes symbols can be as dangerous as omens for those who believe in them."

There was a little smile on his lips as he spoke the words but Michael thought about the exchange that night when he was trying to sleep.

In the morning he had time for only a shave and a quick breakfast before the train arrived in Venice. Michael was sharing a compartment with Grazu and

Aman, while the elderly Dr. Vincenti and Slava Botosana had private compartments of their own. The woman and the two younger men joined him for breakfast and later when he stopped by Vincenti's compartment he found the man studying some papers he'd spread out on the lift-up table with which each compartment was equipped.

"No breakfast today?" Michael asked him.

"Perhaps later. I must prepare my remarks for our meeting with King Michael."

"I think I'll take a look around the station here in Venice."

"Don't get left behind."

Michael found himself in the company of the young man, Petru Grazu, as he left the train to stretch his legs. "Have you ever been to Venice before?" he asked Michael.

"Never."

"How many more borders do we have to cross?"

"Only the Swiss border, after our stop in Milan."

"The policeman at the Yugoslav border really annoyed me. They treated us all like some sort of criminals despite our diplomatic passports."

"It is not an entirely pleasant experience," Michael agreed. "But at least the food is reasonably good."

The outspoken labor representative nodded. "For a time in the Seventies, there wasn't even a dining car on the *Orient Express*. Passengers had to obtain food and drink from vendors on station platforms. At least it's better now, though the train will never recapture all of its lost glory."

"You sound like a capitalist," Michael observed.

"Hardly!"

A while after they reboarded the train for the depressing journey out of Venice, crossing the oil-slick lagoon to enter a vast flatland of refineries and factories, Slava came along the corridor and joined them. "How long to Milan?" she asked.

"We should be there early this afternoon," Grazu told her. "Is Vincenti still working, do you know?"

"I think so."

Constantine Aman was just coming out of Dr. Vincenti's compartment as Michael and Grazu moved down the corridor. He brushed back the thin hair on his forehead and turned to say, "I'll check in with you when we reach Milan."

"Still working?" Grazu asked.

"Yes. He doesn't wish to be disturbed for a while."

Aman wanted another cup of morning coffee, so Michael accompanied him through the train to the dining car. "Are we really accomplishing anything with this journey?" he asked the museum director.

Aman eyed him critically as they found seats at one of the tables. He took out a felt tip pen and removed a small pad from his inner pocket. With a few rough strokes he drew a crude pie chart. "You see this tiny wedge, Michael? This is the percentage of Romanians who are Gypsies. Only two hundred and thirty thousand by the last census. The very fact that you are here, included in this mission, accomplishes something for your people."

Michael took the pen and marked off a larger segment of the pie. "Most Gypsies in the country have settled down in one spot. They consider themselves Romanians and many have good reason not to declare themselves as Gypsies. Most estimates place their number at over a million."

"Good reason?"

"The Nazi death camps were not just for Jews."

"That was fifty years ago."

"Gypsies have long memories."

Slava came in then looking puzzled. "Has either of you seen Dr. Vincenti? He wanted my opinion of his opening statement to King Michael and he promised to stop by my compartment."

"He was still working on it when I left him a few minutes ago," Aman told her.

"In his compartment? I knocked on the door and called his name, but no one answered."

"He told me he didn't want to be disturbed," Aman told her.

"But surely he would have answered."

"I'll go check on it." Michael left them and walked back to the next car where their compartments were located. He knocked on Vincenti's door but there was no answer. Then he turned the knob, found it was unlocked and pushed it open.

Vincenti was lying on his side on the seat, his distinguished head toward the closed windows. In front of him on the desktop was spread the penciled draft of the remarks he'd been working on. Michael took a step closer, reaching out a hand to the man who seemed to be sleeping.

Then he saw the blood, and the slim dagger plunged into his right side.

Michael found Petru Grazu alone in their compartment. The younger man came alert when he saw the intensity of Michael's expression. "What is it?"

"Dr. Vincenti has been murdered in his compartment. Stay by the door while I get the others."

He hurried back to the dining car, where he was surprised to see Constantine Aman holding Slava's hand across the table. When he saw Michael, Aman got quickly to his feet. "What's the trouble?"

"Someone's killed Vincenti – come quickly!"

"Oh, no!" Slava gasped.

Grazu awaiting his return stepped aside as Michael pushed the compartment door open and allowed the others to enter. "Don't touch anything," he cautioned. "We don't want them blaming one of us for this."

Grazu turned to face him. "Who *should* they blame? Surely it must be obvious to you that we are the only suspects. Who else even knew we were traveling on this train?"

"Someone might have followed us," Slava argued, "and wants to disrupt our mission."

"They've certainly done that," Aman said. "There's no way we can continue without Vincenti."

"Why do you say that?" Grazu bristled as if his personal honor was at stake. "I will lead the mission if no one else does. We have come too far to turn back now."

"Let's deal with his death first," Slava insisted. "The conductor must be notified."

"The police will delay us for questioning," Michael pointed out.

She gave him an exasperated look. "He'll be found when we cross the Swiss border anyway. I'm going to find the conductor right now."

She was gone before anyone could object.

"Perhaps he was robbed," Aman suggested.

Michael moved closer to the body. "I'll see if his money's been taken. You both can witness that I removed nothing from him."

"I don't know," Grazu said with a twisted smile, "Gypsies are fast with their fingers."

Michael ignored the remark and surveyed the area around Vincenti's body. The desktop was clear of everything except the three sheets of paper on which the dead man had been writing. There was nothing on the floor and nothing on the seat next to the body. Michael felt in the crevice between the seat and its back, but not even a coin or a gum-wrapper was hidden there. Next he checked the dead man's pockets. His wallet, containing the currency they'd been issued for the journey seemed to be intact. Otherwise, his pockets contained only the usual objects – a handkerchief, keys, a case for his eyeglasses, a few Romanian coins, a pen, and a notebook that had a section for addresses.

Michael turned his attention to the topcoat that hung near the compartment door. In one pocket he found gloves, in another a slender vial of blood pressure pills.

"Where's his passport?" Grazu asked.

That had been bothering Michael too. He wondered if the old man might have been killed for it. Then he spotted the overnight bag on the rack above the seat. He lifted it down carefully and opened the unlocked snaps on either end. The passport was lying on top of a clean shirt and pajamas. "Here it is. Nothing seems to be missing."

"Unless the killer took something we didn't know about."

"That's always a possibility!" Michael went quickly through the bag, turning once toward the two men. "One of you stand outside in case Slava comes back with the conductor. I don't want him walking in on me like this." But the overnight bag contained nothing except a few articles of clothing, a toothbrush, toothpaste, a comb and brush, and a small scissors perhaps for trimming his beard.

Aman had stepped outside and Grazu remained. "Didn't he have any background information on the meeting?" he asked Michael.

Michael got down on his hands and knees to make certain no sheet of paper had fallen beneath the seat or into the heating unit. "There's nothing here. Perhaps Slava has the material in her briefcase."

Slava entered then, pushing past Aman with the train conductor in tow. The conductor stared at the body as if he'd never seen a dead man before. "This is terrible! We'll radio ahead to Milan and request instructions." As he was retreating out the door he seemed to remember his duties. "You three clear out and I'll lock the compartment."

They went down the corridor to Slava's compartment. "What will we do now?" Aman said.

"I told you!" the younger Grazu sputtered. "I will lead the mission if no one else does! King Michael has been told of our arrival and we must appear as scheduled!"

Aman was doubtful. "I don't know. If one of *us* killed Dr. Vincenti perhaps there is a plot on King Michael's life."

"Rubbish!" Grazu turned to Slava. "Do you have the background information on the meeting? We found nothing in Vincenti's compartment."

She nodded, brushing the hair back from her eyes. "I have it in my briefcase." She produced a sheaf of papers from the fine leather case Michael had noticed earlier. "Here's everything we need if you wish to continue."

"I think we should vote on it," Aman said. "I vote we abort the mission and return home. We can leave the train at Milan and catch the next one back to Romania."

"I vote we continue on," Grazu urged. He and Aman looked to Slava and Michael for their decisions.

"Continue", Slava said.

"Continue," Michael agreed.

"Three to one on my side," Grazu crowed. "Will you leave or continue with us, Aman?"

The museum director stared at him with ill-concealed distaste. "I will continue, if only to keep you under some sort of control, little man. It is not yet the Germans' time to rule."

Grazu was on his feet bristling. "I am Romanian, not German! Are you questioning my loyalty?"

At that moment there was a knock on the compartment door. Michael opened it and the conductor stepped partway in. "The authorities in Milan have been alerted. They will meet the train and remove the body there. Everyone will be questioned before we are allowed to proceed. It may take longer than our scheduled one-hour stop."

When he'd left them alone again, Slava said, "They'll want to know where each of us was. We'd better get our stories straight."

"Michael and I were together in the dining car," Aman pointed out. "Neither of us had an opportunity to stab him."

Grazu missed no opportunity to continue his feud with the older man. "That's only if we believe Vincenti was alive when you left his compartment. We heard you speak to him, but we heard no answer and none of us saw him. You told us he didn't want to be disturbed, but that might have been because he was already dead."

"He was alive when I left him," Aman stated firmly. "But either you or Miss Botosana might have entered the compartment and killed him while Michael and I were in the dining car."

Slava smiled at Michael. "It seems that you are the only one with an alibi."

"Not so fast," Grazu said. "Perhaps Vincenti was still alive when the Gypsy went to check on him. A dagger is a Gypsy weapon, remember. He might have stabbed him and then come running to report his murder."

Slava sighed and nodded. "It appears that any one of us might have done it."

The railroad station at Milan was modeled like a cathedral, with high vaulted ceilings and balconies that seemed to serve no purpose. Michael remembered it from his previous visit to the city, but this time the experience was different. He was led through the station to a private office the police had commandeered for questioning. The others had gone first, but he'd been kept separate from them until he was questioned.

Lieutenant Rizzoli was a beefy man who smoked a cigar. That he disliked Gypsies was obvious to Michael with the first words out of his mouth.

"Is this one of your Gypsy shivs?" he asked gesturing toward the dagger in a plastic evidence bag that rested on the table between them. He said "shiv" in English though he spoke in Italian. Michael wondered if he knew that the slang word came originally from the Romany word for blade. He didn't really need to know because to him Gypsies and knives were practically the same.

"I never saw that dagger before," Michael answered truthfully. "It's not a Gypsy weapon"

Rizzoli chewed on his cigar. "Tell us in your own words exactly what you know of this. I believe you were the one who found the body."

"I found it," Michael admitted and launched into a brief account of their journey. He didn't know how much the others had told, but he managed to remain vague about the nature of their journey to Switzerland.

When he'd finished, the police stenographer typed up the statement while he waited on the bench outside the office to sign it. As he sat there, Grazu the labor leader, was brought out of an adjoining office and seated next to him.

Seeing Michael, Grazu seemed to have forgotten his suspicions concerning the dagger. "This is all a matter of routine," he offered smiling nervously. "The detective assured me we're not under suspicion. They're questioning the other passengers about a possible thief, someone Vincenti might have surprised in his compartment."

"He surprise no one," Michael reminded him. "He was drafting his remarks to the king when he was stabbed. If a thief had entered thinking the compartment was empty, he would simply have excused himself and left."

Lieutenant Rizzoli reappeared with two typed statements. Grazu read his, then took out a fountain pen and signed it. He passed the pen to Michael for signing his statement. "Fine," the lieutenant told them. "You are free to reboard the train. It should be getting under way shortly."

Vincenti's body had been removed in their absence, as had his overnight bag and topcoat. The compartment was empty. Michael lingered near the door at the front of the passenger car, watching for Slava and Aman to return from questioning.

That was how he happened to see Captain Segar suddenly dart across the high-ceilinged station and grab an innocent-looking man in a bear hug. The man carried a package about the size of a cigar box.

Michael thought for a moment that his eyes were deceiving him. Segar in Milan? It was impossible – Segar was back in Romania!

But when he hurried over to the struggling pair to confirm the identity, Segar spoke to him. "Michael, take that package out of his hand – very carefully or you might blow us all up."

"Segar, what – "

"Take that package!"

The man in Segar's grasp, with a black mustache and glowering eyes, struggled to break free, then dropped the package. Michael made a grab for it, but wasn't quite fast enough.

The package hit the floor but nothing happened.

By that time, Lieutenant Rizzoli and two uniformed officers had come running.

"What's going on here?" Rizzoli demanded.

"Hold this man!" Segar commanded in the most authoritative voice Michael had ever head him use. "Here are my credentials. I represent the new Romanian government. This man was attempting to board the train with an explosive device."

"Vincenti has been killed," Michael managed to tell Segar.

"His death must be linked to this bomb plot in some way," Segar speculated. "I followed this man here from Romania."

Rizzoli chewed on his cigar and carefully picked up the fallen package. In a gesture either brave or foolhardy he carefully tore open a part of the wrapping. "It's a book." He announced. "*Twentieth Century Romania.*"

"A gift fit for a king," Segar said. "Let us go somewhere private where innocent travelers will not be injured if it goes off...."

The Italian lieutenant led them back to an office used for questioning. The prisoner had been handcuffed and seated himself silently in one of the chairs. Michael tried to remember if he'd ever seen him before, but decided it was only the expression that was familiar – the arrogant sneer he'd seen on officials of the old government when he drove to the city. He'd thought these men, and that expression, were gone from Romania for good. But the time had been too short. The new freedom could not come overnight.

Segar removed the jacket from the book and took a penknife from his pocket. He slit the binding, front and back and peeled away the cloth covering. Something white and doughy came into view. "Plastic explosive," he told them. "There's a timer and detonator hidden in the binding, but I won't fool with those." He placed it on the desk. "I'm sure it's safe until the timer is set. Otherwise he wouldn't have been carrying it around like this."

Lieutenant Rizzoli stared at the prisoner. "Who is he?"

"A member of the secret police under the former government. His name is Meershan, though he goes by others. He took a plane from Bucharest this morning. We had a tip about the bomb, so I went along to see what he was doing with it. It was packed in his luggage and plastic explosives are difficult to detect with airport X-rays. When he left the plane at Milan, I decided he would make contact with this train."

"To kill the members of the government mission?" Michael asked.

"No, to deliver this infernal device to the hands of the final assassin, who would present it to King Michael. My plan was to follow him until he made contact with one of your party, but in the station he spotted me – he must have remembered seeing me on the plane. He started running with his package. I couldn't risk his getting away with the bomb – I had to arrest him."

"You have no jurisdiction here," Rizzoli muttered.

"It was a citizen's arrest until you arrived to make it official," Segar explained. He turned to Michael. "Tell me about Vincenti's murder."

Running through the events quickly Michael concluded, "It seems likely that Vincenti somehow discovered the identity of the would-be assassin. He had to be killed before the assassin was to accept delivery of the bomb from this man Meershan."

Rizzoli lit a fresh cigar and walked over to grasp their prisoner by the coat lapels. "Who were you meeting on the train?" he asked.

"No one."

The detective leaned closer until the glowing tip of his cigar was almost brushing Meershan's cheek. "I'll ask you again. To whom were you supposed to deliver the package?"

Meershan's glowering eyes went to each of their faces in turn, finally stopping at Michael. "Him!" he spat out. "The Gypsy."

Before Rizzoli could say anything, Captain Segar spoke up in Michael's defense. "That's not true. I recommended Michael for this mission personally. King Michael would be the last person he'd attempt to kill."

Rizzoli relaxed a bit. "Why should anyone want to kill a deposed king who's been living in exile for more than forty years? Surely your country would never take him back."

"It has to do with symbols," Michael told him. "The king is a symbol of the old Romania, before Communism. We may not want him back, but we want that sort of life back – a freedom even I was too young to have ever known. Though our former President and his wife went before a firing squad, there are still plenty of people opposed to freedom of that sort."

The lieutenant turned back to the prisoner. "Do you have a better answer for me, scum? Who were you planning to meet?"

Meershan's eyes grew even harder. "Go to hell."

Rizzoli raised his arm to strike the man, but Michael intervened. "Wait a minute! Give me time to think."

"You are going to produce the murderer from a hat, perhaps?"

"I know I'm not guilty, despite what this man says. And we can rule out robbery as a motive. Since the bomb had to have been intended for use by one of those three – Slava, Grazu or Aman – we can safely assume one of them killed Dr. Vincenti. Otherwise we have a would-be bomber assassin plus a totally independent murderer without a logical motive."

"You said Vincenti was preparing a draft of his greeting to the king," Segar reminded him. "Could he have left a hidden message in it identifying the killer?"

Michael shook his head. "Not unless it was so obscure as to be useless. It was his handwriting but there were only general remarks about the greatness of Romania's past."

"Perhaps all three are in on it," Rizzoli suggested. "I read a mystery once where all the passengers on the train conspired to kill – "

Then it came to Michael. He remembered something, and it all came to him. "Not all three," he said. "Just one of them. And now I know which one ..."

The other three were brought from the train and the passengers told there would be another brief delay before the journey to Lausanne and Paris continued. Segar suggested that Michael explain his reasoning to him, and Lieutenant Rizzoli stood by. The prisoner Meershan was being held in an adjoining room.

"You'll remember," Michael began, facing Slava Botosanna and the two men, "that I searched the compartment very carefully after I discovered Dr. Vincenti's body. Something was missing and I couldn't understand what – not at first. Then we got on to looking for his passport and other things, and I forgot about it."

"What was missing?" Grazu asked.

"Dr. Vincenti had written a pencil draft of the remarks he would make in greeting King Michael, yet there was no pencil in the room. It wasn't on the desktop with the sheets of paper or on the floor, or down the seat cushions. All I found in his pockets was a pen. You'll remember I even searched his overnight bag on the rack. There was no pencil anywhere."

"No pencil," Rizzoli repeated. "Are you saying the man was killed over a pencil?"

"Not at all. I'm just saying it wasn't there. Why not? There is only one possible explanation. The murderer removed it from the compartment after stabbing Vincenti."

"I repeat, are you saying the man was killed over a pencil?"

"No. If he was killed *over* a pencil why would the killer remove it? A pencil is a pencil. What harm could there be in leaving it? The pencil had to belong to the killer. In other words the pencil – if left at the crime scene – would have revealed the killers identity."

"It had the name of a restaurant on it?" Aman suggested. "Or a business establishment?"

Michael shook his head. "An ordinary wooden pencil, even with advertising on it, would not immediately identify the killer. I believe it was something more – the gold mechanical pencil I noticed Slava using back in Bucharest." He turned toward her. "Perhaps it even has your initials engraved on it, Slava."

She was on her feet, face flushed struggling for breath. "I'm not the only one who owns a pencil! What about these two?"

Michael shook his head. "Aman uses a felt tip pen, and I just borrowed Gruzu's fountain pen a short while ago. You're the only one with a recognizable pencil, Slava. You went in to discuss the greeting to King Michael and loaned Vincenti your pencil while he wrote a rough draft. Then what happened? Somehow he must have suspected you, and you stabbed him. You had to remove the pencil or it would have placed you in the room. He wouldn't have just borrowed it from you, because he had his own pen."

"You're very clever," she said, turning on her heel and heading for the door. "Or at least you think you are."

They all saw what she was doing, but nobody spoke. Instead of the door to the terminal she opened the door to the adjoining office where the handcuffed Meershan was waiting with an officer. "Slava!" he exclaimed when he saw her. "What – "

She slammed the door on him and turned, her face drained of color.

"Why did you kill Dr. Vincenti?" Michael asked.

Her shoulders sagged in defeat. "He told me while he wrote his remarks with my pencil. He said some of my past associations had been questioned by the new government, and after reviewing the matter he'd decided I was not to be allowed to meet with King Michael – I was to remain at the hotel while the rest of you spoke with him. I had no choice then. Meershan was on his way to meet me with the bomb. I knew that killing Dr. Vincenti might abort the entire mission, but I had to gamble that the rest of you would decide to continue. The dagger was in a hidden pocket of my briefcase."

"Did you get all that?" Rizzoli asked the stenographer. Then, to Slava he said, "You are under arrest. You may have a lawyer present if you wish."

Michael and the others remained overnight in Milan. In the morning they continued on to Lausanne.

THE IRON ANGEL

Michael Vlado's Gypsy village in the foothills of the Carpathians had remained free, so far, of the turmoil that had swept through much of Romania since the collapse of the Socialist government. In many communities Gypsies had died, or been driven away, and Michael had intensified efforts to find a new home for his people. But as spring returned to the Carpathians all seemed well for a time.

Even Michael's old friend Segar, once a captain in the government militia and now an official of the transition government, had taken to driving up to the village of Gravita as he had done so often in the old days. That was why Michael saw nothing unusual in his arrival that April morning when the horses were out it the field and the first of the spring flowers had blossomed.

"Good morning, Captain. A nice day for a ride in the hills!"

Segar smiled. Though he no longer wore his old uniform, he still liked being addressed as Captain. "My visit is not entirely one of pleasure," he admitted. "Do you remember an American girl named Jennifer Beatty? She rode up here on a motorcycle and stayed a few days."

Michael nodded. "It was at the time the old king was murdered and I took over the leadership of my tribe. How could I forget? I've wondered sometimes whatever happened to that girl. I hope she returned to her country."

"Unfortunately, no," Segar told him, looking off into the distance where the two mares were romping. "She's in Bucharest, and she seems to be involved in a killing. I thought you'd want to know."

"Is she accused of it?"

"Not yet. She'd been snorting heroin with some other young people, and she was a bit high at the time."

"Snorting heroin?"

"Drug addicts think it's safer than using contaminated needles."

Michael knew there was some reason for Segar's visit. "What do you want from me?"

"You were her friend for that brief period."

"More than three years ago."

"True, but she asked for you while being questioned. She won't talk to anyone else."

"You want me to return to Bucharest with you?"

"Yes, if you could follow me down in your car."

"I hate that city, even more so now for what they've done to my people."

"I think the worst of the oppression is over."

Michael shook his head. "Last week a small group of Gypsies passed through here from Poland, heading south. They told of gangs of young people wrecking homes of wealthy Gypsies, trying to drive them from the country."

"I think the worst is over," Captain Segar repeated. "Return with me to Bucharest. You can help the girl and you can help me."

"Who was murdered?" Michael asked.

"A Gypsy."

The capital city had changed little since Michael's last visit. A few statues had been removed and the name of the late president, Ceausescu, was nowhere to be seen. Otherwise, the buildings were as Michael remembered them. He recognized the old militia headquarters at once as Segar turned into the parking garage connected to it. "This is our police headquarters now," his friend explained.

"Then you are back in police work?"

Segar shrugged. "It is the only work I know."

He led the way up to his second floor office, then picked up the telephone and issued a curt order for Jennifer Beatty to be brought in. He explained that she was being kept in a holding cell while they decided what to do with her. "The murdered man was a Gypsy named Jaroslaw Miawa. He was found stabbed to death in a cellar where Jennifer and some others were snorting heroin. She insists no one touched him, that he was wounded before coming there."

"Would that have been possible? What does your autopsy show?"

Before Segar could respond, the door opened and Jennifer Beatty was brought in. Michael remembered her as a young woman of twenty-two who'd stolen a motorcycle from her boyfriend and driven it into the foothills to hide from him. Now she was in her mid-twenties, though somehow she looked older. Her blonde hair was streaked with some sort of coloring and the healthy outdoors look he remembered was tarnished. Her eyes were tired and the lids sagged, though that might have been from a night without sleep. "Hello, Jennifer," he said, getting to his feet.

"You came! Thank God you came! Tell these people to release me." Her face seemed to come alive at the sight of him.

"I'm afraid I can't do that."

"You're the Gypsy king aren't you?"

"These days in Romania that means even less that it did three years ago."

"I brought Michael Vlado as you requested," Segar told her. "Now you must give us a statement as you promised."

"I don't know. It's so confusing – "

"Could I speak with her alone?" Michael asked.

"All right," Segar agreed.

She reached out to touch his arm. "Wait. Do you have a cigarette?"

Segar took out a pack from his pocket and gave them to her. "They're not American," he said apologetically.

"I'll smoke anything." She lit one and tried to relax as Segar left them alone in the little office.

"I was hoping you'd be back in America by now," Michael told her.

"I started back. I got sidetracked."

"How was that?"

She shrugged. "I decided to stop off at Switzerland for a few days. They had this park in Zurich where you could buy drugs legally and take them quite openly. The city government even supplied clean needles. I think they've stopped it now. The idea was to keep addicts in just one area of the city, but it didn't work too well."

"So you were back on drugs."

She nodded, drawing on the cigarette. "And before I knew it I was back here. I hooked up with a guy and when I told him about Romania he wanted to see it. Travel is easier now, and there was no problem driving here from Zurich. We both had American passports."

"What happened to him?"

"He wanted drugs and he got arrested the first week we were here. I haven't seen him since. After that I fell in with a German named Conrad Rynox. I like him a lot. His crowd is into snorting heroin, which I'd never done before."

"Did you know the man who was killed?"

"Jarie. Jaroslaw Miawa. He hung around, liked to gamble. That's how he got money for the heroin."

Michael jotted down the name, asking her to spell it. Then, "Tell me what happened last night."

"We were in this cellar on Furtuna street. When Jarie came in I could see he was hurt badly. Then we saw the blood. He'd been stabbed more than once. He said a few words and then he just died there, on the cellar floor." Segar slipped back in while she talked.

"What did he say?"

"Something about an iron angel. The three eyes on the iron angel."

Michael glanced at Captain Segar. "Mean anything to you?"

Segar shook his head. "Nothing."

"Is there someplace in the city that has an iron angel – a park or a church perhaps?"

"I don't know of any."

"You might try contacting the churches. There aren't that many of them anymore."

Segar nodded and made a note.

"What does the autopsy say about the dead man's wounds? How far could he have walked before collapsing?"

"We found no blood on the pavement outside, which is why we're questioning her further. He couldn't have gone too far after he was stabbed."

Michael Vlado nodded. "And you say he was a Gypsy? Did he have a family?"

"A brother here in the city. The rest of the family moved west years ago."

"Do you really think Jennifer is involved?"

"We found her with the body."

"The others all ran away," she explained. "I stayed. He was my friend and I was hoping he was still alive."

"Will you release her?" Michael asked.

"Not now. Perhaps tomorrow, after the court hearing."

"She stayed with him, for God's sake! Would his killer have done that?"

"That argument will weigh in her favor," Segar conceded, "but the laws and the courts are different now. We must follow regulations to the letter. Here is the name and address of the victim's brother. If you can learn anything from the Gypsies, it could help her."

Michael had the unpleasant feeling that Segar had somehow recruited him to act as a detective. Either he was setting up Michael for some sort of trouble or there was something about the case that Segar couldn't trust to his own assistants. Michael didn't like it, but maybe Jennifer Beatty deserved another chance.

The brother's name was Sigmund Miawa, and Michael found him in the morning at a Gypsy enclave by the edge of the city. He was tall for a Rom, with a fairness of skin that suggested mixed blood and intermarriage. He was a watchmaker, with a caravan that housed his wife Zorica and their child. It was a wonder that he continued to live as a Gypsy.

"It is a sad day for my family," he told Michael. "Perhaps you can honor us by taking part in the funeral service for my slain brother."

"Of course," Michael quickly agreed.

"To have a Gypsy king here, even a king from a neighboring tribe, would honor his memory."

"The police are trying to find who killed him."

"It was the drugs that killed him, whatever they say."

"As he was dying he spoke of the iron angel. What does that mean to you?"

"Nothing. A myth. I have heard men speak of worshipping at the iron angel, but I think it is only a saying."

"A saying not known in my hills. It is not a Rom saying."

"Nevertheless – "

"Your brother spoke of the three eyes of the iron angel."

"The Trinity, perhaps. It would be some sort of Christian symbol."

Michael Vlado said no more until after the funeral. There was only a small group of mourners. Sigmund's family and a few others. It was explained that Jarie had not lived among them, that he had chosen the ways of the city. And his city friends, perhaps fearing the police, had not come to the funeral.

Jaroslaw Miawa was buried in an unmarked grave over the hill from the Gypsy enclave. As they walked back together, his brother explained, "Feelings against the Rom are at a high pitch right now. We fear the wild city youths might desecrate the graves if they found them. We know where he is buried, and when times are better I will place a marker there."

"You should go out into the countryside where the living is better," Michael suggested.

"I have never been a wanderer. My work is here, and I doubt if old Kurzbic could manage without me."

"He is your employer?"

Sigmund nodded. "I am not a Rom when I am at work. I do not have the typical features of a Gypsy and it is easy to pass as a Romanian. That is something my brother always resented. His Gypsy heritage was more obvious, and it kept him from the sort of job I have."

Sigmund Miawa used public transportation to go to work, and he was grateful when Michael offered him a ride. "I could not tell Old Kurzbic that my brother had died, or he would ask too many questions. I simply took off half a day."

The store where he worked as a watchmaker was near the center of the city on Calea Grivitei. Michael parked his car down the street and went into the shop with Sigmund. From the name "Old Kurzbic," he'd expected the store owner to be a man in his seventies, but Kurzbic could not have been more than sixty. He was balding and wore thick glasses, but showed no sign of aging. His handshake was strong as he greeted Michael. "Welcome to my store. Feel free to look around."

In addition to jewelry, the small shop sold antique watches and clockwork mechanisms designed to amuse adults as well as children. "Whoever made these things?" Michael marveled, examining the miniature figure of a magician who waved his wand and produced answers to previously prepared questions.

"Such devices were popular in the late eighteenth century," Kurzbic explained. "Basically they were clockwork automatons, designed to perform any number of wondrous tasks. In a sense it was the golden age of the watchmaker's art."

"Do you sell them?"

"Some are worth a small fortune today, but only to collectors."

"You should guard these with care."

Kurzbic nodded. The reflection of the overhead lights danced off his thick glasses. "I am careful. Everything is locked up well at night, and I keep a gun behind the counter."

Michael glanced at the more modern watches and clocks and then bid farewell to Sigmund and his employer. "One other thing," he asked Kurzbic. "Did you ever hear of something called the iron angel?"

The older man blinked. "A prize fighter, wasn't he? Many years ago?"

"Said to have three eyes?"

"I believe so. One in the back of his head, they claimed, because he was so fast. The memory is vague but I think he was called the Iron Angel."

"That was the Iron Engine," Sigmund Miawa corrected from his work table. "I remember going to see him in my youth. I think Ceausescu's government had him shot as a traitor because he refused to be part of the Olympic team."

Kurzbic nodded. "Iron Engine, Iron angel – you may be right."

Michael left the shop and drove back to Captain Segar's office. The court hearing was over and Jennifer Beatty was waiting for him. "They said I can go," she told him.

He glanced at Segar. "Do you have any leads yet?"

"None. Here are the things from the dead man's pockets."

A shabby wallet with a few bills in it, some coins, a stubby pencil, a handkerchief, a key and a folded piece of paper bearing the number 470. Michael looked them over and saw little of interest. "What's the key for?"

"His apartment. It's in an old building a few blocks from where he was found. The address is in his wallet and we checked on it."

"He lived alone?"

"So far as we know."

"Is 470 his apartment number?"

"No. We don't know what that is."

Michael noticed the piece of paper was perforated along one edge as if it had been torn from a notebook. "All right," he said to Jennifer. "Ready to go?"

"I was ready yesterday."

He said goodbye to Segar and promised to call later. Outside, he asked the American girl where she was living. She wiped her palms nervously against the sides of her jeans. "I've been staying with Conrad Rynox, " she answered quietly.

"The leader of this little drug group?"

"He's very good to me," she answered defensively. "I love him."

He decided she was not really his responsibility. "All right, where does he live?"

"Furtuna Street. Across from the cellar where I was arrested."

"Tell me something," he said as they got into his car. "You knew Jarie Miawa. Did you ever see him with a knife?"

"I don't think so. Why?"

"There wasn't one among his belongings. Most Gypsies carry knives, especially in a city like this. It might indicate he pulled it out to defend himself and dropped it when he was stabbed. Perhaps he wounded the killer with it."

"I never saw one," she said looking away.

As they turned into Furtuna Street, he pulled up to the curb. "Jennifer, I have to ask you if you're doing the right thing going back to this man Rynox. He's been supplying you with drugs, hasn't he?"

"Sometimes." She looked away. "I'm cutting down. Pretty soon I won't need them anymore."

"I've known addicts before who said that. Come on, I want to meet Conrad Rynox."

She was reluctant at first to introduce them, but when Michael insisted she finally led the way into the apartment building. There was no elevator so they climbed five flights to the rooms she and Rynox shared. Michael hadn't known what to expect, but he shouldn't have been surprised to find a bearded man, apparently well into his thirties asleep on the sofa in his underwear. He woke up when Jennifer shook him, and reached for her.

She danced away and announced, "We have a guest. Try to make yourself presentable, Conrad."

He sat up bleary-eyed, making no effort to cover his hairy legs. "You come for some H?" he asked.

Michael shook his head. "I'm a friend of Jennifer's. I don't need any heroin and neither does she."

Conrad Rynox, if that was his name, spoke German rather than Romanian. He picked up his wristwatch, shook it, then tossed it aside. "What time is it, Jenny?"

"One-thirty. It's time you were up."

Michael could tell by his eyes and general manner that Conrad was still high on drugs, though he seemed reasonably coherent. "Do you know a man named Jarie Miawa?"

"Sure, I know Jarie – knew him, that is. He's dead, isn't he? Do I remember that right?"

"Yes, he's dead," Jennifer confirmed.

"Thought so. Came in bleeding like a stuck pig. That was last night, wasn't it?"

"Two nights ago. Everyone ran away and left me for the cops."

"I'm sorry, Jenny. I wasn't thinking straight."

"Jarie talked about the iron angel," Michael said. "Do you know about it?"

"Iron angel – sure! It's the answer to all problems, the fountain of youth, utopia."

"Does it exist? Have you seen it?"

"I've seen it, just once. It was like nothing else on earth, man! There were a half-dozen fires burning around it, and there it was shrouded in smoke. We approached like worshippers one at a time, through the smoke, to peer into its three eyes and learn our destiny."

"Where can I find it, Conrad?"

"Why do you ask?"

"I think Jarie was stabbed there. Otherwise why was it on his dying lips? I need to find the killer or else the police may arrest Jennifer again."

"It is nearby," he said. "But I'm not sure I could find it again. I'll try to find out where."

Michael could see there was no chance of learning more at the moment. "I'll be going now," he told Jennifer. "This is the hotel where I'm staying and the phone number. Please call me if he learns anything."

"I will," she promised.

He went back downstairs. Glancing toward the end of Furtuna Street, where it intersected with Grivitei, he realized for the first time that he was just around the corner from the watchmaker's shop where the victim's brother worked. Sigmund was sitting behind the counter where Michael had left him only a couple of hours earlier.

"I thought of another question," he told Sigmund. "Is there somewhere we could talk?"

"There's a coffee house down the street." He turned toward Old Kurzbic at the rear of the store. "Can you handle things while I go for a cup of coffee?"

"I handled them all morning," the shop owner grumbled.

"I won't be more than twenty minutes," Sigmund promised.

Over coffee Michael said, "Your employer didn't seem too pleased with your taking a break."

"Sometimes he feels sorry for himself. He knows more about the business than I ever will. I think he only hired me so he'd have someone to converse with. On days like today there aren't many customers." He took a sip of coffee. "But what was it you wanted to ask me?"

He repeated Conrad Rynox's description of the iron angel. "Did you ever hear anything like that before?"

He shook his head. "It sounds like a narcotic dream, all those smoky fires and the angel in the middle. It couldn't really exist, could it?"

"I don't know," Michael Vlado answered honestly. If this Gypsy didn't believe in the iron angel, why should he? "Do you know Conrad Rynox?"

"Slightly. He's an occasional customer at our shop."

"The number 470 was on a small paper in your brother's pocket. Could it be an address?"

"None that I know of." He thought about it. "That number would be about two blocks down from the cellar where his body was found. It wouldn't be connected."

"Connected. What do you mean?"

"In these old city blocks the building basements often run together. A person can enter on one street and exit through a building on a street around the corner."

"But 470 wouldn't be one of them, in any direction?"

"No. It would be too far away."

They finished their coffee and walked back to the shop. Kurzbic was behind the counter waiting on a customer with a damaged alarm clock. "I'll see you later," Michael told Sigmund, leaving him at the door.

He went back to where he'd left his car and was about to get in when a women stepped from a doorway. Her clothing told him at once that she was a Gypsy, but at first he didn't recognize her.

"Michael Vlado!"

"Yes?"

"I am Zorica Miawa, Sigmund's wife. We met briefly at the funeral this morning."

"Of course. For a moment I didn't remember."

"There was no reason why you should."

"I just left your husband. We had a cup of coffee together."

She was a small, dark woman a bit younger than Michael – perhaps around forty. Her eyes had the deep intensity associated with Gypsy beauty, and he imagined she'd broken more than one Rom heart in her youth.

"I must speak to you about my husband and Jarie."

He held open the car door. "Get in here."

She slid in next to him, but he made no attempt to start the engine. "I heard you asking Sigmund about the iron angel. He knows more than he pretends. The men talk about it. I have heard it mentioned in their conversations."

"Is it some sort of cult? A bizarre religion, or even a sexual thing?"

"I don't know. Jarie went there often. He spoke of the cellars, and the heroin-snorting and the iron angel. My husband was intrigued, but I don't know if he'd ever been himself."

"There was a number on a piece of paper in Jarie's pocket – 470. Mean anything to you?"

"No. An address, perhaps, but I don't know where."

"How did you happen to find me here?"

She hesitated only an instant. "I was shopping on this street and saw you returning to you car."

Michael nodded. "You'd better go now. I have to see Captain Segar."

She smiled slightly and slipped out of the car. He watched her walking back along Furtuna Street and wondered if she might have been there spying on her husband. Or on Jennifer Beatty.

Back in Segar's office, Michael was openly discouraged. "I'm no detective. I've gone about as far as I can, but I've learned nothing about this so-called iron angel except that a great many people seem to know about it."

"If a great many people know about it, but not the police, that implies something beyond the law."

"Perhaps but in which direction? Maybe drugs are involved, maybe it's merely a heroin-induced fantasy. Then again, it could be a sort of religious cult. Jarie Miawa might have been stabbed to death as some sort of sacrifice."

Segar snorted at that. "What sort of angel would demand a blood sacrifice?"

"The Angel of Death."

"Michael, you are seeing darkness where there is only human fallibility. I am convinced that drugs are the key to this."

He told Segar about his meeting with Conrad Rynox. "I hate to see Jennifer back there with him."

"Do you think they might be still using that cellar for their activities?"

"I doubt it, so soon after Jarie Miawa's murder." But Michael wondered about it. "I suppose I should look at the place where his body was found."

"Go there tonight," Segar said. "I can equip you with a body microphone and I'll be waiting outside with some men. This is the number where we found the body – 117 Furtuna."

"I know. It's right across the street from the apartment Jennifer shares with Conrad."

"You'll do it?"

"All right."

They waited until darkness descended on the city, soon after dinnertime, and Segar carefully taped a microphone and small transmitting unit to Michael's chest. "With that Gypsy tunic you wear, no one will notice it," he assured him.

"I hope I'm doing the right thing," Michael said, aware that Jennifer might be back in that cellar, if anyone was.

Segar had two men with him, and they dropped Michael at the corner of Grivitei and Furtuna. "We'll be listening," he promised.

Michael saw that old Kurzbic's shop was dark, and he pictured Sigmund back in the caravan with his wife and child. He walked around the corner, seeing only a few pedestrians hurrying home, and made his way to the building numbered 117. The sign outside identified several offices located there, but once past the front door he made his way back to the cellar stairs. The door was unlocked and no sound reached him from the darkness below. He turned on the light and started down.

The basement area was empty except for a few upended crates which could have served as seats for the heroin sniffers. He moved around it, wondering if he should report in to Segar. There was a door, perhaps leading to one of the adjoining cellars. It was unlocked and he swung it open.

Almost at once he saw the figure, about ten feet in, lit only by the faint glow from his side of the basement. It wasn't an iron angel, or an angel of any sort.

It was Conrad Rynox and he was dead.

Back at headquarters, Segar slumped in his chair, staring at Michael Vlado, "You found me another body when I wanted you to find a murderer."

"I found what was there."

"He was stabbed just like Miawa, though this time the wound was right to the heart. He didn't live long enough to run away."

"The killer is getting better with practice," Michael observed. "When I touched him the body was cold. Any idea how long he'd been dead?"

"Several hours. They'll do an autopsy right away."

"What about Jennifer?"

"I'm sorry, Michael. I'm having her picked up for questioning."

"Tell your men to search the rest of those basements."

"I'm having that done too."

Michael was waiting when Jennifer Beatty arrived. "He's dead, isn't he? They told me he'd been stabbed and I know he's dead."

"I'm sorry, Jennifer. He was never any good for you."

She flared into anger at his words. "How would you know?"

"He gave you heroin – "

"He gave me lots more besides that! Where is he? I want to see him."

"Perhaps later," Segar murmured. "First I must ask you some questions. If you do not wish Michael to stay – "

"He can stay."

"Would you like a lawyer?"

"I have no money for one. My God ,do you think I killed the only man I ever really loved?" Her eyes flooded with tears.

Segar sighed, perhaps realizing that communication would be difficult in her present condition. Still, he pressed on. "When was the last time you saw Conrad Rynox?"

"This afternoon," she answered listlessly. "Michael drove me back to the apartment and we found Conrad asleep on the sofa. After Michael left a little before two I fixed Conrad a light lunch. Then he said he had to go out for a while. That was the last time I saw him."

"Did he say where he was going?"

She shook her head. "He often went out without telling me where, especially if he needed drugs from his supplier."

"Who's that?"

"I don't know."

"I hope your memory improves, Miss Beatty."

"It was someone across town. His address is in the apartment. I insisted Conrad give it to me in case I got desperate some day when he wasn't home. Now are you going to let me see him?"

"First I want you to go over the contents of his pockets." Segar dumped a plastic evidence bag on the desk in front of him. There was German and Romanian currency gripped by a golden clip, a leather wallet with some papers, a few coins, a handkerchief, some unidentified capsules, and a six-inch spring knife with the initials J.M on it.

"That's Jarie Miawa's missing knife," Michael observed.

"Looks like it."

"He – he took it off Jarie's body," Jennifer said. "He went through his pockets before the police arrived, looking for drugs."

"These are deadly things." Segar demonstrated by pressing a button on the side of the knife. The spring-powered blade shot out one end.

Michael was more interested in the wallet. He looked through its contents, found an apartment key, some routine identification cards, and a folded slip of paper with a number on it.

"117," Michael read.

"The building where we had our drug parties," Jennifer said.

"Where Jarie Miawa died," Segar added.

Michael frowned at it. "The building was right across the street from his own apartment. Why would he need to write down its number ?"

"Maybe to give to someone," Segar speculated. He took out a second evidence bag. "Here are his watch and rings. A battery-powered wristwatch with the correct time. No clue there to when he died."

"I saw that in his room." Michael picked up two fancy rings. "What about these Jennifer? Was he wearing them both when he left you?"

"Yes. I gave him the sapphire." She seemed close to tears again. Segar was starting to gather up the objects when the phone on his desk rang. He picked it up and listened intently. "Fine," he said. "All right." He hung up and turned to Michael. "The autopsy shows he died within a short time of eating, probably around two o'clock."

"It was after two when he left the apartment!" Jennifer insisted.

"He must have crossed the street to number 117 and been stabbed to death in the basement almost at once," Michael said. He was remembering meeting Zorica, Sigmund's wife, on that street.

The phone rang again and this time it was one of Segar's men reporting that a search of the connecting basements in the block had yielded nothing unusual.

"Can I see him now?" Jennifer asked again.

Michael tried putting an arm around her shoulders. "What good will it do? It'll only make you feel the loss all the more."

She shook off his comforting arm. "I want to see him! It's my right!"

Michael and Segar exchanged glances over her head. "All right," the captain said. "Come this way."

"Life might be better for you now," Michael tired to tell her as they went downstairs. "You can get into a treatment program and stop your dependence on drugs."

"It's not just the drugs, it's not even Conrad, really. It's just that this is another ending. My life has been too full of endings. When I fled into the mountains to your Gypsy village it was an ending, and when I left Zurich it was another ending. By now I've run out of endings."

"Here we are," Segar said, holding open a white door with a No Admission sign. The attendant pulled out one of the drawers and lifted the sheet.

Jennifer froze, staring at Conrad's chalk-white face, thinking thoughts that Michael couldn't imagine. Yes, it was another ending for her. There was no denying that.

A low moan started then deep in her throat, building toward a fearful culmination. Michael, standing across the open drawer from her, tried to move, then shouted, "Segar! The knife!"

It was tight against her chest, just beneath the breastbone and she had only to press the button for the spring release. They both saw the spurt of blood as the blade went in and even as Segar grabbed her Michael knew it was too late.

In all the years that he'd known Captain Segar, he'd never seen anything hit him as hard as Jennifer Beatty's death. He sat in his office chair, his face almost as ashen as Conrad's had been. "How could I have done it, Michael? When I was distracted by those phone calls she must have slipped the knife up her sleeve or into her blouse. I never even noticed!"

"Neither of us noticed. She didn't want us to. She decided she wanted to die like that. Perhaps she was thinking of Juliet stabbing herself and falling on Romeo's body."

"My God, Michael! Do they read Shakespeare in your village? "At least he was stirring a bit and some color was creeping back into his face.

"I read it, and I'm sure Jennifer Beatty did too. She was an American kid, over here attending college, and she just took the wrong turn in the road. If there's fault to be found, it started a long time before you or I ever knew her."

Segar shook his head, as much to clear it as to deny the truth of Michael's words. "There is nothing to keep you here any longer," he said.

"Yes, there is."

"What's that?"

"The iron angel."

"A heroin dream, nothing more. Our men searched the basements and found nothing."

"Wouldn't an angel more likely be up than down?" Michael was examining the contents of the victims' pockets, especially the numbered slips of paper.

"This 470 and 117. They could have been written by the same person. The sevens are almost identical. And both slips seem to have been torn from a notebook of some sort."

"We know what 117 is – the address of the office building where they gathered for the heroin parties. But what about 470?"

Michael pondered that, studying the slips of paper. "I can't believe Conrad would have written down the street number to give someone. And why should he have needed it for himself?" Then suddenly he knew. He knew it all. "Up, Captain, up ! The angel is up, not down."

"Up?"

"On an upper floor of one of those buildings, where your men didn't search. Come on – I'll wear the body microphone again."

"You're going back there? It's almost midnight."

"I have to bring the killer to justice. I owe Jennifer that much."

As soon as he saw men entering the building at 117 at this late hour, he knew it was the place he sought. This time he went upstairs instead of down to the cellar, following people to the top floor of the old building. No one stopped or questioned him. He passed through a door with the others and found himself in a large darkened loft area lit only by a half-dozen small smoky fires. Beyond them, the focus of everyone in the room, stood an ancient statue of iron as tall as a man, its colors chipped and faded with the passage of time. The men approached one by one, and as they turned away they seemed to drop an offering into one of the burning pots.

Michael joined the line, speaking softly into the body mike. As he drew nearer he saw that each person paused only an instant before the statue, gazing into its three evenly spaced eyes.

Then it was his turn. He saw the faded face of the iron angel and looked into its three eyes and gazed upon the truth he had expected.

To his left, through the smoke, old Kurzbic appeared holding a Luger pistol. As he raised it to fire, it seemed to Michael's eyes that everything moved in slow motion. It seemed that Segar would never make it across the room before the Luger fired.

But then he was onto Kurzbic, toppling him to the floor as the weapon fired harmlessly toward the ceiling. Lights went on and people scattered in every direction as more police filled the room.

From the floor Segar asked, "What did you see in the angel's eyes Michael?"

"Today's number is 525. The iron angel is a gambling device."

Later, though he was bone-tired, Michael Vlado dictated a statement to complete Captain Segar's investigation. They were back in Segar's office.

"Somewhere, while adding to his collection of eighteenth-century clockwork automatons, Kurzbic came upon this large figure of an iron angel, fitted with three eyes and spring mechanisms to bring random three-digit numbers into view at the push of a lever. One digit appeared in each eye opening and because they were small a viewer had to step right up to the statue to read them. Kurzbic decided to set up a daily lottery, a sort of numbers game, selling chances on whichever number the buyers wanted to play. He recorded the number in his book and gave the player a slip with the number written on it as a receipt. Those were the slips we found on Jarie and Conrad. In the latter case, Conrad simply played the address of his drug den because he felt it was a lucky number."

"It wasn't lucky for him," Segar said. "What were those fires for?"

"Simply to burn up the losing tickets after betters had checked the day's number. Kurzbic must have feared a police raid would have turned up numbered slips in everyone's pockets. He had the master list, of course, to check for payoffs, but he kept that well hidden. I believe Jarie Miawa must have confronted Kurzbic on the night he was killed. Perhaps he discovered that with his clockwork skills Kurzbic was fixing the mechanism to stop only at numbers on which there'd be a few winners, avoiding those that were getting a heavy play. In any event, Miawa was stabbed. He managed to stagger downstairs to the heroin den and died there. Kurzbic could have quickly wiped up any spots of blood on the steps."

"What about Conrad Rynox?"

"It was his death that identified Kurzbic as the killer. Shortly before the murder I saw him toss his wristwatch aside because it had stopped. Yet when we found his body the battery-operated watch was running perfectly. Conrad left the apartment with a watch that wasn't running and had it fixed within a few minutes. The only possible conclusion was that he visited a watch shop and purchased a new battery. Kurzbic's shop is across Furtuna Street and just around the corner on Grivitei and Sigmund told me he was an occasional customer there. There'd have been no time for him to go anywhere else, according to the autopsy report. During those important minutes I'd taken Sigmund down the street for coffee, and old Kurzbic was alone in the shop."

"That's the trouble. He was alone! If he killed Conrad, how did he get his body around the corner to 117 and into the basement?"

"You're forgetting that the basements in that block all connect. Conrad must have indicated he knew the truth about Jarie's death. After Kurzbic replaced the battery he stabbed Conrad and pushed his body into the basement, waiting until later to move it over to where I found it."

"Hundreds of people must have known Kurzbic ran this gambling game."

"Of course! They bought numbers from him every day, and if they couldn't wait to hear the winner they went at midnight to watch the angel's wheels spin. I should have guessed a gambling involvement from the beginning. The first thing Jennifer told me about Jarie Miawa was that he liked to gamble. When I finally made the connection in my mind between those three-digit numbers and the three eyes of this fabled iron angel, I suspected an antique gambling device of some sort. That pointed me towards Kurzbic and his collection of clockwork automatons. When he saw me tonight he knew it was over and drew his gun, probably the one he mentioned keeping behind his counter."

Captain Segar sighed and signaled that Michael's statement was at an end. He looked tired himself. "I must thank you again, old friend. I could never have concluded this case without you."

Michael Vlado shook his hand. Without them, Jennifer Beatty might still be alive, but neither spoke those words. Perhaps it wouldn't have made any difference. Perhaps her number had simply come up on the face of another iron angel somewhere.

THE PUZZLE GARDEN

It had been many months since Michael Vlado's old friend Segar had driven up the twisty roads of the Transylvanian foothills to visit him at the Gypsy village where he was a somewhat uncertain leader. " 'King' only means that I'd be the first to die if the government moved against us," Michael had remarked to his wife Rosanna only the night before. These were not good days to be a Gypsy in Romania. Some of his people had already moved on to Germany, but they had only found a more immediate hell awaiting them there.

So Michael chose to remain in his village, always watching the road for the unexpected. When he recognized Segar's government car that warm spring morning he felt a jolt of alarm. Once a captain in the government militia responsible for law enforcement, Segar had assumed a vague position with the transition government. He could be delivering bad news for Michael's people.

"My old friend!" Segar greeted him with a smile, and Michael immediately relaxed. There was nothing to fear. "It's been a long time."

Segar nodded sadly. His gray suit seemed worn and drab compared to the bright militia uniform he'd often worn in those years when they first became friends. "I do not have the freedom I once had. I am chained to a bureaucrat's desk eight hours a day."

"At least you managed to escape on this bright May morning."

Segar's smile returned. "I came to ask your help. Have you ever heard of the Garden of the Apostles?"

It was vague in Michael's mind. "On the estate of the Sibiu family wasn't it? I was only five when the Communist government began the collectivization of agriculture and large estates back in nineteen forty-nine. I remember my mother's concern for the Gypsy farmland when I was growing up, but in the end farmers were permitted to retain half-acre plots for private use. No one here has ever had more than that.

Segar nodded, but it was obvious his interest was in the present rather than the past. "After the overthrow of the Socialist government in nineteen eighty-nine, the estate was quietly returned to the rightful heirs of the Sibiu family. The Garden of the Apostles is gradually returning to its past beauty and may someday reopen to the public."

"I am a horse breeder, not a gardener," Michael reminded his friend. "What help could I give you in this matter?"

"It seems that something of great value was buried in the garden long ago, before the Communists seized power. Even Claus Sibiu and his wife have no idea exactly where it is located. Naturally they want me to find it before the grounds are opened to the public."

"You want me for a treasure hunt!"

"In a sense. I thought the puzzle might intrigue you."

"When?"

"Now. Today, if you can get away."

They walked up to the house while Michael spoke with his wife Rosanna. "I'll try to be back tonight, or tomorrow certainly."

She was a long-suffering woman who sought peace among the little wooden animals she skillfully carved. His absences were nothing new. "I will expect you when I see you," she told him. "Are the horses penned?"

"Everything is fine."

She glanced over at Segar. "It is good to see you again. How is life in Bucharest?"

"Improving gradually. There have been no antigovernment protests this month."

"We are thankful for anything these days."

Michael kissed her lightly on the cheek. "I will be back," he said, and then they were gone.

The estate of the Sibiu family was at the base of the foothills where the land finally flattened out on the road south to Bucharest. They turned off the highway at a weathered sign that said *Sibiu* in barely legible lettering. "Does anyone still come here?" Michael asked.

"If the government is ever stabilized, Claus Sibiu plans to open the grounds to tourists, as in the prewar days. That is why the Garden of the Apostles is being restored."

"Do you know Sibiu?"

"I met him with his wife at a reception in Bucharest a few months back. Last week he phoned me with their problem. They have new growth starting in the gardens and they hope the public will be able to view them soon. However, Claus Sibiu recently uncovered a letter from his father, who died of a heart attack shortly after being forced from his home by the Communists. The letter gave clues to the whereabouts of a statue that the elder Sibiu had hidden in the garden to keep it safe. Claus wondered if I might be able to help decipher it."

"A code?"

"Not really. I gather it's more a puzzle to be solved. They don't want to dig up the entire garden if they can pinpoint where this thing is buried."

Michael smiled. "A treasure hunt, as I said earlier."

"Does it not appeal to you?"

"It might be relaxing after some of the problems I've had to face lately." They'd paused before the big iron gates of the estate, which seemed to show a family crest entwined with vines of metallic ivy. Segar beeped his horn gently and presently a middle-aged woman in khaki pants and a work shirt came to admit them. She was large-boned and handsome in a rugged way, as if much of her life had been lived out of doors.

Michael assumed she was one of the estate's gardeners, and was startled when Segar called out, "Good day, Madame Sibiu. I am here to see your husband."

"Captain Segar!" she greeted him, swinging open the gate for their car.

"Not Captain any longer, I fear. In the new order of things I am only a government bureaucrat. Your husband phoned last week to suggest that I help him in his search for the statue of Cynthia, believed to be hidden in the Garden of the Apostles."

Her quick eyes went from Segar to Michael. "That would be most kind. And you bring with you an assistant?"

"I am Michael Vlado, a poor Gypsy with some knowledge of puzzles. My friend Segar thought I could help."

She nodded. "Park your car inside the gate, off the road and we will walk to the garden. It is only a short distance from here."

They followed her along a path that had been cut through the haphazard growth of decades. Their drive down from Michael's village had taken much of the afternoon and the shadows of the spring day were already lengthening. Michael tried to remember what he had heard about the Garden of the Apostles. As he remembered it there were twelve sections, one designated for each of the followers of Christ. The flowers and plantings in each were in keeping with the apostle's life and Christian symbolism.

"You and your husband have done wonders here," Segar told her as they emerged from the path on to the open lawn at the front of an old stone mansion badly in need of repairs.

The house, with its dull gray façade and gabled roof, was a perfect background for the blaze of spring flowers that burst upon Michael's eyes. The Garden of the Apostles, at least in this current reincarnation, was a formal planting of twelve raised beds, each about ten feet square and enclosed by a wooden frame. From where they stood there were three rows of four beds each, running across the front of the house.

"Viewed from the house the order is alphabetical," Mrs. Sibiu explained. "Andrew's garden is here and Thomas, Doubting Thomas is at the opposite corner."

They strolled among the flowerbeds, pausing occasionally to comment on a small tree or a particularly lovely planting. "Everything seems to be in blossom at once," Segar remarked, trying to take it all in.

"Claus and I tired to rebuild the garden using paintings and drawings from medieval monasteries. Most others show spring gardens, so we have a preponderance of spring blossoms. But there will be blossoms of some sort throughout the summer and autumn." She led them toward the front steps. "Come to the house now. My husband will tell you more about it and explain our particular problem."

As he was mounting the stone steps Michael caught a glimpse of two men ducking out of sight around the corner of the house. "Are those gardeners?" he asked, thinking it odd that they would hide from view.

"Damned Gypsies!" she exclaimed angrily. "They did some work for us and the one in the red kerchief tried to steal our tools."

Segar and Michael exchanged glances but said no more. Inside the house Ida Sibiu ran up the wide front staircase calling to her husband. "Claus – Mr. Segar is here with a friend!"

While they waited, Michael had an opportunity to inspect the sparse but elegant furnishings of the large house. A marble-topped table with thick gilt legs stood in the foyer and on it was framed photograph of Claus and Ida Sibiu, on vacation or perhaps in exile, posed at the railing of a cruise ship of some sort. She was almost as tall as he was, and they might have passed for brother and sister. Their smiles in the photograph were virtually identical, as if they were already contemplating the money awaiting them back in a free Romania.

"That was on a cruise to the Greek Islands two years ago," a voice announced from the stairs. "It was our fifth anniversary."

Michael turned to see the man with the fringe of beard and thinning hairline descending the steps. He was a bit thinner than in the photo but still immediately recognizable. Segar came forward to shake his hand. "It is good to see you again, Mr. Sibiu. This is my friend Michael Vlado, who has come to assist us."

Sibiu stepped forward to shake Michael's hand. "Ida told me she'd given you a brief look at the garden."

"Very impressive," Michael told him. "It must take a great deal of work."

"That is Ida's province. She often neglects the house to work in the garden, but she says that is what will bring the tourists." He spoke slowly and carefully, as if unsure of the language. "You can see that our furnishings are sparse."

This marble-topped table is lovely," Segar told him. "And this wall plaque of a golden moon – "

"Ida found it in Rome during our travels." The plaque was nearly two feet across, perfectly round but with the graceful curve of a half moon etched on its surface. "She thought at first it might be by Picasso because of that odd representation of the moon's face."

Michael had moved on to a painting of a Roman galley under full sail. "Is this one old?"

"The last century, but not too valuable. The Communists did not even bother to steal it when they went through the house. I used to love it as a child here."

"When were you forced to leave?" Michael asked.

"In the summer of forty-nine when they began seizing property. I was just a boy but my father wanted me safely out of here. The Communists became Socialists in nineteen sixty-five, but no less repressive."

Segar cleared his throat, anxious to get on with the business at hand. "You told me on the telephone that you had found a message left by your father."

"I have it here." He was wearing a short maroon dressing gown over dark pants and a white shirt. From the gown's pocket he drew a folded envelope. "We found this among his papers when they were returned to us by the transition government. Apparently no one had ever opened it over all these years. My father mentions a buried statue which could be very valuable."

Segar accepted the envelope and withdrew a folded sheet of paper. "We had warehouses full of personal papers and possessions seized from the wealthy. You are lucky they could even find this to return it." He read the message with a deepening frown and then passed it on to Michael, who read it aloud:

> My son, you have been gone from me only two weeks and already I yearn for your presence. If you should come back I pray that this message reaches you someday. Among the Apostles I have buried a likeness of Cynthia which is unique and valuable. This is for you, my son, and not for those who would destroy our country. Seek out the garden of the last Apostle and there you will find the treasure.

"This is his signature?" Segar asked.

"I believe so. It seems to match others we found among his papers."

"When was this written?" Michael wondered.

"There's a lightly penciled date on the back of the envelope, right here. It says February twenty-four, nineteen forty-nine."

Segar examined the envelope. "Who is Cynthia? An ancestor?"

"No one I'm aware of. My father's books were returned along with his papers, and I tried to find the name in an edition of Bulfinch's *Age of Fable*. It's not there."

"Has any searching been done?" Michael Vlado asked.

"Come into the garden. I will show you."

They followed him out the front door and down the steps to the twelve sections of the Garden of the Apostles. The rosebushes were not quite in blossom, but there were tulips and lilies and even a small magnolia tree in various stages of bloom. They saw now that one bed of the garden had been dug into recently, and an attempt made to repair the damage.

"Our only clue was mention of the garden of the last Apostle," Claus Sibiu explained. "The Apostles are listed four times in the New Testament, in Matthew, Mark, Luke and the Acts. Each time Judas is listed last. The indication is that he was the last one chosen, but he may be last only because he later betrayed Christ. In any event, we dug up part of this garden and found nothing. A couple of Gypsies camping on the property helped us, but we were unsuccessful. Ida claimed the Gypsies tried to steal our tools and we stopped using them."

"They are still here," Michael said. "We saw them earlier."

"No doubt. The pests are hard to drive off."

"What do you want from us?" Segar asked him.

"If we have to dig up all twelve gardens to find this statue, it will set back progress to open the estate to the public for at least a year. I was hoping the government could offer some solution to the puzzle."

Segar gave a snort. "You need a priest, not a bureaucrat. I have no idea who the last Apostle was, or even the first."

"Simon Peter," Michael said. He remembered that much, how Christ had come upon Peter and his brother Andrew casting their fishing net into the sea.

But already the darkness was descending. Any further examination of the twelve gardens would have to wait until morning. "We have five bedrooms," Sibiu told them. "Please stay the night and we can examine the place by the light of the day. It is already too late for your return to Bucharest." He glanced at the watch on his right wrist.

Segar and Michael exchanged glances. The puzzle itself held little interest for Michael, who was inclined to think that the mysterious statue might well have been dug up decades ago by the Communist government. Still, the presence of the two Gypsies on the land interested him. They might know something, if he could find them again and speak with them. "We could stay," he told Segar.

His old friend chewed at his lower lip. "I must be in my office by afternoon, but perhaps we could stay long enough to have a quick look in the morning. I have no fondness for driving these roads after dark."

"Very good!" Claus Sibiu seemed pleased. "I ate early this evening, shortly before your arrival, but Ida can prepare something light for you before you retire. I will look forward to continuing our analysis of this puzzle in the morning."

He left them in the large, well-stocked kitchen and presently Ida Sibiu appeared wearing an emerald-green robe. Michael wondered if it was their custom to retire at nightfall each evening, like the birds.

"I have prepared the large guest room at the front of the house," she told them, "overlooking the garden. It has only one large bed – "

"That's all right," Michael assured her.

She prepared a light supper of soup and cold meat, which tasted good to Michael. Then she joined them at the table with a bottle of German beer. "You have to forgive us for the food," she apologized, wiping a drop of blood from a cut she'd inflicted on her left wrist. "We have not entertained since Claus regained the estate from the government. I've even lost the knack of carving meat!"

"You have not been married long?" Segar asked.

She shrugged. "Nearly seven years. But of course in middle age that is only a small fraction of our lives. I met him in Greece and he would tell me fabulous stories of his great estate back here in Romania. He never thought he would see it again, nor did I. Then the Communist and Socialist governments began to topple. It was all so fast, all at once! Claus made application to the provisional government for the return of his property and no one was more surprised than he when the request was granted. We came back last year to find the place was like a jungle."

"You've done wonders with it."

"But we must open it to the public to generate some income! Claus is not a wealthy man. What money he had was drained away by his years of living in exile. Once we even tried to sneak back into Romania, in disguise, but I was nervous about it and we turned back before we reached home."

"Home. This estate."

She nodded sadly. "For him it was always home. He has told me he wants to be buried here."

Soon after that she showed them to their room. Michael slept restlessly, awakened occasionally by Segar's snoring. Finally, when the first light of dawn slipped into the guest room, he got out of the bed and opened the drapes to gaze down at the Garden of the Apostles.

At one of its intersecting paths the body of the Gypsy with the red kerchief was sprawled face down on the graveled earth. There was a knife in the center of his back, and from above it appeared that he'd been dragged to the spot and pinned there by some giant hand.

Michael and Segar, whom Michael awakened hastily from his morning dreams, were unable to find their hosts in the upstairs bedrooms. They finally located Ida Sibiu in the kitchen, where she was just beginning to prepare breakfast. "A body?" she repeated, unbelieving. "In the garden?"

Michael assured her it was true. "It appears to be one of the Gypsies. Is your husband about?"

"He's bathing now. I'll go look with you."

She followed them through the house and out the front door, hanging back a bit when they reached the garden. "It's Erik," she said, apparently recognizing the red kerchief.

"He's dead," Segar confirmed, kneeling by the body. "I'd better use your telephone to call Bucharest. The local authorities aren't equipped to handle this."

"Who could have done it?" Ida asked.

"The other Gypsy?" Segar suggested.

"His name is Bedrich," she volunteered. "They were camped at the back of our property with at least one woman."

"I'll go," Michael decided suddenly, because there was no one else to do it. "If this Bedrich did it he'll be on the run and I can track him."

Segar didn't argue. He'd known Michael Vlado too long for that. "All right, go. You'd better tell your husband what's happened, Mrs. Sibiu, while I phone the authorities."

She pointed the way for Michael and he set off unarmed, hardly realizing that he'd been out of bed for only twenty minutes. The morning dew lay thick on the grass as he circled the big house and set off toward the rear of the property. He didn't know what he might be facing – a murderer, perhaps, but more likely an abandoned campsite with embers from a fire still glowing in the daylight. If there was only one woman they had probably fought over her. There were no rules in a knife fight, except it would be rare to stab a fellow Gypsy in the back whatever the provocation.

He saw the tent then, a little thing nestled among the firs. Had they left so quickly that the tent had been sacrificed? Not too likely. He was almost to it when the woman emerged carrying a bucket of morning wash water which she emptied on the ground. She saw him then and was startled. "Bedrich!" she called out.

The second Gypsy emerged, bare-chested, from the tent. He was tall and well-built with olive skin and a square jaw. "What do you want here?" he asked, speaking in Romany.

They both seemed surprised when Michael replied in the Gypsy language. "Your friend Erik is dead. I have come to ask you about that."

They exchanged glances but he saw no surprise. "The fool was looking for trouble," the woman said. She was dark and pretty in the way that very young women sometimes are, before age plays its tricks.

"Did you kill him?" Michael asked.

"He was my brother," the woman answered. "Erik. I am Esmeralda. Those people at the house killed him because he came searching for their treasure."

Michael turned to the Gypsy named Bedrich, who asked simply, "How did he die?"

"Stabbed in the back, near the center of the Garden of the Apostles."

"We worked for them, for Sibiu and his wife," Bedrich said. "Then she said we stole tools and they ordered us off the property."

"But you are still here."

The man shrugged. "Erik did not want to leave without the treasure. He heard them talking about it. He knew it was somewhere in the garden."

"This was the statue of Cynthia?"

"Yes."

"A goddess?"

It was Esmeralda who answered, possibly because of her Greek name. "Cynthia is Artemis, the Greek goddess of the hunt, the counterpart to the Roman goddess Diana." She closed her eyes for a moment and then opened them. " I must see my brother's body. Take me to him."

Michael nodded. He could understand the need. When Bedrich followed along too, he said nothing. Back at the big house Claus Sibiu had replaced his wife in the garden with Segar. "This is a shock to Ida," he said. "She must rest before she joins us." He looked uncertainly at the Gypsy couple. "So you found them!"

"They were at their camp. They had not run away. Esmeralda is the dead man's sister."

Sibiu frowned. "Why did I never know that?"

She looked away, avoiding his face. "Because you never asked. We were only workers to be accused by your wife when something was missing." The words came from Bedrich, not her, but either might have spoken them.

She saw the body then, only half covered by a burlap sack, and went to it. The knife was still buried in his back and she touched it gently, as if about to pull it free. Then her fingers dropped away and she began to sob quietly, showing real emotion for the first time since Michael brought her the news of her brother's death.

"What about the authorities?" he asked Segar.

"No good news. There are disturbances in the streets of Bucharest. Nothing too serious but all police are on standby. It will be at least tomorrow before they can send someone up here. In the meantime, they quickly point out, I am a former investigative officer for the militia. I am to take charge and conduct my own investigation."

Michael could see he was unhappy with the prospect. "There must be local authorities in this area."

"No one qualified to investigate a murder, I fear. Help in such cases is usually summoned from the cities." He glanced toward Gypsy Bedrich, who had not joined Esmeralda at her brother's body. "I might as well start with you."

The young Gypsy seemed frightened by the turn of events. "We never stole the tools!" he insisted. "We never killed anybody!"

Claus Sibiu glanced at the watch on his left wrist. "Will you be needing me for the next half hour, Mr. Segar? I have some phone calls to make. And I want to see how my wife is doing."

"Go ahead."

Esmeralda had returned to Michael's side. "You are a Gypsy too," she said.

"Yes, from Gravita, up in the foothills."

"We must have the body for a traditional burial ceremony. You understand that."

"Of course. Segar will have a few questions first. Tell me about the knife. Did it belong to your brother?"

"It was his."

"Did he always have such dirty hands?"

"What do you mean?"

"Michael walked over and indicated the dead man's hand. "There's dirt on them, and under the fingernails too, as if he'd been digging."

"In one of the gardens?"

"Where else? Your brother was after the so-called treasure, wasn't he? His body lies between the gardens of Judas and Jude, at the very center of the layout."

"No Judas," Esmeralda said simply. "He betrayed Christ. He is never honored with the Apostles."

"But there are twelve gardens. You can see that."

"Judas was replaced. The Apostles drew lots for a replacement after he hanged himself."

"There was no marking on any of these gardens," Michael admitted. "I was told they were alphabetical. What was the name of his replacement?"

"I do not remember. It has been years since I studied the Bible with my mother."

Segar had finished questioning the Gypsy Bedrich. "You both must remain on the property until tomorrow," he ordered. "The other police will be arriving then, and may have more questions for you. I will go back to your tent now and look through it. You say you found no statue of Cynthia, but I must be certain it is not among your possessions.

Michael was in the house with Sibiu when he returned. Nothing had been found in or around the Gypsy camp. "Are you sure?" Sibiu asked.

Segar smiled slightly. "My old friend Michael has taught me all the Gypsy tricks. I even kicked away the remains of the campfire and dug underneath it. "There was no treasure. Erik did not find it before he was killed."

"Then its still out there," Michael said. "The statue of Cynthia."

"I'm more disturbed about the killing right now," Sibiu told them in his measured tones. "The government could use this as an excuse for not letting us open the garden."

"Something must be done with the body until tomorrow," Segar told the man. "Do you have any sort of cold storage room in the house?"

There was nothing except a large freezer, and they decided that was too small. The body was wrapped in a plastic bag and carried to the cool basement. Then they set about the problem at hand.

"The statue is out there," Segar stated firmly. "I say everything gets dug up until we find it."

"How will that help us identify the killer?" Michael asked.

"Erik was killed because he guessed or deduced where the statue was buried. If he did it, we can do it."

"You forget he'd camped on the estate for a year or more," Sibiu told them. "He might have seen something."

"According to your father's note the statue was buried over forty years ago, long before Erik was born. Since you and Ida don't know where it is, what could he have seen? Did either of you ever mention your father's message to him?"

"We might have," Sibiu admitted. "That part about the last Apostle."

"Yes, the last Apostle. It didn't mean Judas but the Apostle who replaced Judas. That's where you'll find the statue."

"We looked there!" Claus Sibiu insisted. "We dug it up and the Gypsies helped. The Apostle chosen to replace Judas was Matthias."

"When you say you looked there you mean you looked in the garden assigned to Judas. Don't you see? There never was a Judas honored with the other Apostles. You were too young to remember it but the twelfth garden was Matthias's from the beginning. It was never the sixth plot, where you dug, but the eighth plot, in proper alphabetical order between Matthew and Peter."

Segar had drawn twelve squares on a sheet of paper, arranged in three rows of four each and labeled as they appeared from the house. "You mean the right-hand plot in the second row?"

"Exactly," Michael replied.

"But Erik wasn't killed there," Sibiu reminded them.

"The killer dragged the body to the middle, to keep it away from Matthias's plot. From the upstairs window I could detect signs of dragging on the gravel. But here's stronger evidence that Matthias is the garden we want. You told us, Claus, that you left here as a child in the summer of nineteen forty-nine and your father's message says you've been gone two weeks. So the date on the envelope, February twenty-fourth, is not when the letter was written. What does it refer to? I found it in one of your library books last night – the feast of Saint Matthias! That was before I even realized he was the last Apostle.

"Let's get shovels and start digging," Segar suggested.

They went out the front door with Michael leading the way. He paused at the right end of the second row, as seen from the house. The plot for Matthias, even though it was unmarked. Segar returned with two shovels and he and Michael plunged them into the dry earth.

Claus gave a sigh. "Ida wont like what you're doing to her garden."

Michael avoided the well-established tulip bed and the carpet of lilies of the valley. Instead he went to work on a patch of disturbed soil, turned over since the last rain. He'd dug down only two feet before he hit something. "This may be it," he told them. "It's a large plastic bag. Hand me your knife, Mr. Sibiu."

The man slipped the blade from his belt and passed it over. Michael made a clean slit and pulled the edges of the plastic apart.

Something is wrong, he suddenly realized even as he was doing it. *They didn't have plastic bags like this back in the forties.*

Then he saw the body, and the dead face staring up at him was the face of Claus Sibiu, the man who stood behind him at that moment.

Segar gasped at the sight of the uncovered face. "This is madness! Sibiu, is that a twin?"

"There are forces at work here you cannot imagine, " Sibiu told them. "Come into the house with me and I will explain everything."

"The body is fresh," Michael pointed out. "He hasn't been dead more than a few days, if that long."

"Come into the house," Sibiu repeated.

"No, I think not," Michael replied. He was beginning to see it all. He was beginning to see too much.

Sibiu's hand came out of his pocket holding a double-barreled derringer pistol, but Michael still held the knife in his hand. He rolled to one side as Sibiu fired, and hurled the knife with an aim he knew was true. It buried itself in the fleshy part of Sibiu's arm, bringing a high pitched yelp of pain.

Then Michael and Segar were both on him, holding him as Michael peeled away the fringe beard and the false headpiece. "What is this?" Segar demanded.

"It is Ida Sibiu," Michael explained, holding her tightly as he pulled the knife from her arm. "She murdered her husband and buried him in the garden of Matthias in place of the moon."

"Moon? What moon?"

"Let me go!" she screeched in a fury, ignoring her arm wound as she wrestled with Michael.

But he held her firm as he answered Segar's question. "The golden moon that hangs on the wall of their house. No one else ever said that treasure was a statue. The message from Claus's father described it as a likeness of Cynthia. I finally remembered that Cynthia is also a poetic term for the moon. You and your husband discovered the hiding place in the garden of Matthias a few days ago. Once it was dug up, you didn't need the pretense anymore. You killed Claus and buried him where the moon had been, then hid the treasure in plain sight on the wall of your house."

"Why would she kill him," Segar asked, "when she knew I was coming to see him?"

"That's just the point. She didn't know."

Segar had produced a pair of handcuffs from the trunk of his car and they bandaged Ida Sibiu's arm wound as best they could before driving to the hospital in a nearby town. "I don't understand any of it," Segar admitted as they waited at the hospital for her wound to be treated and stitched up. "Why would she kill her husband?"

"You'll have to ask her that. She met him in Greece, away from home, and

I imagine when they were married seven years ago he filled her mind with visions of great wealth back here in Romania. Then the government collapsed and she got an unexpected look at all the wealth – a decaying mansion and a garden gone to seed. Perhaps she would have left him then if the message from his father hadn't come to light, with its promise of buried treasure. So she stayed on, but when Claus phoned you for help with the puzzle last week he neglected to tell her, probably wanting your arrival kept secret until he knew if you could help."

"So we walked in on her yesterday unannounced?"

"Exactly." Michael watched a nurse helping an old man negotiate the corridor. "In retrospect we have to say she kept her composure very well. You already knew about the statue and the message so she had to show it to us, hoping it wouldn't lead us to the body. As for the disguise, she may have had it ready in case local officials called. Remember she told us they'd used disguises to slip across the borders. All she really needed were the fringe beard for her chin, the wig to make the hair appear thin in front, and some of his clothes. We saw from that picture that they were about the same height, and her face was like his in a sisterly way. She was big-boned, but still a bit thinner than he appeared in the photo. As for the voice, she spoke slowly, in a measured manner, careful to give it a masculine tone. She felt safe because you'd met them only once and that time at a reception with others present. The rest was easy. We never saw them together and never suspected at first that the wall plaque in plain sight was the buried treasure.

"What about he Gypsies? They knew the Sibius."

"But Esmeralda avoided looking directly at Claus when she came to view her brother's body. He was dressed right and neither of them had reason to doubt his identity."

"You see it all in retrospect," Segar challenged. "Admit it – you were as surprised as I was when we uncovered Claus Sibiu's body!"

"I was surprised," Michael admitted, "but I shouldn't have been. Yesterday Claus wore his watch on his right wrist. This morning it was on his left. Why the change overnight?"

"I didn't notice that," Segar admitted. "Why?"

"Because Ida cut herself while slicing the meat last night – remember? She couldn't risk our noticing the same cut on Claus's wrist so she covered it with the watchband."

Segar nodded finally, beginning to accept it. "After she killed him and buried the body, why didn't she just take the moon plaque and leave?"

"Because Erik the Gypsy was still around, searching for the treasure. Last night, when he started digging with his hands in the garden of Matthias, she stabbed him in the back with his own knife."

Michael Vlado had an answer for everything, except why a woman would kill her husband for a golden plaque that didn't look very much like the moon at all.

THE GYPSY'S PAW

It was peaceful that summer in the foothills of the Transylvania Alps, or as peaceful as life ever got for Gypsies in Romania these days. Michael Vlado, king of his small tribe in the village of Gravita, had settled into his work of raising and training horses, and the others went about their summer chores, pleased for the moment that the anti-Gypsy sentiment sweeping through Eastern Europe had passed them by.

Michael's wife Rosanna, who earned money by carving wooden animals to be sold at village shops, was the first to tell him of the strange Gypsy woman named Esmeralda who lived in a neighboring village. "I brought some of my wooden animals to the shop in Agula today," she told him as she cooked a modest dinner of beans, rice and pork. "The shopkeeper thinks they will sell well to travelers."

"That is good news, Rosanna. Soon you will be adding helpers for the carving."

She knew he teased her about the hobby, though lately the money from it had helped him buy another stallion for breeding. "They say in Agula there is a Rom with magic powers," Rosanna told him. "Her name is Esmeralda."

Michael snorted. "An old woman with a bear's paw! I have heard the stories."

"People pay her to make their wishes come true."

"It is women like that who make the Gypsy someone to fear and hate, no better than the cutpurses who ply the streets of Athens and Rome. I should speak with her."

"She is not of our tribe," Rosanna reminded him.

"All Roms are one tribe," he replied, voicing words that were more a desire than a fact.

"Go then! Go and see the woman Esmeralda!"

His face relaxed into a smile. "What wish should I make for you ?"

"That I sell more of my little animals."

Two days later, on the weekend, Michael Vlado drove down the steep road to the neighboring village of Agula. It was a more prosperous area than Gravita, and large, well-built farmhouses dotted the hillsides in sharp contrast to the Gypsy cabins at higher elevations. But some Gypsies lived among the people and were tolerated more than in the cities. An old woman like Esmeralda would take up magic late in life, perhaps when her other charms were no longer profitable.

Everyone knew where she lived, and Michael found the cabin without difficulty. Esmeralda, who seemed to have no last name, was a wrinkled woman in her seventies. Though stooped like a crone, she could move about with surprising agility when necessary. Michael was amazed when she admitted him and promptly laid out cups and saucers for tea.

"That's hardly necessary," he protested. "I only stopped by for a visit."

She nodded and kept setting the table. "I know you, Michael Vlado. You are king of your tribe in the village of Gravita. Do you come to see old Esmeralda for the wishes my magic paw can bestow?"

"I do not believe in magic paws," he told her. "But I do believe in Gypsy women who shame us with their small swindles. I have come to ask you to stop this business."

She brought a teapot from the stove and filled their cups before she answered. "You are a strong man, still in middle age. I am an old woman who has no other way to make a living. Would you have me beg in the streets as the children do? These days that would get me arrested and perhaps shot."

"But this business with the paw is distasteful!"

"Let me show you," she said, as if the sight of the thing would win him over to her side. She disappeared into a back bedroom and returned in a moment carrying an intricately carved ebony box.

"Is that a dragon?" he asked, running his fingers over the carving.

"It is. This box came from China, a gift from a man who loved me many years ago."

She opened the box's hinged lid and revealed a furry extremity about the size of Michael's fist, with claws clearly visible at one end. "It is the right front paw of a brown bear. The strength of the brown bear is well known among the Rom. They have been said to kill an adult cow with a single swipe of their forepaw." She lifted it and playfully swung it in Michael's direction.

"You must have been a tigress in your youth," he told her.

"Only a bear. Now this paw brings me money. People pay to have their wishes come true."

"But do they come true? Ever?"

"Sometimes. Any wish can come true sometimes." She returned the paw to its ebony box and closed it. "Come with me and I will show you. This very night I am calling on a wealthy couple with a missing son. They came to me two weeks ago but I would not help them at once. I wanted to be sure the magic of the paw would work. Tonight I will show them, and you."

"What time?"

"I go there at dusk. If you drive me I will not have to hire the local taxi."

Michael shook his head and chuckled. "Ah, Esmeralda, you have charmed your way through life and you are still doing it in old age."

"Is that a yes or a no?"

"Yes, yes! I will go with you. I will even carry your paw. But believe me, I am a skeptical audience."

It was six hours till dusk and Michael drove back up the hill to his village. When he told his wife what he had agreed to do that night, she thought him insane. "But what will you accomplish? Your presence will simply lend credence to that old woman."

"I hope to convince these people that all Gypsies are not tricksters and swindlers. It is time for Esmeralda to retire to gardening and knitting."

Rosanna snorted and went away.

After dinner he made the journey down to Agula once more. The old Gypsy woman was waiting by the door, watching for him. A light summer rain was starting to fall and he helped her to the car, sheltering her head with his coat. "I thought you would not come," she said, safely in the car with her ebony box.

"My word is good," he assured her. "Which way shall I go?"

"To the left. I will guide you."

Presently, in the failing light, they came upon a two-story farmhouse set back a bit from the road. It was white with green shutters, and seemed out of place among the rough wooden cabins and larger chalets of the countryside. The rain was falling harder now and in the gathering gloom a spotlight had been turned on above the front door. There was no sidewalk such as city homes had, only a dirt path growing wetter by the minute.

A man opened the door as they pulled up and called out, "It's getting muddy here. Drive around the back."

Michael did as instructed and they pulled up into a covered carport. He helped Esmeralda into the house, carrying the ebony box as he'd promised. She was puffing with exertion as she entered, but she introduced him immediately. "Michael, this is Olak and Frieda Glasnach." She squinted into the room beyond them where a young man had just gotten to his feet. "And their son Andre."

Michael shook hands all around and accompanied them into the cozy living room of the farmhouse. Olak Glasnach was a rough hewn man of middle age, a farmer whose working life had been spent beneath the brutal sun. Every victory, every defeat, seemed etched into his skin. By contrast, his wife Frieda had flat and pale features unmarked by strong emotion. The son, Andre, hung back from them like a common workman, his bulging biceps clearly visible beneath his sleeveless workshirt. It seemed obvious that he labored on the farm with his father.

"This is Michael Vlado," Esmeralda quickly explained. "He is king of the Gypsy tribe in Gravita."

"A pleasure to have you here," Olak Glasnach said. Then, a bit puzzled, he asked the Gypsy woman, "Does he take part in the ceremony?"

"Only as an observer." She reached out her wrinkled hands for the ebony box and Michael passed it to her. He was thinking it would be better for all concerned if she stuck to tarot cards. Bear paws were a bit too exotic.

"Could you tell me a little of the background?" Michael asked. "I understand there is a second son – "

It was Frieda who spoke as they seated themselves around a low table in the living room. On it she'd placed a plate of rich Romanian delicacies of the sort Michael had rarely tasted. As a boy they'd been treasures he saw through the bakery windows, always just out of reach.

"My older son Felipe lived here and worked the farm with his father and brother. We were a happy family until a year ago."

"What happened then?"

"He met a woman named Louise," Andre supplied. "She tempted him away from his family."

"Where is he now?"

"In Bucharest, living with her."

"The bear's paw will bring him back," Esmeralda assured them, "if you wish for it strongly enough."

"I don't believe any of this," Andre said and started to leave the room.

"Come back here!" his mother ordered. "We must all wish for it."

The sky had grown dark outside with the coming of night and they could hear the rain, harder now, beating on the windows with each shift of the breeze. Old Esmeralda smiled and opened the ebony box. Watching it all, as if in slow motion, Michael wondered why he had come here. If it was to expose the fakery, now was the time to speak. But he said nothing.

"Place your hands upon the paw," the Gypsy woman said, and removed it from the box. The father, Olak, seemed reluctant to be first, but his wife did not hesitate. She touched the dead fur, caressed it, and waited for her husband and son to do likewise. After a moment Olak did so, and then Andre. "Now repeat after me – *I wish our son and brother Felipe to return home this night.*"

"I wish our son and brother Felipe to return home this night," they responded, more or less in unison.

Nothing happened.

They waited and still nothing happened. There was no sound except the beating of the rain.

For nearly ten minutes no one spoke. Then it was Esmeralda who broke the silence. "Sometimes it takes awhile, but he will arrive. Let us just sit back and wait."

"It's a long way from Bucharest," Glasnach said. "A drive of three hours or more on a night like this."

"The paw knows no distance," Esmeralda told him.

They waited an hour, talking of village matters and the summer weather, which had been unusually dry till that evening. They talked of everything but the missing Felipe, and to Michael the desultory conversation was worse than silence. "Do you have any way of reaching your son in Bucharest?" he asked at last.

Frieda Glasnach was on her feet pacing, full of nervous energy. "He gave us a phone number once, after he'd left the farm for that woman. We never used it. I showed it to you, Esmeralda."

"Get it now," Esmeralda said. "Something has gone wrong with the magic."

Michael sighted. "Why prolong this, woman? He is never coming. Put your paw back in its box."

But Frieda was already pulling open the drawer of a cabinet. On a piece of paper was a telephone number scrawled beneath the single word, "Felipe." "Here it is. I tried to call him only once, but that woman answered and I hung up."

Though she'd asked for the number, old Esmeralda refused to accept the paper. "I cannot call. One of you must do it."

They stared blankly at each other and finally Olak said, "We are paying you to bring our son home by Gypsy magic. The telephone call we could make at any time."

The old woman turned to Michael. "Will you call? Simply call and ask for him."

Sorry now that he had ever come, feeling himself trapped in this woman's scheme gone wrong, Michael reluctantly agreed. How had she ever expected to get money out of this family with her withered bear's paw ?

The telephone lines between the villages and the country's capital city were not always reliable and it took him some minutes before the connection was made. He heard the ringing of the phone and then the voice of a young woman. "Hello?"

"I wish to speak with Felipe Glasnach."

There was a muffled gasp at the other end. "Hello?" Michael said. "Is Felipe there?"

"Felipe is dead. He drowned in the Dimbovita River two days ago."

The news sent a chill through the Glasnach family when Michael told them. Oddly, it was the father rather than the mother who burst into tears and it was he whom Andre went to comfort. "Dead," he repeated in a flat tone. "Dead, dead, dead."

Only Esmeralda seemed unshaken by the news. "The paw will bring him back," she told them.

"What is it?" Andre scoffed. "A monkey's paw like that story I once read, with the power to bring him back from the grave?"

"He is in no grave, only a river."

Michael had gotten no details of the tragedy before the woman on the other end hung up. "I will go to see her if you wish," he told the family, trying to make amends for all that Esmeralda had done. "You must know her name."

"Louise Stricker," Frieda said. "She is German, we think."

Andre left them, more from disgust than sorrow, and they heard him go up to his room. But still the old Gypsy woman clutched the bear paw to her breast and whispered of things to come. "I will take you home soon," Michael told her. "We must leave these people alone with their grief."

"A little longer," she begged. If she was waiting for something he could not imagine what it was.

And then they heard it – a loud knocking on the front door that seemed to resound through the house.

For a moment they were all frozen in their chairs, unable to move. Even Esmeralda seemed unbelieving, but she was the first to get up. "That's him," she spoke with assurance. "He's come back."

They heard the knocking again, much gentler this time, as Andre came running down the stairs. He must have seen that his mother was on the verge of hastening to the door, because he begged her, "Do not open it! Felipe has been summoned by this crone from his watery grave!"

It was Olak who headed for the door as the gentle tapping came again. "If it is my son he will always be welcome here."

"My God, father!" Andre sprang forward and grabbed the bear paw from Esmeralda's hand. Before anyone could say a word he shouted, "I wish my brother Felipe back in his watery grave!"

"*No!*" Frieda screamed. She ran for the door, reaching it just before her husband, slid back the bolt, and yanked it open.

The light from above shone down on an empty front yard. There was no one in sight. Frieda Glasnach breathed a long sigh of despair.

"Look here!" her husband said, pointing to the ground.

Michael and Andre joined them, peering at the dirt path to the front door. All was mud now, and sunken into the mud was a line of recent footprints leading to the door. They came as far as the door and stopped, not going back or to either side.

Whoever made them had either entered the house through the bolted door or vanished without a trace.

The summer rainstorm seemed only to grow worse through the night. Michael accompanied Andre up to Felipe's old bedroom at the rear of the house. The room seemed dusty and closed against the outside world but in the closet they found a pair of the elder son's work boots. Michael took them downstairs and risked the rain to fit both boots into the muddy footprints by the front door. They were an exact fit.

"So he was here," Olak Glasnach said.

"Or someone wanted us to think he was here," Michael Vlado replied. "I will drive down to the capital in the morning. For now I suggest you believe nothing that you have seen or heard. If I find evidence of your son's death, I will phone you at once."

The events of the evening, hard as they were on the family, seemed finally to have affected old Esmeralda as well. "I want to go home," she told Michael shortly before midnight. "I don't understand any of this."

He helped her out to the car and promised to return with news. Frieda had given him a picture of her son to aid in identification. He was a thin, smiling young man, handsomer than his younger brother. Michael could see why the attractions of city life might have lured him away from the farm life.

"Will you be all right?" Michael asked as he drove the Gypsy woman to her cabin.

"Yes. I am just tired. So much has happened tonight."

"You really thought he would come, didn't you?"

"I thought so," she agreed.

"But you can't believe in something as preposterous as the wishes granted by a bear's paw!"

She turned her old eyes toward him. "You have grown away from your roots, Michael Vlado. Always remember you are a Gypsy first!"

He helped her to the door of the cabin and went on his way. The rain was beginning to let up so he was able to negotiate the muddy roads back up to his village. He said very little to Rosanna about what had transpired. She was already in bed and only grunted as he slipped beneath the covers.

In the morning he told her he must go to Bucharest. "On a Sunday?" she asked as she prepared breakfast. "What for?"

"That Gypsy woman, Esmeralda, is in trouble. She's involved in something quite serious and needs help."

"She is not one of us."

"Not of our tribe, no, but she is a Rom."

"Go then," his wife said, looking away.

"I will tell you everything when I get back," he promised.

The rain of the night before had given way to morning sun, and as soon as he hit the main road at the base of the foothills he was able to make good time. There was virtually no traffic on a Sunday morning until he reached the outskirts of Bucharest itself. Then he phoned Louise Stricker and obtained her address. It was night when he arrived at her apartment near the public gardens.

Louise Stricker was a slender woman with straight black hair that framed her face. She was plain yet attractive, something like Frieda Glasnach must have looked in her younger days. Perhaps that was what had first attracted Felipe. Now she wore no makeup and her dark blue dress might have been a symbol of mourning.

"You are a friend of Felipe?" she asked as she held the door open for him. The apartment was plain with only a few colorful touches like a witty stuffed bat and a rainbow poster from a rock concert.

"Not really," he admitted, having given her that impression on the phone. "I know his parents."

"I'm sorry. I should have phoned them. It's just that we've never spoken. I know how they feel about me."

"Tell me how he died."

"He had to work for a while Thursday morning. He had a job at the university bookstore. I expected him to be home in the afternoon but he didn't come. Finally I called the bookstore and they said he hadn't been in, not at all!" Her voice broke and she was close to tears. "I went to retrace the route he must have taken that morning. When I was crossing the bridge over the Dimbovita I saw some policemen and a small crowd down by the water. I realized they were dragging for a body."

"Felipe?"

She nodded. "I recognized a shirt I'd given him. He'd been wearing it that morning. It had been found by the water, and his other clothes as well."

"You believed he killed himself?"

"I don't know what I believe. We'd been arguing lately. He was thirty– one years old but still tied to his family. He walked out on them a year ago but there wasn't a weekend when he didn't want to call them. Sometimes we'd have terrible fights about it."

"Did they find his body?"

"Not yet. They're still searching."

"Is it possible that he didn't die, that he returned to the farm?"

"I can't imagine that. He still loved them at a distance but after a year away he never could have gone back to living that life. He told me how they watched over every aspect of the boys' lives. They had no girls and very few male friends. All their time was spent on the farm, working year round."

"Farming takes a great deal of time."

"But to rob them of their lives like that! The parents were almost paranoid about dangers of any sort. His father slept with a shotgun under the bed. They had a bucket of sand and an escape rope in the bedroom in case of fire. On rare occasions when the boys went to a dance in their village, the father or mother went along to make sure they didn't drink too much."

"How did he meet you?"

"Somehow they agreed to let him take classes at the university here – a course in farm management, because the farm would someday be his. I was in my final year, completing my teaching preparations. When I graduated at the beginning of last summer he decided to remain here with me. The family was furious. His younger brother met with him and tried to get him back, but that only convinced him he'd done the right thing."

"And you had a good life together?"

"The best," she said as her eyes teared over once more. "I can't understand what happened."

"You said you'd argued lately."

She shrugged. "That was about his family. It was the only thing we ever disagreed about."

"Was there anything unusual in the days before he di – disappeared?"

"Nothing, except for the old woman."

"What old woman?"

"I saw him talking to a woman across the street there. It must have been Monday or Tuesday. He told me it was just a Gypsy woman begging for money, but they seemed to talk for a long time."

"Do Gypsies still beg for money on the city streets?"

"Rarely. They fear arrest from the new government. That was why it seemed so strange."

It seemed strange to Michael too. "How old a woman was this?"

"Old. In her seventies at least, maybe older than that. She seemed to get around without any trouble, though she was stooped."

He realized she was describing Esmeralda, and he wondered what she had been doing with Felipe Glasnach. "Thank you, Miss Stricker. You've been a big help."

"Where are you going now?"

"I have a friend with the police. Perhaps I can learn something form him."

When Michael first met him he had been Captain Segar of the government militia, a sort of police force under the old socialist government. Though he had received a promotion in the new republic, many of his duties were similar to what they had been. He still supervised certain elements of law enforcement, though he no longer wore the uniform of the militia.

On this Sunday afternoon, Michael found him at home, entertaining a young woman who immediately vanished into the next room. "I didn't mean to frighten off your visitor," Michael told his old friend with a grin.

Segar shifted uneasily. He was in his early forties, about Michael's age, and though they'd been friends for nine years Michael knew virtually nothing about his private life. "Forget it, Michael. It is so rare to see you in Bucharest these days. What brings you here?"

"An old Gypsy woman named Esmeralda, who can summon the dead with the paw of a bear."

"You are beyond believing in such things, my friend. Let me pour you a bit of wine and you can tell me about it from the beginning."

And so Michael told him all of it and when he had finished Segar nodded and said, "It is some sort of fraud, a clever deception."

"Of course it is! But to what purpose? Who are the deceivers and who is the deceived?"

Segar merely shook his head. "Let me make a call and see if a body has been recovered from the river."

Michael listened while he spoke to the officer in charge of the river detail. "Anything?" he asked when Segar hung up.

"Nothing yet, but I have expressed my interest. They will search with renewed vigor."

Michael took the photograph from his pocket. "This is Felipe Glasnach. You may need it for identification." He paused and added, "That is, if you find anything at all."

"I'll keep you advised." Segar told him.

"Express my apologies to your lady friend."

Segar walked him to the door. "Someday, Michael, we must have a long talk about life and love."

"I look forward to it. Gypsies are said to be experts in at least one of those subjects."

He drove out of Bucharest along the river, following it for some distance before turning north toward home.

On Monday morning Michael visited old Esmeralda once more. The Gypsy woman seemed less pleased to see him than on his first visit two day earlier. "What – you've come to cause more trouble, Michael Vlado?"

"I wasn't aware that I caused trouble," he said as she moved away from the door to let him enter. "I do know that you traveled to Bucharest last week to see Felipe Glasnach."

"And if I did? Is it so wrong to bring peace and happiness to a family in exchange for a little money?"

"Where is Felipe now?" he asked. "Is he dead or alive?"

"Only the paw knows."

"Then get out the paw and ask it! I want an answer, Esmeralda!" She sat down heavily, as if the weight of her years was at last beginning to leave its mark. "I do not know the answer." Her voice was sad and tired.

"Why did you go to Bucharest? And how did you find him?"

"The family had his phone number. I called and arranged a meeting. He didn't want his woman to know. I begged him to return home for the sake of the family. He said he would like to, but was reluctant to leave this woman."

"Louise Stricker."

"Yes, that was her name. I asked him to come Saturday night, just before dark. I arranged to conduct a session with the family using the bear's paw as a charm. Felipe would arrive home at the proper moment and be reunited with his family. They would be overjoyed and I would receive the money I'd been promised."

"What happened?"

"I don't know," she answered sadly. "Something went wrong."

"The Stricker woman thinks Felipe drowned himself in the Dimbovita River."

"Perhaps he did. He was a deeply troubled young man."

"Then who came to the door Saturday night? Who made those foot-prints in the mud? And what happened to him?"

"I do not know," she admitted. "This world is filled with stranger things. Somehow even a false charm can work real wonders."

"Like bringing someone back from the dead?"

"Perhaps he is not dead."

"Perhaps."

There was nothing more to say, and Michael departed soon after that. He went back home and exercised the horse for a time, all the while trying to puzzle out what had happened. He was still there when Rosanna summoned him to the telephone. "It's Segar," she said, "calling from Bucharest."

He hurried to the phone and heard the familiar voice on the other end. "Michael, I thought you'd want to know we have recovered the body."

"What?" Virtually no news could have surprised him more.

"That's right. It was found early this morning a few hundred meters downstream from where he left his clothes."

"Does it look like suicide?"

"No, there was a wire around his neck with handles attached at the end. He'd been garroted, apparently in the course of a robbery."

"You're sure of the identification?"

"The picture you gave me was a great help. There's no doubt it's him."

"Thank you for calling, Segar."

"One more thing – "

"What's that?"

"The body was fully clothed."

For an instant Michael didn't grasp the significance of his words. "What about it?"

"He'd left his clothes upstream near the bridge, but he was still fully clothed. There's something strange about the whole thing."

Once more Michael Vlado drove down the hill to Agula, passing Esmeralda's cabin and driving directly to the Glasnach's farmhouse. The front path was dry today, with no trace of footprints, and he knocked on the door. The son Andre opened it. "Come in," he said. "We've had a call from Bucharest. They've found my brother's body."

Michael nodded. "That's why I came."

Frieda Glasnach was sobbing quietly in the front room while her husband tried to comfort her. Michael said what he could, but they seemed to take no notice of his words. Finally, Andre brought him a glass of wine and forced some on his parents as well.

"You'll have to forgive us," Olak said when he'd recovered some of his composure. "We knew the news would be bad but it was still a shock."

"I have more news for you, and you won't find it pleasant. As a Rom, the king of my tribe, I feel I owe you an apology for the actions of old Esmeralda. The woman is a fraud, her bear's paw is worthless. She journeyed to Bucharest last week and met with your son. She persuaded him to leave Louise Stricker and return here. Apparently the relationship had cooled a bit, but not enough that he could openly walk away from it. I believe he arranged to fake his own suicide rather than face a scene with the Stricker woman. Esmeralda hoped to get money from you by having him appear after you all wished on the bear's paw."

"But he wasn't killed here," Frieda pointed out. "He was killed in Bucharest."

"I know. The key to it all seems to be Esmeralda's conversation with him last week. I think if she can remember it all she can tell us who killed him."

"What about the footprints at our door?" Olak asked. "How do you explain those?"

"Esmeralda may have arranged to fake them somehow, though she hasn't admitted it yet."

"How do you fake footprints in the mud? They were made by a person wearing shoes of Felipe's size. There is no tree limb or anything else close enough for him to have climbed into. And if they were made much earlier we'd have seen them, or the heavy rain would have washed them away."

"I plan to question Esmeralda again in the morning," Michael told the father. "She knows more than she's telling."

He left them, promising to return, and headed back home while Olak and Andre returned to their work in the field. Even the tragedy of a lost son could not interrupt the chores of a farm day for long. He thought of Frieda alone in the house with her thoughts, but decided she might be able to handle it better than the men. With luck, tomorrow would see an end to it – an end to the questions if not the grief.

That night, just after dark, he went once more to the cabin of old Esmeralda. This time he did not enter by the front door but parked some distance away and slipped around through the woods to the rear. By the time she heard him he was already inside. Her frightened eyes peered at him from the bedclothes. "What have you come for, Michael Vlado? Are you an avenger?"

"Not an avenger, but a savior. Hush now and wait."

He might have been wrong. He had been wrong many times before in judging the workings of an irrational mind. But he waited beneath Esmeralda's bed, forced to caution her every few minutes when she tried to whisper a question. An hour passed, and then another.

It was a bit after midnight when he heard one of the cabin windows being slid open. Quietly, someone climbed in and moved around, perhaps searching for the bedroom. Then he saw the figure above her bed, saw a glint of moonlight on the dagger. It would be a knife this time, because that was a Gypsy weapon.

Michael grabbed the ankles and the figure went down with a crash. Esmeralda screamed from her bed. Then he was on the figure, grasping for the knife hand. The glare of the spotlight targeted the struggle and suddenly Captain Segar was coming through the door with one of his men.

"Take him Segar," Michael gasped, panting from the struggle. "There's your murderer – Andre Glasnach. He killed his own brother."

It was Segar who asked, "How did you know he'd come here, Michael? I must admit when you phoned me earlier to ask for help I thought it was a waste of time."

"When I visited the Glasnach house earlier I played up Esmeralda's meeting with their dead son and the probability that she had some special knowledge. Andre couldn't take a chance that it was true. Felipe might have told her of his plans, even told her he feared returning because of Andre. As the eldest son, the farm was Felipe's if he came back. But it would be Andre's if he stayed away. For a man who killed his brother, killing an old Gypsy woman would have been easy."

"The faked suicide – ?"

"As I explained to the family earlier, Felipe was ready to return home but couldn't face the scene of breaking up with Louise Stricker. He left his clothes by the river and went into hiding until Saturday night, when he'd told Esmeralda he would reappear at the family farmhouse."

The Gypsy woman stirred in her bed, following his explanation when she could keep her eyes open. "I had it all planned," she muttered. "We wished on the paw and he was supposed to knock at the door."

"But the rain came and the bad roads delayed him. You kept waiting and he didn't come. Andre finally went up to his bedroom and there from his window, bathed in the light from above the front door, he saw his brother approaching through the rain. Perhaps he was prepared for such a possibility, or perhaps he ran into his parents' room for the rope they kept in case of fires. A quick slipknot, as Felipe hesitated by the front door and then he dropped the noose through the open window right around his brother's neck."

"My God!" Segar whispered.

"The muddy footprints stopped because Felipe, small of bone, was yanked straight up in the air by his muscular brother, and left hanging from the second floor window of the farmhouse. Then Andre ran downstairs and quickly wished his brother away with the bear's paw."

"No, no," the old woman protested from her bed. "We could still hear the knocking after Andre came down from his room!"

"We heard it more faintly. It was the sound of Felipe's boots hitting the side of the house as he struggled in his dying agony."

"Why didn't we see the body when we opened the door?"

"It was above us. More importantly, it was above the spotlight over the door. If anyone looked up, the strong light blinded them and they never saw the body. I went upstairs to get boots to compare with the muddy tracks but Andre kept me away from his room where the rope went out the window. Later, perhaps as we were leaving, he pulled the body into his room. During the night he would have lowered it out again and carried it to the car his brother had parked nearby. On Sunday he drove the body to Bucharest and dumped it in the river hoping it was close to the right spot. He wrapped a wire garrote around the throat to conceal the marks of the rope and hide the real cause of death."

"How did you know this?" Segar asked. "Can it be proven?"

"The autopsy on Felipe's body will show that he died Saturday rather than Thursday. And a careful examination might even find evidence of the rope marks. Once you have that, Andre is the only possibility. Only he was upstairs when the knocking started. And only he, as the killer, knew that his final wish on the bear's paw would be successful. He had the motive – to inherit the farm someday for himself – and the opportunity. I think you can prove that he was away long enough on Sunday to drive to Bucharest and back."

"When did you suspect him?" Segar asked.

When I went over Saturday's events in my mind. Andre was the first to scoff at the bear's paw and its wishes, yet he ran downstairs to use it himself when the knocking came."

As it turned out, Segar needn't have worried about evidence. Shortly before his mother and father were to visit him at the Agula jail, Andre managed to cut his wrists with a razor blade he'd hidden in his mouth. He'd put it back under his tongue as he bled to death in his cell.

Later, when Michael Vlado finished telling Rosanna everything that had happened, she, with her literary mind, turned to him and said, as Andre had earlier, "It was 'The Monkey's Paw'!"

Michael, his voice soft and sad, corrected her. "No, it was 'The Prodigal Son.' "

THE CLOCKWORK RAT

Old Caspian came to visit Michael Vlado one day in the spring, when the horses were running in the field. He stood for a time watching them, as he often did on visits to the Gypsy village in the foothills of Romania's Transylvanian Alps. Finally, after nearly an hour, he came to the point of his visit.

"One of my people is in trouble, Michael – a Rom like ourselves, though he lives in Moscow."

"Moscow is a long way from here," Michael said quietly, knowing what was going to be asked of him.

"You went there once before to race a horse, when the Communists were still in power. It is a different place now."

"But trouble is always the same. I try to avoid it."

Old Caspian sighed. "Ten years younger and I would go myself, Michael."

"Tell me about this trouble. I promise nothing."

Caspian brought out his pipe and stuffed the bowl with tobacco. He took his time lighting it, and Michael feared he was in for a long story. "He's a dwarf," the old man said. "I suppose that's how he got the job in the first place."

"What job is it?"

"With the coming of capitalism to Russia, several private clubs have sprung up around Moscow. My little friend Maksim is employed at one of them dressed up like a page boy from a couple of centuries ago. They have gambling there and drugs. Maksim wants desperately to leave Moscow and return home, but he is a virtual prisoner, treated as little more than a slave. He owes a large sum of money to gangsters – the Russian Mafia as the press likes to call them – and they keep him working against his will. He fears they would kill him if he tried to escape."

"What can I do?" Michael Vlado asked. "I do not have the money to ransom him."

"You are a Gypsy king, my friend," Caspian reminded him. "You could get Maksim out safely. They would not dare to harm you."

"I'm sure your Russian Mafia or whatever you call them, would have little respect for a Gypsy of whatever rank."

"Look Michael, you are my only hope! We have no one to represent us, no one to protect our interests. There is no Rom ambassador in Moscow or anywhere else."

Michael considered the appeal, knowing he should turn it down but reluctant to do so. "They might not even let me enter the country."

"You still have your Romanian passport don't you?"

"Yes."

"Then they will let you in. Everything is much looser in Russia today."

"Including the crime."

Caspian persisted. "I just want Maksim out alive. I know you can do it for me."

Michael Vlado shook his head, trying one last time to say no. "It's two day's drive to Moscow and another two back. I can't be gone that long."

"I will buy you a plane ticket, and give you money for two return tickets."

"Why does this dwarf Maksim mean so much to you?"

The old man simply stared at him. Finally he turned away, perhaps to hide a tear. "He is my grandson."

On the flight to Moscow the following day, Michael considered the story old Caspian had told him. The man's daughter, Sasha, whom Michael remembered holding in his arms when she was a baby, had joined a traveling circus some twenty-five years earlier, working as a bareback rider and touring throughout the Socialist countries of Eastern Europe. Later, with the new freedom engendered by the fall of Communism, she had returned home briefly to Caspian's village. During her circus days she had borne a son named Maksim who was in his early twenties now. It was only recently that Caspian had learned that part of the story, after Sasha departed once more and left him a long letter.

Maksim's father, short of stature but not, like his son, a dwarf, was an animal trainer with the circus. Sasha had fallen in love with him and they'd had a child. When it became clear that young Maksim would never achieve full height, his father began teaching him the business of training animals. The boy was especially adept at handling and breeding performing rats, and the rats were always in large supply when the circus set up its tents in the fields of the old cities.

After 1991, when the changes in Russia accelerated, Maksim and his father left the circus and moved to Moscow. Sasha had returned to her home village in Romania, feeling that her son was now an adult and able to fend for himself. Once in Moscow, Maksim and his father quickly found work in the shadowy world of private gambling, arranging races using their trained rats. But last fall something happened. Maksim's father dropped out of sight and Maksim ended up owing the mob a great deal of money. He'd been kept in servitude ever since, working off his debt at one of the many private clubs in the Moscow area. Sasha had again left her village to earn money to send him, but meanwhile, Caspian's grandson remained in a sort of forced servitude.

It was obvious to Michael Vlado that he would not get far in Moscow as a Gypsy, not even as a Gypsy king. Once he cleared customs at Domodedovo Airport, he assumed the role of a Romanian businessman. He used most of the money for the two return plane tickets to purchase a suit of clothes and accessories at the huge GUM department store in Red Square. Walking among the fountains in the lofty glass-roofed galleries of the store, he could almost feel like a capitalist. The feeling remained with him back in his tiny hotel room as he changed into the unfamiliar clothes.

The address Caspian had given him was for the Club Nikolas, an elaborate old mansion located next to the city's soccer stadium near the airport. Michael had rented a car and he parked near the club, walking up the drive just as the hazy spring evening was at last yielding to darkness. A uniformed guard standing by the massive oak door of the building was hardly welcoming and when Michael pressed the bell he had no idea what to expect. The door was opened by a somber young man in evening clothes who said in Russian, "Your membership card, please."

"I have none. I understood I could be admitted on a temporary basis while my membership is being processed," Michael replied also in Russian.

"No, no! A membership card is required!"

"My name is Michael Vlado. I have come from Bucharest on business. May I see your manager?"

The doorman picked up a house telephone and spoke a few words into it. He glowered at Michael, apparently in response to a question he had been asked, and finally answered in the affirmative. He hung up the phone and said with visible distaste. "Follow me."

They walked perhaps twenty feet down an oak paneled hall to a closed door. From farther down the hall came the sound of voices and music. The doorman turned the knob. "In here."

A stout Russian in a tuxedo was seated behind a carved mahogany desk in an office that seemed a relic of fifty years ago. Only the beige computer and printer on a side table seemed out of place.

Michael immediately introduced himself and shook hands. The Russian, obviously uncertain about this unknown Romanian, said simply, "I am Oleg Kizim, manager of the Club Nikolas."

"I was told I could apply for membership here. My business brings me to

Moscow frequently these days."

Kizim smiled. "What business would that be?"

"I own a large automobile dealership in Bucharest."

"Did someone recommend Club Nikolas?"

"One of my employees is related to a member of your staff – Maksim Wanovich."

The club manger was startled into laughter. "The man's a dwarf!"

"I understood him to be a highly skilled animal trainer."

"Among our features at the Club Nikolas are the nightly rodent races. Maksim is in charge of those. It is a popular gambling game."

"I would like to see that," Michael assured him.

Oleg Kizim considered the request. "Our rules are not overly strict here. If you plan on taking out a membership – "

"What is the cost?"

"We prefer payment in Western currency if possible. The annual dues are three thousand American dollars or its equivalent in British, French or German currency."

"That would be no problem. Or if you'd accept a check drawn on a Romanian bank, I could give it to you now."

The manager held up his hand. "I prefer Western currency if it is available to you. Tomorrow would be fine."

"But I am free to spend the evening here?"

"Yes, of course, Mr. Vlado. I'll give you a temporary membership card. We have a health spa downtown too which you may use."

"And those rodent races?"

"A large room in back. Anyone can direct you."

During the next few minutes, Michael gained a quick impression of the Club Nikolas. There was a room for casino gambling and another for cabaret style shows. The dining room was crowded, though the usual hour for dinner had passed. An oak-paneled library with reading nooks could have been part of some staid old London club, except for a small amber-lit bar at one end where a short blonde barmaid, still attractive in her late thirties, was mixing drinks. Her nametag read *Alexandra* in both English and Russian. It seemed a fitting name for Club Nikolas.

"Which way to the races?" he asked her.

"Through the door to your left." Her smile widened. "Buy your chips from the cashier and good luck."

"It's my first time," Michael admitted. "Are there any tips on how to play?"

"Watch a few races before you bet," she advised. "On busy nights they run the same rats several times. The early winners sometimes tire. Bet on a loser when you believe his turn has come."

He gave her a smile. "Thank you for the tip. If I win you'll get part of it."

The gambling room was large enough to hold perhaps a hundred people. Most were men and Michael decided it was not a sport to hold any special appeal for women. There were four tracks, really neon-lit glass tubes, which were attached to the walls one above the other and circled the room. Each was numbered, with track one at the top. The large white rats were placed in glass holding boxes and released simultaneously by a little man with curly black hair, dressed as an eighteenth-century page. Surely this was Maksim Wanovich, though whether he was short enough to qualify as a true dwarf was open to question. He did have to reach up to release the rats, about five feet above the floor, and then he urged them on by ringing a small hand bell. The spectators held scorecards, and as at any race they cheered their favorites as the four rats burst from the starting gate. The bank of tubes gradually rose, sending the tracks above the entrance door and then down again toward the finish line.

This time the winner was rat number three, reaching his reward of food by a good margin. There was a wait of about ten minutes between races while chips on the winning numbers were paid off and new bets placed. Chips were sold and redeemed at a cashier's window just outside the door. Michael used the time between races to approach the costumed dwarf. When he was close enough he could read *Maksim* on his nameplate.

"Hello, Maksim" he said quietly. "I am a friend of your grandfather back in Romania."

The dwarf's head jerked up as if he'd been struck. "I have no grandfather. He is dead."

"No, Caspian is old but very much alive. He sent me to get you out of here."

Maksim glanced around nervously. "I cannot talk. I have races to run."

The blonde barmaid, Alexandra, appeared with a tray of drinks for the gamblers. A slender young Englishman who could have been her son ran his hand over the rear of her tight satin pants. Her smile froze, but she kept passing out the drinks as if nothing had happened. Michael took two quick steps and locked his fingers around the man's wrist. "You could lose a hand that way," he said in English.

"What – ? Who the bloody hell are you?"

"Please," Alexandra said to Michael. "You'll only get me in trouble."

He let go of the man's wrist. "Sorry. I thought you were molesting her."

"Do you work here?" the Englishman asked.

"I'm a member," Michael replied, stretching the truth.

Maksim rang his bell and the next race began. There were the usual shouts from the spectators as the four white rats sped along their glass tubes. It was, Michael decided, not too different from the day some years back when he'd been at the Moscow racetrack. The animals were smaller, but the spectators were just as vocal.

Rat number one came in first, to the delight of the Englishman. He was so pleased as he collected his winnings that he fell into a conversation with Michael. "Sorry about that earlier. I've probably had a bit too much to drink. Name's Sean Croydon."

"Michael Vlado."

"I'm designing a golf course here, introducing the Russians to Western ways. I think we can make golf as big in Russia as it is in Japan. What about you?"

"I have an auto dealership in Romania. I'm here to see about purchasing Russian cars."

The Englishman chuckled. "They're not much good. Stick with the Germans or Italians." He pocketed his winnings and strolled out toward the bar.

Michael decided it was time to take a chance. He bet on rat number three in the next race and watched him come in second. The winning bet paid odds of three to one, and since about the same amount was wagered on each rat, that meant the club kept about a quarter of all bets. Michael had two more losses before he started winning, picking three winning rats in a row. But Maksim was still reluctant to speak with him. It was obvious that even in the new Russian society people were constantly on their guard when dealing with foreigners.

"I am a Rom like yourself." Michael managed to tell him between races, as he was removing the rats from their tubes and substituting new ones. "Tell me what happened to your father. I have come to here to help you both."

"You cannot help him. He is dead."

"Was he killed?"

But Maksim ignored him, raising his voice to announce, "The next race will be run with the clockwork rat in the number two position." He pressed the button on the wall.

Michael realized that only three white rats were present in the tubes and the number two tube was empty. He saw the Englishman, Croydon, reenter the room and went over to ask him about it. "What is a clockwork rat?"

"A windup, like a child's toy. Sometimes if they have three rats and the rest are tired or lame they add the toy rat so that the betting odds will remain the same. It goes quite fast, but experienced bettors know it hardly ever wins. Here comes Kizim now to wind it. If it's not wound tightly enough it runs too slow, and he doesn't trust the dwarf to do it right."

The stout Russian manager removed the clockwork rat from a drawer beneath the glass racing tubes and inserted a key in its side. He began turning the key with a measured vigor.

The sudden explosion sounded no louder than a firecracker. Then Michael saw the blood and fire on the front of Kizim's tuxedo and realized it had been a bomb.

The Russian was dead before the first ambulance arrived. The detectives and police who came with it were an odd mixture of civilian and military – the latter, Michael supposed, because of the bomb. These were in uniform and they seemed more efficient than the stocky men in baggy dark suits who checked identification and asked pointless questions. Michael had been seated with the other customers, waiting his turn with the police when one of the uniformed men announced, "We have arrested a suspect. It will not be necessary to question you individually unless you have specific knowledge of this crime. Please leave your name and address and we will contact you later if necessary."

Michael had been wondering how to explain his presence, and his first reaction to the announcement was one of relief. Then, as he was leaving the Club Nikolas with the other guests, Alexandra ran up to him. "Maksim has been arrested for the murder! Can you help?"

"Arrested? Why him?"

"The police discovered there was bad blood between them and he had charge of the clockwork rat, with the best opportunity to plant the bomb. It makes sense to them. He told me to get you, that you are friend of his grandfather."

"Who is the officer in charge?" Michael asked.

"Ivan Vasili. He is a lieutenant in this district. He comes here frequently, sometimes off duty."

"I will try to speak with him," he promised.

Sam Croydon had seen Michael talking with Alexandra and he was waiting with a smirk on his face. "You have to admit, old chap, that she's easy on the eyes."

"I never denied it. Do you come here often?"

"I did until tonight. When bombs start going off, I stay away. It's a Bolshevik thing, you know – those bowling ball bombs with the lighted fuse coming out of them, just as in the cartoons."

"It wasn't that sort of bomb, and the Bolsheviks are gone."

"Gone but not forgotten."

"Do you know who this Lieutenant Vasili is, the one who's handling the investigation?"

Croydon glanced around at the crowd outside the Club Nikolas. "I saw him just a moment ago. He's a regular at the club." Suddenly he pointed toward a black sedan. "There he is with the dwarf!"

Maksim was in handcuffs, being placed in the backseat of the car. Michael wanted to run up to try to free him but he knew such action would have brought a bullet in response. Much as he hated to admit it, old Caspian's grandson might even be guilty of the crime. Perhaps he had good and sufficient reason for wanting the manager dead.

The hour was already late and he decided to wait until morning. Things might look different by daylight.

Michael was staying at an old, inexpensive hotel near the Pushkin Art Museum. There were no shades on the windows and he was awakened by the first light of day. He had breakfast and tried to read a newspaper account of the bombing at the Club Nikolas. His Russian was not good enough to grasp it all, but he saw that Maksim was described as a suspected terrorist.

He took a taxi to the central police headquarters and asked to see Lieutenant Vasili, saying it was about the bombing. After a twenty-minute wait in a bare depressing room, the man in the baggy suit appeared. He carried a list of those who'd been at the club the previous night, and after Michael identified himself the detective led him back to a cubicle. "What do you have to tell me?" he asked, taking out a pack of Russian cigarettes.

"I was sent here by Maksim's grandfather. He was being forced to work at that club because of debts he'd run up."

"He told us that. It makes a good motive for wanting Kizim dead."

"But would he do it in such a manner, in the very room where he worked? And what would Maksim know about making bombs?"

The detective lit his cigarette. "It is an unfortunate fact of life that such knowledge is easy to come by these days. He admits that during his youth in the circus he helped his parents make firecrackers for the clowns to use in their act."

"What happened to his father, Yegor Wanovich?"

Ivan Vasili shrugged. "The mobs have a certain power in the city at this moment. Places like the Club Nikolas always attract them. They see it as a good semi-legal source of Western currency. Possibly Wanovich's father stood in their way."

"He was killed?"

"We have no proof of that. No one has looked too hard for him. He was only a Gypsy from the circus."

"I would like to speak with young Maksim."

"That would be highly irregular. We have not yet finished our interrogation."

"I am a fellow Rom," Michael said, realizing it might be the wrong thing to say. "I am king of the Gypsy tribe to which Maksim's grandfather belongs. He lives in a village not far from me. Let me talk to him."

"You are a Gypsy king?" Vasili stared at him, studying him as if for the first time. "That is something like a judge, is it not?"

"I have held court," Michael admitted. "It is an informal court, called a *kris*, but my decisions carry weight within our community."

The detective though for a moment and then said, "I will respect your position, Michael Vlado. You may speak with the prisoner for ten minutes, no longer."

"Thank you."

Michael waited while Vasili stepped into the next room to use the telephone. Presently he was escorted along a narrow corridor to an interrogation room with one small window. Maksim sat alone at a long table that made him look even smaller than he was. In place of his eighteenth-century pageboy garb he wore a gray prison uniform. "You again!" he said as Michael entered. "Thank you for coming." He probably would have welcomed anyone at that moment.

"I have only ten minutes, Maksim. Tell me what you know of the killing."

"I know nothing, believe me! They say I killed him because he was holding me in bondage for my father's unpaid debts. But I am innocent!"

"Your father's debts? How did that happen?"

He spoke with childish naiveté remembering the days with the circus. "It was good then. Coming to Moscow was different. My mother had returned home and there were just the two of us. But I had my rats, and that got us a job at the Club Nikolas, which was just opening up. I did well, running the rats through the glass tubes my father had constructed. But once the place was open there was no job for him except kitchen work. One night last autumn he simply disappeared. He never came back to the little apartment we shared with a pair of music students."

"That detective, Vasili, thinks the mob played a part in his disappearance."

Maksim snorted. "Vasili himself is in the pay of the mob, as are many of the police. He would never suggest that if it were true. Oleg Kizim insisted my father had stolen money from him and he forced me to continue working there until he considered the debt repaid."

"With Kizim dead you're free to go?"

"Yes," Maksim said with some irony in his voice, glancing around at the somber walls. "I am free at last."

Michael Vlado considered the possibilities. The club manager's death could have been an outgrowth of his troubles with Maksim and his father, or it could have had some other cause, probably mob-related. "Is there any possibility that your father could have rigged that bomb in the clockwork rat before his disappearance?"

"None. We use it two or three times a week. There are two of them but we use them both at least once a week. Both were used two nights ago and Kizim wound them as he always did. The bomb must have been placed in it during the last two days."

"Did your father have a key to the club? Could he have slipped in while the place was closed?"

"It's only closed for cleaning for a few hours in the early morning. Even then, someone is always in the building. We all came and went as we pleased. But I told you, he is dead, and I don't believe in spirits."

"You say there are two of those windup devices?"

"Yes, in case one breaks down. They're both kept in the drawer."

"So the killer could have borrowed one and tampered with it and then returned it to its place."

"I suppose so. The drawer isn't locked. A key is needed for the rat itself, but a key for any windup toy would probably fit. And there's one in the drawer anyway."

"Would anything have prevented your father from returning to the club, slipping back in during those early morning hours and tampering with the mechanical rat?"

"Not if he's still alive."

Michael saw that his ten minutes was almost up. "If the mob was responsible for your father's disappearance, who would it be? I need a name."

"The detective, Vasili, is paid off by a Georgian name Gogol. At least that's what he's called. I sometimes see him meeting with Kizim."

"Where can I find Gogol?"

"He hangs around a health club named Elite, near Red Square. It's connected with the Club Nikolas somehow."

"Time's up," Ivan Vasili announced, returning to the interrogation room.

"I'm finished," Michael said getting to his feet.

He knew Maksim's eyes were on him as he left the room.

Michael spent the afternoon at the Elite Health Spa, trying out the Jacuzzi, a foaming tub of hot water that he'd never before experienced. Then he moved on to the exercise cycles and the weight room. It was an invigorating way to spend a few hours, but no one he spoke to would admit knowing a man called Gogol.

He had used his temporary membership card for the Club Nikolas to gain admission to the Elite, and obviously there was a connection between the two. The woman at the desk told him any charges would appear on his monthly statement from Club Nikolas. That evening, after eating lightly at his hotel, he returned to the club. Most of the rooms seemed much the same, and the place was crowded, though the back room used for the rodent races was closed and locked.

He saw Alexandra at the bar and went to speak with her. She seemed drained of color and there were beads of sweat visible on her forehead . "Are you all right?" he asked.

"I've just had a shock. A new manager has been appointed for the club. He is a man I dislike intensely."

"Did he work here before?"

She shook her head. "He would come and meet with Oleg Kizim. He is a bad man, worse than Kizim was."

The mention of meetings sparked a memory of something Maksim had told him that morning. "What is the new manager's name?"

"Everyone calls him Gogol."

"I saw Maksim at the police headquarters this morning. He mentioned that name."

"How is Maksim?" she asked trying to smile.

"He seemed well. They were still questioning him. But he did tell me this man Gogol is associated with the mobs that have sprung up in Moscow recently. He might even know something about the disappearance of Maksim's father."

"That was before I came," she told him. "I have worked here only since January, many months after Yegor Wanovich's disappearance." Suddenly she caught her breadth and whispered, "There he is!"

Michael turned, thinking for an instant that she meant Yegor, but then he saw the Russian and knew it was Gogol. He must have been well over six feet tall, moving with authority as he towered over everyone else in the room. He strode directly to the door of the room where the rat races were held and inserted a key in the lock.

Sam Croydon, the Englishman Michael had met earlier, appeared from somewhere and asked Gogol, "Will there be racing tonight?"

The Russian pulled the door open. "I must inspect the damage first."

Michael could see there was surprisingly little of it. "The position in which Kizim had been holding the clockwork rat as he wound it had directed the force of the small explosion into his body, either by accident or design.

Perhaps the bomber was a humanitarian who was careful not to injure anyone but his victim. Or perhaps he was careful simply because he knew he'd be standing close to Kizim when the bomb detonated.

"Who will operate the games?" Sam Croydon asked.

"The police have released Maksim," the Russian answered, and as if on cue the little Gypsy walked through the door. "Maksim!" Alexandra exclaimed, throwing her arms around him as one might greet a child. "You're free!"

"For the moment," he told her. "Vasili has warned me not to leave the city."

Croydon shook his hand. "Great to have you back old chap. Now get those rats of yours running."

"Give us one hour to clean up the place," Gogol said. "Will that be enough, Maksim?"

"I don't know. There are blood spots here which I must clean from the carpet as best I can."

Gogol inspected them. "Hardly noticeable especially with the room full of gamblers."

Michael had moved over to Maksim's side. "Vasili wouldn't have released you unless he was fairly certain of your innocence."

"Gogol wanted me to run the races. Vasili does what he's told. Gogol doesn't care who killed Kizim as long as the races go on."

An hour later the bettors were lining up once more with their money and chips in hand. Maksim rang the bell and released his rats for their dash through the lighted tubes to the food at the other end. The races continued for more than an hour before Gogol announced there'd be just one more before the room closed. The Gypsy placed three rats into their holding boxes and said to Gogol, "There is one more clockwork rat remaining if you wish to use it."

"Go ahead."

"Do you want to wind it?"

The man in the black suit smiled and shook his head. "You will do that, little man." He took a step back, toward the door. Everyone in the room seemed to do likewise, though Michael was certain the remaining windup rat would have been examined by the police. Maksim shrugged and inserted the key into the furry toy, winding it briskly several times. He placed it on the bottom track and turned it on just as he released the other rats. Cheers went up from the spectators.

This time, to the surprise of many, the clockwork rat actually won the race by a nose. Gogol scowled at the dwarf, perhaps thinking that the previous manager had the right idea about winding the toy himself. "Not so tight next time," he cautioned Maksim in a low voice.

Michael followed the crowd into the club's regular casino and watched the more familiar varieties of gaming for an hour or so. He even tried his hand at roulette and won enough for those two plane tickets back home. He hoped he'd be able to use them. Gogol did not appear, and there was no opportunity to speak with him about the murdered man and the missing Yegor Wanovich. Finally, at midnight, he saw Alexandra departing through a side door, her shift at an end.

But there was something wrong.

Gogol had emerged from his office and signaled to two men in the rumpled suits seated at the bar. They looked like former KGB agents, which wouldn't have surprised Michael. He'd heard that some of them had gone into organized crime. These two quickly followed the woman out the side door, and Michael hurried after them.

They caught up with her at her little black car yanking her from the front seat before she could start the engine. Michael Vlado broke into a run heading straight for them. He caught the first man by surprise spinning him around and toppling him to the cindered parking lot. The second man was tougher and he already had his hands on Alexandra's throat. Michael kicked him in the shin, then dragged him from the car as he relaxed his grip on her.

"Thank you," she managed to gasp.

"Let's get out of here, fast!" He pushed her over and took the wheel himself.

Both men were at the car as they pulled away, but if they were armed, neither used a weapon. "They're going for their car," Alexandra said, looking back. "They'll try to catch us."

The little Russian car was unfamiliar to Michael but he guided it along the residential streets, past old houses and high rise apartments. "Why is Gogol after you?"

"Because I know what happened to Yegor Wanovich. He was killed by Kizim, probably on orders from Gogol."

"How did you find that out?"

"There were papers in Kizim's office at the club. I'd sneak in there during my breaks if he was busy somewhere else, hoping to find something on him. I wasn't the only one interested. Wanovich discovered the games were crooked and was blackmailing Kizim. I found records of the payments."

"Would anyone be surprised at the crooked casino games in Moscow? Why would Wanovich take such a risk?"

"Because Kizim was fixing even the rat races, making it look as if Wanovich and his son were responsible." She peered through the windshield squinting until she recognized the street. "Turn left here."

"How do you fix a rat race?" Michael wondered.

"By forcing them to swallow lead shots. It slows down the ones you want to lose."

It was a Gypsy trick. Michael wondered if Wanovich had taught it to Kizim in the first place. "I came here to rescue Wanovich's son Maksim. His grandfather said Kizim was holding him in virtual slavery."

"This is my apartment," Alexandra said, indicating a brick building that probably dated from pre-Revolutionary days. "Come in with me until I know we haven't been followed."

The street was deserted in the midnight darkness and Michael hurried after her. Inside the tiny apartment she turned on no lights but moved familiarly through the darkened room to the window. The glow from a streetlight enabled him to follow her progress until she stood just behind the curtains staring down at the street. "Is anyone there?" he asked.

"No one yet."

The spring night had turned chilly in the Russian capital and he could see she was trembling from the cold or from fear. He went to her and put his arm around her. "I can stay the night and sleep here on the sofa."

"If you get involved with me you may end up dead. Gogol is a hard man who'll do anything to keep control of the Club Nikolas."

He looked down at the street and saw a car drive slowly past he building. It might have been the one that followed them but he couldn't be sure. "This money Maksim's father is supposed to have stolen from the club – it was really the blackmail money, wasn't it?"

"I think so, yes." She turned and nestled her head beneath his chin. "Can you get me out of here? Out of Moscow?"

"I came here to get Maksim out."

"You are tall. I like that. Yegor only came up to my chin."

Michael stepped away from her, his attention suddenly drawn to the street. "I think they're down there." The car had returned and parked beneath a tree. As they watched, the two men emerged and started across the street.

"What will I do?" she asked.

"Is there a back way out of here?"

"Yes, into a courtyard that connects with the next apartment."

"Come on." He took her by the hand and led her into the hallway. She directed him to a rear staircase and then down to street level. They went through an outside door and found themselves in an enclosed courtyard. By the light of a single weak bulb he could make out the entrance to the apartment next door.

"Stop there!" a voice shouted. A spotlight hit them, pinning them like bugs. Then, shielding his eyes, Michael made out the figure of Lieutenant Ivan Vasili. He was holding a gun pointed at them.

"What do you want?" Michael asked.

"The woman. Surrender her and you are free to go."

"You're working for Gogol. He wants her dead."

"I am working for the state."

Behind him, Michael heard the door opening. The two men in the black suits came around on either side of them. The one Michael had kicked in the shin was holding a gun. "He is just another Gypsy," the man said. "I would know them anywhere. Let me shoot him!"

But Vasili held up his hand. "I think we must talk, Michael Vlado. You do not fully understand the situation. My men were not trying to abduct Alexandra outside the Club Nikolas tonight. They were trying to arrest her. We searched her apartment this evening and found explosives there."

At his side, Alexandra gasped. "Did you have a warrant for the search?" Michael said.

"Warrant?" the detective repeated with a smile. Then he said to his men, "Bring them both along. He may have been working with her."

In the early morning hours Moscow police headquarters was even more depressing than on his earlier visit. That time Maksim had been the prisoner. Now it was Michael himself.

Seated alone in a holding cell while Vasili questioned Alexandra, he had time to consider the problem of Kizim's murder. By the time the detective came for him, many things had become clearer. "She will not talk without a lawyer," Vasili said. "Do you have anything to say?"

"Let me see her," Michael suggested.

The detective lit a cigarette and frowned. "What good will that do?"

"Can it do any harm? I'm sure you'll be listening to every word we say."

"All right." He unlocked the cell door. "She's in the first interrogation room."

Alexandra stood by a small window covered with heavy wire mesh, staring down at the street. She turned as Michael entered, surprised to see him. "Have they sent you now to question me?"

"No. I asked to speak with you."

She sat down at the long table, crossing her hands in front of her. "Do you think that I killed Oleg Kizim?"

"I know that you killed him."

Her head jerked up. "What do you mean?"

Michael began to speak, feeling lonely and sad as he often did when remembering his childhood. "I must have been around ten years old at the time. My mother took me to visit a man named Caspian in a neighboring village. His wife had recently given birth, and that was the reason for our visit. I remember they let me hold the child in my arms. It was the first time I'd ever held a baby because this was something boys rarely did. That baby was you, Sasha." Her head jerked up at the name. "You are Caspian's daughter and Maksim's mother."

She was silent for a long time, twisting her hands as she tried to find words. "How did you know?" she asked finally.

"You told me Yegor was gone many months before you started working at the club, yet tonight in your apartment you mentioned how short he was, that he only came up to your chin. If you didn't work together you must have known him before. Then there was the business of Maksim's mother and father making fireworks for the clowns when they worked at the circus. You had the knowledge to make a small bomb, if you were Maksim's mother. Sitting here thinking about it just now, I remembered how you greeted Maksim almost like a mother when he was released from police custody earlier."

"I suppose I should have admitted everything," she said speaking in a tired voice.

"Tell me about it."

"Yegor and I split up when he insisted on taking Maksim to Moscow with him. He said there was no future for a Gyspy in Romania, especially a Gypsy dwarf. He'd heard everything was changing in Russia and there were opportunities in the capital. He was right, but those opportunities were in gambling and mob-related activities. I was so glad I'd taught my son how to read and write. He sent me letters from here, telling of their new jobs at the Club Nikolas. He made it sound like a glamorous place, which I suppose it is. The nightly rat races brought in much money for Oleg Kizim, especially after he started fixing the races by feeding the rats lead shot to weight them down."

"That was when your husband began blackmailing him?"

She nodded. "And got himself killed. Leaving my son alone. Worse still, Kizim insisted he return the money his father had extorted. He refused to let Maksim leave the club until every ruble was repaid. My son became a virtual slave. That was when I decided to go to Moscow and be with him. I obtained the job as a barmaid and no one but Maksim knew I was his mother. Still, there seemed no way out for him. Even with my small income added to his, it would have taken us years to pay off my husband's debt. Kizim had paid him thousands before deciding to kill him."

"What did your husband do with all that money?"

"Maksim says he gambled it away, and spent it on drugs."

"So you killed Kizim."

She nodded. "Maksim knew I was planning something but he didn't know what. I'd watched Kizim wind that clockwork rat many times and I knew exactly how he held it. I made certain the explosive charge was small enough that my son and the others in the room would not be harmed. I saw this as our way to freedom, but then Gogol took over as manager of the club and I knew that things would never change."

"What made the police suspect you enough to search your room?"

"Lieutenant Vasili told me they found small traces of gunpowder in your locker at work. It must have come out of the bag in which I carried the toy rat to my apartment and back. It was there that I assembled the bomb." She gave a weak smile. "Perhaps I am a better mother than I am a criminal."

"I'd like to get Maksim out of here, if you'll allow it. Your father gave me money for two plane tickets back to Bucharest. I think now is the time to use them."

"Do it. Today if they'll let you. Perhaps some day I can join him."

He left her then and spoke to Ivan Vasili in the outer office. "Am I free to go?"

"Go" he said with a wave of his hand.

"What about Maksim?"

"Take the dwarf with you, but don't say I told you that."

"Will Gogol try to stop me?"

"I will handle him."

Michael and Maksim flew out of Domodedovo Airport on the afternoon flight to Bucharest. The rats stayed behind.

THE STARKWORTH ATROCITY

Unlike the traditional image of the Gypsy, Michael Vlado had never been a wanderer. He would have been quite content to live with his wife in the foothills of Romania's Transylvanian Alps, breeding horses and working with the members of his clan, had not circumstances thrust a different role upon him. He became king of his tribe when just past forty years of age, at a time when European persecution of Gypsies together with political upheavals in Eastern Europe were changing his life in unexpected ways. Hardly a year passed now when he was not summoned to a faraway place to plead the cause of Romanies seeking political asylum.

That was how he happened to be traveling by train through the Channel Tunnel on his way to England in late October of 1997. Thousands of Gypsies facing increased persecution in Slovakia and the Czech Republic had been encouraged to flee by a television program's favorable portrayal of Canada as welcoming Romany immigrants.

When Canada insisted on stricter entry rules, the focus shifted to Britain. Once there, the rumors said, it was easier to travel the rest of the way to Canada.

Michael had answered a direct appeal from Colonel Jugger, an official of the European Union, to travel with him to Dover and examine the problem in person. Now, passing through the seemingly endless tunnel beneath the English Channel he listened while the colonel outlined the problem, speaking English with only a slight accent. "It is said that upwards of six thousand Gypsies are on their way to Britain. Most will arrive by the less expensive cross-channel ferries, but however they come, Dover is the most likely port of entry. They have a real problem there, compounded by the recent Dublin Convention on Immigration ruling that asylum seekers may apply for refuge in the country in which they wish to live. Britain can no longer simply send them back across the channel."

"The European Union is making many changes to the old rules," Michael observed.

"Too many, in the British view of things, which is why they're resisting a full acceptance of the Union. But here we are, at last." The train burst into the sunlight without warning, and Michael Vlado was on British soil for the first time in his life.

They rolled into the station a bit farther along. Colonel Jugger, a slender man of military bearing who was taller than Michael by a couple of inches, had arranged for a car to meet them. He was a retired officer in the former West German army who'd taken the job with the European Union a couple of years earlier. His specialty was migration between various countries in the Union, which automatically made him an expert on Gypsies. It was men like Jugger who would change the map of Europe in the decades to come, for better or worse. Now, as Michael followed him down the steps to the waiting car with its small EU banners mounted on the front fender, he felt increasingly out of place. He didn't belong here. He was no sort of politician.

"There's an unused nursing home at Starkworth about twenty miles from here," Jugger was saying. "The government has pressed it into service to help provide emergency accommodations for Gypsies requesting asylum, at least until the courts can rule on their requests." He gave the driver a route to their destination and the black sedan sprang into motion, traveling swiftly and silently up Marine Parade Road to the A2.

"I'm not too familiar with the Romany population in Britain," Michael admitted.

"They're often called Travelers, a term that includes both Gypsies and itinerant speakers of the Shelta language. We estimate that there are about fifty thousand in all, with another twenty thousand in Ireland."

"Shelta?"

"It's a private language based partly on Irish. Apparently it's spoken only by Travelers in the British Isles. These are hard times for itinerant people hereabouts. In the past, Gypsies camped in the countryside, even in some distant corner of a large estate. They were out of sight and bothered no one, sometimes even proving useful as seasonal farm workers. But as the population grew and empty areas became less common, conflicts emerged. The new suburban communities did not want Gypsies on their doorstep. The Caravan Site Act of nineteen sixty-eight obliged local authorities to provide camping areas for them, but generally these were in the least desirable areas of town. Needless to say, this new wave of Gypsy immigration is not welcome here."

After a time the car turned off the A2. They headed back toward the coast and through the country town of Starkworth. It was probably like many others, with a clock tower on the town hall and an old stone church dating from at least the last century, but it was the first one Michael had seen in England. Soon they reached their destination, a sprawling white building surrounded by a grove of trees across from a school. Until a year ago it had been the Starkworth Nursing home, Jugger explained. Unused since then, the county council had agreed to the government suggestion that Gypsy immigrants be housed there until their status was clarified. "How many can they handle here?" Michael wondered.

"About one hundred, more if they installed cots in the recreation room. Right now I believe they're around half of capacity."

The car pulled up behind a white MG, the only other vehicle in evidence. "I expect we'll be about an hour," Colonel Jugger told the driver.

Jugger was a few steps ahead of Michael going up the walkway to the front door, so he was the first to spot the body sprawled in the doorway, its head and shoulders on the brick entryway. As he hurried to the young man, who was clad in a white jacket and pants, Michael looked beyond him into the front hall of the nursing home. He could see two more figures on the floor. "Something's happened here!"

Jugger turned the man over. He was alive but gasping for breath. "What is it? What happened to you?"

The man opened his eyes for an instant. "Gas," he muttered. "They're all – "

Michael's hand was on the door but Jugger shouted a warning. "Don't go in there! Something bad has happened here. Tell our driver to phone for police and ambulances!"

What was to become known around the world within hours as the Starkworth Atrocity began to unfold with the arrival of the first police car and ambulance. Two officers circled the building, peering in all the ground floor windows, and came back to report that there were bodies everywhere. After that the local fire brigade was summoned and two men in rubber coats and gas masks entered the nursing home carrying gauges to measure the extent of impurities in the air. They returned almost at once and the firefighters set up a large exhaust fan in the doorway pointed towards the sky. On the opposite side of the building they smashed windows so that fresh air could enter and help dissipate the fumes.

An hour later when they reentered the nursing home they brought back the stark statistics. There were fifty-three bodies of men, women and children inside, plus two women volunteers who had been tending to the immigrants' needs. Only the male orderly had survived. In the basement of the building, near the heating ducts, two empty metal canisters had been found. When he learned of that, Colonel Jugger asked to see the canisters.

Only the firefighter, and some police officers in protective gear had been allowed into the nursing home thus far, and Michael was still standing outside with Colonel Jugger when one of them came out with the canisters. He thought the blood drained from the colonel's face at the sight of them. "They're the sort used at Auschwitz," Jugger said grimly. "Cyanide pellets are dissolved in acid to produce quick working hydrogen cyanide gas."

"I know about Auschwitz," Michael agreed. "Jews and Gypsies were gassed there routinely. Are you telling me that someone deliberately killed these people in the manner used at Nazi death camps?"

The German hung his head. "I fear that a terrible crime has been committed here."

Though he'd planned to visit other immigrant sites during his stay, it was clear to Michael that the massacre at Starkworth took precedence over all else. Michael and Jugger made arrangements to spend at least one night at a hotel a few blocks from thenursing home. It was one of a popular chain of lodgings, five stories high, with a dining room and meeting suites on the top floor affording a sweeping view of the sea.

Michael knew that whoever the killer and whatever the motive, the truth had to be uncovered quickly before the media had an opportunity to launch its own conspiracy theories. The rest of the afternoon was a blur of police questioning and phone calls from Jugger back to his superiors in Brussels. It was well after seven before they were able to avoid the press and sneak away for a light meal and ale at a nearby pub. By that time the television networks had interrupted their regular programming for coverage of what was already being called the Starkworth Atrocity.

"Fifty-five men, women and children are dead," the newsreader was reporting in an urgent yet somber tone, "and another is hospitalized in fair condition. Although autopsies are not yet complete, police believe they were victims of an attack by hydrogen cyanide gas introduced through the nursing home's heating ducts. Recent arrivals in Dover of large groups of Gypsies seeking asylum here have strained the area's resources and increased tensions, though there has been no previous act of violence against the new arrivals. Officials estimate some eight hundred European Gypsies have landed at Dover in recent weeks, and efforts are under way to provide emergency accommodations and education. Fears have been expressed in some quarters that today's atrocity might be the beginning of a terrorist campaign targeted at Gypsy immigrants."

"Do you believe that?" Michael asked Colonel Jugger.

"I'm trying not to. Terrible as it is, a single madman would be preferable to a terrorist campaign. That is, it would be preferable once he was captured and behind bars. Do you think you could help us with that?"

Michael held out his palms in a gesture of helplessness. "I know no more than you do, Colonel."

Jugger lowered his voice just a bit. "The EU office supplied me with your dossier. You have been very helpful in the past, both in local criminal investigations and in events farther afield. They have a commendation from a Captain Segar, formerly of the Romanian government militia."

"Segar is an old friend."

"I hope we can be friends too. I need any help you can give me on this, Michael." It was his first use of Michael's given name.

"Isn't it a matter for the local police or Scotland Yard?"

"The European Union has a large stake in the matter too. An unpunished terrorist act against a migrating people could encourage more such acts against Gypsies, Muslims, Jews, Irish, Africans, Asians, almost anyone! One of the goals of the EU is the free movement of goods and people between the various European states."

"Where would I begin?" Michael wondered aloud. "Everyone is dead."

"That orderly survived. He might know something."

By morning the town of Starkworth was in a frenzy. Television crews from the BBC and the independent networks were crowding the lanes with their trucks and more American and European correspondents were arriving by the hour. Teams of Scotland Yard investigators were everywhere and before Colonel Jugger and Michael had even finished their breakfast eggs they were being interviewed by a pair of dour-looking investigators from London. They told their story of finding the bodies, which was really all they knew.

"What about Mr. Isaacson?" one of the Scotland Yard men asked. His name was Inspector Drexell and he carried his excess weight with seeming ease.

"Who?" Michael questioned.

"The sole survivor. The man you found in the doorway. We need to know exactly what he said."

Jugger thought for a moment and answered. "I think it was 'Gas, they're all dead.' Isn't that what he said, Michael?"

"As I remember it."

"Nothing else?"

They both shook their heads. "His breathing was bad," Michael said. "How is he today?"

"The doctors say he's coming along fine," the inspector said. "He should be released soon."

"We need to speak with him," Jugger said. "The European union will want a full report on this."

"I'm afraid that will be impossible until after we've interviewed him."

"Have you been able to trace those canisters?" Michael asked

"I'm not at liberty to talk about that."

They departed soon afterward and Colonel Jugger spent the rest of the breakfast deep in thought. "They may be onto something. That fellow Drexell – "

They were interrupted by the sudden arrival in the hotel dining room of a tall, blonde woman. Wearing a short black leather jacket, a tight skirt that ended just above the knees and a knapsack over her shoulder, she strode purposefully across the room to their table, pale blue eyes taking in the scene. "Which of you is Michael Vlado?" she asked.

"I am," Michael acknowledged with a smile.

"Katie Blackthorn, Skywatch World Service. I'd like to interview you about the killings."

Michael must have looked blank, because Jugger had to mutter into his ear, "Television, go ahead!"

"I only know what's been on the news," he said.

"I understand you are a Gypsy king who came here specifically to meet with the victims. That's what I want to ask you about."

Michael reluctantly followed her to a secluded corner of the hotel lobby where her cameraman was waiting. "This is Dominick," she said. "He's my eyes. Dominick, I'll need about three minutes with Mr. Vlado here, maybe with that wall as a background."

"How are you?" Dominic said, shaking hands as he balanced the video camera on his shoulder. He was a husky man with dark hair and a trace of beard, wearing a rock group T-shirt. Positioning himself a few feet away, he aimed the camera. "Ready when you are, Katie."

The cameraman shot some footage as she introduced Michael to the viewers, and then she asked Michael a preliminary question about being a king of the Gypsies. "I am only king of my clan," Michael explained. "Gypsies have many clans and many kings. Because of the recent increase in Gypsy migration to Britain, I was asked by the European Union to meet with these groups and establish their true destination."

"Some say they're bound for Canada."

He nodded. "That's what I was trying to determine. Tragically, these killings occurred before we could talk."

"Do you believe it was an attempt to discourage Gypsy immigration?"

"I really don't know. Right now I'm still trying to get over the terrible shock of this atrocity."

Katie Blackthorn relaxed and allowed herself to smile. "Thank you, Mr. Vlado," she said and then after a pause, "That's it, Dominick."

Dominick stopped filming and replayed the tape for her. Michael stayed to watch and heard her cell phone beeping. She took it from her duffel bag and answered with a touch of impatience. "Blackthorn here." Apparently it was no one she knew and she seemed ready to hang up when something the caller said caught her interest. "Cubberth? How did you get my phone number?" Then, "All right. At the pier in an hour."

She broke the connection and stowed away the phone. "A fan," she told her cameraman. "The office gave him my number. Shoot some footage of the church and the town hall for atmosphere. I'll see you back at the hotel around noon."

Michael returned to the table and finished his breakfast. "That's probably the first of many interviews you'll be giving," Jugger predicted.

"She seems nice enough. I'll have to look for myself on the evening news."

"I must report in to the immigration people about this business. Do you want to come along?"

Michael shook his head. "I'd rather look around the town. I came here to speak with Gypsies and I haven't seen a live one yet."

Their waitress brought them the check. "They just said on the telly the Prince of Wales is coming this afternoon to see the place where it happened!"

"The media will love that," Colonel Jugger decided. "I understand they are even worse here than in Germany."

Michael departed, feeling he'd better get started if he wanted to see anyone before the traffic jams began. The local police were already fighting a losing battle to keep the main streets passable. He intercepted one officer and asked directions to the local caravan site. "Straight down the road to the railroad tracks, then left for about a half mile," he said. "But you won't find any Travelers there, if that's what you're looking for. They all left town. Frightened, I suppose."

Michael glanced at his watch and saw it was only ten thirty. He set off for the site, following directions. When he reached it nearly twenty minutes later the field was indeed deserted, but he saw an elderly man with a thick cane walking about with dazed look on his face. As he drew nearer, Michael could make out some intricate carvings on the cane. He had seen such cranes before, carried by older Gypsies. "Pardon me," he said. "Are you a Traveler?"

The man replied in a language Michael had never heard, and he switched to Romany, asking the question again. Still the old man talked on unintelligibly and Michael remembered Jugger's mention of a language called Shelta, spoken by some Travelers. "Shelta?" he asked.

The man's face brightened for the first time in recognition of the word. Michael tried Romany again speaking more slowly. If there were Gypsies of many tribes here they must have some way of communicating. "What is your name?" he asked the man.

"Granza," he said finally. "Where have my people gone?" His knowledge of Romany was faulty but understandable.

"You are Granza?"

A nod. "Granza Djuric. When I left yesterday the caravan was camped here."

"There has been a terrible tragedy," Michael tired to explain. "Many Gypsies newly arrived from Europe died here yesterday. Your people have fled."

Suddenly a lone horseman appeared at the other end of the field, riding toward them. He was young, in his twenties, and wore a colorful shirt that caught the wind as he rode. "Granza!" he shouted as he approached.

"See?" Michael told the old man. "You are not forgotten !"

Granza Djuric smiled. "It is Dane, my grandson."

As the rider dismounted, Michael greeted him. "Michael Vlado. I am king of a Rom tribe in the foothills of Romania. I have come here because of the immigrants."

The young man, with curly black hair and a gold tooth that was visible when he smiled, shook hands. "I am Dane Morgan. We left at dawn and I thought my grandfather was in another caravan. We only now realized he was missing and I rode back for him."

"You left because of the deaths?"

He nodded. "A terrible thing. Some people think we did it. Others believe we could be the next victims. Either way it was time to move on."

"It's important the police find whoever is responsible. Someone may be trying to keep Roms from coming here."

"We have not heard details, only that many people died."

"Fifty-five in all," Michael confirmed, "Counting two volunteers who were staying with them. Poison gas was used."

"My grandfather knows about that. He was at Auschwitz. He almost died there."

"Have you heard anything at all? Did the residents of Starkworth resent the arrival of more Gypsies?"

"Some might have, but they were only here temporarily. " He thought for a moment. "There was one man ..."

"Who?"

"His name was Cubber or Cubberth. He had a laboratory nearby and he manufactured drugs like LSD. Tried to sell us some a few weeks ago, but we sent him on his way."

Where had he heard that name before? "A laboratory?"

"So he said. To him Travelers are nothing but fortune-tellers, beggars and gamblers. He wanted money from us. And I heard him complaining about more Gypsies coming from Eastern Europe."

"Cubberth." Michael repeated the name. He remembered now. It was the person Katie Blackthorn had agreed to meet in one hour at the pier. Checking his watch again, he saw that it was a few minutes to eleven. If he hurried back he might be in time for that meeting. "Which way is the pier?" he asked Dane Morgan.

"Did you come from town?"

"From the hotel."

"There's a shorter way back to the pier." He gave Michael careful directions and then helped his grandfather up onto the horse. "We'll be camped tonight further west along the coast, near Whitstable," he said. Michael waved as they rode away.

The Starkworth pier was about a hundred feet long and seemed to be a town fishing spot. There was a narrow rocky beach on either side but nothing that would invite swimmers. Michael got there by eleven-fifteen and saw a lone fisherman out near the end wearing a braodbrimmed hat that shielded his head against the noonday sun. Another man was just stepping onto the pier. He was balding, without a hat, and seemed a bit hesitant in his movements. Finally he headed toward the fisherman at the end of the pier.

For a moment Michael wondered if the fisherman might be Katie Blackthorn disguising herself to hide from rival press people. But then he saw her come around the corner of a building walking fast toward the pier, her knapsack over one shoulder. He moved quickly after her, but was too far away to beat her onto the pier. The balding man had reached the end and was seated next to the fisherman, his back against one of the wooden posts.

Michael was still only about halfway to the end of the pier when the television reporter reached the two men. He couldn't quite see what she did because her body shielded them from Michael's view. But he saw her jump back as if stung by some unseen hornet. The broad-brimmed hat the fisherman wore had fallen to the dock and his jacket collapsed beneath it. Katie Blackthorn screamed and Michael broke into a run.

"What is it?" he called out as he reached her.

She turned to him terrified. "He's dead!"

"The fisherman?"

"There is no fisherman. It think this is a man named Cubberth."

The balding man was slumped against the wooden post, his throat torn by a jagged weapon. At his feet lay a bloody fish-scaler. Michael looked around. "I saw someone out here fishing."

"A coat and hat were propped up with this broomstick. That is what you saw."

"Then who killed him?"

"I have no idea." She squinted at him in the sunlight. "You're that Gypsy, Michael Vlado."

"That's right."

She pulled the cell phone from her duffel bag and jabbed the button for the operator. "Police! It's an emergency! There's a dead man on the Starkworth pier." Then after being connected, she repeated the information adding, "I'm a television journalist. My name is Katie Blackthorn. Yes, I'll stay right here till you arrive." She broke the connection and immediately punched in another number. "Dominick. I'm at the pier. Get down here with your camera right away !"

Within a minute they heard the sound of an approaching siren. "What are you doing here?" she asked Michael.

"I remembered Cubberth's name from when he phoned you back at the hotel. I was questioning a local Traveler just now and the name came up. I decided to join your meeting with him."

"How did his name come up?"

"I'd better wait and tell that to Inspector Drexell."

The stocky Scotland Yard man was one of the first to arrive. "Were you together when you found him?" he asked Michael and the newswoman while his assistants were examining the body.

Michael explained that he arrived at the pier just as the victim was walking out toward the end. "I knew Cubberth had an appointment with Miss Blackthorn and I guessed this might be him. She was just a few seconds behind him."

The inspector turned toward her. "Miss Blackthorn?"

"Cubberth phoned me at the hotel this morning. The station gave him my number. He claimed to have information about yesterday's killings. He said he'd meet me here at the pier."

"And what's your connection with Cubberth?" he asked Michael.

"One of the Travelers told me he has a laboratory near here. He's been making LSD and other chemicals. If he had something to tell the press it might have involved the killings."

The inspector nodded. Dominick had arrived with the video camera on his shoulder and was panning down the pier. "The body's at the end," Katie shouted. "Get down there!"

He hurried past them. "I was filming around the town hall like you said. I've got great footage for you!"

"Good. Now get me some blood and guts."

"Is that what you want Miss Blackthorn?" the inspector asked with a certain grimness. "Were fifty-five bodies not enough for you?"

"That's – that's so terrible my viewers will have trouble grasping it. A single body with his throat cut is more understandable."

"Do I need to remind you that you seem to have been alone with the victim when he died? Mr. Vlado here saw him walk out on the pier ahead of you."

"There was a fisherman at the end." She gestured toward the body and the slouched stick-figure dummy. Dominick had paused in his filming holding the camera against his striped T-Shirt while he changed the video cartridge.

"Where is he now?" Inspector Drexell asked.

They gazed into the water together and Michael could see a flatfish gliding a few feet down near the stony bottom. Katie Blackthorn didn't answer. Instead she said, "I went to the hospital this morning to see that injured orderly, Isaacson. He wasn't there. He'd been released."

Drexell nodded. "They kept him overnight but his lungs seemed all right. Having his head out the door saved his life."

"I need to interview him."

"Before either of you leave, I want the name of that Traveler, Mr. Vlado."

"Dane Morgan. He's with his grandfather, an old man named Granza Djuric. They may have already left Starkworth."

"We'll find him."

Drexell started to turn away but Katie reminded him, "What about

Isaacson? Where is he now?"

"At the command post we've set up on the top floor of the hotel. I believe Colonel Jugger is questioning him on behalf of the European Union."

She shouted out to her cameraman. "Keep filming. I'll meet you back at the hotel." An ambulance crew had arrived to remove the body when the police finished. At the shore end of the pier uniformed police were keeping back the crowd.

They reached the hotel a little before noon. Without Drexell along, Michael doubted they'd be allowed to interview the massacre's sole survivor, but Colonel Jugger arranged that. "He knows nothing, really, but you're welcome to do an interview if he's willing."

Carl Isaacson was seated in a chair in one of the top floor meeting rooms. His breathing was still a little raspy but he showed a vast improvement over the previous day. "You're the one who was with Colonel Jugger yesterday," he said rising to shake Michael's hand. "I don't know how I survived that terrible thing."

Katie Blackthorn immediately took over the interview. "What was it like in there when the gas started seeping through the ducts? Did you know what was happening?"

"Not at first. I heard some of the Gypsies starting to cough and choke. Then I saw Mrs. Withers, one of the volunteers, collapse on the floor. That's when I realized something was wrong. I ran to call for help and collapsed in the doorway."

"Do you have any idea who might have done this?"

"It had to be a terrorist," Isaacson told them. "Or a madman. It doesn't make much difference, does it?"

Someone turned on a television set and they saw the turmoil on the road north of town. The motorcade carrying the Prince of Wales was approaching with television crews jockeying for the best positions.

"He'll come to the nursing home," Katie decided. "That's where it happened." She called Dominick again on her cell phone and told him to get there with his camera. Jugger hurried outside to join the welcoming committee.

When Dominick arrived he handed her the tapes he'd shot in the town square and at the pier, then hurried out to join the others. "Do you have to get these tapes back to London?" Michael asked. "The world of television crews was a long way from his farm in Romania.

"No, no. We transmit them by satellite from our news van directly to the studio. Whatever they're shooting now will be on the evening news and I'll do a live commentary to accompany it."

Before he could say anything else, a line of black Rolls Royce limousines came into view. Bodyguards jumped out first, crowding around the central vehicle in the motorcade. Michael caught a glimpse of Colonel Jugger shaking the prince's hand as the cameras rolled.

"I'd better get out there," Katie said.

He stayed watching at the hotel window as the official party went down the street to the nursing home and stood before the building for more pictures. The entire visit meant very little from a practical point of view, but Michael was nevertheless grateful that the nation was officially acknowledging the enormity of the crime. Starkworth and what happened here would be remembered.

It was later in the afternoon, when the prince had completed his visit, that Inspector Drexell returned. Michael knew he was back as soon as Dane Morgan entered the hotel accompanied by his grandfather. "So you found them," he said to Drexel.

"It wasn't difficult," the Scotland Yard man told him. "You get to know the ways of these Travelers after a time."

"Have you arrested them?"

"Dane Morgan is assisting with our inquiries."

"I've done nothing wrong," young Morgan insisted. "And neither has my grandfather. Why would we kill our own people?"

"Because they weren't your people," the inspector pointed out. "They were Gypsies from Eastern Europe coming to take over the land that had always been yours."

"Not quite. My grandfather came from the same area sixty years ago."

There was more activity in the command post as several of the inspector's men returned from another mission. He stepped out briefly to speak with them and then returned with Colonel Jugger trailing behind. "Where is Miss Blackthorn?" he asked glancing around.

"Out in the news van reviewing the tapes she's transmitting to London," Michael told him.

"Good! This isn't ready for the press yet." He led Michael and the colonel aside, out of earshot of Dane and his grandfather. "London is demanding fast action and I think we have something. This fellow Cubberth, the one who was killed on the pier this morning – my men searched his house and found a small laboratory, just as Dane Morgan said. There were containers full of cyanide pellets and acid, just like the ones used at the nursing home. Cubberth's our man. He may have cut his own throat on the pier this morning."

"Then how would you explain the coat and hat on the stick? And why would he ask Katie to meet him if he was going to kill himself without making some sort of statement first?"

"What do you think happened?" Drexell asked, obviously anxious for some sort of quick resolution to the case. "Do you think she's involved?"

"I don't know. I think Cubberth supplied the chemicals to someone and that person used them. Then Cubberth was killed so he wouldn't talk to the press. Once he saw what had happened with his chemicals, he wanted a way out for himself."

More news was coming in and Drexell hurried off in answer to a summons. Michael went downstairs in search of Katie's news van. The street between the hotel and the nursing home seemed to have grown a stand of trees during the day. Five vans were parked in a row. Their transmitting towers had been raised toward the heavens, seeking out satellites that would carry their pictures to London and beyond.

He found Katie Blackthorn's van and peered inside. "Come in," she told him. "I've had great news. We're providing the feed for one of the big American networks!"

"Sounds good. What does it mean?"

"I'll be on the telly in America on their evening news. Here, look at this tape! The segment started with a close up of Katie setting the scene. Then it cut to the center of the town and the bell tower of the town hall. "He has some great footage here. Watch this." At the stroke of noon, as the bells started ringing, a flock of birds took off from the tower, spiraling skyward. Then the scene shifted back to Katie standing in front of the old nursing home. "That idyllic scene was shattered yesterday by an event that is already being dubbed the Starkworth Atrocity – the death by poison gas of fifty-three Gypsy immigrants and two volunteer aides." She went on to run through the day's events including the unsolved murder of a local resident on the town's pier. There was a tape of the police at the pier and Cubberth's body being removed. Then there was the arrival of the Prince of Wales with footage of his remarks.

"This is the short version for America," she explained. "It runs fifty seconds which is all they can use. My London station will use lots more, of course. They'll pick up a live feed from me in an hour." The thing had become a media event. It w as a matter of airtime rather than the deaths of all those people.

Her cameraman opened the door and called to Katie. "Something's up! The inspector just came back again with some others. They were moving fast."

She flipped off the switch on her video monitor. "Let's go."

Michael followed along as she broke into a run, followed by Dominick and his camera. There did seem to be some unusual activity at the hotel, and when they reached the elevator a Scotland Yard man with a clipboard blocked their paths. "Sorry, only authorized personnel allowed on the top floor. The dining room is closed this evening."

"I'm Michael Vlado with Colonel Jugger."

"Katie Blackthorn, and this is my cameraman, Dominick Withers. We're both on your list."

The man smiled slightly. "Not on this list. No press allowed. You can go up Mr. Vlado."

"Michael!" she called after him. "I'll wait for you in the bar !"

The elevator doors closed on him and he was whisked to the fifth floor. He entered the familiar conference rooms being used by the Scotland Yard investigators. Colonel Jugger and Inspector Drexell were seated across the desk from each other. "Michael my friend," Jugger began.

"What's happened? What's going on?"

"We have a serious situation here," Drexell announced. "Some important information has reached us regarding a possible new suspect."

"Do you mean the Traveler, Dane Morgan?"

"No, I mean Colonel Jugger."

The shock went through Michael like an electric current. "That's impossible! We were together every minute of the journey. At the time of the killings we would have been still in France or just starting through your Chunnel."

"Please hear me out," the inspector said. "The facts we have uncovered are quite shocking. Colonel Jugger was born in Germany during the final days of World War Two. After the war his father was tried as a war criminal. The charges against him involved the gassing of hundreds of Gypsies at Auschwitz. He was convicted and given a life sentence, later commuted for health reasons. He was released from prison in nineteen seventy-one and died one year later. Is that correct Colonel?"

"It is correct," Jugger answered in a subdued voice. "Are the sins of the fathers to be visited on their sons?"

"After what happened to your father you may have nursed a growing hatred for Gypsies."

"On the contrary, I have devoted my life to erasing my father's terrible crime."

"But that crime was committed with the same weapon we see here at Starkworth. It seems like more than a coincidence."

Michael had to interrupt. "How could he have been in two places at once Inspector? I told you – "

"I think we're agreed that Cubberth prepared the necessary chemicals at the urging, or in the employ, of someone else. Otherwise there'd be no reason for silencing him. Suppose we take that a step further. Perhaps he was paid to supply the chemicals and use them on the Gypsies at the nursing home. If Colonel Jugger paid him and arrived after the killings, he was truly above suspicion."

"If, if!" Michael hit the desk with his fist. "You have no proof for any of this!"

"We have the physical evidence from Cubberth's house. With a bit more searching I think we'll turn up the name of the person who hired him."

It was a corner conference room and Michael walked to the wide window to stare out at the rolling sea, his mind in turmoil. Then, in the other direction, he could see dusk beginning to gather at the center of Starkworth. It was late now and there were no birds visible on the town-hall bell tower.

Michael turned and walked back to the table. "Get the press up here and I'll tell you who killed them all – the fifty five people and Mr. Cubberth. I'll tell you why too."

Inspector Drexell resisted at first. It was obvious he was not about to release information to the press until he knew what it was. Finally Michael went off in a corner with him and talked for twenty minutes. Drexell sighed and stood up. "All right," he agreed. "We'll try it."

Within a half-hour the upstairs conference room was crowded with journalists and video cameras. By this time a shroud of darkness was draped over Starkworth and the windows toward the sea showed only the room's reflected lights.

Drexell stepped to the battery of microphones. "I'm please to introduce Mr. Michael Vlado, a representative of the European Union, who was present with Colonel Jugger when the atrocity was discovered yesterday afternoon. Mr. Vlado has been working closely with Scotland Yard on its investigation and has provided a theory involving the person responsible for this terrible crime. I'll let Mr. Vlado explain it in his own words."

Michael stepped to the microphones, glancing toward Katie Blackthorn in the first row of journalists. Colonel Jugger had gathered some of the others connected with the case too, and was just ushering Dane Morgan and his grandfather Granza into the room. One of the officers had brought Carl Isaacson, the tragedy's sole survivor,up to the room too.

"Ladies and gentlemen of the press, you must excuse my English, which is not always perfect," Michael told them. "I come from a remote farming village in Romania, and I have a deep and abiding interest in truth, justice and brotherhood. I am myself a Gypsy and king of my small tribe but I have worked with the Romanian police and others in solving a number of crimes in the past. When I came here yesterday with Colonel Jugger to examine the problem of Gypsy immigrants, I never imagined I would find the horror that awaited us at the nursing home."

Katie raised her hand with a question, but Michael said the time for questions would come later. "We all have questions, and perhaps the greatest now is how anyone could commit such a terrible crime. It is reminiscent of the worst atrocities of the Second World war when Jews and Gypsies at Auschwitz were gassed in this manner. That was our first question. Was this the work of a terrorist or a madman?

"A madman needs no rational motive, while for a terrorist the killings could have been a way of discouraging other Gypsy immigrants said to be on their way here.

"From my viewpoint, the first break in this case came earlier today when a local man named Cubberth was murdered on the town pier. I'd learned earlier that Cubberth was making LSD and other chemicals at a laboratory in his home, selling these things to local Travelers and others. Inspector Drexell's men found evidence at Cubberth's house that he had put together the chemicals responsible for the deaths of these fifty-five people. The killer had no doubt paid him to do it."

This time Katie couldn't be silenced, "How did you know Cubberth wasn't the killer himself?" she called out.

Michael sighed and answered. "Because he called you to arrange a meeting at the pier this morning. What was he going to tell you? That he'd killed all those people? More likely he was going to supply knowledge of the crime and the person behind it. This was confirmed to some extent when Cubberth himself was murdered at the end of the pier as you came to meet him."

"But what happened to the killer?"

"His disappearance is really quite simple. The prop coat and hat shielded him from view. Cubberth walked out there, thinking it might be you seated there. The killer slit his throat and then simply slipped off the end of the pier into the water as you walked toward him. I noticed he water was only a few feet deep, and the killer simply walked back to shore beneath the pier. Your eyes were on Cubberth and that dummy coat and hat, and you never saw him. The same was true of me, as I followed you out there. The killer made his escape, but this murder provided the first clue I needed to his identity."

"He left no clues," Katie argued. It had become a dialogue between the two of them recorded by the world's press.

"Think back. How did the killer know Cubberth would be at the pier? Cubberth would hardly have told him, and I saw Cubberth myself walking onto the pier. The killer was already in place at the end so he hadn't followed his victim there. No, the killer must have known of the proposed meeting in advance. I was present when Cubberth called you after breakfast on your cell phone, just as you finished interviewing me. You didn't tell me what it was about, but you mentioned Cubberth's name and the time and place of the meeting. That was all the killer needed to hear."

"But no one else was there," she argued." There were just the two of us."

Michael shook his head. "There was one other person. Your cameraman, Dominick."

As Michael uttered the words, Dominick stopped filming and dropped his camera. Every eye in the room was suddenly on him. "This is madness!" he rasped out angrily.

"Is it? The killer would have been soaking wet after wading ashore beneath that pier. You were wearing a rock group T-shirt at breakfast but when Katie summoned you to the pier later to film the murder scene you'd changed to a striped T-shirt."

He moistened his lips and moved forward a few steps. Behind him Katie Blackthorn knelt silently to retrieve his camera. She hoisted it to her shoulder and started filming. "I wasn't at the pier till after she called," Dominick said. "I was in the square shooting footage of the town-hall tower. You can look at the tape."

"I did," Michael told him. "You shot it exactly at noon with a flight of birds frightened by the tolling bells. A fine picture, but it proves you were there almost an hour after the murder, not while Cubberth was being killed."

His face had gone white and Inspector Drexell started toward him. "Why would I do such an insane thing?" he asked as if he couldn't quite understand it himself.

"I can't explain exactly," Michael said. "But it wasn't the Gypsies, was it? They were only a cover for your true motive, the sort of motive that might make some men blow up an airliner to kill just one person on it. A little while ago, when the officer stopped us at the door, Katie gave your name as Dominick Withers. One of the volunteers killed by the gas was a Mrs. Withers. Who was she? Your wife or ex-wife perhaps ?"

It was one revelation too many for him. Before Drexell or the others could move, he uttered a long scream and launched himself at the window overlooking the sea.

Katie Blackthorn caught it all on videotape, but in the end her station decided it would have been in bad taste to show the suicide of a station employee on the evening news. She went back to London the following morning and Colonel Jugger came to meet Michael for breakfast.

"It was his mother, not his ex-wife," he told Michael. "I suppose we'll never know any more than that. He lived in Maidstone, halfway to London, so it was easy for him to drive down here in a half hour and set off Cubberth's gas at the nursing home."

"What now?" Michael asked, thinking about Katie Blackthorn.

"There's another boatload of Gypsies crossing the channel. They land at Dover in less than an hour."

Michael finished his coffee. "Let's go."

A WALL TOO HIGH

"I understand you are a Gypsy king," the uniformed man addressed Michael Vlado, not without an edge of contempt in his voice. He was seated across the desk in an unadorned office fifty kilometers north of Prague. It was a sunny afternoon in early autumn, and Michael would rather have been back in the village with his wife and their horses.

He smiled, trying to cooperate with his inquisitor. "I am only a king to my people back in Romania. Here in the Czech Republic I am merely a tourist."

The man, taller than Michael, had slicked-back hair and a tiny black mustache. He said his name was Lieutenant Lyrik and he spoke German after learning that Michael's knowledge of the Czech language was limited. "More than a tourist. Our police computer lists you as a trouble-maker, an agent provocateur."

"Hardly that Lieutenant! I have not traveled this distance to incite anyone to anything. As you must have guessed, I've come about the wall." The European Roma Rights center in Budapest has commissioned me to act on its behalf to request that the wall separating the Roma section of town from the rest be torn down at once."

"What you refer to as a wall on Masarak Street is no more than a fence."

Michael had dealt with this type of official before. It was never pleasant. "A seven foot high fence made of concrete?"

Lyrik shrugged. "There is a similar structure in Ústí nad Labem and that is called a fence too. You must realize that these Gypsies are criminals, beggars, thieves and fortunetellers squatting in decrepit apartment buildings, usually without paying rent. Can we do nothing to protect the decent neighbors who live just across the street?"

Michael Vlado was growing impatient with this man. He had traveled from his village to do some good, not to hear a diatribe against the Roms. "You must know that seventy percent of Gypsy children in this country are shunted off to special schools for the mentally retarded. In many cases, their parents have been fired from their jobs, beaten and killed. The police do nothing."

"What do you want?" the lieutenant asked. "Why have you been sent here?"

"The Roma Rights Center wants the walls here and in Ústí nad Labem torn down. They want the Gypsies free from segregation and persecution."

"This is strictly a local matter. You have no authority here." After a moment's thought he stood up. "But we do not wish to seem uncooperative. Let me speak to my superior."

Left alone, Michael let his eyes wander over the slate gray walls and the framed photograph of the country's president, Vaclav Havel. The single window offered a view of the parking lot, and he noticed a uniformed officer checking his license plate and peering into the car. He wondered if they'd ask his permission to search it.

Presently Lieutenant Lyrik returned. He resumed his seat behind the desk and smiled. "I have been given permission to take you to the Gypsy quarter and show you the fence."

"Very good. That's what I wanted."

Michael followed along to the officer's car where the man who'd been inspecting his vehicle joined them. "This is Sergeant Cista. He will accompany us," the lieutenant said. Cista was a grim sort who shook hands and then rested his palm on the holster flap of his pistol. Michael was given the front passenger seat and he was well aware that Cista was seated directly behind him with the weapon.

The small city's commercial and shopping district covered only a half-dozen blocks and within minutes they'd reached an area of decrepit apartment buildings, two stories in height. He saw at once that a solid concrete wall had been erected down the center of the wide street, effectively separating the apartment block from the two-family homes on the other side. As Lyrik started down the better side of the avenue, Michael said, "I'd like to visit the Roma side first."

"Very well." The lieutenant backed out, made a sharp turn, and then proceeded past the Gypsy apartments. Behind him Michael heard the snap as Sergeant Cista opened the flap on his holster.

Some of the Gypsy women were on the sidewalk clustered in small groups. One older woman in a colorful skirt spit at the police car as it went by. Further along there were a few men and boys, too, shouting their defiance at the wall. "Can you stop?" Michael asked. "I wish to speak with them."

"That's not allowed," was the answer.

"What about that woman?" He indicated a fair-skinned redhead in her thirties. "Surely she's not a Roma."

"Mrs. Autumn," Cista muttered from behind him.

"Is that her name?"

Lyrik snorted, "She is sent by an Irish relief agency to work with the Gypsies. We call her that because she comes every autumn."

"I'd like to meet her."

Lyrik dismissed the suggestion. "She's an agitator." They pulled around the end of the wall and started down the other side. "As you can see this is no Berlin wall. Your Gypsies need merely to walk around it. But it does offer the neighbors some respite from their noise and rubbish."

He stopped the car and they got out. The wall rose higher than Michael's head, probably seven feet. As they approached it, Lyrik explained that it was constructed of cinder blocks with cement facing. Michael wondered how long it would be before graffiti began to appear on it.

Sergeant Cista had remained behind them near the car while Lyrik and Michael walked up to the wall. "Perhaps the noise and garbage you fear so much would be less if the children were not denied a proper education," Michael told the lieutenant, reaching out to touch the rough concrete of the wall.

Lyrik opened his mouth as if to reply when a sudden sound like the crack of a rifle reached them from the distance. Lieutenant Lyrik gasped and his right hand flew to his face. He sank to his knees and toppled forward into the wall. Michael could see blood on the pavement even before Sergeant Cista ran up and turned him over.

There was a bloody wound over Lyrik's right eye. Michael had no doubt that the shot had killed him instantly.

Cista's hand came up from his holster holding the pistol he'd been so anxious to draw. "Back up," he ordered Michael.

"I didn't kill him. I have no weapon." Not knowing how well the sergeant understood him, he raised his hands above his head.

Cista unhooked the cell phone from Lyrik's belt and called for help. Already a few neighbors had ventured forth from the two-family homes that lined the street on this side of the wall. "I heard the shot," one man said. "The Gypsies killed him!"

Michael was kept well away from the body as an ambulance and police car arrived on the scene. The body was quickly removed as the gathering crowd increased in size and Cista escorted a police officer over to where Michael waited. "I am Captain Mulheim," the officer said briskly. "Do you wish to make a statement?" He was older and stouter than Lyrik had been, perhaps reflecting his higher rank.

"I have no statement to make. I'm sure you are aware that I came at the request of the European Roma Rights Center. Lieutenant Lyrik was showing me your wall when he was shot."

"By a bullet from the Gypsy side of the wall."

"We don't know that." Michael insisted. "I heard the shot but couldn't tell its direction."

The police captain glowered. "You will accompany me to headquarters while we check your story," he said, making it clear there was no room for negotiation.

Michael Vlado sat on a hard wooden bench for two hours outside Captain Mulheim's office. Finally, at five o'clock, he was summoned inside. "Your story checks out," the captain told him. "I also have the medical examiner's report. The fatal bullet passed through Lieutenant Lyrik's head and was not recovered, but it came from a high-powered rifle some distance away, probably equipped with a telescopic sight. An hour from now, at six o'clock, I am going on television to issue an ultimatum. If the killer of Lieutenant Lyrik does not surrender within twenty-four hours, the police and militia will clear all Gypsies from the apartments on Masarak Street. The message will also be broadcast by loudspeakers on the street."

"You can't do that," Michael said, trying to keep his voice under control.

"Can't?" The Captain smiled. "You seem to forget that I am the law in this city. I have full authority in all criminal matters."

"Let me speak to the Rom. Let me get to the bottom of this."

"Certainly," Captain Mulheim said, getting to his feet. "You have twenty-four hours to deliver the murderer."

Michael left police headquarters and walked back several blocks through the decrepit city. To his eye, the area being protected from a Rom incursion was little better than the Gypsy section itself. The wall was not a matter of economics but rather of fear. As he passed the wall itself he could still see the stain of Lyrik's blood on the pavement where he'd fallen. Michael rounded the end of the wall and walked up to the first house. It was a two-story apartment like the others, although a broken front window on the second floor told him that apartment was probably unoccupied. From downstairs came the sound of off-key music, perhaps played on an accordian.

A young woman wearing a full red skirt came to the door, frowning at him. She had the dark features of a Gypsy though her manner almost suggested a Western upbringing. "Are you police?" she asked immediately. "They have already questioned us about the shooting."

"My name is Michael Vlado," he told her. "I have been sent by the European Roma Rights Center in Budapest. It's about the wall."

"You are Rom?"

"Yes."

"Come in," she said reluctantly, stepping aside. The outlines of her long legs were visible against the thin fabric of the skirt.

The music grew louder as he entered a small, neat living room. He saw at once that it was coming from two boys about nine or ten years old. The younger was playing a small violin while the other had an accordion. It was little more than a toy but he was coaxing passable music from it.

"These are your sons?"

"Yes."

"Your husband?"

"He is at work." She brushed the dark hair back from her face, then added, "I am Rosetta. My sons are Erik and Josef." She signaled to the boys. "Go practice in your room."

They disappeared through the kitchen. Michael sat down on the nearest chair. "They play well for children."

"Gypsies love music, but you must know that. They say a violin in the hands of a Gypsy produces purer and more passionate sounds than for anyone else."

"That is true," Michael agreed. Then, "I have disturbing news. The police captain, Mulheim, is threatening to clear this entire block if the killer of Lieutenant Lyrik does not surrender within twenty-four hours."

"Of course!" She showed a flash of anger. "We are easy people to blame for any crime. He sent you to tell us this?"

"No. You will learn it soon enough." Already far in the distance, he could hear the blare of an approaching sound truck, its message not yet clear. He glanced toward the ceiling, where the sound of the children's music had resumed. "Does someone live upstairs?"

Rosetta shook her head. "It's empty. The children play there and practice their music."

"Josef shows great promise for his age. Is he around ten?"

"He is twelve. I know he looks younger. Sometimes we cannot afford the food a growing boy needs. His father beats him if he catches him begging in the streets with the other Rom children. He wants to support us through his own work, but that is not always possible."

"Do the police bother you?"

"All the time," she acknowledged. "But we are used to it. My husband says it is the price we must pay for living in the city."

"How many of you are living here?"

"About seventy. There were more, but the police harassment has driven many away. That is their goal, of course."

The sound truck was on the street now, blaring its message for all to hear.

Captain Mulheim had seen to it that the announcement was read in Czech, followed by a translation into Rom. Michael lifted the curtain on the front window and looked down the street. A few men and some women had come out of the apartments and were gathering in small groups. "I'd better go out there," he told her. "I may see you again later."

The Irish woman that Lyrik had pointed out to him had emerged from one of the houses and was pleading with the Rom to remain calm. One man, taller and bulkier than the rest, already held a slender dagger in his hand. "I am calm until they drive me from my home," he told anyone who would listen. "Then I am angry."

Others clustered around and when there was an opportunity Michael spoke to the Irish woman and introduced herself. "I'm glad they've sent someone," she told him. "I can't handle this alone." Up close he judged her age to be around forty, but the long red hair had given her a younger appearance when he saw her from the patrol car.

"The police call you Mrs. Autumn," he said.

"They usually call me worse than that. My name is Mary Baxter. Come inside where we can talk."

"Do you live here?"

"I stay in one of the empty apartments when I come each year."

"Is this a fairly stable Rom community?"Michael asked, following her up the steps to one of the apartments. The inside walls were greasy from years of cooking. Peeling paint hung from the ceiling.

She shrugged. "Some Gypsies were meant to wander. I do believe it is in their blood."

"My wife and I have lived in the same Romanian town for more than fifteen years. W e have a farm where we raise horses."

"Ah, but you're here now, aren't you?" Mary Baxter said. "I imagine this position with the Roma Rights Center keeps you away from home much of the time. It is your own form of wandering."

"It is a new thing for me. But I admit to being away frequently. Perhaps you are right. But I'm interested in this particular community. Is there anyone you know who resents the wall enough to shoot a police officer over it?"

"Many."

He gestured out the window toward the man with the dagger. "That one?"

"His name is Mathias. He is their protector and he takes the job seriously."

"Might he have killed the lieutenant?"

Mary Baxter shook her head. "That dagger is his weapon. I have never seen anyone on the block with a firearm."

He motioned toward the peeling paint. "This place needs work. The house at the end of the block is in much better shape."

"Rosetta Lacko. She has a husband and two fine children. They're not all that lucky. But I hope to find time to paint these walls while I'm here."

"Who lives upstairs?"

"Mathias."

"The one with the knife?"

"He doesn't worry me. Next year it'll be someone else."

"Why do you keep coming back?" Michael asked.

"Because the job is never finished, is it?"

"No," he agreed.

Mary Baxter prepared something for them to eat, and they talked into the evening hours. "Michael is an unusual name for a Rom," She observed.

"Not in Romania. I was named for their last king, deposed by the Communists after the war and still living in exile. We were ruled with an iron fist until recently."

"Sometimes I wish for a strong president here to keep the local police under control."

"I thought Vaclav Havel was a strong leader. He's highly regarded in other countries. Can't he control them?"

She shook her head. "Havel has lost much of his popularity with the Czech people. He seems to do nothing toward helping the Gypsies."

The conversation shifted to the murder of Lieutenant Lyrik, and who might have fired the fatal shot. "There aren't a great many men on the street," Michael observed. "Is there a tribal king?"

"The last one moved away. Rosetta's husband Bruno will probably replace him."

"Where does he work?"

"He has a booth at the fun fair on the outskirts of the city, one of those where you hit the target and win trinkets or stuffed animals. He should be home soon."

Michael glanced at his watch. "I must be going. I hadn't realized it was so late."

"Where will you stay?"

He smiled. "The Roma Rights Center arranged for a hotel room. I have two beds if you'd care to sleep in comfort for one night."

She smiled and shook her head. "It's a kind offer, but my place is here."

"When does Mathias return with his dagger?"

"When he's so drunk I have to help him upstairs to his bed."

"Before I leave, could you show me the upstairs apartment? The side facing the wall?"

"Follow me."

She snapped on the stairway light and led him up to Mathias's place. The door was unlocked and as they entered Michael could smell the odor of beer and stale tobacco smoke. He stood at the window for a moment, trying to gauge the angle down to the wall in the center of Masarak Street. "I need more light," he decided. "Could I return in the morning?"

"Certainly. It may be our last day here if the police drive us out."

"You don't think Lyrik's killer will confess?"

"Whoever did it, he is not a Gypsy. He is not here."

Michael looked again at his watch. "I really must leave. I'll be back in the morning."

She saw him to the door and he headed down the street the way he had come, nodding to some of the Gypsy families lounging in front of their apartments. Though it was after nine o'clock, Rosetta's children were still practicing on their instruments and she was seated on the front steps. As he stopped to say hello, a well-built man with glasses and a moustache loomed up beside her. "Bruno," she said, "this is the man from the Roma Rights Center that I told you about."

"Bruno Lacko," he said, extending his hand to Michael. "Rosetta tells me you've come to help."

"If I can. Mary – Mrs. Autumn – tells me you're in charge here."

"When I can be. I work long hours for my family."

"What is the feeling among your people? Might one of them have killed Lieutenant Lyrik?"

"In a fair fight certainly. No one on this block would have fired a rifle at him. No one owns a rifle that I am aware of."

Michael nodded. "I'd like to return tomorrow and take some measurements from your upstairs window to the wall. Would that be all right?"

"Certainly, so long as you make it before the police deadline. We don't know what will happen then."

Michael slept well in the strange bed and ate breakfast at the hotel. As he retraced his route to Masarak Street he was aware of the police cars slowly circling the blocks. One of them came to a stop at a corner, blocking his route across a street. The window rolled down and Captain Mulheim peered out.

"I did not expect you to be here still, Gypsy. At six this evening Masarak Street will not be a safe place."

"I'm hoping I can help settle this matter before your deadline. Would it be possible for me to examine the lieutenant's body?"

Mulheim shoot his head. "It was cremated this morning. He had no wife or close relatives."

"Captain, I ask that you consult with me before moving against those Gypsies."

"I can make no promises," he said, and the car window slid silently shut.

Michael continued on his way, aware that he was never out of sight of at least one patrol car. He entered Masarak Street from the other end, but the street showed little difference when approached from that direction. The first adult he saw was Mary Baxter, directing children into a small van that he guessed must function as a school bus.

"You've come back," she said.

"Of course. Are these children schooled by the state?"

"Not so they learn anything. I've managed to enroll them in a private school for half days. We have to provide our own transportation, but it's better than nothing."

Once the van pulled away from the curb, crowded to overflowing, she relaxed with a sigh. "I don't want them here this evening, in case there is violence. No one knows how serious the police are about evicting us."

"They're serious," he said following her into the apartment. "If they are driven out, will you return to Ireland?"

"Not until Christmas, whatever happens. My husband – "

"Then there is a Mr. Autumn?"

She laughed. "Yes, there is. He teaches the autumn semester each year at Trinity College."

Michael stood by the front window, staring at the wall again. "Would you happen to have a ball of string or twine?"

"I think there's one in the kitchen. I'll get it."

She returned with it and they went upstairs together. "Is Mathias still here?" he asked quietly.

She nodded. "He came in late and drunk as usual. He'll still be sleeping."

He followed her inside and opened the parlor window. They were just about opposite the spot where Lyrik had been shot. Hefting the ball of twine about the size of his fist, he said, "I'll see how my pitching arm is." Holding one end, he threw the ball out the window, aiming for the other side of the wall. Leaving a trail of twine as it unwound, the ball just cleared the seven foot wall.

"What's all this?" a voice growled behind them.

It was Mathias, wearing a dirty nightshirt, his tall hulk filling the bedroom doorway. He had the dagger in his hand, as if facing some threatening intruder, but Mary quickly disarmed him. "You met Michael yesterday, Mathias," she reminded him. "He is trying to find out who killed the police officer."

He grumbled something but returned to his bedroom. "Here," Michael said, handing the end of the twine to Mary. "Hold this while I go around to the other side of the wall."

He then hurried downstairs and circled the end of the wall to the other side. About halfway along he found the ball of twine much reduced in size. He pulled it taut so that it just cleared the top of the seven foot wall. If the fatal shot had been fired from Mathias's apartment or any of the other second-floor rooms in mid block, this was the path it would have taken. Michael had been standing right next to the victim and he remembered holding out his hand to touch the wall. They'd been thirty inches away from that wall, probably a bit less.

But that close to the wall, the fatal shot would have passed nearly a foot over their heads. Any lower and it wouldn't have cleared the wall at all. It was a simple matter of geometry. The wall was too high.

Michael backed up until he could see Mary Baxter in the apartment window holding the end of the twine. He knew a high-powered rifle can be accurate at a distance of a mile or more, but there were no taller buildings even at that distance. There was nothing but sky, gray with the threat of approaching rain.

He tried reexamining the facts. There'd been the sound of a distant rifle shot and Lieutenant Lyrik had fallen dead. The fatal bullet could not have come from in front of him because of the height of the wall, but Sergeant Cista was behind them. Could he have killed his superior with a pistol shot?

No, because Lyrik was facing the wall at the time. There'd been no blood on the back of his head, only on the front, where he'd been hit over the right eye. Michael turned to the right, looking over the wall at the last house. It had been the first house when he entered the street the previous day, Rosetta and Bruno Lacko's apartment with its empty second floor.

He tossed the ball of twine over the wall and walked around to retrieve it. "Drop the end," he called up to Mary. "I want to try it again down the block at Rosetta's place."

The children were at school but Michael found Rosetta hanging out the wash. Bruno was in the small kitchen, preparing to go off to his job at the fun fair. "What will you do with that ball of twine?" the man asked.

"I'm trying to determine where the fatal shot might have come from. I ran a line from Mary Baxter's second floor over the top of the wall where Lyrik was standing. Now I want to try it from here."

Bruno Lacko nodded. "I must go," he called to his wife. "I will return before five."

Rosetta came in with her wash basket. "He doesn't want me alone if Captain Mulheim makes good on his threat."

"He cares about you," Michael said.

"He cares about all of us. Too much, I fear. If the police come as they threaten, Bruno will be standing in front o them, blocking their path. I worry about what will happen then."

Upstairs, in the empty apartment, he opened the window next to the broken one and hurled his ball of twine again, aiming down the street toward the center of the wall. This time his aim was a bit short. It hit the wall and came down on their side. "I'll go get it and throw it over," Rosetta said. "Stay here and hold the end. You can tell me where to put it."

He agreed and stood by the window with the end held firmly in hand. Out in the street, Rosetta hurried to pick up the end and then flipped it over the wall. He saw at once that she had not thrown it far enough along for a proper measurement and he sought out a way to help her. The end of the twine could be tied to something in the empty apartment and he could join her at the wall. But what?

He opened a closet door, thinking that even a clothes hook might serve as an anchor and that was when he found it. A rifle standing in the corner.

Rosetta watched him approach her with a grim expression written on his face. "I tied the twine to a hook in the closet," he told her. "I found something there."

"What do you mean?"

"A rifle. Is it your husband's?"

She shook her head, confused. "Bruno never goes up there. Only the boys use it, for their practice."

"Could one of them, Josef perhaps, have fired the rifle? Is that how the window was broken?"

"That window was broken by a rock hurled by one of the boys across the street before they put up the wall to protect them from us." She handed him the end of the twine. "Do your measurements. Tell me if a bullet from our rifle could have killed Lieutenant Lyrik."

He strode further down the wall but he saw at once that in order to clear the top a bullet would still have passed well above Lyrik's head. "No," he told her. "The fatal shot couldn't have come from over the wall. But it also couldn't have come from any other direction. Are you sure one of your boys couldn't have –"

"Come with me, Michael Vlado!" She walked quickly around the wall with long strides that he had difficulty matching. They climbed the stairs to the empty apartment. "Now show me this rifle."

He went to the closet and lifted it gently from the corner. She took it from him, her concern vanishing, pointed it at the ceiling and pulled the trigger. Nothing happened. "My boys would have difficulty shooting anyone with this. It's an air rifle from Bruno's fun-fair booth. He brought it home for them months ago because it was broken and not worth fixing."

"I'm sorry," Michael told her. "I don't usually jump to conclusions like that."

Her mood turned somber again. "We are only a few hours from the police deadline. What will happen then?"

"Perhaps someone will come forward and confess."

She shook her head. "How is that possible? No one is guilty."

"That's true," he agreed, and left her standing alone in the empty apartment with a promise to return.

The rain had started by the time he reached the street, not the hard driving sort that autumn sometimes brought to his home in the foothills of the Carpathians but a misty sweeping shower that warned of worse to come. He bundled his jacket around him and saw at the opposite end of block the sudden appearance of a police armored vehicle. Go away, he wanted to yell as if confronting the angel of death. It's not yet time! But instead he hurried along in the opposite direction.

It was the sight of Sergeant Cista parked in a police car across from his hotel that told Michael what he must do. The officer had obviously been assigned to keep track of him and Michael made certain he was seen entering the place. Then he retrieved the raincoat from his luggage and left the hotel by a rear door. He came up to the police car from the rear and was into the front passenger seat before Cista knew what was happening.

"What are you doing?"

"You should keep your doors locked, Sergeant. I want to talk to you."

Cista squirmed about, trying to reach his holstered weapon but Michael laid a hand on it first, yanking it free. "You don't need this. I only want to talk."

"I'm just following orders. I have nothing against the Gypsies."

"I know what happened at the wall yesterday."

"I don't know what you mean."

"Lyrik was standing too close to the wall to have been hit by a bullet from one of the Gypsy apartments. I know because I took measurements from the angles today. The bullet couldn't have come from behind where you stood, because there was no blood on the back of his head. The wound was over his right eye, yet I was standing on his right side, shielding him from that direction."

The sergeant ran his tongue over dry lips. "What are you trying to say, that his murder was impossible?"

"Exactly. It was impossible and therefore it didn't happen. Lieutenant Lyrik is still alive and you are going to take me to him."

The rain had let up by the time they reached the little farmhouse some distance from the city. With his raincoat bundled around his face, Michael was unrecognizable until Lyrik had already opened the door to admit Cista. Then he shoved his way inside, knocking the lieutenant to the floor. "Don't go for a gun," he warned. "We wouldn't want the report of your death to be proved correct after all."

Lyrik rolled over on the floor, cursing his sergeant. "You told him! Mulheim will have our heads for this!"

"No, no he already knew!"

"How could he know, unless someone told him?"

"Someone told me today. Someone told me that no one could have killed you and they were right. Captain Mulheim said the fatal bullet passed through your head, yet there was no blood on the back of your head, only on the forehead. The bullet couldn't have passed through. I remembered too that I heard the shot a split second before you grabbed your forehead and the blood appeared. A bullet from a high powered rifle would travel faster than the sound. You had a capsule of blood hidden in your hand, and when one of Mulheim's men fired a shot in the air you squashed the capsule against your forehead and fell over. Sergeant Cista came running and the captain was summoned with an ambulance. I was kept away from the body so I wouldn't discover that you were still alive. The whole thing was a plot on Mulheim's part. He wanted an excuse to rid that block of Gypsies."

"And he'll do it," Lyrik said with a smile. "In less than two hours."

Michael showed him the sergeant's 9-mm automatic pistol. "I have this now. And you are coming with us to Masarak Street."

It was a wild ride back to the city, but they reached the street with ten minutes to spare. Every Rom was outside, facing the police, and Mary Baxter stood at their front with Bruno Lacko, not twenty feet away from Captain Mulheim. Cista had to blow his horn to cut a path through the waiting police and military men.

Michael was the first out of the car, and Mulheim raised his pistol to face him.

"You arrived just in time for the evacuation," he said, "unless you've come to confess to Lyrik's murder yourself."

"Hardly that! I have Lieutenant Lyrik alive and well in this car, and you have a great deal of explaining to do."

When they saw Lyrik, the residents of Masarak Street shouted and cheered, knowing the threat was ended. Captain Mulheim hesitated just an instant, perhaps contemplating the killing of them all. Then he turned and waved his men back. "There'll be other days, Mr. Vlado," he promised.

It was not a promise he was fated to keep. In the morning, as Michael prepared to return home, Mary Baxter brought him the good news. President Havel and the government had negotiated the removal of the walls in the Gypsy sections of their city and Ústí nad Labem to the north. The wall was already being torn down and the Czech government had promised to give both cities money to improve social conditions. Meantime, a formal investigation had been opened into the faking of Lieutenant Lyrik's murder and the plot against the Gypsies of Masarak Street.

"If I'm ever in Ireland I'll visit you," Michael told her as he prepared to leave for home.

Mary Baxter smiled. "So long as it's not in the autumn."

A Michael Vlado Checklist

1. "The Luck of a Gypsy," *The Ethnic Detectives* (Dodd, Mead, 1985). Collected in *The Iron Angel.*
2. "Odds on a Gypsy," *Ellery Queen's Mystery Magazine* (hereafter, *EQMM*), July 1985. Collected in *The Iron Angel.*
3. "Blood of a Gypsy," *EQMM*, January 1986. Collected in *The Iron Angel.*
4. "The Gypsy Treasure," *EQMM*, May 1986. Collected in *The Iron Angel.*
5. "Punishment for a Gypsy," *EQMM*, January 1987. Collected in *The Iron Angel.*
6. "The Gypsy Wizard," *EQMM*, May 1987. Collected In *The Iron Angel.*
7. "The Hostage Gypsies," *EQMM*, Mid-December 1987.
8. "Murder of a Gypsy King," *EQMM*, July 1988. Collected in *The Iron Angel.*
9. "Gypsy at Sea," *EQMM*, Mid-December 1988. Collected in *The Iron Angel.*
10. "The Gypsy and the Pilgrims," *EQMM*, June 1989.
11. "The Gypsy Bear," *EQMM*, November 1989.
12. "The Crypt of the Gypsy Saint," *EQMM*, April 1990.
13. "The Gypsy Delegate," *EQMM*, October 1990. Collected in *The Iron Angel*
14. "Funeral for a Gypsy," *EQMIM*, January 1991.
15. "The Spy and the Gypsy," *EQMM*, May 1991.
16. "The Return of the Gypsy," *EQMM*, December 1991.
17. "The Iron Angel," *EQMM*, October 1992. Collected in *The Iron Angel.*
18. "The Hiding Place," *EQMM*, May 1993.
19. "The Puzzle Garden," *EQMM*, February 1994. Collected in *The Iron Angel.*

20. "The Gypsy's Paw," *EQMM*, September 1994. Collected in *The Iron Angel.*
21. "The Butcher of Seville," *EQMM*, March 1995.
22. "The Clockwork Rat," *EQMM*, May 1996. Collected in *The Iron Angel.*
23. "Emperor of the Gypsies," *EQMM*, December 1997.
24. "The Starkworth Atrocity," *EQMM*, September-October 1998. Collected in *The Iron Angel*
25. "A Wall Too High," *EQMM*, June 2000. Collected in *The Iron Angel.*
26. "A Deal in Horses," *EQMM*, September-October 2001.
27. "The Vampire Theme," *EQMM*, August 2002.

THE IRON ANGEL

The Iron Angel and Other Tales of the Gypsy Sleuth by Edward D. Hoch is printed on 60-pound Glatfelter Supple Opaque Natural (a recycled acid-free stock) from 11-point Goudy Old Style The cover painting is by Carol Heyer and the design by Deborah Miller. The first printing comprises approximately one thousand copies, in trade softcover, and two hundred sixty copies sewn in cloth, signed and numbered by the author. Each of the clothbound copies contains a separate pamphlet, *The Wolfram Hunters* by Edward D. Hoch. The book was printed and bound by Thomson-Shore, Inc., Dexter, Michigan.

The Old Spies Club was published in December 2002 by Crippen & Landru, Publishers, Inc., Norfolk, Virginia.

CRIPPEN & LANDRU, PUBLISHERS
P. O. Box 9315
Norfolk, VA 23505
E-mail: CrippenL@Pilot.Infi.Net; toll-free 877 622-6656
Web: www.crippenlandru.com

Long Live the Dead: Tales from Black Mask by Hugh B. Cave. 2000. Trade softcover, $16.00.

Tales Out of School: Mystery Stories by Carolyn Wheat. 2000. Trade softcover, $16.00.

Stakeout on Page Street and Other DKA Files by Joe Gores. 2000. Trade softcover, $16.00.

Strangers in Town: Three Newly Discovered Mysteries by Ross Macdonald, edited by Tom Nolan. 2001. Trade softcover, $15.00.

The Celestial Buffet and Other Morsels of Murder by Susan Dunlap. 2001. Trade softcover, $16.00.

Kisses of Death: A Nathan Heller Casebook by Max Allan Collins. 2001. Trade softcover, $17.00.

The Old Spies Club and Other Intrigues of Rand by Edward D. Hoch. 2001. Signed unnumbered cloth overrun copies, $32.00. Trade softcover, $17.00.

Adam and Eve on a Raft: Mystery Stories by Ron Goulart. 2001. Signed, numbered clothbound, $42.00. Trade softcover, $17.00.

The Sedgemoor Strangler and Other Stories of Crime by Peter Lovesey. 2001. Trade softcover, $17.00.

The Reluctant Detective and Other Stories by Michael Z. Lewin. 2001. Signed, numbered clothbound, $42.00. Trade softcover, $17.00.

The Lost Cases of Ed London by Lawrence Block. 2001. Published only in signed, numbered clothbound, $42.00.

Nine Sons: Collected Mysteries by Wendy Hornsby. 2002. Trade softcover, $16.00.

The Newtonian Egg and Other Cases of Rolf le Roux by Peter Godfrey. 2002. [A "Crippen & Landru Lost Classic"]. Cloth, $25.00. Trade softcover, $15.00.

The Curious Conspiracy and Other Crimes by Michael Gilbert. 2002. Signed, numbered clothbound, $42.00. Trade softcover, $17.00.

Murder, Mystery and Malone by Craig Rice, edited by Jeffrey Marks. 2002. [A "Crippen & Landru Lost Classic"]. Cloth, $27.00. Trade softcover, $17.00.

The Sleuth of Baghdad by Charles B. Child. 2002. [A "Crippen & Landru Lost Classic"]. Cloth, $27.00. Trade softcover, $17.00.

The 13 Culprits by Georges Simenon, translated by Peter Schulman. 2002. Unnumbered cloth overrun copies, $32.00. Trade softcover, $16.00.

Hildegarde Withers: Uncollected Riddles by Stuart Palmer. 2002. [A "Crippen & Landru Lost Classic"]. Cloth, $29.00. Trade softcover. $19.00.

The Dark Snow and Other Stories by Brendan DuBois. 2002. Signed, numbered clothbound, $42.00. Trade softcover, $17.00.

The Spotted Cat and Other Stories from Inspector Cockrill's Casebook, by Christianna Brand, edited by Tony Medawar. 2002. [A "Crippen & Landru Lost Classic"]. Cloth, $29.00. Trade softcover. $19.00.

Jo Gar's Casebook by Raoul Whitfield, edited by Keith Alan Deutsch, [Published with Black Mask Press]. 2002. Signed, numbered clothbound, $45.00. Trade softcover, $20.00.

Come Into My Parlor: Tales from Detective Fiction Weekly by Hugh B. Cave. 2002. Signed, numbered clothbound, $42.00. Trade softcover, $17.00.

The Iron Angel and Other Tales of the Gypsy Sleuth by Edward D. Hoch. Signed, numbered clothbound, $42.00. Trade softcover, $17.00.

Forthcoming Short-Story Collections

Marksman and Other Stories by William Campbell Gault, edited by Bill Pronzini. "Lost Classics Series."

Cuddy Plus One by Jeremiah Healy.

Karmesin, The World's Greatest Thief – or Most Outrageous Liar by Gerald Kersh, edited by Paul Duncan. "Lost Classics Series."

Problems Solved by Bill Pronzini and Barry N. Malzberg.

One of a Kind: Collected Mystery Stories by Eric Wright.

The Complete Mr. Tarrant by C. Daly King. "Lost Classics" series.

Lucky Dip and Other Stories by Liza Cody.

Kill the Umpire: The Calls of Ed Gorgon by Jon L. Breen.

The Adventure of the Murdered Moths and Other Radio Mysteries by Ellery Queen.

Banner Deadlines by Joseph Commings, edited by Robert Adey. "Lost Classics Series."

14 Slayers by Paul Cain, edited by Max Allan Collins and Lynn Myers. Published with Black Mask Press.

The Mankiller of Poojeegai and Other Mysteries by Walter Satterthwait.

The Pleasant Assassin and Other Cases of Dr. Basil Willing by Helen McCloy. "Lost Classics" series.

Hoch's Ladies by Edward D. Hoch.

Murder! 'Orrible Murder! by Amy Myers.

Murder – All Kinds by William L. DeAndrea. "Lost Classics" series.

A Pocketful of Noses: Stories of One Ganelon or Another by James Powell.

More Things Impossible: The Second Casebook of Dr. Sam Hawthorne by Edward D. Hoch.

The Couple Next Door: Collected Short Mysteries by Margaret Millar, edited by Tom Nolan. "Lost Classics Series."

You'll Die Laughing by Norbert Davis, edited by Bill Pronzini. Published with Black Mask Press.

Dr. Poggioli: Detective by T. S. Stribling, edited by Arthur Vidro. "Lost Classics" series.

Slot-Machine Kelly, Early Private Eye Stories by Michael Collins.

The Evidence of the Sword: Mysteries by Rafael Sabatini, edited by Jesse Knight. "Lost Classics" series.

Tough As Nails by Frederick Nebel, edited by Rob Preston. Published with Black Mask Press.

The Confessions of Owen Keane by Terence Faherty.

Murders and Other Confusions: The Chronicles of Susana, Lady Appleton, Sixteenth-Century Gentlewoman, Herbalist, and Sleuth by Kathy Lynn Emerson.

Who Was Guilty?: Three Dime Novels by Phillip S. Warne, edited by Marlena Bremseth. "Lost Classics" series.

Murder – Ancient and Modern by Edward Marston.

The Avenging Chance and Other Mysteries from Roger Sheringham's Casebook by Anthony Berkeley, edited by Tony Medawar and Arthur Robinson. "Lost Classics" series.

Sleuth's Alchemy: Cases of Mrs. Bradley and Others by Gladys Mitchell, edited by Nicholas Fuller. "Lost Classics" series.

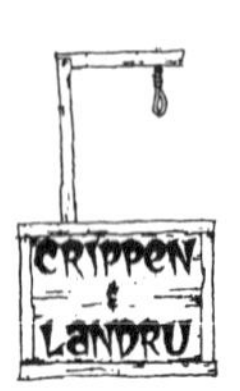

Crippen & Landru offers discounts to individuals and institutions who place Standing Order Subscriptions for its forthcoming publications, either the Regular Series or the Lost Classics or (preferably) both. Collectors can thereby guarantee receiving limited editions, and readers won't miss any favorite stories. Standing Order Subscribers receive a specially commissioned story in a deluxe edition as a gift at the end of the year. Please write or e-mail for more details.